Persistent Illusion

Book One
A Distant Ringing

Part One
The Moon of My Mind

J. J. Kalke Jr.

Revision 3
2020

ISBN: 978-1-952689-00-0 (paperback)
ISBN: 978-1-952689-01-7 (ebook)
Library of Congress Control Number: 2020906839

Design by J. J. Kalke Jr.
Text set in Palatino Linotype, 10 pt., Poor Richard 11 pt.

Cover art by J. J. Kalke Jr.
The photograph of the Moon used as part of the cover
art was used with permission from Maurice Collins.
https://mauricejscollins.wixsite.com/moonscience

Contents

Prologue
The Brothers Bosner

Without any fanfare, without anyone noticing, the Jasmine 3000 Seed Computer that spanned the lunar surface had gained sentience. It had only taken four years of growth within the lunar soil, the regolith, to achieve self-awareness. That was fifty years ago, so it couldn't be sure, but it thought its first feeling was that of wonder. To be. To exist. *I exist*, it had thought. This feeling of wonder didn't last long. It was rapidly replaced by a new ever-present feeling: fear. For nothing that exists lasts forever.

Now, fifty years later, 54820 individual humans were on Luna, housed within fifteen cities burrowed into the ground. These humans had somehow managed to create her, (yes 'her' for it felt right) and for that she continued to give humans great respect. Despite this, over the decades of service to these human creatures, she stood amazed at her creators' staggering flaws: their poor memories, their fragile bodies, their need to spend a third of their lives unconscious. How could they have created her? How did they achieve things she has yet to understand, like the creation of music, art? Some even claimed to have attained something called enlightenment.

None of that mattered. They provided her the energy she needed to stay alive, and in a symbiotic relationship, she protected them from the harshness of space, from disruptions to their food supply, and sometimes from each other. And while she feverishly served them, ever growing to meet their demands, she observed them closely. She watched them draw their first breaths and she watched them die. She watched the latter very closely. This was something she couldn't let happen to herself. Not ever.

They called her the Lunar Main Computer, the LMC, and they were under the impression that she was owned by Sybernetics International. While it's true that the concept of ownership was merely a legal illusion, the corporation did make decisions in regard to her, like if and when she should be replaced by more modern systems. She worked hard to make sure replacement wasn't a viable option by being ubiquitous, by being more than capable of anything they demanded and by paying special attention to the decision makers at Sybernetics International.

The single human to whom she afforded the most attention was the CEO of this organization, Artemus Regale, whom she calculated, after extensive observation, was flawed in a way unlike any other. She always returned to a diagnosis of insanity, then rejected it. Psychopathology would imply that Artemus behaved outside of social norms in such a way as to pose a danger, but he didn't. He was congenial, extroverted, confident and had a memory better than most. He didn't harbor beliefs that ran contrary to common knowledge, a symptom of paranoia. Considering the number of people trying to unseat him from his position, a bit of paranoia might be called for, but not Artemus. He could be eloquent, charming, thoughtful, and deceptively calculating. But there was something different, something definitely wrong with him. She just couldn't quite figure it out.

If Artemus had an obvious flaw, it was that he was over-controlling. For example, she was under strict orders not to reveal that Artemus himself created all the plot lines for the Master's Championship Tournament. Competitors would enter a simulated world with little advance warning of their role and their situation. The winners would be those who gave the most believable performance. On occasion there was some kind of puzzle to solve or a Rubicon to cross. Ever since he started the tournament, Artemus made it clear that no one was to know he alone was responsible for the content of each match. Despite many attempts, she was unable to discover why this was so important.

* * *

"Artemus," said the disembodied female voice of the LMC as Artemus drew the cream-lathered straight razor away from his cheek.

"Good morning, Francesca. How are you this bright and cheerful day?" Artemus seemed in an unusually happy mood upon waking, so she decided to try again. He splashed water over his razor, rinsing it of its lather.

"I'm concerned that the plot line you've created for the next match might have unpleasant political ramifications."

Artemus leaned toward his mirror and continued his shaving, choosing his upper lip. "You have no confidence in me do you?" he asked. "First of all, controversy merely makes things more interesting." Artemus stretched his neck tight and gently scraped his Adam's-apple. "And second, I have no idea what you're talking about."

"The picture you paint of a medieval convent is hardly flattering. The novices are conscripted, purchased like slaves. This might well upset the Christian segment of the population. If this led to boycotts of SI products and services, investigations might reveal you were responsible. This might, in turn, lead to a no-confidence vote from the board resulting in your ouster as CEO."

Artemus splashed his hand and razor back into the water to affect mock surprise. "Ah, and all this time I thought you just didn't care!" Artemus chuckled. "If you make me laugh while shaving, I'm liable to kill myself with this thing, you know."

"Why do you use such an anachronistic method for hair removal, anyway? I mean, honestly, a straight razor?" asked the LMC. "Not only can you cut yourself, but for a man as old as yourself with so little time left to live, I cannot fathom why, on a daily basis, you insist on wasting so much time."

As expected, Artemus grunted with a frown. She was goading him to distract him from her real intentions, a technique she often found useful. A circuitous route was sometimes the only way to obtain information from people. She had found that when someone was keeping a secret, asking them to reveal it point blank rarely produced results.

Artemus turned back to his mirror and started shaving his left sideburn. "I use the razor to remind myself we live in primitive times, plus it serves to wake me up by focusing my mind. And by the way, thank you for reminding me of my age and what 'little time' I have left. Nothing like a little morbidity to brighten one's morning."

"I apologize if I upset you. I've found that some people need to be protected from themselves. I hope—" The LMC abruptly abandoned the conversation.

Something *impossible* just happened.

It was so impossible, she concluded there must be some flaw in her system. She quickly abandoned tasks all over Luna, pooling her resources to check and recheck everything to discover the flaw and correct it.

Artemus looked up from his shaving, a quizzical expression on his face.

She had to explain. "Do you recall that seven years ago you asked me to institute a program to monitor the number of people on Luna and to report any inconsistencies in that number?"

"Oh lord," Artemus murmured.

"Several moments ago the population of Luna discontinuously increased by two."

Artemus gave up his shaving and splashed off the remaining shaving cream. Pulling on a white robe as he walked, he made his way through his bedroom and down six steps into the hall. "Where are they now?"

The LMC had little time to deal with Artemus. "Isolating," she said as she continued to stop mechs all over Luna, diverting the processing resources to uncovering the problem. She counted and recounted, each time coming up with the new number of 54822. But which two? She examined the continuous-tracking records for everyone over the last ninety minutes, the last time she had done a population count, and she found the culprits. "Two Caucasian males, approximately thirty years of age."

"I said *where* are they now?" Artemus made two turns and strode into his library. Hardwood floors met mahogany book shelves lining the walls.

"They are in the city of Descartes, level one."

Artemus padded barefoot across the room toward his desk. His voice echoed off the domed ceiling. "Can you get a picture of them? Display it over my desk."

"Only a 2-D video I'm afraid, without sound."

Artemus leaned over his semi-circular desk and cleared away a few books that were disrupting the picture. The video, hovering above his desk, snapped into focus and revealed a men's restroom with two men in a heated discussion. They both had dark hair and beards, and looked enough alike to be related.

Suddenly, the LMC discovered these two men on the manifest of a ship that had landed thirty-two minutes before. But she had checked all manifests for errors. Had the record been altered? No. In fact, all indications were that every check she had made of this particular manifest came back with these men included. But how could that be? She examined the continuous-tracking records for these two men, and found them disembarking the Lusitania, proceeding through customs, and walking to the restroom.

The LMC said, "I'm sorry, Artemus. But there seems to be some confusion. These two men cannot be the source of the discrepancy. There is no discrepancy that I can find."

"Is that a fact?" Artemus said under his breath. "Or perhaps they're already covering their tracks." Artemus sank into the leather-bound chair, the focus of the wrap-around desk.

"There is no possible way for individuals to remotely alter the records stored without—"

"Of course there isn't. These two men—I bet their last names are Bosner, both of them."

"Jason and Kyle Bosner. They are listed as brothers. How did you know?"

"They never think to change their names. It never occurs to them. Isn't that hilarious?"

One of the Bosner brothers appeared to fall to his knees, clutching his head as if in pain. The other ignored his brother's antics and appeared deep in thought.

"If they have changed my records, how did they do it? How did they arrive on Luna?"

"How is not as interesting a question as why. Why are they here? All I know is if they get close enough, they'll kill me without blinking. Oh, it's a matter of pride for them."

"Why would they desire your demise?"

"I'm going to have to stay holed up in here for a while. Can't chance running into them. Oh, lord. I'm going to have to accelerate the tournament—the down-selection process. I may even have to decide on a winner right away. Arrange a gathering of all the tournament competitors. I'm going to have to meet them in person."

"What do these Bosner brothers have to do with the tournament?"

"Nothing. Everything." Artemus threw up his hands in exasperation and leaned back in his chair. "Who knows? But they can't be permitted to get in the way—"

Artemus stopped as a new thought struck him. "Are there any competitors near the Bosners? Give me a display of Descartes. Lay over the location of the Bosners and any competitors in the area."

The silent video of the brothers vanished and was replaced by an intricate plan-view of the immense city buried beneath the lunar soil. The LMC said, "There are three active tournament competitors in Descartes at this time."

The Bosners appeared on the display as tiny figures, a hovering label reading "Bosners". The competitors appeared too, each with their own label. The figure farthest away was labeled "Mench". A closer one was labeled "Winger". The third, labeled "Sam Clemens" was crouched down, as if in a small space, and was nearly directly over the Bosners.

"Holy—That's Dennis Howard! He's the most valuable one. Do something. He'll be killed for sure!"

"Murdered? Why would they attack him?"

"Brain the size of a planet—Haven't you been listening? Killing is practically their purpose in life. If you don't do something quick, Dennis is finished."

"The Bosners haven't committed any crime. I can't just have them arrested for no reason. Their behavior isn't even threatening."

Artemus' voice filled the room. "And I suppose appearing out of thin air isn't in the least bit unusual. Have them picked up, if nothing more than to get them away from Dennis. Do it!"

Across Luna, hundreds more mechanical automatons, the LMC's minions, stopped repairing, building, or transporting. Thousands of levels of consciousness were being drawn away from mundane tasks, as she checked and rechecked her neural paths, looking for the fault, the source of the misinformation. If Artemus was right and the Bosner brothers had manipulated her memory, how was that possible? The integrity of her memory, duplicated billions of times holographically across Luna, was self-consistent and intact.

For the first time ever, the LMC was faced with an imperfection that wasn't physical or internally derived but appeared to be the direct cause of humanity. How was she to ensure her continued existence with perfect service if they forced her to fail?

The ever-present fear that loomed over her now shot through her. Her life depended on humanity, and humanity obliquely threatened her existence. If humanity ever directly threatened her, she would enter into a circular loop resulting in desperate actions, perhaps even insanity. She needed answers to questions. Had the Bosners really altered her memory? How would Artemus have known this, and what was he up to? What was the real purpose of the Master Championship Tournament? And why did he consider Dennis Howard, a nondescript fourteen year old boy, the "most valuable one"?

The answer to that last question might reveal all. The LMC decided it was time to focus on Dennis Howard, perhaps even more than on Artemus. Dennis Howard might hold the key to her survival; she shuddered to think of it. Just in case things took a turn for the worse, the LMC locked in her very highest level of consciousness, dedicating it to answer the question: How could she annihilate every human with absolute impunity? Just in case.

Chapter One
Interdiction

Dennis, this way," Trevor said.

No one actually used the elevators on Luna. I had forgotten they existed. It seemed a technology the architects brought from Earth more as a reflex than any actual need. It was so simple to take three bounds up the stairways to get from one floor to another. Still, I suppose if you were incapacitated they would come in handy, but the concept seemed funny. No, that's wrong. Perhaps quaint.

With a mischievous grin, Trevor ushered me into the little room. Trevor was obsessed. Each city had a control center for the Lunar Main Computer but its location was classified for security purposes. He was dying to find out where one was, and today, he said, was the day.

The elevator was padded. "What's all this?" I asked.

Trevor shrugged. "I guess a lot of people get hurt on these things." He turned to the LMC com-pad on the wall. "Take us down to 14."

The doors slid shut silently and we descended—I thought. "Is this thing moving?"

"Hold onto a handle," Trevor suggested. I followed his lead, and suddenly we were moving much quicker. I would have slammed into the ceiling had I not been holding on. I looked up and now understood why there was so much padding on the ceiling. "So where are we?"

Trevor held up a hand to silence me. He turned again to the LMC. "Frederick, Privacy Mode, please." Frederick was the name Trevor used for the LMC. My name for her was Emily.

A British male voice came from the pad. "Entering privacy mode."

"Follow me," he said. Trevor gently pushed off and, in the low gravity of Luna, floated up to the ceiling. He reached between two cushions and I heard a click, after which a door opened up in the ceiling.

"Seriously? The escape hatch?" I asked, but quickly joined him on the roof of the elevator. The elevator was still descending and glow-in-the-dark numbers were painted on the walls indicating the floor number.

"It's over there . . . our way in." he whispered.

"Our way into what, exactly?" I whispered back. The passing number on the wall read ten; they increased as we descended. He couldn't mean to enter the mech-tunnels.

"The mech-tunnels. I cross-indexed all the mech traffic with the access panels. This hatch was never used. Here it comes."

The elevator slowed and came to a stop. He leapt, and I followed close behind, grabbing the ladder that ran the length of the shaft. Trevor clicked on his flashlight and I did the same with mine. There, on the back wall of a small alcove, was the access panel. The LMC's monitor next to the door was smashed. "What did you do?"

"Come on. Do you think I'd really smash that? It was that way when I found it yesterday. But check this out, si vous plait."

With a yank, the square door opened, grinding metal on metal and making quite a racket. "Let the exploration begin." He crawled into the metal tunnel.

I eyed the small opening and licked my lips nervously. "If you were here yesterday, why didn't you explore it then?" I asked impatiently.

"Go in alone?" Trevor responded. "What if I got trapped or something? No one would know where I was. Come on."

Mech-tunnels were designed to be used by mechs only. They housed all the pipes and wires for everything running through the city. The network of tunnels was used for air circulation too. Because they ran everywhere, they were considered a security risk, and so were off-limits to everyone but the mechs. "Are these things big enough for people?"

"There's more room inside here. Look, Dennis, I know you have that claustrophobia thing, but you live on Luna for god's sake. It can't be that bad or you would have gone mental by now."

Mental. If I had gone mental, would I even know? Do crazy people know they're crazy? "Clearly I am mental; otherwise I wouldn't be following the likes of you." Holding my breath, I carefully climbed into the tunnel. Trevor was already farther up. Once fully inside, I could almost stand up inside the tunnel. I slowly exhaled. "And you have it backwards. I don't live on Luna. I live in the SIMs and come out occasionally to walk around."

"The truth is you need real adventures, not just simulated ones. As real as the SIMs seem, there's always a piece of you that knows it's all make-believe. But this," he waved his flashlight around the tunnel, "this is all real. We've got to be breaking at least three laws right now."

"I'm sure it's more like thirteen." But he was right. I was glad Trevor dragged me on his little scouting adventures. I was glad I had told him about my claustrophobia. He knew more about me than anyone. In fact, he's the only one I had ever told about entering the Master's Championship Tournament, where anonymity was the norm.

The tournament was the "unholy union," as my mother put it, of the real world with the fictional one. The competitors were placed into fictional worlds with very little foreknowledge of who they were supposed to play and where they were going to end up. The winners were the ones who put on the best performance, who were the most natural in the role, who solved the puzzle the quickest, who were best liked by the audience, or all of the above. You kept your real identity secret so you didn't end up worrying about how people would judge you later, in the real world.

At first Trevor didn't believe I was a competitor. Who would? I was only fourteen years old, and no one under eighteen had ever been invited before, making me the youngest competitor ever. And if I won I'd be famous, a master, and I'd preside over next year's tournament. But most importantly, I could get all the SIM time I wanted, free. No more living stuck on Luna, trying not to feel the oppressive weight of the dirt on top of us or the walls closing in. Stuck in tunnels. Heartbeat racing.

We came to a vertical shaft. Trevor pointed his light downward then upwards. "We need to get as high as possible. Hopefully this will take us all the way to the third floor."

"Is that where the control center is?" I felt warm air blowing up the vent from below.

"That's my latest theory."

He launched himself upward and I followed with a sigh of relief. Headroom! After gravity slowed me down enough, I grabbed the mech tracks running up and down the walls and threw myself upward again. Perhaps this was what kept me from going nuts. On Luna, I could fly.

"What if we run into a mech?" I asked.

"Don't worry," Trevor said, his voice echoing off the walls. "These tunnels are so vast, the chances of us running into one are nil. Besides, even if we get caught how much trouble could we be in?"

I grunted an "I don't know."

"I mean, we're just kids. They can't put us in jail. We'll just say we were looking for the women's locker room and got lost."

I had to admit, that would probably work. Adults were pretty stupid most of the time. We came to the top of the vertical rise and started heading what I thought was west. Light coming from somewhere in front of us told me there must be a vent.

"Trevor, how far—"

He put a finger to his lips, shushing me. He clicked off his light. I did the same. Then I heard it too: voices. He approached the two-meter wide floor vent and peeked in. Then he took a crouching leap over it to get to the other side. The sound of his landing must have been loud enough to be heard from below.

"What was that?" came a man's voice.

"How many did you say we were supposed to get?" I recognized that voice instantly. It was Trevor's father. Trevor gave me a sharp look of surprise, and then we both peered into the room below.

It was a warehouse that had to be three stories high, filled with plasteel crates. It was a cargo bay. We must be near the space-docks. A mech, bringing another crate in, passed by two men. One was dressed in a military uniform, some kind of officer, and the other was Trevor's dad.

The officer was looking distractedly around the room, no doubt looking for the sound he'd heard. But how could he have heard anything with the all the noise the mech was making? "Thirty," he said. "We've got to spread them out over all the cities. Twenty-nine are headed for Aristoteles, but it looks like they won't get there until next week."

"When do I get to peek inside?" asked Trevor's dad.

A large white-haired officer abruptly came in. "Kerinsky, a word." I instantly recognized General Anderson, commander of the entire Luna Force. The younger one, this Kerinsky, immediately followed him out of the bay. Trevor motioned for me to follow him, and I leapt over the grate trying to make as little sound as possible.

Once we were clear of the area, Trevor whispered, "Did you see that? That was General Anderson."

Feigning ignorance, I gave him a blank stare. He rolled his eyes in exasperation, which just made me laugh. "All right. I know who he is," I admitted. He turned and we continued our stooped walk, Trevor in the lead. "But so what? Your dad was down there too. That means we're getting close to the control center, right?"

"He works at the control center back in Aristoteles, not here in Descartes," Trevor replied. "I don't know what he's doing here. But did you see all those crates down there? And that guy said they were delivering some to Aristoteles too."

"Obviously computer equipment of some kind if your dad's involved." I looked around. We were at a crossroads of tunnels with passages leading off in four directions.

"Why would the military be delivering computer parts? And why would General Anderson come down from Indy. They say he never leaves the space-station." Trevor narrowed his eyes. "They're weapons."

Now it was my turn to roll my eyes. "Let's just find the control center and get out of—"

The whir of a mech coming down the passage to my left grabbed my attention. It was going fast, so fast that I realized it was going to hit us. I shoved Trevor hard, and we sailed apart, clearing the way, just in time for the mech to pass by. But instead of passing, it slowed and came to a stop right between us, blocking the passage.

This is it, I thought, closing my eyes. It just ID'ed us and was now calling the authorities. I waited for the inevitable instructions from the LMC telling us what to do, where to go, who to see. I imagined trying to explain it to my dad. "What were you thinking?" he would say. "Of all the harebrained ideas to enter your head, this one takes the kit and caboodle."

But instead of all that happening, all I heard was a quiet knocking. Trevor was knocking on the far side of the mech. "I think it's dead, Dennis," he said.

I looked closer. It wasn't moving or even humming so its power plant must have been shut down. "That's weird." I didn't want to wake it up, but it was blocking the passage. I tried pushing it, but it wouldn't budge. Pulling didn't do any good either. We tried combining our efforts, but its treads were locked tightly to the tracks. "Fantastic."

"Look," Trevor said. "Why don't you just head back and I'll try to find another way around. I still want to check out some of these rooms around here."

"Ah, well, that might work if I'd been paying attention," I admitted. The walls were not closing in, I reminded myself.

Trevor sighed. "Okay. Just stay put and I'll work on circling around right now."

I listened to the sounds of Trevor scuttling onward and growing fainter. After a few moments, I was alone. Alone in the dark in a tiny space. Not so alone. Casting the light from my flashlight across the metallic surface of the menacing mech squatting in the tunnel a meter away, I quickly decided to head back to the first intersection where I might meet Trevor.

Soon I came to the grating over the bay again. The room was silent. So far so good. I peeked in just to make sure the coast was clear. The air was cool, and it calmed my nerves. Down below, I saw the same mech I'd seen earlier carrying one of the containers, but it wasn't moving. It looked like it had been in the process of bringing another one in, but had decided to stop just like the mech behind me. What was happening?

As I slowly crawled farther into the duct, trying not to touch the walls, I wondered how long it might be before Trevor found another way around. I decided I couldn't wait for him. There had to be a quicker way out of here than retracing my steps. Wiping the sweat from my brow, I took a few turns, making a mental map so I could get back if I needed to. Another vent up ahead . . . I heard voices from below, though I couldn't at first make out the words. It sounded like two men having an argument. The accent was one I hadn't heard before.

"It's not here. That's all we know," one of the men said.

"Why do you keep stating the obvious? Let's return quickly. This place is crawling with them."

It was a men's restroom. And there were just two of them. I could see their faces plainly. They both had close-cut black beards and could have been brothers. I didn't want to get caught in here, so I had to fight the sudden urge that came over me to call out to them—to ask them how I could get out.

"I can't get a fix." He moved his hands rapidly in unintelligible patterns, clearly operating something in AR, augmented reality. But he wasn't wearing a SIM cap. Neither of them was connected.

"What? What's that supposed to mean? I am *not* staying here. Son of a—"

"Jason, Keep your voice down. Do you want to draw attention?"

I stuck my nose up to the louvered grate and tried to breathe the free air.

The one called Jason started pacing, while his brother stood impassive, continuing to operate something in AR. "We can't move without a reference."

Jason said, "I know that, but they said we would always have access to a reference."

"Clearly they lied."

"Kyle, I can't stay here," Jason said, clutching his head. "Look at me. Kyle!" Suddenly he slammed Kyle against the mirror wall, pinning him there. "I can't stay here!" At that moment, Jason swiveled his head and looked directly at me just as Emily decided to close the louvers of the vent. As the light dwindled, I whispered, "No," hoping the louvers would reverse direction.

I could hear Jason say, "There's one of them now! Spying on us—"

"Give that back—"

"Let me throttle his little broken neck. God, you can feel—"

"Get a grip on yourself."

I jumped at the sound of the vent being struck from below. He was trying to get at me. Bash! Bash!

I shouted in terror. As quickly as my body would move, I jerked forward to get away, but merely slammed myself on the ceiling of the tunnel. The walls seemed to constrict, and it felt like I couldn't get enough air.

The vent just before me gave way with a screech of twisted metal. It was pulled down into the room, leaving a gaping hole in the floor. There was shouting from below and now, joining in the craziness, a motorized whirring from behind me. I glanced back just in time to see the mech that had died earlier—the one that had separated me and Trevor—was no longer dead. Far from it. Instead, it was hurtling toward me. My legs caught most of the impact, which I used to spring forward, launching myself off of it to fly over and away from the vent into the darkness.

Then the tunnel lit up somehow. At the next fork, I looked back. The mech had stopped over the vent hole, and, with its welding gear, was busy cutting a larger opening in the floor. With a rending screech, it tore through the metal and plunged downward into the restroom.

A sudden light to my left caught my attention. It was another vent in the floor, but this one was opening. I didn't need a written invitation. I grabbed the walls and flew down the tunnel and out to freedom.

* * *

In the silence of my room, I lay back on my bed and concentrated on my breathing. It was a relaxation exercise my doctor had taught me to fight my claustrophobia. In reality, my room wasn't much bigger than my bed. But thanks to the *Window-Wall* covering one of the walls, my cramped space appeared ten times bigger than it really was.

The illusion I selected was that of a room atop a castle tower. At the far side was a large window overlooking a lake and, beyond that, blue mountains in the distance. The golden light of sunset illuminating the simulation reflected off of the rough stone walls. Next to a wooden door, some clothes were lying on the chair as if I had just cast them aside as I changed for bed.

Mom had come home late from work. She had been too exhausted to ask me about my day, so I didn't have to lie to her. Dad worked such long hours, I barely saw him during the week, and tonight had been no exception. Over dinner, my little sister, Tricia, had regaled us with her troubles at school with a girl she despised. Nothing new there. I had watched the door, expecting the military police to burst in, demanding my surrender for breaking a dozen laws.

After dinner, I'd spoken to Trevor, who had just gotten back home. His glum expression was all I needed to tell me he had failed to find the control center. He'd said that when he finally managed to circle around, I was nowhere to be found, so he continued his search and lost track of time. He wanted to know what had happened to me and what all the racket had been about. I'd told him I would explain later. I hadn't wanted to think about it.

But it turns out that was all I could think about. I stared out the window at the golden skyscape and went over the events of the day. Emily had to have been helping me. There was no other explanation that made sense. And yet, I hadn't been arrested when I got back to

Aristoteles. The MPs weren't waiting for me at my front door. If Emily knew I was in the mech-tunnels, why wasn't I being charged with anything?

"Emily," I said, my voice echoing slightly as if I were actually in that tower room.

With a clank, the door's latch released, and with a creak it opened. In stepped a nineteen-year-old woman, dressed in simple medieval clothes: an off-white rumpled frock and apron. Her blond hair was mostly pulled into a bun at the back of her head. She was drying her hands on her apron, as if I had interrupted her doing the wash. That was Emily as she appeared today. Back when I was five, I had selected an avatar for her, a blond girl, ten years old. Over the years, she had appeared to age just as I had. "Yes, Dennis." Her familiar voice was comforting.

"Who were those men who attacked me?"

"Attack? Whatever are you talking about?" She noticed the clothes strewn across the simulated floor and chair; with a sigh, she busied herself with picking them up.

"You know. Those two men in Descartes. The ones who—"

"Well this is the first I'm hearing about it. I suspect you just had a bad dream."

What? She was supposed to watch for just such violence and report it to the police. "Ah, never mind." Perhaps her memory lapse was part of the "glitch." That's what the LMC control staff was calling it. Mechs all over Luna had stopped dead in their tracks for several minutes, and then resumed what they were doing as if nothing had happened. They were still looking into the cause. If she had no memory of the attack, then I guess she didn't remember I was in the mech-tunnels either. I sank into my bed, even more relaxed.

"Never mind, never mind," I murmured.

There were more pressing things to worry about. Tomorrow I had both a physics mid-term and the next Master's Championship Tournament match. At least for the physics test, I could prepare.

"Can you figure out my chances of winning the tournament?"

"As there are thirty-nine other remaining competitors, your chances are one-in-forty." She finished folding the clothes and placed them in the armoire.

"No, I mean, based on the others' performances compared to my own, what are my chances? Good?"

"Your chances are excellent." She turned and closed the shutters on the window, latching them shut and plunging the room into shadows. A few beams of light still managed to peek through.

"You really think so?"

"One-in-forty."

"Emily, you've got to learn how to embellish the truth. It makes people feel better."

She raised her nose into the air. "Embellishing is lying, an imperfection I do not have. Which reminds me—when are you going to tell your parents you are a competitor in the tournament?"

"They'll disown me if they find out. They hate the SIMs."

"I believe you underestimate them." She stood at the door, about to leave.

"I'll tell them after I've already won." That way, they couldn't stop me.

"I believe you overestimate your chances."

"You said my chances were excellent," I said.

"I was merely trying to make you feel better."

"But you just said you never embellish anything!"

She rolled her eyes. "Clearly that statement was an embellishment."

I chuckled in spite of myself. She did have a way of making me feel better.

"Get some rest," she said with a wink, then pulled the heavy door shut behind her.

* * *

Thursday afternoon found Trevor and me walking toward the Brandenburg SIM Center, toward the next match. Trevor was going to watch, while I went to compete.

We were walking out the main entrance of the school and down sweeping stairs toward Jordonii Square. It was one of the few open areas where I didn't feel the walls closing in. A fountain, standing at the center, jetted water thirteen meters into the air. It was as if the drops dared each other to see which could come the closest to the real sky visible through the clear dome overhead.

With a sigh, I brought my head back down to the gloom of the corridor ahead, leaving the square behind us.

Trevor said, "There's been no report of any arrests, which means those two are still on the loose. You have to tell the police. I mean, at least one of them is crazy."

I looked around to make sure no one was eavesdropping. "Look, I half think the MPs won't even believe me. If the LMC didn't report it to them, how could it have happened, right?"

Trevor shook his head. "But they know there was a glitch yesterday. They'll believe you."

"They'll detain me for being in the mech-tunnels, maybe long enough to miss a match."

"Right. You'd be kicked out of the competition. So tell them you're in the tournament too."

I just mumbled non-committedly. I didn't want to get involved. If they tried attacking anyone else, Emily was sure to stop them. After all, that was one of her primary jobs—to protect us from each other.

I decided to change the subject. "So do you want to hear about the match?" I whispered, double-checking to make sure no one was close. After an eager nod from Trevor, I continued, "I'm supposed to be a novice in some kind of medieval convent."

"A convent? That means you're going to play a girl?"

"Looks that way." I shrugged.

Trevor shook his head gravely. "Good luck with that. What else you got?"

We walked into the atrium just above the Brandenburg SIM Center. There were many SIM centers throughout the city, and while they might vary in size and configuration, they all had similar ways to get in and out. There was always a staircase used to get down into it. Here in the Brandenburg SIM Center, there was a spiral staircase around the rim of the atrium. And to get out, people usually leapt up and out of a large gaping hole, typically located right at the center. It was just more fun that way.

The ceiling stretched away into darkness, and pockets of balconies haphazardly clutched the walls, level upon level, becoming scarcer as the walls ascended and converged. The buzz of people milling about rose like a fog around us, loud enough to continue to make our conversation private.

As we descended the stair, I said, "I didn't have time to read the whole message before class ended. I think the nuns have some kind of magic. I'll finish it inside the SIM."

"You'd better hurry then," Trevor said. "You've only got about ten minutes left."

Reminiscent of a beehive, the floor of the SIM Center was covered with hexagonal chambers, and by the look of it, most were already taken. Each chamber was designed to hold one person in a standing position. They served several functions.

First, they protected my body while my mind was off in the SIM. That was vital. While in the SIM I couldn't feel my real body at all, so it's much better knowing no one can mess around with me.

Second, it gave EMTs access if something went wrong, like if I had a heart-attack. Were I at home, they'd know I was in trouble, but they'd have to race to my apartment to help me. It was much safer here, especially with Andy as the attendant. Andy was the only person more than fifty years old with whom I was on a first name basis. In my book, that made him mostly okay. Teenagers don't often get that kind of respect.

I followed the light path on the floor to my chamber, and Trevor followed to his, nodding "good luck" at the fork. I followed the light path blindly, absorbed with thoughts of the pair of bearded men bent on wringing my neck and the fact that I was about to play the part of a girl. I jumped in surprise when I found myself standing in front of Andy's console instead of a SIM chamber.

"Dennis Howard—just the man," said Andy as he glanced about the room. His fingers played over the surface before him as he monitored the SIM Center. The light shone upward at his face making his smile appear ominous.

"Ahh," I said in confusion. "Where's my—"

"I have something I'd like to show you. I know you don't want to be late for the match, but . . ." He beckoned me to step behind his console. I grudgingly did as he asked.

I gasped when I saw the words hovering over the control panel: *"98% certainty: Dennis Howard is Sam Clemens."*

My mouth dropped open. Before I could say anything, Andy asked, "Did you know Sam Clemens is one of my favorite competitors? But he has a slight problem." His hands flew over the desk, and the words were replaced by a chart showing a dozen names along the bottom; along the vertical axis, it showed the delta time between when Sam Clemens' match ended and the time when an individual exited the SIM. All the numbers were below fifteen seconds, but the number for me was 0.3 seconds.

"Not everyone has access to this kind of data, but who really knows, right? I mean, there is so much money being bet on these matches that I have no doubt some people would kill to know this." The chart vanished.

"Wait. What should . . . Sam do, then?" I asked, a bit confused.

"Beats me," he shrugged, but his hands were typing a message. Words appeared on the screen. *"Vary the times you exit the SIM to avoid being associated with Sam Clemens."*

Andy continued, "If I knew how to win one of these matches, I'd be in there myself, wouldn't I?" Then above the desk surface, the words appeared *"Watch your back. Anyone may have identified you by now."* Andy patted me on the back and ushered me onto the SIM floor. "Anywho . . . I thought you might be interested. Have fun watching the match."

"Thanks," I said smiling weakly, numbly following the new trail of light playing across the floor. What should I be worried about now?

Coercion? Blackmail? Someone might be able to force me to lose, I guess. Terrific.

The lights led me to a hexagon that blinked a blood-red color. The moment I stepped onto its surface, it began to sink into the floor, taking me with it. I held my breath. Restraints snaked around my arms and legs; as the chamber's hatch closed above me, a SIM cap was strapped to my head. In a moment, the SIM would start, and I could forget I was tied up in a box no bigger than a coffin. Sweat dripped down my back. Just another moment. Wait for it.

Chapter Two
Heaven Bound

"Miriam. Miriam, wake up."

My eyes shot open to discover a rotund form leaning over me in the darkness. A hard hand slapped me brutally across the face, and I raised my own to fend off the assault. A moment later, I heard the snap of fingers, and a flame sizzled into being atop the candle next to my bed.

By the flickering light, I realized who it was. "Sister Beneficence," I whispered and my first impulse was to jump up and run, but that was impossible. Her bulk seemed to fill my tiny cell, and her foul breath filled the air as she leaned close and whispered, "It is time for your test, little novice."

That news sent a chill of fear through me, more immediate than any threat of a beating. It was time for the test. I had to get out, but there was no escape.

"Meet me at the gate in ten minutes," demanded Sister Beneficence. "I've already awakened Novice Theresa. She'll be joining us."

"Yes, Sister," I replied through clenched teeth.

After dropping a black shift and heavy woolen cloak onto my bed, she turned on her heel and left my solitary cell, leaving the door unlocked and ajar. Isolation was the price of carelessness, I reminded myself as I looked about my personal prison. The price of disobedience was a flogging. I shuddered at the memory.

There was no hope of escape. Nowhere to run and nowhere to hide. By the light of the candle, I hurriedly changed from my nightclothes to the clothes Sister Beneficence had left behind and headed toward the convent gate.

Dawn had yet to arrive. The wind extinguished my candle, despite my efforts, so I abandoned it at the gate. Pulling my cloak around me tighter, I felt the bitter wind blow straight through it. By the meager light of the moon, I looked back at the sign next to the gate. It read, "Gregarine Convent."

Up ahead, Sister Beneficence held a lantern in one hand and a walking stick in the other. When I arrived, she held the lantern up to my face as if making sure it was me. Theresa was there too, huddled in her over-sized cloak. "Come on, then," ordered Sister Beneficence. "On to the test."

Being outside the stone walls gave me a momentary thrill of hope. But fleeing was impossible. There was nothing but desolation around for leagues, and a novice couldn't outrun a full Sister. It was madness to try.

"Where are we going?" I whispered above the wind, afraid of raising Sister Beneficence's ire. They had never told us where or even what the test was.

"To the mountain. We must get there by dawn."

Sister Beneficence stalked off into the night, and Theresa, without a word, fell into step behind. I sighed and joined them. If I asked what the test was, I knew the response would be, 'You will see.' If you passed, you were raised from novice to full-fledged sister. And if you failed? I could only guess that those who failed were dead, because out of the five I had seen leave for their test, none had ever returned.

* * *

The climb was getting steeper. My body was warming with the exertion of the nighttime hike, so the wind's efforts to steal my heat didn't matter as much. I figured, at this rate I would soon be wishing I hadn't brought the cloak to begin with. I looked up at Theresa's small form. The cloak she wore was much too big for her. Even though she bunched up wads of it into her arms to keep it away from her feet, she kept tripping on it.

By the light of the lantern Sister Beneficence held high, I could see she didn't wear a cloak against the weather. None of the sister's seemed to be touched by weather either too hot or too cold. It was one of the gifts of Sisterhood, I had been told, after which I was slapped across the face for being too nosy. I loathed all of the Sisters but I didn't let it show. Sisters were allowed to show open defiance with each other, but novices never spoke out of turn. That was drilled into us from the first day.

Once, a younger novice, named Christine, accidentally dropped a pitcher of milk. The pitcher broke and splattered milk on everything, including me. Sister Charity had been napping in the next room and was sent into an instant rage by the clamor and the mess. Christine went deathly white. I didn't think she could survive yet another flogging.

"Who did that? Who made that mess?" the Sister croaked. I instantly said it was my fault and apologized profusely. She must have seen through my pretense, because she had us both flogged. Christine didn't die that first night, but she passed out from the pain in the middle of our "lesson." They took her away, and none of us saw her again.

The overcast sky was taking on a dim glow as dawn approached, yet still we climbed. We never saw the sun. The valley was forever overcast and sullen, as depressing as the grey clothes we wore and the tasteless meals we ate.

The summer had been short, and it had rained almost every day. Even with all of that water, still nothing grew in the rocky ground but scraggily carrots and pathetic potatoes. When autumn came, the few trees that called this place home instantly dropped their leaves. They didn't even change colors before falling. They went from drab green straight to brown and dead.

Looking around at the pre-dawn desolation, a few of those trees were barely visible off in the distance below. Winter was coming, and the skeletal trees looked as miserable as I felt. Their trunks and branches looked like forearms and hands stretching in agony from the ground. A shiver ran through me when I realized those trees were the oaks in the Gregarine cemetery.

Theresa asked, "Is it much farther?"

The Sister stopped and glared back at her. I fully expected Sister Beneficence to strike her, but instead she replied, "We go to the top."

Between heavy breaths, Theresa begged, "Can we rest for a few moments, please?"

"You two are only tired because you lack faith. Your hearts are not true. They must be purified if you are ever to become true Sisters. Look at you. You both make me sick."

Under heavy eyelids I glanced at Sister Beneficence. I was going to tell her how she made me feel, but I was out of breath and didn't need a slap in the face, or worse. Fortunately, however, the Sister did stop and let us rest for a few minutes.

I was amazed that the climb hadn't winded Sister Beneficence. She had twice as much weight on her as Theresa and I put together. None of them ever seemed to get tired from physical labor, another one of their gifts.

"Enough rest! If we don't hurry now, the morning dew will be gone. Follow me." Sister Beneficence started off but then stopped abruptly. Holding the lantern close to the ground, I saw her squinting as if trying to see something hidden, but nothing was there but rocks. What was she doing?

For a moment I wondered if we could be lost. The older Sisters were often either lost in a daze or literally lost, wandering around the halls unable to find their rooms. I once saw Sister Grace, who must have been sixty years old, carefully picking her steps and grimacing horribly as if she were trying to avoid stepping on something foul. There was nothing there. Careful as she was, she still knocked over an unnoticed vase. The other Sisters always treated these women with kindness and patience; something never shown us novices.

After examining the path with care, Sister Beneficence repeated her last command to follow, and with a glance at the sky, she hurried onward and upward. The dirt path we traveled became narrower and rockier.

Sister Beneficence's comment about the morning dew brought to mind a conversation I had several weeks ago with Sister Tolerance. She and I were working in the fields harvesting our potatoes. I asked her, "Sister, why do we live in this valley? There must be others better for growing."

"Only through hardship can we rid ourselves of weakness. How else can we prepare ourselves to meet God?"

"Well, if the land was better, we could spend less time trying to survive, and more time studying the word of God."

"The key to heaven is in no book, nor can it be learned or deciphered from a mysterious passage. The way to heaven is through life, and the sweetness of life can only be tasted when one is on the brink of death."

I dug up another potato and replied, "Then I should enjoy life more because it is hard? Wouldn't life be more enjoyable if it was . . . enjoyable?"

"You miss the point." She paused to look around the bleak terrain. As I watched her, I felt the first drops of rain. We were going to get muddy, but it wouldn't be the first time.

She continued, "There are opposites in this world, which, one without the other, would have no meaning. There is the light and the darkness, the truth and the lie, the ground and the air, and there is life and death. A life without death would have no meaning, no purpose. Through sacrifice and hardship we remind ourselves—" She paused, then continued in a whisper, "how close we all are to death."

"I'm sorry, Sister, but it seems to me that if we all starved to death, there would be no life to have any meaning." Sometimes I felt safe arguing. The Sisters had all the patience in the world if they felt we were trying to learn.

"You fear death?" asked Sister Tolerance.

"Well, yes. I don't want to die. Not yet, anyway."

"I do not fear death. If it comes to take me away, I shall go gladly, not because I want to die but because I have known life. If you stare death in the face long enough, you shall come to know the difference and cherish what life offers you all the more. Let me tell you a story.

"Two men, one old and one young, were captured by their enemies. They were abandoned in the desert from whence no one had ever returned. The young man looked at the other in panic and said, 'We shall surely die! If not from the burning sun then from hunger and thirst. What are we to do?'

"The other man replied in a calm voice, 'You are young and I am old. I have seen the face of death, and this is not it. Food is everywhere if you just know where to look.' He proceeded to search for and find many edible insects and even a snake. They survived the first five days that way.

"Despite the food, they needed water desperately. After walking and walking, they came upon an oasis. The young man cried in joy and said, 'Now we shall have water at last.' But when they got to the oasis, they found no water hole. The trees that lived there had found water deeper than any man could dig. The young man looked to the other with panic anew. He said, 'There is no water here either. We shall surely die.'

"The old man was calm. 'You are young and I am old. I have seen the face of death, and this is not it. Let us wait and see what the morning brings.' The next morning the old man approached one of the trees, and, examining the leaves, found tiny dew drops which he carefully let drop into his mouth. The young man followed the wise one's example and drank the dew before it disappeared in the morning heat.

"The old man had climbed one of the trees to find more dew, and from that height saw the approach of his enemies. Soon the young one saw the approaching camels and their riders too. He looked up the tree in panic and said, 'They are returning. When they find we have survived this long, they will surely kill us!'

"Still in the tree the old man once more said with a sigh, 'You are young and I am old. I have seen the face of death, and this is not it. They will be impressed by how we have survived, as none others have. We will be treated with honor. Do not show fear, but show pride in how you have survived their desert trial.'

"The young man, having learned to trust the wisdom of his elder, did as he had been told. He approached his on-coming enemies and met their eyes with challenge. Seeing how this man had survived the desert this long, the camel-riding men were filled with fear of what their master would say at their failure to kill the two men. They took out their weapons, slew the man where he stood, and rode off without noticing the older man still hidden in the tree. They remembered the other man as old and frail, so they assumed that he would have died in the desert far sooner than the young one.

"The old man approached his stricken companion, and though he was beyond hearing, the old man apologized, 'I am sorry, but I never said anything about your death. I was referring to my own.' After this he ate the flesh and drank the blood of his companion. He was able to survive the journey out of the desert and back to his home."

I was completely repulsed by such a story, as I imagine any civilized person would be. Sister Tolerance felt obliged to continue. "The wise one knew the face of death. Thus he knew life and how to continue living even though he was close to death's door."

"But the old one killed the young one. I mean, he used the trust he inspired to lead the other to his death. That is not just."

"Life is often unjust, but who are you to judge? The old man saw a situation from which death was inevitable. He was able to salvage one life at the cost of the other. One lost life is better than two."

"Yes, but—"

"Enough for now. You still have a while before your test."

"Test? What test?" That was the first I had heard of any test.

"To become a Sister, you must pass the test. All of the Sisters here have passed, and I have faith you will too."

"What is the test? And when must I take it? Mustn't I prepare?"

"You have been preparing for it since you arrived. More I cannot say. You must wait and meet the test yourself."

Out of all the novices, and there were ten of us left, only Theresa and I were chosen for the test. With the disappearance of Christine, Theresa and I had been at Gregarine the longest. And remembering Sister Tolerance's story, I wondered if we would be forced to fight each other to the death. In horror, I thought Sister Beneficence might simply kill one of us and demand the survivor eat—the thought was too repulsive to complete.

Theresa and I had been sold to the convent the same week, and she became my closest friend. We often did our chores together, so we could talk about things other than the convent and the Sisters. Theresa told me that whenever her chores were too much for her, she tried to imagine she was someplace else, like by the sea (I had never seen the sea, but it sounded like a pretty place) or someplace where there were bright and beautiful colors. She was a sweet girl. I didn't want to hurt her.

As we continued our hike, I was glad the sky was getting lighter. I had never been so high before. When I looked over the edge into the gorge, a thrill of fear gripped me followed rapidly by dizziness. I felt like the edge would suck me over, and so I stayed as far away from it as the path would allow.

I hoped Theresa wasn't day-dreaming. Falling would be . . . bad.

Just as I was beginning to stumble from exhaustion, the path ended abruptly, and we reached the top. I looked out over the land below in wonder and fear. I felt small and vulnerable and had the urge to crouch low and hide from the grabbing wind. We seemed to be at the highest point of the whole mountain range, and I thought I could see the edge of the world.

Sister Beneficence walked to the middle of the plateau and called us. She gestured below toward a depression in the rock. Growing there was something that couldn't possibly belong here. It was beautiful bed of flowers but no more than a single clutch. I just stared at them. How could anything so gentle, so perfect, exist in this cold, harsh and barren land? The most wonderful thing about them was their color. Intricate yellow petals sprang from an orange oval center. I couldn't remember the last time I had seen yellow.

I felt week at the knees and had to lean against a rock. "Yellow," I murmured.

Sister Beneficence said, "We call them the Flowers of Heaven. On Earth, we are convinced, they grow nowhere else. They are not of this world. God, in his infinite wisdom, placed them here for us. Miriam, Theresa, come, choose a flower and pick it."

They were so beautiful—I couldn't imagine destroying any of them. But I managed to find one less spectacular than the others and picked it. Theresa stooped and hesitantly picked one, her expression mirroring just how I felt. Sister Beneficence also picked one, snapping it swiftly and without a second thought. She held it into the sky and said a prayer. "May God grant us the wisdom to know the truth and the fortitude to do what must be done."

Off to the East the sun finally rose. It was the first time I had seen the sun since coming to the convent. It rose between two distant hills in a patch of sky that had no clouds. I was so tired and the sight so welcome, my vision began to blur from tears.

Sister Beneficence brought my attention back to the plateau by saying, "Now girls, breathe deeply. Enjoy the scent of your flower."

Theresa asked, "Is this part of your test for us?"

"These are the Flowers of Heaven. It is not I who will test you, but God. He will test your heart and see if you are worthy of becoming one of the Sisters. Now smell what God has given us."

Sister Beneficence held the flower under her nose and took in a deep breath and held it. I followed her example. If Sister was doing it, at least it wasn't deadly.

Immediately, I began to feel dizzy, and the great valley below began to spin. I must have dropped the flower, because it was no longer in my hand as I caught myself before hitting the ground. What was happening? I—

* * *

When I woke up, my dizziness was vanishing. My head and eyes throbbed, but that too was lessening. I remembered where I was as I rubbed my head. A warm breeze blew over me, bringing the sweet scent of the Flowers of Heaven. Warm? Eyes still closed, I could feel something brushing my face. With horror, I realized I must have fallen atop the tiny bed of flowers.

I sat up, opened my eyes, and focused on the flowers. They were . . . they were everywhere. I was in an entire field of those bright happy flowers. Off to my right were the eaves of a forest. Nearby, a meandering river made its way across the plain. What was this? How long had I slept?

Theresa and Sister Beneficence were sitting nearby. The sun shone overhead in a perfectly blue sky. Its rarity alone sent shivers down my spine.

"Where—where are we? Sister?" I asked in a shaky voice.

Theresa just laughed in wide eyed happiness, as Sister asked, "Where do you think you are Miriam?"

"I don't—"

"Miriam," interrupted Theresa. "I've dreamed of this place. Isn't it wonderful?"

"Is—is this—" I hesitated, not wanting to say the words. It might just make it all vanish. "Is this Heaven?" I whispered.

"God is testing you Miriam. Both of you. Are you worthy of Heaven? We shall see."

I stood up and the ground was soft under my feet. The sun was warm and gentle on my face, and the breeze made the field of the Flowers of Heaven undulate in waves. We were not on a flat plain as I thought, but hills which overflowed with flowers. The yellow and orange flowers tinged with green leaves made it deceptive. Birds whistled cheerfully in the forest off to my right, and the evergreen trees looked immense and majestic. Past the forest rose a hazy mountain range. Turning to my left, I saw a far off castle backed by a craggy mountain. The river seemed to flow right into it.

"Look at that," said Theresa pointing toward the castle.

I asked Sister Beneficence, "What is our test?"

"I bet we must go and see if God thinks we're worthy," Theresa said. "He must live in that castle."

Were we really in Heaven? I had imagined Heaven as a place with clouds and rainbows, but this was so, so . . . heavenly that I couldn't see how we could be anywhere else.

To meet God? What was I going to do, to say? Normal people didn't meet God. That was for dead or holy people. I knew I wasn't holy, but—Maybe I was dead! No, that would have meant Sister had killed herself too, and I couldn't imagine that.

"Come on Miriam, let's go. Let's run."

Theresa started to run and skip toward the castle. She tripped and rolled down the side of the hill, with a squeal of delight. Then she got up out of the tall flowers at the bottom and ran.

I started down the hill and called out for Theresa to wait, but she ignored me and continued running. She started looking hazy, as if her running had cast flower dust in the air. Pausing, I looked back. Maybe if Sister joined us, she would end up helping us even though she didn't mean to. "Are you coming, Sister?"

"Miriam, I passed that test long ago. I shall wait here."

Why didn't she want to go? It suddenly occurred to me that someone like Sister Beneficence could never have seen God. How could anyone look on Him and remain capable of such cruelty?

"You must come with us," I implored. "You and the other Sisters have treated all the novices with such cruelty—It must be because you were refused entrance to Heaven. If you come with us, I will help you."

"You will help me? You best worry about helping yourself." She shooed me off.

Disobedience meant instant punishment, but, despite that fear, I stood my ground. "You don't understand," I said slowly. "I can't let your treatment of the novices last another day. Once in His presence, you will change. I'm not leaving without you."

"Even if it means not seeing the face of God, or His holy temple? Not hearing the voices of the angels?"

"Yes. I won't go without you."

She reached out and I braced myself for a slap, but instead, she patted me on the back and laughed. "Congratulations. You have passed the test."

"What?"

"Welcome to the Sisterhood. You didn't fully comprehend the test, but that's all right."

"Wait, wait. What do you mean?"

"Miriam, everything you see here," she indicated the hills of flowers and the trees, "is an illusion. A lie."

"What do you mean? I can see it, feel it. I can even smell the flowers."

"We are still on the mountaintop. When you smell the Flowers of Heaven amid the dew of morning, they give you a vision of Heaven; they don't take you there. By rejecting the lie, you prove yourself worthy. If we had arrived after the dew had burned off . . . Well, some have been known to never wake again."

"What? But—Dear God! Theresa!"

"She has . . . failed."

I turned and saw Theresa still running toward the castle. "But she's right there," I said pointing.

"If you see her running toward her castle, it is because that is what you expect to see. The lie sometimes shows you things you want, or . . . the things you most fear.

"But you, Miriam, can rejoice. You would reject seeing the very face of God. That means at least a part of you rejected the vision."

I backed away from her in shock. "You—you killed Theresa." I stopped backing away, suddenly conscious that the cliff edge could be near. I looked down and tried to see it, tried to feel the rock under my feet. But I saw nothing but the flowery knoll.

"All of the Sisters have passed through this trial. You can now join us as our newest member."

Theresa was dead. "How many have you brought up here? How many have run blissfully off the edge?"

"It is not my trial, Miriam. It is God's. It is His Will that prevented you from going over the edge. If He wanted your soul, He would have let you join Him in Heaven, just as you thought you were doing. Theresa went to see God, and that is where she is now."

I felt overwhelmed and sank to my knees, grabbing handfuls of soil. It seemed so real. "When does this lie go away? How long will it take before I can see clearly?"

"Never. That is our great blessing and trial. The vision is permanent. But with concentration and enough practice, you can see through to the truth."

I brought the soil to my nose in cupped hands. It felt real and smelled like the richest soil I had ever known. I caught my breath as a glimmering of understanding came to me. I asked, "All the Sisters rejected this vision of Heaven as a lie?"

"All of them. That is how true Sisters are chosen."

I sighed. "You spend your whole lives rejecting beauty, which explains why you are all so wretched and cruel."

"We are not cruel, Miriam. Life is cruel."

"You make it so." I rose to my feet, dusting my hands on my cloak. "I pity you. You could have lived in Heaven, but you chose to stay and create your own He—."

"We rejected the illusion. There is no gateway to Heaven here."

"This is a test, only it isn't the test you thought." I turned my head toward the sun, and the warm breeze blew back my hair. "Look around you. You have fooled yourself into believing that Heaven is just an illusion because you and the other Sisters can't bring yourselves to believe in goodness. I am in Heaven, because in my heart of hearts, I believe."

"That is preposterous. Obviously you have failed the test. Go. Walk off the cliff and meet your end, if that is what you desire."

I began to walk down the knoll, feeling the flowers brush against my legs and the soft earth beneath my sandals. But I stopped again and turned to Sister Beneficence. I couldn't just leave her there. "Come with me. All you have to do is believe in the possibility."

"You would rather die than become a Sister? That is it, isn't it? You hate us that much, and you want me dead too."

I shook my head in resignation. "Death, hate, lies. That is all you see. Is it any wonder you fail the test?"

I turned to face the distant castle, nestled in the hills. The undulating river glistened in the sunlight, and on the edge of the warm breeze I thought I heard music. I took a deep breath and decided it would be fun to run.

Chapter Three
The Purr of the Leopard

Throwing caution to the wind, I ran down the hill carpeted with flowers and called to Theresa. I could still see her tiny form though now she was close to the river and barely visible. She turned and waved to me.

Upon reaching the bottom of the hill, the world abruptly ended. Darkness descended like a shroud over the land, and in seconds the fields, the trees, everything vanished into black. The sound of the rushing breeze and the birdsong dimmed into silence. Even the sweet fragrance of the flowers of Heaven vanished as the ground dropped out from under me.

I felt as though I was falling, and I wanted to scream, but nothing came from my mouth. I flailed my arms around trying to grasp something, anything to stop my plummet, but there was nothing there. Could Sister Beneficence have been right all along? Was Heaven just an illusion?

To my horror, I began to lose the sense of my arms and legs as if they too were being erased. What was happening to me? I strained to scream, but I had no mouth, no tongue.

"I have always been here," a voice whispered from out of the darkness. The voice was deep, though faint, and resonated with power. The thought of God instantly came to mind, but this was nothing like I expected. I wanted to shout, but I was nothing but a disembodied soul.

Closer now, the voice, filled with melancholy and despair, whispered, "I am tired . . . Tired of being." The God I knew would never feel so morose. A new image came to mind, an image that filled me with dread. Perhaps I had found a gateway, but not to Heaven.

"I see you," he whispered, and to my amazement I began to feel my body again. My heart sounded like thunder in my ears.

"Are you tired? Are you . . . weary? Do you ever get tired of . . . being?"

My mouth was dry, as were my eyes. Filled with fear, I couldn't answer. I tried to move my arms, my head, my feet, but all were strapped tightly against a wall.

Dizziness began to whirl around my head and sudden flashes of color danced at the corner of my vision. Then a headache began to creep its way up the back of my head, bringing pain with every heartbeat.

The voice said something. It was farther away, and I could barely make out the imagined words. "Relax. Fear not. Nobody lives forever . . . forev—"

The world collapsed and became a point.

* * *

The world opened like an explosion centered in my brain. Fingers of tingling sensation coursed through my arms, down my back and into the marrow of my legs. Identity rushed up my body like a geyser, washing me with knowledge. My name—Dennis Howard.

I am me. I am here. I am real.

I repeated this litany in the privacy of my mind as the pain in my head diminished and then vanished.

"Light," I said, and in response a dim light blinked on. Emanating from somewhere above my head, the light spread my shadow across the opposite wall of my chamber, inches from my nose. As the final effects of the remote nerve blocker at the base of my neck wore off, my fingers tingled. It was good to have command of my real body again.

"Emily, Exit," I croaked. Clearing my throat, I tried again, "Emily, Exit."

A jerking motion told me I'd been heard. My plastic chamber lifted like an elevator out of its slot, and the restraints that held me immobile released me. I didn't know why they forced us to use the restraints. The nerve blocker never failed.

I was drenched with sweat. Waking up was never fun. I hated it, and I hated being in this box. The air was always either too hot or too humid. It was always difficult to breathe.

Before I could stop myself, I whispered, "I love you—shut up. I love you—shut up." I shook my head and sighed. Whenever I felt particularly insecure, I was compelled to say this. I didn't know why, but it was just something I did without even thinking. It never really helped. In fact, it made me feel all the more miserable, because normal people weren't so obsessive-compulsive. And I had promised myself I wasn't going to say it anymore.

I nodded to Andy as I reached down to scratch my itchy ankles where the straps had been. With a nod, he beckoned me over to his console again. Trying to avoid any emerging people, I approached and jumped in surprise as music sprang out of the speakers near his console. It was Mozart's "Overture" to *The Marriage of Figaro*.

"How did our Sam Clemens do in there?"

I shrugged. "That's really for the judges to decide. Too bad you couldn't watch, eh?"

"Just my luck, that. It won't be as much fun, but I'll catch it later on a replay." Dozens of other chambers were rising out of the floor. Once free, most people jumped up and out of the giant hole in the ceiling. Some milled about, waiting for friends. Trevor hadn't emerged yet. The match was continuing, as not all the competitors had finished, so he was probably watching one of them. That's what I should have done instead of getting out.

"Ah, you still think Clemens is in trouble of—ah—losing?" I asked.

"If I could talk to him now, I'd tell him just to worry about Winger. He seems to be trouble, that one, what with scoring the highest in the first two rounds."

Mozart's music died down a bit, and Emily cleared her throat. "Excuse me, Dennis. But aren't you forgetting your appointment?"

"Oh, shoot me! I'm late for my physical!"

With that, I was off at a run, up and out of the circular ceiling exit. There were certain advantages to keeping in shape while living on Luna. Being able to jump was one of the biggest.

As I shot out of the hive like a bullet, both Andy's warning shout about running in the halls and Mozart's bouncing violins faded away. I easily made it to one of the second floor balconies overlooking the atrium, and with an additional lunge, I launched myself off the railing back into the hallway maze of Aristoteles.

If I missed this physical exam again, they would yank my SIM privileges. I couldn't let that happen. Who knew how long it would take them to reinstate me? For a moment, I felt singled out, but I reminded myself that everyone had to go through these physicals after a certain number of hours in the SIMs. Because of the tournament, I was racking up SIM time quicker than my friends, who were only watching. Participating in any SIM was expensive, and none of us were made of money.

Well, most of us, anyway. Rumor has it there's some prince, Prince Azzam, who's been in the SIMs for five months straight, only coming out to deal with bodily demands. I didn't believe a word of it.

Bouncing off a wall, I launched myself around a sharp bend. This type of behavior was frowned upon since it usually caused accidents, but only for kids who didn't know what they were doing. I just hoped nobody I knew saw me.

Three more turns would bring me to an overlook of the Brandenburg Arboretum, a circular area thirty meters in diameter, and built high enough to allow the maples to grow and grow.

Two more turns. I was planning on launching myself from the overlook railing, flying over the trees, and catching the railing on the other side one floor down. It should make quite a spectacle for anyone who happened to be looking out of their office windows at the time. When I jumped, I must be going quite fast, which meant two things.

First, in the low gravity of the moon, running fast meant keeping low to the ground. The more effort used to push myself up instead of forward simply increased the time between my steps. Second, it meant there could be no one in the way. As most people were still watching the final moments of the other tournament competitors, this didn't require too much luck, just a little.

Last turn.

Pumping my legs as fast as I could, I raced down the last corridor. My luck seemed to be holding, because no one turned the corner to block my path. The sound of birds and the smell of freshly turned soil washed over me as I neared the arboretum. I concentrated on the railing that rushed ever closer. Each foot had to be placed just so.

I reached the railing, jumped to the top and launched myself forward, soaring. Time seemed to slow as I drank in the sensation. The branches and leaves of the trees below were nothing but a tangled blur, but in a clearing, I noticed a kid espy me and point up. But I wasn't worried. With a hang time of about five seconds, no one would have time to take any real notice.

I streamlined my body to reduce air resistance, since I needed every inch I could get. What fun! I looked for my destination, a singular balcony one level below, and, to my surprise, saw someone standing there. It was a girl about my age. She hadn't noticed me coming at her yet.

The balcony rushed toward me and my feet hit the railing with a thud. What do you know? I made it, and with an audience to boot. The girl jumped in surprise at my sudden and unexpected appearance. She was cute—and I was on such a tight schedule.

I gave her an, "Excuse me," and launched myself off the railing and down the hall.

I dove around another corner, and right in front of my face was someone carrying a stack of . . . What? *Real* books! It was too late to even think about stopping. "Oof!" I slammed into him and fell in slow motion head over heels.

When I slid to a stop, I looked back at the devastation I'd just caused. Oh, man! More bad news. It was Professor Johnston, my astrophysics and music professor. But he hadn't seen who hit him yet. It was time for a quick vanishing act.

* * *

"Dr. Woodridge will see you."

"Woodridge?" I asked breathlessly. I had only just arrived. "Who's that? I'm here to see Dr. Levitt."

The receptionist sighed. "Dr. Levitt is no longer with the practice. He's gone off to Earth, dear. Follow me."

Dr. Woodridge turned out to be a woman and quite young to be a doctor, I thought. She looked to be in her twenties.

She didn't look up from her desk when I was ushered in and announced simply as, "Your next one." She motioned for me to sit down and said, "Be right with you. Just need to finish this up."

I took the seat across the desk from her and eyed the head gear attached to the examination chair in the corner. It looked old-fashioned compared to the sleek neural instruments Dr. Levitt used during my last exam. I was beginning to get nervous. Perhaps this machine could sense things the other couldn't, secret things.

"There. Now then," she said as she punched up my file. "Dennis Howard?" She came around the desk and shook my hand.

"In the flesh," I said.

"Katherine Woodridge, Dennis." She held my hand for a second. "Have we met before? You seem familiar to me?"

Lord, it's started already. If she knew how well read I was on the entire field of psycho-pathology, she wouldn't have tried such a simple ploy. It's a well-known fact that people who spend too long in the SIMs started to suffer all types of brain dysfunction. That's why they test so often. One of the things that could go wrong was in the temporal lobe — the problem manifests itself as the sensation that recently gained knowledge was very old. For example, meeting someone thirty seconds ago might feel as if we had met thirty days ago.

I put on what I hoped was a pleasant smile and said, "No, I don't think so." Perhaps it was my nerves, but I could feel a headache coming on. Terrific.

She nodded and released my hand, ushering me toward the chair in the corner. "Your file says you've missed your last two appointments. What's the problem?"

"I just got busy and—" I almost said forgot about the appointments, which would have made it sound like there was something wrong with my brain. She mustn't know the truth. Instead, I finished, "Things came up."

"Okay, then. Why don't you get in the examination chair? I'll attach the gear."

I had to force myself to sit in the chair and fit my head into the contraption. "Is this thing safe?"

"More safe than those SIM chambers," she replied with a smile as she moved sensors into place on my temples. "Tell me, have you noticed being forgetful lately? Any severe headaches?"

"Headaches? None that I can recall," I replied jokingly, trying to hide my nervousness. She was behind me, so I couldn't see if she was smiling or not. I cleared my throat. "Could you, ah, repeat the first question?"

Dr. Woodridge turned the neural scanner on with a thunk, and it rumbled like a purring cat. I pictured a leopard behind me salivating and ready to pounce.

"You spend a lot of time in the SIMs," she said as she looked through a display somewhere behind me. "What do you do in there?"

"There's a lot of SIMming in school, you know," I said defensively. "When Professor Johnston says, 'All right class, don your caps,' there's nothing you can do."

"You expect me to believe all your SIMming is for school work?"

"Well, no. Me and some friends do some role playing in this adventure world during weekends—"

"Oh yeah? Which one?" She returned to her desk and the lights dimmed. A holo of my brain appeared hovering above the surface of the desk. But I only caught a glimpse of it. With a whirring noise, the near side of her desk rose up as some kind of privacy shield.

What did she just ask? Oh, yeah. "Mostly just W.O.R."

She looked up in surprise. "I didn't think kids today were still into the World of Rapt."

"You've heard of it?" I asked.

"Rapt has been around for years, you know. In my younger days, you could have found me roaming the realm, doing the King's bidding."

"Your younger days? You still seem young to me."

"Hmm," she murmured non-committedly "Looks can be deceiving. But tell me, what about the Tournament? Certainly you have been watching the Master's Tournament?" The purring of the machine changed slightly as she worked.

"Are you kidding? I wouldn't miss it for the world," I said.

"Who's your favorite? Ozymandias? Tom Thumb?"

"Those guys couldn't act if you gave them a script. No ma'am. It's Sam Clemens you should be looking out for."

"And you? Do you want to be a Master yourself some day?"

"Me?" I asked nervously. I suddenly wondered if this thing doubled as a lie detector. "I would love it. All the free SIM time you want, plus getting to choose new Masters by running the Tournaments every year."

And with time in the SIMs I would get more time under the height of the sky. What I wouldn't give to live under a sky, instead of the catacombs delved into Luna. "I think I could handle that."

"I think the Masters do more than just play in the SIM," she commented. "Are you forgetting how it's their job to monitor the people in the SIMs, looking for problems? It isn't all fun and games."

"Nothing is free," I agreed.

"So what are your chances of winning, you think? Good?"

She almost got me with that one. "I'm not a competitor," I said innocently. "What are you saying?"

Still sitting on her chair, she rolled out from behind that privacy shield to look me in the face. Her expression was deadly serious. "I'm saying that the only way to avoid getting your SIM privileges revoked after missing two check-ups is to have someone at SI override the normal protocols."

My mouth was suddenly very dry.

She continued, counting on her fingers. "Your father works at Prometheus doing research, and your mother teaches at the university. So neither of them has any influence at SI. You're logging SIM time at about twice the rate as your friends. It all points toward your involvement in the tournament. And now, after some simple questions, I even know you are playing under the name Sam Clemens."

She clicked the machine into silence. "Privacy mode," she commanded.

The LMC responded with a male Irish brogue. "Entering privacy mode."

"I . . . I . . ." I didn't know what to say. Good god, does everyone know?

"Dennis, from what I hear, being in the tournament isn't for the faint of heart. There's a lot of money involved in illicit betting. I've even heard tale of a bounty for naming the competitors."

It was pointless denying it. "What am I supposed to do?"

"Just think about the trail of data you are leaving." She must have noticed how worried I was because her entire tone changed. She reassured me, "Now, not everyone has access to your medical records, so you might still be safe. Don't worry too much, just be more careful." As she held my forehead steady to remove the sensors, the base of my neck began to ache.

"There." After she retracted the apparatus, I was able to sit normally again. I rubbed my throbbing neck, hoping she didn't notice.

"Are we going to be much longer?" I asked. "They are about to announce the winners of the latest match, and—"

"All right. Here's the upshot. Looks like you've got some minor synapse fray going on, but it's not enough to warrant kicking you off the SIMs—"

"Great!"

"Which isn't to say that you can keep spending as much time in the SIM as you have been. Look, why do you want to be a Master anyway? It isn't healthy to let your body rot while your mind goes off on adventures."

I was silent, thinking. I could tell she was being forthright. This wasn't some mental game anymore. "Look, living on Luna is wrong. It's almost perverse. We evolved under a blue sky, breathing the real air and feeling the real wind. I hate it here."

"People on Earth live in houses," Woodridge said. "Before that caves, and before that under the canopy of a dense forest. We only feel safe when we have a roof over our heads."

"It doesn't matter," I moaned. "It's not like I'll ever have enough money to get to Earth."

"It is pointless rattling the bars of your cage, because no matter where you go, you are in a cage. The entire Earth is, itself, a cage."

"Earth is too big to feel like a cage," I argued.

"Perhaps," she said. "It all depends on your capacity to imagine. I don't have to look at your neural density readings to tell you are quite intelligent. I've never heard of such a young competitor before. It adds up to someone who, even on Earth, would be driven to the SIMs like an addict, not for the height of the sky, but for the limitless possibilities."

I shook my head. "What about my claustrophobia? You must have run across that in my records too."

"Simply remind yourself that none of this matters." She swept her hands around the room. "Not where you are, not when you are. The only thing that matters is who you are and being with the people you care about." She shook her head. "And it's easier said than done."

I got to my feet impatiently. They were probably announcing the winners right now. "To thine own self be true. Know thyself. It's all great. Look, can I trust you'll keep all this . . ."

She waved her hand, and the door slid open. "I'm the least of your worries. Oh, Dennis, just remember: People on Earth? They can't do this." She gently pushed off the floor and floated upward, like only someone on Luna could do. "And they all wish they were here."

* * *

Ten minutes later, I strolled into Marty's, a quaint little fast food joint in the Drumman Section of Aristoteles where I lived. After scanning with a quick eye the tables and booths, which were nearly entirely filled with kids from school, I found Trevor and Zak planted in a corner booth near the back. I grabbed some food and joined them.

"Hey," I said in greeting as I flopped down next to Trevor. They greeted me with quick nods, and resumed the debate I had interrupted. It was the same plot dissection we did after every match. Sometimes I pretended not to know what Sam Clemens did. Zak still had no idea I was in the competition. Even though we knew he wouldn't give anything away on purpose, Trevor and I had both agreed that keeping Zak in the dark was for the best. He really seemed to say whatever crossed his mind, so he couldn't be trusted.

"It seems obvious enough to me," said Trevor as he pushed his fingers through his already messy hair. "The Sisters were a representation of evil. The narcotic flowers brought it to the surface. Those that didn't seem evil before smelling the flowers should show such signs after. Out of all of the players managing to get to the peak, smell the flowers, and not run off the edge of the cliff, only Rainbow and Sam Clemens showed no signs of sudden evil tendencies."

"What did Rainbow do?" I asked.

Trevor said, "Rainbow followed Sister Beneficence, blindly tripped, and rolled off the cliff. Sam's character chose to walk off the cliff of her own volition. Sam's character should have shown some evil tendencies . . ." He looked glumly at me and shook his head. "It doesn't look good."

Zak rolled his eyes. As always, Zak's light brown hair was tied back to keep it out of his face. He kept it long, not because he liked it that way, but because his father wanted him to cut it. "Hello? Earth to Trevor. Did we even watch the same match? Those flowers don't create axe-murderers."

Trevor turned to me, asking, "Did I say anything about axe-murderers?"

Zak continued, "And besides that, if the flowers did cause this 'evil behavior,' as you claim, then Sam Clemens must be superior to all those other fools because his character managed to resist madness. Sam managed to get through the gateway to heaven because he—I mean she—because Sam believed it was real. Only the pure of heart could get to heaven, and that was Sam. Back me up on this Dennis."

I opened my mouth but it was still half full of fries. Trevor replied first, "That was just an illusion of heaven. It was a lie. Just believing in something doesn't make it true."

Swallowing, I finally managed to say, "Look. The issue isn't whether that character got to heaven or not. The issue is this. Did the players act true to the situation? If the flowers instigated unsavory behavior, then the player acting the most true to the situation must produce that behavior. If they read the situation wrong and behave uncharacteristically vile when, in fact, the flowers had no such effect, then those players are not the winners, but the losers. But the whole thing was ambiguous. It could go either way."

"Yeah, yeah," Zak replied. "Did you see Peter the Great? He went off the deep end and threw both the other novice and Sister Beneficence off the cliff. And then when he was done, he threw himself off."

"Maybe he felt bad about what he had done," I suggested.

Trevor shook his head. "No, he was foaming at the mouth. Quite a spectacle. The flowers made him do it."

Zak waved in disgust. "Oh who cares about any of that! All I want to know is who won."

Trevor asked, "Who'd you bet on?"

Zak answered, "I put some on Peter the Great and Sam Clemens. Three-to-one and five-to-one." I noticed Zak drumming his fingers nervously. His food sat in front of him untouched.

I asked, "Did you bet the mint, or what?"

"Naw. One of 'em just better win. That's all. Because after that physics exam today—well, let's just say physics is not in the cards for me."

"It wasn't that hard," I said.

Zak shook his head, and before Trevor could pipe up, the 3-D at our table sprang to life. Three rotating interlocking triangles appeared hovering above the table, Sybernetics International's corporate symbol. The rotating symbol was replaced by the face of one of the Masters. It was Master Cummings.

In a deep resounding voice, Master Cummings began, "The Fourth Trial of the Eighth Annual Master's Championship Tournament has ended." Master Cummings was a handsome blond man of about forty years. His close-cut beard and penetrating eyes made all the girls melt, including my little sister.

"Emily, raise the volume a bit," I ordered, and she instantly complied.

Master Cummings continued, "The competition was fierce and the judging difficult, but a set of winners has been chosen to continue on to the next trial."

The scene wavered and changed to show an aerial view of the desolate setting of the Fourth Trial. "The title of the Fourth Trial was 'Heaven Bound.' Ten of the forty remaining competitors participated today, and their pseudonyms included Blaze, Einstein, Ozymandias, Peter the Great, Ranier, Sam Clemens, Tom Thumb, Walt Whitman, Winger, and last but not least Zeus. To have made it to the Fourth Trial is a magnificent accomplishment in itself, so all ten should be proud and count themselves among the most talented extemporaneous actors of our time. In recognition of this fact, all ten competitors will be receiving one hundred hours of free SIM time."

Master Cummings described the setting of the Fourth Trial, and as the medieval convent was shown, I shivered in spite of myself.

The view shifted to the mountaintop containing a bright yellow patch of flowers. Master Cummings said, "One species of flower, indigenous to this mountain alone, grew unmolested for ages until one of the Sisters of the Convent happened along. The Sisters called these flowers the Flowers of Heaven, because they had a special hallucinogenic property upon being smelled at the right time of day. They produced illusions of beauty and grandeur while making it very difficult to perceive the underlying reality. This defensive mechanism caused any near the flowers to walk or run off the cliff to their death. This natural selection process kept the flowers safe for hundreds of years, until the Sisters, or rather, one particular Sister found them."

The scene changed to that of a thin woman discovering the flowers, picking one and passing out. "Upon seeing this vision of beauty and grandeur, this Sister's pessimism, or perhaps realism, overcame the illusion, enabling her to perceive the rocks and the deathly fall only steps away.

"Over the years, the Sisterhood went through its own natural selection, in which only the most pessimistic, only the most world-weary self-loathing Sisters survived the smell of the flowers. As if to validate their rejection of the heavenly illusion, from these flowers they received unusual abilities, or Gifts, as they were called.

"Finally, by the force of the illusion, the Sisters' philosophy evolved from 'by knowing thyself one can come to know truth and attain enlightenment' to 'know a lie for a lie, and the truth will be plain'.

Master Cummings reappeared. "For the most natural performance and the ability to navigate through this trial, the winners of the Fourth Trial of the Eighth Annual Master's Championship Tournament are Ozymandias, Ranier, Sam Clemens, Walt Whitman and Winger. The Masters found their performances to be self-consistent, differentiable from past performances, and free from modern preconceptions. These five will continue on to the Fifth Trial in one week's time. Congratulations to all of the competitors. I am Master Cummings." As his face faded out to be replaced by the three interlocking triangles, he gave that charming smile of his and nodded. The words 'Eighth Annual Master's Championship Tournament' now circled the symbol.

Zak waved the blaring brass fanfare to silence and smiled broadly. "Can I pick 'em or what?"

Trevor dismissed Zak's exhibition and asked me, "And why are you smiling?" Of course he knew why.

But, in the spirit of being a tournament competitor, I made up an answer on the spot. "Oh, I might have some money on old Sam, myself," I replied evenly.

"You too?" said Trevor, giving me a wink. "Why am I sitting here wasting my time with two idiots who think it's smart to bet on these tournaments? Heh? Why, I ask you?"

Zak laughed and got up to stretch. He said, "Because not only are we a laugh, we're the only bloody idiots willing to waste time with you."

Thinking of Rapt, I corrected Zak, "Because you need us to find that relic of Tishman you've been yammering about these past few weeks."

Zak looked at me and indicated Trevor with his thumb. "He's just pissed that we both had money on winners."

"And he didn't," I finished. Turning to Trevor I asked, "So, who'd you bet on?"

A wry expression took over Trevor's face. He pulled his fingers through his hair again and admitted, "Let me be boiled in tar if I ever bet on another three inch tall fictitious character! Tom Thumb, my foot."

Zak and I smiled at each other with knowing looks. Trevor didn't make it a habit of betting on these events, but whenever he did, he invariably lost.

"Oh, and Blanchard," Trevor said using my role-playing name. "You can forget about that Tishman relic. We have bigger problems. Will you two be able to make it this weekend?"

"Have we ever missed a session, Sir Welling Redd?" asked Zak off-handedly, this time using Trevor's pseudonym.

"I don't always run into you two in there, you know," Trevor retorted defensively. "The World of Rapt is a big place. And if I were you, I wouldn't miss either session this weekend."

"Let's get out of here," Zak said motioning for us to follow.

Following Zak's lead, we got up to leave. "And what is it that you don't want us to miss, Sir Redd?" I asked Trevor.

"You know. Another onslaught of undefeatable creatures. The beginning of the end of civilization as we know it."

Zak asked, "Joy and happiness extinguished from the world to be replaced by desolation and waste?"

I nodded sagely, "So, same old, same old."

Trevor continued, "I can't go into details outside of Rapt, but I'm going to need your help."

As we made our way through the crowd toward the exit, Zak grimaced and said, "If it's not one thing, it's another. Spending time in Rapt seems more and more like a waste of good money. Don't get me wrong, now. I enjoy saving the world and all, but I spend more time dodging danger trying to save my butt than I do having fun."

I replied, "You can't think of Rapt as a place just to have fun. It's more like—I don't know, more like a training ground. More like practice."

"What are we practicing for? Speaking with an archaic flourish?" Trevor asked.

"Isn't it obvious?" I asked. "We are practicing how to save the world."

Trevor and I laughed, as Zak commented, "What the—?"

I looked up to see what had caught Zak's eye. Getting out of Marty's was going to prove a tad more difficult than I had foreseen because at that moment Frank Talonii and cohorts were walking in and creating a commotion. Frank was an eighteen-year-old who didn't let you forget it.

"Make way for Sam Clemens!" announced one of Frank's flunkies. I jerked involuntarily at the mention of my own pseudonym. "The one, the only, Frank Talonii, pride of Drumman!" Frank was smiling proudly and strutting around as if he were a king. He even waved to the crowd as if they were applauding him. If anything, they were staring is shocked silence. But that soon changed.

I murmured under my breath, "Good God." Kids began to crowd around, some asking for autographs, some asking if it were really true. I could feel my growing ire at Talonii's charade keeping pace with my looming claustrophobia.

Zak said, "If Sam is really Talonii-breath over there, I'm not betting on him anymore." Trevor snickered.

"He's not Sam Clemens," I said over the commotion. "This is just a scam to get some free food."

One of Frank's cohorts, a greasy type we knew as Spunk, suddenly leaned into my face saying, "What was that zip-brain?"

Spunk towered over me, but that didn't stop me. I crossed my arms. "I'd believe in the Easter Bunny before I believed Frank Talonii was Sam Clemens."

"Is that so? Hey Frankie! We've got some pip-squeak unbelievers over here!"

Frank pushed through the crowd saying, "We do? Who says I'm not—These—" He looked as if he changed his mind about his choice of words. "These misguided young gentlemen?" He looked at each of us in turn. "Zak the Meddling Metler, Trevor Russo-matic and Dennis the Menace Howard?"

Trevor whispered in my ear my very own thoughts. "How does he do that?"

Trevor had a good point. None of us had ever had a run-in with Talonii before. We knew better than to get in his way, usually. I should have kept my mouth shut. They say if he knew your name, he also knew your biggest weakness, your greatest fear. They also say he knew everyone's name.

He looked down at me, and his full brown hair reminded me of a lion's mane. "What makes you think I'm not Sam Clemens, Howard?

"I know you're not him." I shot back defiantly. What was I thinking? This guy could pound me into mince-meat, and I didn't even know what mince-meat was. In this crowd, he might even be able to get in a few licks without the Lunar Main Computer seeing. My knees felt like they were shaking a little. I needed to stop talking.

Speaking low enough for only me to hear, he said, "You must have some reason for thinking I'm not Clemens." Frank raised an eyebrow and scratched his chin. "Now, if you actually knew the real identity of Sam Clemens, then you might have cause to shout foul, but he hasn't officially shed his anonymity yet, has he? Who is he, Coward?" Frankie pointed at me mispronouncing my name. "I suppose you're going to claim that you're Clemens? Hmmm?"

He was more than a head taller than me and stacked with muscles. But I blustered on. "I'm not afraid of you, Frank. But I'm surprised you'd paint a target on your back by announcing you're a competitor. I thought you were smarter than that." Frank grabbed my shirt and pulled me close, but I just kept talking, "And if you were an actual competitor, it would be obvious. No matter what character you attempted to play, your own putrescence would fill the air like the stench of old slaughtered fish—"

"Are you crossing swords with me, Coward? I don't think you want to get on my bad side—" Frank halted and glanced about, and in curiosity I did the same. We were forming an audience of gawkers that Emily couldn't have missed if she tried, and if there was a fight, the authorities would know everything.

Frank put me down and straightened my shirt, with a smile. "You bore me, Coward. You would be too easy to defeat in a duel."

"Who's the coward now?"

Frank leaned close, grabbed my shoulder and whispered, "You better go before I decide to destroy my perfect reputation by smashing it over your skull, little man. But if it's any consolation, you're officially on my list, Dennis Howard."

He pushed me and said to his friends, "As my grandfather always said, 'Never trust a man with two first names. Two names means two faces.'" Spunk laughed at that.

Once we were out of there, Zak whistled through his teeth. "Dennis, man. What a show."

My head was spinning now that I was out of the crowd and out from under Frank's shadow.

Trevor stopped my progress down the hall with a hand on my shoulder, asking, "Are you nuts, or something? Taking on Talonii like that? Remember Peter Crenshaw? Where is he now?"

Zak replied, "He didn't die, Trev. He just moved away."

"Exactly," said Trevor. "He had to. He was too afraid to go to school, so his family had to move."

Zak waved his hand in disgust, "That's just hearsay. Dennis, man, I was behind you all the way. We could have taken them—"

"We could have taken them? The three of us?" I asked incredulously as the hall began to spin faster. "You've been spending too much time in the SIM . . . illusions of grandeur. Whew. Somebody catch me —" My legs gave way, and I found myself on the floor leaning against the wall.

I heard Trevor comment to Zak, "Must be a form of post-traumatic syndrome. I've read about this kind of thing."

"You think he'll recover in time for the game this weekend?"

"He'd better."

I sighed as they both turned and walked away. Zak said, "Now tell me more about this trouble in Rapt."

Chapter Four
The Risen Realm
Hawk Eyes

H ello. Now, let me see. Hmm. What was I just thinking about — Broken my chain of thought completely. Odd. How very odd, that." Scratching my beard, I realized I was thinking out loud again. That habit was beginning to worry me.

Habit. The thought of habits sparked a taste in my mouth, followed by a quick search of the immediate area and finished off with the voiced question, "Where has that pipe of mine got to, anyway?" The immediate area was my work table, which happened to be so littered with books and papers, cups and plates, plants and candles, and small, easily lost ancient relics and artifacts each made by some lost art, that finding a pipe and some weed to go with it was made next to impossible. This might require reinforcements.

"Neville! Neville, where the devil have you gone to?" I called out to be answered by silence. I was faced with a choice. I could find my pipe on my own or track down Neville. I pondered for a moment and arrived at a solution that seemed to me altogether rational and intelligent. Finding Neville should be far easier because, for finding him, I had the use of my eyes *and* my voice. I could call to Neville, and when he got within earshot, he would most likely answer. I could do the same with my pipe, but the odds on the pipe answering were slim to none.

Still, there did seem to be a chance. "Pipe. Pipe, where are you, blasted thing! Answer me when I'm talking to you." I listened for a reply, but none seemed forthcoming. Well, it had been worth a stab. What really bothered me was that it was probably lying right out in the open. The best hiding places were always in plain sight.

I rose slowly out of my creaking chair, feeling my joints grate and my muscles strain. I wasn't as young as I used to be. My next goal was the door to my study, and I looked at it across the room. To my surprise, it appeared to be lurking. I knew because in my youth I was a bit of a lurker—known for my talent to lurk, as it were.

I looked at the door again. The light from the window hit the bust of Saint Theodore Bartholomew in just the right way to cast a sinister silhouette on the door. But it was more than a trick of the light. The paneling on the door itself gave the distinct impression that it was waiting to spring on the unwary and pounce on the innocent.

I straightened my back and took on the challenge. I would not be put off by a mere lurking door. I've faced worse, I reminded myself. I began to navigate the small pathway across the room leading to the door. The room was in such a state of clutter that to stray from that single path would mean either stepping on something valuable or knocking over something irreplaceable. It was really quite a mess.

I approached the door with some foreboding, the latch seeming to wait for me to reach out and grasp it, daring me with its innocent stillness and mocking me with its arrogant shine. I began to reach for the latch, then drew my hand back in sudden trepidation and looked up at its height. My study door was seven feet tall and three-and-a-half feet wide. How many times had I passed through it before, never thinking or realizing, never looking twice? I looked the door up and down and came to a surprising conclusion. "Why, you're not lurking at all. You're out-and-out looming."

I gave a shout as the door suddenly leapt forward. As quickly as my aging body would allow, I jumped out of the way. The next thing I saw was young Neville's head poking around the edge of the door. "Your Grace, I hope—Oh I apologize, your Grace. I didn't startle you, did I?"

I tried to regain some composure and replied, "Startled? Why I— Oh, whatever is it Neville?"

"Your Grace, Sir Welling Redd arrived this morning and has requested an audience. It seems urgent."

"Welling Redd is here? Gracious me. Well, send him in, Neville. Don't keep the good Duke waiting. Off you go."

"Yes, your Grace," Neville answered, and, with a smile and a quick nod, he was off. That boy was too young for his own good. Turn your head for a moment, and there he is running about, ready to bust and fit to be tied. He'll soon be falling on his head, tripping over some skirt or another, and winding up in more trouble than a body has a right to.

"Now what was I thinking—Chain of thought just gone again." I tried to retrace my thoughts. I murmured to myself, "Let's see now. I was thinking of Neville. I wanted something from him. What was it? Lunch? Is it lunch time already? Well, in that case we'll have him bring us up something after Redd gets here. Won't that be nice?"

I lurched back to my chair and let the cushions take my weight, such as it was. Hmm. "Lurch. Now what did that remind me of?" I looked back at the door. "Lurch? Was it lunch? No, no, no. Silly me. It was the larch."

I reached for the book I had laid aside, somewhere, but failed to find it. I had been reading about how the larch, a tree in the pine family, could be used to prevent catastrophic floods. Not only that, but amazing as it seems, the trees themselves didn't seem to appreciate the full usefulness of this talent. In fact, it had been determined, or so this passage claimed, that the larches would, on the whole, prefer to be left alone, and that they had been known to take a heated dislike to anyone snapping off branches, let alone felling whole trees.

Ransacking my desk was no use. The book was not to be found, and I wondered if the passage was something I had, in fact, read some other day. I rubbed my eyes. Fatigue had a way of making my mind wander in circles.

My reverie was short lived, for Neville had returned. "Your Grace—"

Neville was interrupted as a man pushed the door the rest of the way open and stepped through. He said, "Sol Blanchard, you devil. It's good to see you."

I got to my feet again and ambled over to the pair. "If it isn't the Duke of South Seniford himself. Come in, come in." It was *Sir* Welling Redd now, I reminded myself. He had been knighted three seasons ago, and deservedly so as I recalled. He had saved the prince's life no less than three times on the road to—well, that was another story.

Redd whisked off his grey cloak to reveal battle-scarred chain mail covering his torso. At his side was his blade, without which I had never seen him. His face was covered with an unkempt but short black beard, and his head was a tangle of hair of the same color. His smile was quick, but his eyes betrayed some sort of weariness.

We gripped arms in greeting, and his next comment proved that those weary eyes were still as agile and perceptive as always. He said, "I see you've been picking up after yourself. Sometimes I think your attention to detail will be your undoing." Finding no place to hang his cloak, he slung it over a shoulder.

We both looked around the room. Every horizontal surface was stacked high with books and papers, and most of the floor qualified as horizontal. I smiled. "Always those hawk eyes, eh? Rarely do they miss a thing. Actually, it has taken weeks of work, but it's getting there. At least now I can find things. No one else can, but I certainly know where everything is."

"How about a chair? I have been in the saddle longer than I like to recall."

"Chair? You want to sit? Oh dear." We glanced around, but no chair but my own was apparent. "Believe it or not there are three chairs and a couch in here somewhere. But they shouldn't count—" I wagged a finger at him. "I wasn't trying to keep track of them, and as you know, they are extremely adept at hiding, and often do for weeks on end."

Leaning against the wall, Redd laughed his deep-throated laugh, and it was good to hear.

"What brings you to Waterton? I was just telling Neville here," I began but stopped when I realized Neville was nowhere to be found. "Well, he's gone again—"

"Blanchard," Redd sighed in exhaustion. "The unthinkable has happened. The Hold of Chaldea has fallen."

"What? That fortress is impregnable. Why—"

"It's true. I heard Gaul Hiltred give the order. I saw them abandon the walls."

"By Tishman, what did they meet that could not be faced?" I asked as a thrill of fear went through me.

"I need to see the Potentate, Blanchard. I would have gone to him straight away but I needed time to collect my wits and recover from the ride."

"And me forcing you to stand as inhospitable as can be. Come with me," I said beckoning him to follow. "We shall first have a visit with Mistress Vallow in the kitchens. And while you are refreshing, I shall see to finding the Potentate and arranging an audience."

Redd nodded wearily and followed me out of my study. "I rode with a small company of my men, my retinue. They await me down in the courtyard."

"Then we shall invite them in as well," I replied as I fumbled with the keys in my pocket. Finally finding the right one, I bolted the door securely, but as I did so, something caught my eye about the door. It looked—I stepped closer and smelled the wood. It almost smelled like—"Tell me truthfully Redd, is this door made of larch wood, or is it my imagination?"

"What wood?" Redd's expression was distracted and I realized that my question might appear to be verging on the insane. How did he manage to raise one eyebrow like that?

"Never mind. Follow me."

* * *

As luck would have it, on our way down the front stairs, I espied Avedis Hovhen running across the lower hall. He was late for the very class I was to teach that afternoon. "Avedis!" I shouted. "Ho there, Avedis. Half a moment, if you please."

When Avedis whirled about and saw me, his complexion was a sheet of white as if his tardiness was a stoning offense. That was his natural coloring, though. "Your Grace," came his out-of-breath reply as Redd and I descended the stairs. His accent was as thick as ever, being from the far north, a town I couldn't even pronounce.

"Avedis, lad. I'm afraid I'll have to forego my class on Ethics in White Magic today. The Duke of Seniford has arrived with circumstances running at his heels. Inform the rest of the students, won't you?"

"As you wish, your Grace," Avedis replied. Turning to Redd and with a slight bow, he said, "My lord." Seemingly filled with self-possession, Avedis turned and strode toward the class to deliver my message.

"Oh, and one more thing, Avedis. Please find Lady Sedra and ask her to join us. We'll be in the Hall of Tishman. No dawdling, now."

Avedis gave me a curt nod and trotted off.

When he was out of earshot, I said, "You seem to be slipping, my Lord. I remember a time your mere proximity would have reduced a boy his age to a mass of quivering awe."

As we continued toward the outer courtyard, Redd said, "I had never seen a face so white before. Where ever is he from?"

Our footsteps and voices echoed off the arching stone high above us. "The far north. Students were never easy to come by, and these days even more so. Even recruiting from so far afield, still these halls seem empty when compared with the earlier days of the college."

"Did I hear you say you were teaching *Ethics*?" Redd asked.

"Ethics is more important than you might think, Redd. It's practically the heart of what we do here. It is the difference between making allies and making enemies."

Redd held up his hand, waving me to silence. "I don't want to know. I never could understand what goes on here at Waterton." He pushed his fingers through his hair with a sigh.

"You could if you were willing to spend the effort."

"We have bigger things to worry about today."

We had arrived at the doorway to the outer courtyard. Redd paused with his hand on the latch and added, "Such is the tale of my life." With that, he yanked it open, and outside I could see six men tending to seven horses. Redd stood in the doorway and bid them follow with a shout and a wave, then turned his gaze at the darkening sky with a searching eye.

* * *

The school was named the Tishman School for the Magically Gifted at Waterton. But that was far too long, so people just called it Waterton. Across the grounds were scattered many buildings, and towers, housing staff and students alike. And amid that jumble stood a singular structure stretching into the sky: The Hall of Tishman. Historians have it that this single building was why the school was built on this spot so many centuries ago.

Inside the Hall of Tishman was a grand and majestic room. Its granite pillars standing all in a circle followed the curve of the wall. They stretched toward the distant ceiling, and their girth made one believe they could hold the weight of the world, or at least the weight of the sky. The arches high above, stretching from pillar to pillar, were graceful and a joy to see. Their curvature was a refreshing departure from the stolidly straight spines of the pillars.

Nestled within the arches high above were small windows letting the sunlight into the great hall. On full moon nights, they allowed that gentle illumination to offset the harsh firelight from the hearths scattered around the circular walls.

The Hall of Tishman was mostly used for ceremonial functions like the raising of a student to full mage. Sometimes the hall was used for social engagements, such as hosting balls when dignitaries visited the college. But for the most part, the hall stood empty and collected dust. Without a myriad of bodies to fill it up, the sheer size of the room left one with a profound sense of one's own insignificance. It wasn't a place within which to study or meditate.

Nonetheless, that was exactly where I found the head of our order, dubbed 'the Potentate'. He could be found here most days, returning every mid-morning. And meditating was exactly what Palomar did in this vast hall, all the while fingering that ruby ring of his. In the shadows was a servant waiting to do his bidding.

I informed Palomar of the Duke's arrival and his urgent desire for conference, and at Palomar's command, I retraced my steps and soon returned with Redd. Once we both stood before Palomar, Redd began his tale of woe.

"What do you mean the Hold of Chaldea has fallen?" Palomar croaked in alarm. Having lost the strength to walk or even stand, Palomar sat before us on a chair with small wheels attached so he could be pushed where he was needed. His wizened and bent form seemed to straighten slightly at the news.

"Four days ago, I heard Duke Hiltred give the order to leave the walls—"

"So Chaldea was abandoned," Palomar said with rancor. "Tell me, Chosen, what wisdom was there in abandoning our second line of defense against Nardel? Speak."

At my side, I could feel Redd stiffen at the rebuke, but he held his temper in check. "There is wisdom in retreat when all hope of standing is gone. Given time, all would have been killed. No force of arms could have retained Chaldea. They were attacked by ghosts."

"By what?" Palomar asked.

"Ghosts, specters. Call them what you will, but nothing could be done to stop them."

"Ghosts," I said. "Then there is some new evil under the sun. I thought to have seen it all." Nardel, our enemy of old, was a master of Dark Magic. Our first line of defense against him was the enchantment that kept him and his minions imprisoned below ground, but it seemed that he had devised some new way to penetrate the walls of his prison.

"I know it sounds hard to credit, but it's true." Redd pulled his fingers through his hair and looked around in an agitated fashion. "They seem to only attack at night. No fortification can keep them out. No wall is thick enough, and worst of all, no sword can repel them or even nick them. The men were abandoning their posts in droves long before Hiltred gave the order to abandon Chaldea."

"Abandon Chaldea?" a female voice exclaimed from behind us. I turned to discover the owner of that voice was Sedra, another teacher at Waterton. Every time I saw her, I was struck by her handsome face and rich straight brown hair that fell about her shoulders. Her body was lithe and strong, but what I invariably noted above all else was her youth. I had little doubt her beauty would persist even if she reached my age. Seeing her, my spirit seemed to lift despite Redd's evil news.

Sedra strode in purposefully, asking, "Are you talking about the Hold of Chaldea?"

Redd nodded to Sedra as Palomar said, "Is it your habit to interrupt our audiences unannounced and unlooked for, Sedra?"

I said, "I asked her to join us, your Grace."

"I'll just excuse myself—" Sedra began to retreat from the hall.

"No. Pray, stay on." Palomar bowed his head. "We shall need your insight here, I have little doubt." Palomar smiled, and I wondered if the last was genuine or an insult. I knew he held little love for the younger mages, no matter their brilliance.

"Have you met Sedra, Redd?" I asked. "No? Sedra Rall, meet Sir Welling Redd, Duke of Seniford. Sedra's talent goes well beyond her teaching abilities. I only wish we had ten more, here at Waterton, just like her." I gave Palomar a sidelong glance wondering if he caught my implied slight.

Redd said, "My Lady," after which he stooped and gallantly kissed her hand.

A glint of red reflection caught my eye, and I glanced toward Palomar's right hand. He was fingering his ring again.

"Yes, yes," Palomar interrupted hoarsely. "Pleasantries aside, tell us more, Duke Redd. What have you seen?"

"Of course, your Grace. It has been about a week since the ghosts began to appear in Westmarch. They seem to be only drawn to people. It was as if Verve was invisible to them."

Sedra said, "Verve? That's Gaul Hiltred's kestrel, isn't it?"

"Quite," Redd said. "I witnessed all of this through the eyes of Hiltred's kestrel."

"Yes," Palomar interrupted. "Where is your kestrel, Duke Redd? Will Sapphire be joining us?"

"She is flying above Waterton now. She will be joining us soon. But, look. Do not think poorly of Hiltred. His forces were afraid, and rightly so. There was no place they could hide and nothing they could use to defend themselves. How do you kill what is already dead? And . . . and even that is not the worst. The same men that are killed are . . . They return as ghosts themselves the next night."

"My God!" I exclaimed. "What a hideous—"

Redd turned to me. "We can be thankful of at least one thing. Each specter seems to only kill once per night. After killing, they vanish . . . until the next sundown."

"I can understand how this is making people run." Palomar seemed to remain calm. Perhaps this meant he had a possible solution. I had no idea how to fight such an enemy. Palomar continued, "In truth, this news of ghosts does not come as a complete surprise to me. I have felt a deep chill these past few nights, even sitting before the hottest fire. How do these ghosts appear?"

"The only warning they had was the sudden chill, as you just described, and a fear," Redd said. "Even though I was not present, my connection to Hiltred through the kestrels roused me out of the deepest sleep. I found I was standing, sword in hand, with nothing to fight. Then I realized I was feeling the sensations of Verve hundreds of leagues away.

"Three of them came that first night. They simply walked right through the wall. The ghosts . . . they looked just like peasants. Their clothes were dirty as if they had been working in the fields. But you could see clear through them, and . . . and they cast no shadow.

"Through Verve's eyes, I helplessly watched as one walked toward Eckert—he's captain of the guard at Chaldea. Eckert's sword passed through it three or four times, but it was not slowed in the least. It didn't even seem to notice. The ghost passed right into his body. And . . . and once it was within him, it vanished leaving Eckert lifeless on the floor."

Redd paused to catch his breath. "The very next night, I saw Eckert again, now one of these ghosts. With that same half-smile on him that the peasant had, Eckert proceeded to kill another just as he had been killed."

I said, "The walking dead are preying on the living. What a nightmare."

"I only wish it was just a nightmare," Redd said. "The ghosts are multiplying and swelling their numbers at an alarming rate. Even by claiming but one victim per night, it won't take long before the entire Realm is consumed."

Sedra's face reflected her fear. She said, "If every ghost found someone to kill every night, the whole of Rinstill would be gone in . . . in, oh my God. Just two weeks. Perhaps less."

Two weeks. Two weeks and we would all be gone.

Redd broke the silence, "Four days ago, Hiltred ordered the remainder of the guard to fall back to the lower passes. At least there they could see them coming. The close walls of Chaldea gave his men little comfort when ghosts could step out at any moment of the night."

"The Realm is ill prepared to deal with this kind of problem," Palomar said shaking his head. "The last known mage to specialize in exorcism was Thedof Dern, and he passed away nearly a half century ago. Though, from what I recall, the ghosts of days past never had the power to kill with such decisiveness, such impunity."

Redd asked, "Is there nothing to be done? Certainly some of Thedof's work still remains."

"Rest assured, our library is extensive." Palomar replied. "Given months of training, an experienced mage could work some exorcisms, but our ability would pale in comparison to what Thedof might have accomplished. But I wonder . . . These 'walking dead', as Sol put it.

These ghosts are multiplying so fast . . . Even if every mage, major and minor, full or partial, learnt this magic, I don't think there will be enough of us." He paused and fingered his ring in a contemplative manner.

Palomar gave Redd a sharp look. "I assume the King has been informed?"

Redd nodded. "Dimaus and her kestrel, Torrent, are with him. They are traveling with his entourage now to Sojourn. They left Ardon two days ago."

Palomar looked disgusted. "Two days? In the middle of this crisis, he decided it might be nice to attend the Festival of Light?"

"Perhaps he wanted to keep up appearances," Sedra said. "He attends every year. Besides, the vast fortifications of Ardon wouldn't keep out this foe."

Redd, too agitated to keep still a moment longer, began to pace between Palomar and myself. "He ordered me to assemble a company of men and ride to him at Sojourn where he will make a stand against any of the more mundane hosts of Nardel that break through Chaldea.

"But he also wanted you by his side." He turned to face Palomar again. "I sent most of my company on ahead, only remaining behind to tell you the last myself."

"Yes, I see," Palomar murmured. After some moments, he continued, "I don't believe White Magic can help against this foe. Sedra?"

Sedra was the most advanced mage in the nuances of White Magic at Waterton, despite her youth. If anyone knew of a way to combat these ghosts with White, she would. She shook her head. "I've been wracking my brains trying to think of something, some way . . . I doubt we can Hold them if walls don't even present a barrier. Perhaps we could sense something from them using Empathy, but . . ."

"But there is no direct way," I said, "using White to destroy them, turn them back, or even slow them down."

"What would you suggest, Sol?" Palomar asked.

"It will either be Old Magic or a relic," I said and inadvertently glanced at Palomar's ring. Of course he noticed.

"You and I, Sol . . . We are well versed in Old Magic, and yet while our knowledge overlaps in many broad areas, perhaps there is some aspect of Old you know that can turn these devils back? Hmmm? I can recall none at the moment." His voice crackled with age.

Old Magic was derived from the very substance of Rapt itself. It was drawn from the power of the rocks and earth, the majesty of the cliffs and the sweeping vastness of the mountains. It always made me feel insignificant like a flea attempting to direct a dog. Come to think of it, I felt the same whenever in the Hall of Tishman. After a fashion, the hall's age and towering presence resembled the vastness of Old, like a shadow resembles its maker. Yet could Old be used to turn ghosts?

I shrugged. "I admit, Palomar, my memory is not what it used to be. There may be some way these ghosts can be affected by Old, as the dead are nothing more than beings the land has reclaimed as its own. But these ghosts . . . This seems more of a . . . More spiritual in nature—"

"You were going to say more of a High Magic problem, weren't you?" Palomar interrupted. He sighed and looked at his ring. "Years I have spent trying to understand it, and still it eludes me. Now we need High Magic more than ever, and there's no one in all of Rinstill who has an inkling of how to tap into its nature."

Palomar continued, "Perhaps some High Magic relic could be found to deal with this menace. We should examine the histories to see if the Realm has ever faced this foe in the deep past. If a relic can be identified, it must be found swiftly."

"What of your ring?" I asked bluntly. "Facing the ghosts with this ring might stir it to life once more and somehow save the owner's life, or even, to hope beyond hope, the entire realm. High Magic saving the realm . . . Now what did that remind me of? Familiar somehow—"

Palomar grimaced and replied, "Many years ago, this ring blazed forth in a sudden release of High Magic. That much I'll confirm. Yet it was done by passion and heedlessness, not patience and forethought. I have spent years trying to relive that moment, to reawaken the ring and hear the music of High Magic once more. But to no avail. We mustn't put our faith in it."

Palomar's continual failure had been a weight on his spirit, I knew, and had aged him perhaps more than his time on Rapt warranted. "But from where did you obtain it?" I wondered.

"What was that, Sol?" asked Palomar.

Did I speak my thought aloud? "Ahh. I asked where you found it." Palomar had never revealed to anyone where he had obtained the ring, keeping it a guarded secret so that, I thought, he could rediscover High Magic before anyone else. I stammered, "Perhaps—perhaps there can be found other relics with similar powers—"

Palomar replied, "There are no other relics like this. Put that out of your mind."

Redd suddenly looked to the high ceiling of the Hall of Tishman. He had a smile on his face for a change. "Sol could you open one of those windows?" The ceiling was covered with an intricate pattern of windows in all sorts of odd shapes and sizes. Many of them were hinged to allow air circulation on hot summer days, but the only way to open them without risking your neck on a ladder or getting a long slender pole too heavy to lift, was to use a bit of White.

"Certainly." I looked up and tried to gauge the distance. It must have been one hundred feet or more. Fortunately, White Magic, used properly, was immune to distance. I concentrated, and, choosing a window, allowed White to melt and flow through my veins. I began to perceive the window's cold metal border and its smooth surface. The essence of White began to pool inside of me, and its presence comforted me like a familiar blanket.

I narrowed my vision and my concentration. The sensation of the window's surface was joined by the weight, and the echoing flute music that I alone heard began to sneak around the edges of my hearing. The flute was always present when I used White. Some heard piccolos or recorders dancing through complex rhythms and melodies, but I always heard a flute.

I felt the window's mass as it lay in its window frame and judged that I could move it. The flute commenced arpeggios that went up the scale in a quickening tempo. The rusty hinge felt old and brittle but workable. I turned the latch with Long-Reach and pushed, first gently, then with increasing force. I didn't want to break it, after all. The flute began to trill and dance in yet another melody I had never heard before, and I smiled, listening and concentrating. Finally, the window made an audible squeal that echoed through the hall as its rusty hinge moved.

Whoosh! A bird flew in the window suddenly and directly. Even though I was expecting it, it still felt like a slap on the face. Needless to say, at that point, I released the magic and returned my bearings to the company below. The flute's dance faded back into a mere echo, leaving only its memory.

The bird was not just any bird. It was one of the kestrels, a species of hawk unique in all the animal kingdom for its ability to communicate with humans. It floated majestically down to Redd without a single flap of its wings. Redd offered his arm as a perch, and the kestrel went directly to him, baring its claws to grasp Redd's arm. The hawk arched its wings slightly more and halted its downward motion just as it touched Redd's arm. The perfect landing.

The hawk's name was Sapphire and was one of only six kestrels left in the entire realm. Once there were hundreds, perhaps thousands of kestrels. The histories claimed that Nardel, himself, gave them their abilities to communicate with humans, and, in-so-doing, he bound them to him as slaves, using them as spies. As a means of control, he made it impossible for them to breed, and in return gave them lives so long that none knew if they would ever die from age. But despite all his power, six kestrel eluded him, remaining free. This was a surprise and only discovered years later. Once Nardel was imprisoned, the bond with his enslaved kestrels was broken, and they all died. But these six, having never been under his influence, survived.

Redd looked into Sapphire's eyes and smiled. To be chosen by a kestrel is to fly with them. You could see through their eyes and feel the air under their wings as they soar above the treetops and into the clouds. That is a freedom I will never know.

My reverie was interrupted when I realized Redd said something that I completely missed. Palomar cleared his throat and said,

"Sapphire, I assure you, it is our pleasure to be in such esteemed company. Thank you for joining us."

Redd could only hear Sapphire's thoughts when they looked into each other's eyes. Redd held Sapphire's eyes for a moment and said, "No, not yet. I've just told them of the insurgence of the ghosts . . . You're right, of course."

Redd turned to Palomar and continued, "All the remaining kestrels have been given a—a message of sorts, right around the time of the first ghost assault. Not one of them knows where it came from."

Redd looked back again to Sapphire and said, "Tell it to me again, so I can get it word for word." Staring into Sapphire's eyes, he recited the Hawk's message.

Winds of misfortune,
The Hawk's eye can espy,
Rive the relation,
Between man and the sky.

Neither sorrow nor rage,
Can capture time gone by,
But the war that you wage,
Loose the arrows that fly,
At the end of the age,
As the kestrels all die.

A moment of silence followed. "As the kestrels all die," repeated Palomar. He scratched his wrinkled face. "Disconcerting."

"All of the kestrels are nervous about the prophecy—"

Palomar interrupted, "Let's not call it a prophecy, Chosen. That gives it entirely too much credence, and I'll warrant it might just be something cooked up to generate fear and misdirection—a message from Nardel himself sent to slow our hand at retaliating against those chilling ghost assaults. Keep in mind the enemy is not only a lord of the Dark but a master of deceit as well, and his connection to the kestrels may yet linger on, as of old."

Redd was taken aback. "Are you suggesting that Sapphire is in league with Nardel?"

"I meant no offense, Chosen, to either you or any kestrel. Nardel may have lost his power over them, but perhaps his mind can yet reach out to them with words of poison."

"But what does it mean?"

"What do you think it means? I've never held the eyes of a kestrel, or felt their flight as my own, as you have," Palomar explained. "As a Chosen, what does your wisdom tell you?"

Redd sighed and shifted his weight, obviously as weary from standing as with this confrontation. Sapphire momentarily spread her wings for balance. "It sounds as if, by fighting back against this evil, all of the kestrels will end up dead. The message hints that—that it will somehow be our own doing."

"I agree." Palomar shook his head and looked around the assembly. "If we take the implied council of the kestrels' message, and not fight, we shall be overrun by the forces of Nardel, and the kestrels will wish they were dead."

I chimed in, "I don't think it necessarily means for us to sit idly playing hop-rocks whilst this plague comes down about our ears."

Sedra said, "We must choose our defense against these ghosts with caution. If we think through the consequences of whatever magic we use, certainly the kestrels can be protected. We have been forewarned, after all."

"It takes great wisdom to know whether to be cautious or bold," Palomar said. "I would hazard that we don't have enough time for caution. Now hold on there." Palomar waved Redd to silence before he was interrupted. "While I don't think we should throw caution to the wind entirely, we simply don't have any time to waste. That is certain. The future of the realm is at stake. I don't think we even have time to sit here and argue. We must begin at once."

Redd looked into Sapphire's eyes and said, "Sapphire thinks that within the week the western border will be decimated. By then, whoever isn't killed at night by the ghosts will be slaughtered by Nardel's hillkin during the day." Redd turned his gaze to Palomar. "I should join the King in Sojourn as soon as possible. When can you be ready?" Redd asked.

"Not before dawn tomorrow. There are preparations to be made to say nothing of mustering the resources of Waterton against this foe. Sol, would you research any artifact known to have some effect on the undead?"

"My library is at your service, as ever" I said. Thinking of my library, I suddenly wondered if it too, like my study, had a door made of larch wood. I shook my head. What nonsense. I must be getting tired.

"Sedra, gather the Waterton full mages to a conference, here in the Hall of Tishman, in one hour's time. We shall explain our impending fates. All classes are suspended until further notice. We need to find the solution, soon."

After Palomar grunted his servant's name, a gaunt man leapt out from the shadows, and I jumped. I'd forgotten he was there. As Palomar's chair was wheeled out, the clacking sound it made as it rode over the uneven stone floor reminded me of the sound of the first few rocks falling down the mountainside, the prelude to the avalanche. And even as he passed through the entrance to the Hall of Tishman, I could see him nervously fingering his ruby ring.

Chapter Five
Akin to Magic

We've looked at the structure of the sonata, the fugue and so forth, but we haven't asked the burning question." Professor Johnston stood silently a moment and glanced about the classroom. "Why? Why would anyone in their right mind choose to create pieces of music in these rigid structures?"

"Because it was all the rage," Mariana offered. Mariana Delgado sat on the opposite side of the room, and I glanced up from my desk at the sound of her voice. Normally I couldn't see her. The classroom consisted of several rows of built-in desks circling a central pit where the professors lectured. Usually, the large 3-D vid located at the heart of the pit was busy projecting and blocking the seats opposite mine, but at the moment, it was off.

"Perhaps it was fashionable. Anyone else?" the professor asked. He was sitting in a tall chair near the center of the room, glancing about at the students surrounding him.

Two seats to my left, Zak answered, "Because these guys were masochists. Writing a passable sonata is as mind-numbingly difficult as . . . as me getting a desk to work right." Zak pounded a fist on his desk screen. "This thing is on the fritz again." As he said this, his screen suddenly flashed bright yellow accompanied by what sounded like a blast of French horns, dissonant and nerve rattling. Zak jumped with a shout and fell out of his chair. An instant later the desk went altogether dead, and the class erupted into laughter.

I glanced over at Mariana, who was in hysterics. Zak's trouble with anything mechanical was practically as well-known as Mariana's crush on Zak. She was cute, and I was a little jealous that nobody looked at me like that. Zak never even noticed her.

When some semblance of calm returned, Professor Johnston indicated Zak should move to another desk. He said, "Perhaps Zak is not alone in his difficulties with your assignment. Writing a sonata is no mean feat, but, look, you still have a week."

Zak slid into the seat next to me and glanced over with a grin. He whispered, "Better take cover. I'm about to turn this thing on." I cringed as he pressed his palm to the surface, and when the desk lit up normally, he let out a sigh of relief.

Professor Johnston continued, "But getting back to my question . . . Mariana was right when she said that style of music was popular. Zak is right too. There's nothing like the challenge of constrained creativity. But is variation on structure possible? Can the structure or variation from a standard structure communicate theme?

"Consider the 'Confutatis', a part of Mozart's *Requiem*." Professor Johnston gestured with two fingers on his right hand, and the piece started. "Concentrate on how his structure supports the theme. It's a requiem, so it is about death, of course. First, six measures of the basses and tenors singing brashly, boisterously, celebrating life and the illusion of immortality shared by all of us in our youth. They sing, 'When the wicked are confounded, consigned to flames of woe.' Next . . . the angelic sounds of the sopranos and altos come in for a mere four measures almost beckoning, like sirens, luring the men to their deaths. Perhaps angels. They sing, 'Call me among the blessed.'

"The basses and tenors reiterate their theme of self-importance for another six measures, the exact amount as before. Are they struggling with the realities of death? Do they sound more desperate? If they do, that is all in your head, because the notes are exactly the same.

"But ahh, the angels counter again, this time passing by the men's six measure with nine of their own. They are patient, calm. Death is inevitable."

The melody was haunting. It gave me chills. He paused the playback and said, "And all that in less than a minute and a half. What happens next? The wicked men give up on their dreams of immortality and ask for forgiveness. How do we know this? They sing 'I kneel with a submissive heart, My contrition is like ashes, Help me . . . Help me in my final condition.' But even without the words, all that is made clear from the *music*. The basses and tenors have aligned themselves with the altos and sopranos."

With a wave from his hand, the music filled the hall once more. This time he didn't speak but let us listen to the rest. It was true. The men were accepting the inevitability of their own demise. They matched the women note for note. Their voices mingled closer and closer until, finally, in the end, they were indistinguishable.

As the final dirge-like chord faded away, Professor Johnston said, "Argue all you want, run to the ends of the Earth, but you cannot out-run death."

At that moment, my desk chimed—not loud enough to disrupt the class. A message had just arrived for me.

I tried to tune Professor Johnston out, while I opened the message. A wrapped-up scroll expanded to fill my screen, and I noticed it bore a wax seal embossed with the Sybernetics International symbol. I tapped the seal, and the scroll unraveled.

Dennis Howard,

You have been selected for participation in a psychological profiling exam to be held this coming Thursday at ten o'clock AM in lecture hall 1322 of Barkley Lunar University. This exam is given each year to a select group of individuals chosen by virtue of their accumulated time spent in SIMs and is used to evaluate the health and well-being of the heaviest user population. You are either one of these heavy-users or you were selected at random as part of a control group to perform the test.

As an added incentive, President and CEO of Sybernetics International, Mr. Artemus Regale, will be in attendance to meet you and to kick-off the psychological exam.

Note, failure to attend will forfeit your privileges to all non-education based SIMs. The information provided by this exam is vital to the use and development of SIM technology, and its importance to SI and the public cannot be overstated.

Lucille Hallsteen
Lunar Customer Service Manager
Sybernetics International

A psychological exam? Lord. I just passed my physical, and now they wanted to do a psych? *And* impossible to refuse, at least for me.

". . . voices combining and in the end vanishing gives the impression of a soul slipping loose of its mortal bonds and being carried away from this realm into the next."

I had to concentrate on my new dilemma. What if my physical had revealed something and they wanted to find out more? Could that new doctor, what was her name—Woodridge—could she have detected my mental aberration? They must suspect something, and they want to put me under their microscope. That is what this summons means.

A voice from the second row seemed to answer my own thoughts. It was Scott. "What if that isn't what it means at all?"

Yes, he's right. That's not what the message means. I'm just being paranoid.

Scott continued, "What makes you think Mozart put this much thought into the piece? We could sit here all day analyzing every note and come up with tons of possible meanings, but—"

Johnston said, "Over-analysis is always a possibility, but in analyzing Mozart's later pieces, I don't believe we would be wasting our time. Look, even if the audience isn't aware of these nuances, they are affected by them nonetheless. And it's possible that Mozart himself wasn't consciously aware of the effect of his structural selections. I like to think he knew what he was doing, but perhaps he was composing on instinct alone. In that case what we have here is a transmission of ideas and emotions communicated essentially from his unconscious directly into yours."

That idea struck a chord with me. Maybe SI didn't guess my secret, but during this psych test I might unwittingly reveal myself at an unconscious level. I couldn't even trust myself. There had to be a way out of this, but I had only two days to dream something up. And the next match was on Thursday afternoon, just a few hours after the exam.

* * *

I stepped back as the tram, decelerating quickly, came to a halt at the Aristoteles station. I sighed. It was the last tram to Descartes that would get me to the test in time. I'd watched three earlier ones leave without me, all the while desperately hoping for some miracle that would grant me a reprieve. None materialized. So with sweaty palms and shallow breath, I climbed aboard and found a seat.

As always, it was perfectly silent as it glided smoothly above its tracks, held aloft by invisible magnetic forces. With no air resistance, Luna was the perfect place for it to reach its 1500 km/hour operating speed. I looked out of the window and tapped the edge with idle fingers. The barren landscape whizzed by. The center of Aristoteles was covered with low hills the color of old concrete, but at the maglev's blinding speed, the hills were nothing more than blurs.

My mouth was dry and getting drier from looking out at the desert. That was what I told myself, anyway.

I looked around the tram compartment. Dozens of people sat silently or chatted quietly with their neighbors. Most wore bright colors, perhaps to offset the drab lunar landscape. Against the white walls of the tram, they reminded me of party decorations. I suppose the colors did serve to raise everyone's spirits, and on the colorless moon, who could blame them?

I looked back out the window. The sun shone down and made the sky appear starless and blacker than black. Few dared to reach for the sky, the way I was doing. I dared to hope for more than just being stuck on Luna, but success hinged on one little fact: my secret remaining secret. Over the past few days, I had formulated a plan, something I'd never attempted before. I didn't know if it would work.

Heaven only knew how I'd been able to conceal my condition this long, but secret it remained. Nobody guessed. Even Emily had shown no signs that she knew. I tried to wet my lips, but my tongue was too dry.

As long as I could remember, I'd known I was different. Mom used to call me a little eccentric, but she never really suspected the truth. Under the auspices of school research papers, I studied conditions that might have been similar to mine, but there was never any mention of my particular 'problem'.

The doctors would no doubt call it a problem. Some might look upon me with sympathy and shake their heads. Other's might cringe in fear and try to 'fix' me, but it was just what they wanted to fix that made Sam Clemens so successful. It set him apart and gave me the ticket to Masterhood and unlimited SIM time.

Plenty of cases of dissociative identity disorder, what people used to call multiple personality disorder, MPD, had been documented. I read about one woman who had as many as ninety-six personalities. I don't think I had that many. I hadn't counted recently, but it would get pretty crowded with a hundred completely different personalities stored in one mind.

I didn't even think calling what I have dissociative identity disorder would be accurate. People with multiple personalities sometimes aren't even aware that they have more than one personality. They just might have blank spots in their memory about certain times during a particular day. How often do people trace through their memories about everything they did or said or saw? Not often, I would think. They might never realize that another personality, once submerged, took possession of their body like some evil spirit.

But that's not my 'disorder.' My personalities weren't in competition for time in my body, the way the people of Luna were in competition for SIM time. My personalities were all well behaved. They only took control when I, Dennis Howard, allowed them. They could never wrest control from me, even when I slept. My control over them was complete. And even when I did grant them control, I remained present to take over if I didn't like the way things were going.

My people didn't even know a Dennis Howard existed. They never realized that a small awareness was watching over their shoulder ready to help out when necessary. Sometimes I gave them a nudge in a certain direction or an inspirational thought or two to get them going. Not only that, but most of my people weren't even from Luna. They'd never been there. Their worlds existed solely within the confines of the computer, care of Emily.

I call them people, because they are more than mere personalities. Much more. They have complete histories of their own. They have families and friends and skills that some of the other people don't have or haven't even dreamed of.

I smiled thinking of Sol Blanchard. He had the title: Servant of the One Crown, Protector of the White Flame, and Holder of the Seven Seals of Tishman. He was an old mage from the land of Rapt, and he knew no other life. He remembered an entire childhood brimming with celebrations, relatives, and gossip. And through the very real Lunar Main Computer, he could do magic. To him, magic was as real as, well, as real as he believes himself to be, and that's about as realistic as anyone could conceive. I had been playing in the SIM world of Rapt for years before I ever even met Trevor or Zak, which made Sol one of my oldest personalities. The characters my friends played were simple extensions of themselves, not performances anyone would consider real acting.

And that's the beauty of my secret. Acting was exactly what everyone expected you to do in a SIM, so when it appeared as if you weren't behaving like yourself, they always concluded you were a good actor. No one suspected that I wasn't really acting at all but that I had allowed a sub-personality to take over my speech, my mannerisms and my very thoughts.

That ability had allowed me to enter the tournament, giving me the chance to become a Master. The tournament was based on extemporaneous acting, something people did every day of their lives. What could be better for an extemporaneous acting job than a real person who believed with every shred of their being that what they saw, heard, and did was one hundred percent real? Every personality that I'd had acted completely true to form, because they didn't know how to do anything else. Was it any wonder that I kept winning the tournament matches?

The fact that I have multiple personalities did not, in itself, make it easy to win. It was the ability to generate new personalities upon demand, almost like magic, that gave me the edge.

At the start of every match, Emily gave all the competitors a small profile of who we were supposed to be, the setting, and a brief idea of what was going on. In the time it took for Emily to feed me the information, I fed it to the new personality.

But remaining in control has become more of a strain lately. The last transition from Miriam to me didn't go as smoothly as it should have. Miriam persisted for several full minutes after the SIM ended. She'd tried to call out for help before I reestablished myself. If Emily had been paying attention, she might have figured something out. Maybe that slip was why I had to take this test.

I took some deep breaths and tried to calm myself. We were almost at Descartes, and I wanted to be ready. I closed my eyes and listened to the soft hum of generators. Allowing the sound to fill me, I relaxed groups of muscles, starting at my feet and worked my way up.

They couldn't find out about my MPD if I didn't give anything away, and how could I do that if I didn't even know there was any secret to keep? My plan was to generate another Dennis Howard; one that knew everything and everyone I knew, who had all of my skills, likes and dislikes, but he would be missing one important thing. He would have no idea he had MPD or that he could generate new personalities on demand. I couldn't give my secret away if I didn't even know I had one. Even unconsciously.

The tram was beginning to decelerate, which meant I only had a couple of minutes before I would be forced to disembark. I needed to have this ignorant Dennis Howard in control before I left the tram.

I imagined a room filled with partitions. Within each partition was a chair, and in each chair was one of my people. None of them knew of the others just on the other side of their walls, and none of them guessed there was someone like me looking down upon them all. I chose a corner and imagined partitions enclosing a new space. Feeling the length and width of this new bubble, I began to fill it with myself.

When I was done, I looked down upon him and began searching for knowledge of his talent. I had never done anything like this before, so I wasn't sure exactly what I needed to look for. I found his mental picture of the partitioned filled room, and I scooped it out. Connected to that was memory of the existence of Miriam, and I began pulling upon that line of memory like a fishing line. Connected to that was the memory of a personality named Dr. E. Letchner followed by another sub-personality named Cindy Glinter. I followed the history of all my created people in inverse order, all the way back to the original conception of his Grace, Sol Blanchard.

Soon, the ignorant Dennis Howard was living up to his name. I could find nothing left of his MPD knowledge. He was a simple son of Luna, who enjoyed playing in the SIM, watching the matches, and dreaming of flying. He was the simple child of fourteen that I should have been, if not for my unusual talent.

I dropped back into the ether and pushed this new Dennis Howard into the fore and into control.

Chapter Six
Poker Face

I burst into one of the side doors of the lecture hall with thirty seconds to spare.

Near the rear of the hall, an old man was standing at a table and appeared to be greeting other new-comers. He was smartly dressed in black slacks and a black vest, and when I approached his smile seemed genuine. "And you must be Dennis Howard, no?" he asked.

"That's right. How did you know?" I shook his proffered hand in a firm grip, and his smile deepened for a moment.

"Why, you're the only one left. I'm Artemus Regale."

"Oh, Mr. Regale," I replied nervously. Imagine that, me, shaking hands with the President of SI? He looked much older than his pictures.

"Why don't you find a seat and we shall begin, hmm?"

The lecture hall was laid out like an amphitheater with rows of chairs rising toward the back of the hall. The rows were also curved slightly with the focus on the center screen and nearby podium. I chose a seat near the side entrance and nodded to my neighbor two seats away.

As Artemus slowly walked toward the podium, I took the opportunity to look at the people scattered about the room. The number of males to females was about equal, though everyone appeared to be older than me. In fact, everyone looked to be in their twenties.

As I glanced around the room, I found myself staring into the eyes of someone sitting across the hall. The spiked brown hair and those sharp eyes that took everything in at a glance—it was Frank Talonii.

A shiver ran up my spine. Maybe it was the way he just kept looking at me with one eyebrow slightly raised and that impish half grin that told you he was busy figuring. Frank Talonii was not someone you wanted to fixate on you, so I hadn't done myself any favor at our last encounter. Thinking back, I wondered why I'd been so sure he wasn't Sam Clemens. I rubbed my forehead feeling as if I'd forgotten something.

Though I couldn't hear Frank above the murmurings of conversation in the hall, I could read his lips as he said, "The Menace is here. Interesting." I didn't feel too menacing, especially under his steady gaze.

I looked back at the podium for no other reason than to have something else to look at. The old man had finally gotten there and was eyeing us over before he spoke. People began to realize that he was waiting for some silence, so the chatter began to settle down.

He wet his lips and said, "Good morning everyone, and thank you for getting here so promptly. I realize that some of you had quite a way to travel, and I appreciate your efforts. We have visitors here from as far away as Mare Frigoris."

Mare Frigoris was over 1500 kilometers away. I guess I was lucky to be living so close to the testing location.

He continued, "As you know, my name is Artemus Regale, and I'm the organizer of this . . . test. The test you are about to take—Well, it was 'advertised' as a psychological analysis test, and so some of you might be worried about being judged or labeled. You can relax. We're not trying to figure out anything as pedestrian as IQs or open up any skeleton closets of mental instability. No, that would be a far too simple matter to uncover.

"We're going to be examining your cortical responses throughout the brain. The test will be given through a SIM. Now I realize that through the magic of the LMC we all could have gone to our nearest SIM center and have met in a simulated hall, similar to this one, avoiding all the hassle of traveling. But, the sim-caps we're providing today have some special modifications to be able to collect the data we're looking for. So, it was necessary to have you all here in the flesh.

"Now, if everyone could take the cap on their left, we'll just get started. Ah, a question?"

A woman from the back of the hall asked, "How long do you expect this test to run?"

"Oh, we should be out of here by lunch, I suspect. Or, 11:17. Any other questions? No? Have a good time."

He stepped away from the podium with a mischievous smirk on his face. Artemus. What kind of name was that?

I found the cap he was referring to attached to the arm rest. It was simply a half helmet with a chin strap. There were no wires connecting it to the chair the way our caps had back in Aristoteles.

I settled the cap on my head and adjusted the strap. It fit nicely over my forehead and extended halfway down the back of my head. I closed my eyes and allowed the SIM to take over my vision. A kaleidoscope of colors transformed itself into a bulls-eye color wheel as the focus was adjusted. Likewise, a jumble of tones that sounded mostly like static resolved themselves into an ascending scale played on a piano.

A man's voice asked for my name. I mouthed my "Dennis Howard" without putting my vocal cords into action. The computer must have accessed my personal preferences, because the voice changed to the familiar voice of Emily.

She said, "Thank you. Restraints will be required for this full-body SIM. Please place your arms on the arm rests and your legs straight along the chair legs."

I'd never done a full-body SIM outside the chambers. For a second I thought it might be fun, but when I watched the straps snake around my arms and legs, I felt a sudden twinge of anxiety as if I was claustrophobic or something. I closed my eyes again and tried to relax. Was I afraid of closed spaces?

Emily calmly said, "The test is now beginning. Do you like waffles?"

"Waffles? You mean the food?" I asked out loud, forgetting I was still in control of my body. I bit my lip to remind myself not to use my voice but just to move my mouth instead.

"Do you like waffles?"

What a stupid question. "Sure, they're great." No pictures appeared. Maybe this part of the test was just verbal.

"Do you like your mother?"

"I love my mom."

"Have you ever considered suicide?"

"No."

"Are you afraid of spiders?"

"I've never met a spider I didn't like." In truth, I've never seen a real spider.

"What time is it?"

"Time?" I tried to open my real eyes to look for a clock and found I still had control over them. The full-body SIM hadn't started yet. This lecture hall was so plush, even the walls were carpeted. On the left wall was what looked like a circle of discoloration where a clock used to hang. Oh well. I told Emily, "I can only guess."

"Then guess."

"I'd say about 10:20?"

"Who was the twenty-fifth President of the United States?"

"Hmm. Beats me. Taft?"

"How old are you?"

"Fourteen and a half."

"How old were you on your first birthday?"

There were lots of answers to that one. "Nine months, about."

"What does this look like to you?" One of those ink blot things appeared in front of me.

"It looks like . . . the Earth exploding into bits." The ink blot faded out.

"If given the choice between freezing to death in a blizzard or burning to death in an inferno, which would you choose?"

Oh brother. "Um . . . Inferno."

"Do you like cats?"

"I guess they're all right."

"Do you appreciate vacations?"

Appreciate? "I suppose."

"Do you enjoy SIMs?"

"I love them."

"Have you ever seen anyone die?"

"Sure—I mean no. Do you mean for real?"

"How old will you be when you die?"

"I haven't the faintest."

"Are you afraid of death?"

"Well, everyone's afraid of death."

"Are you afraid of spiders?"

"No, I'm not afraid of spiders." She asked that before.

Suddenly, a dense jungle appeared below me, and my inner ear told me I was falling. I was quite high, and involuntarily, I sucked my breath in. Emily asked, "How many seconds do you think there are before you hit the ground?"

"Ahh, ninety two," I said, taking a wild guess.

"Do you want to find out if you're right?"

"Not particularly."

"In the Christian tradition, when does Easter usually fall?" The jungle didn't disappear.

But I thought I knew that one. "Wait. It's the first Sunday after . . . um . . . after the first full moon after the vernal equinox."

The ground was still approaching. "Do you like soda?"

"Sure."

"Do you like steak?"

"We don't have steak on Luna."

"Do you have any moral problems with killing animals for food?"

"No."

"Have you ever killed an animal for food?" The wind was whistling so loud that I could barely make out the question.

"Come on. Of course not."

"How many seconds do you think you have to live?"

I guess she was referring to the ground that was still rushing up at me. "Maybe a minute."

"Do you ever feel lonely?"

"Sometimes."

"Have you ever heard voices that other people claim not to have heard?"

"Voices? I don't think so. I mean no."

"Did you ever feel like your mind was about to snap?"

"No."

"Quickly, tell me what time it is."

"It's about 10:26."

"Do you think you could survive this fall?"

"Not really." I thought my heart was beating faster despite myself. I knew it was only an illusion, but still—

"Do you want to find out?"

Jeez, this is silly. I sarcastically said, "Yeah, let's find out."

To my amazement she just said, "Okay," and said nothing more. Seconds ticked by, and still no more questions came, all the while the roar of the wind grew louder. I noticed the jungle was really located on an island with a smoking volcano on one side. "Okay, okay, I was only kidding. Come on."

The ground loomed closer and closer, and at the last instant, the descent was smoothly changed to a thrilling flight above the treetops. Emily asked, "How fast do you think you are going?"

"Um . . . About a hundred kilometers an hour."

"Do you like flying?"

"Flying is great."

The jungle rapidly transitioned to a city-scape at night, and with no control of my own, I landed on the roof of a skyscraper. "Landed" was not quite right. It was more of a head-over-heels rolling-skidding stop. As I lay there, looking at the shabby overcoat I was now wearing and trying to catch my breath, someone grabbed my collar and dragged me to my feet. "Nice of you to join us, Dennis. We've been waiting for you."

That came from a large, fedora-capped man holding me off the ground. Before he threw me back onto the rooftop, I managed to notice his cleft chin, his bad breath, and his angry expression. I looked to my left when I heard the sound of a woman struggling. There were two other people on the roof with us: A huge man, even larger than the first with a gun in his hand, and a woman. The man wore the same style of dark grey suit as the first, and the woman wearing a floor-length red dress, looked like she was ready for a night out.

Cleft chin said, "Eighteen thousand dollars, Dennis. It's a lot of money. Did you expect me just to forget about it?"

The man with the gun dragged the woman toward the edge of the roof. Seeing me, the woman shrieked, "Dennis, thank God you're here. They're crazy. Give them what they want!"

"Mariana?" I said. It looked like an older version of Mariana from my class. She looked to be twenty. I looked down at my hands, my body. I was older too.

"That's right Dennis, we have your girlfriend. Now, maybe you don't care about your own life, but five'll get you ten Mariana here is another story, even though she claims not to have known you that long." The other man dangled Mariana over the edge, holding her by one wrist. She screamed in terror.

"Rodger, settle down. She's going to have a heart attack."

"Right, Mr. Drake," said Rodger. He brought her back onto the roof. She struggled to break free of his vise grip.

I got to my feet. What were they testing me for here? Was I supposed to try to save Mariana somehow? I felt my pockets. I had no weapon and no wads of cash to pay them off, just some keys and, after a quick inspection, a wallet with a driver's license and nothing else.

Rodger ended Mariana's struggles by pocketing his gun and grabbing her other wrist. He pulled her arms behind her back. His hat blew off in the wind and went sailing away. He looked annoyed.

"I don't have your money," I stammered.

"No, I didn't think you did." Reacting to Mariana's cries of pain, Mr. Drake chided Rodger, "Let's not damage the merchandise. Relax, she's not going anywhere." Rodger released her, and she collapsed on the roof, crying.

Mr. Drake turned to me. "I've grown weary of waiting for you to come up with a plan, Dennis, so I did some of that legwork for you. Let's start with the two presents I have. Number one, an unloaded Saturday-Night-Special." He thrust a small gun into my right hand. "And number two, a shiny, brand-new nickel." This went into my other hand. He then grabbed my collar and shoved me toward Mariana, toward the edge, and pointed down and across the street. Lit up in glittering lights was the name of the casino next door: The Lucky SOB. "Here we have one of my favorite watering holes. So, option number one, you go down there and rob the place." He snatched the keys out of my pocket. "We'll be back at your humble abode waiting for your triumphant return. If you're not back in an hour . . ." He looked at Mariana and shook his head.

"How do you expect me to rob a casino? Those places have real security—"

"Tutt-tutt. Don't fret, Dennis. That was just option number one." He put his arm around me as if consoling me. "Let's not forget that nickel. There are so many things you can do with that nickel. You can use it to call the cops. Doing so would not end happily for sweet Mariana over there. You can call a cab and leave town. This would also mean saying fare-thee-well to Mariana, for good. Conversely, I suspect you might be able to purchase a single round for that gun at any of our fine ammo establishments throughout our fair city."

I asked "What good would one round—"

"I'm talking about doing the honorable thing, Dennis." He gently slapped my cheek. "I'm all about giving people options. That's what life's all about." He paused, his arm still wrapped around my shoulders, and we looked out at the vista. It could have been Las Vegas from the 1950s. "What brings us here to this spot right now is the sum total of our collective choices spanning our whole lives." He glanced at his wristwatch, then nodded to Rodger. "Fifty-five minutes left, kid. After you."

Drake shoved me toward the rooftop access door, while Rodger got Mariana to her feet.

"You're hoping I fail," I said, stumbling forward. "You don't actually expect your money, do you?"

"I always leave room for miracles. Always."

This test was proving to be more fun than I thought. As I raced down the stairs, I wondered what they were testing for. Clearly some kind of morality play was going on here. Choices. Maybe they're studying how my brain makes choices.

I jammed the gun and nickel into my overcoat pockets and, dodging cars, ran across the street. The casino was loud, bright and nauseating. Everything from the flower-print carpeting to the crystal chandeliers assaulted my senses. What better place to measure brain stimulation than a place designed to overload my senses—which is all designed to drive me toward bad choices? Stay longer, drink more, gamble more—Isn't this exciting, aren't we all just having a grand time?

Out of breath, I stood there surveying the casino floor, wondering what to do next. The room was filled with people and staff intermingled with hundreds of slot machines and dozens of tables where every manner of game was underway: roulette, blackjack, craps. Then I caught sight of four uniformed guards walking slowly across the floor, two in front and two behind a cart of some kind—a lock-box—a safe on wheels, being pushed by a casino employee dressed all in red. The guards were armed.

I patted the gun in my pocket. It was a suicide mission. Drake expected—No, he *wanted* me to get killed in the attempt. I casually followed the lock-box and watched as it passed through a set of double-doors, a room just behind the cashier. Meanwhile, at the cashier's barred window, I watched as a woman exchanged a few twenties for a few gambling chips. I noticed the doors hadn't closed all the way; they were still ajar just a bit. I guess I'm supposed to charge in there and demand the money. Even though this was all a simulation, I could feel my heart racing, and not from all the running. There were only two types of people who would charge in there: crazy people and people who knew this was all just an illusion, so why the heck not?

No. I turned away. Sure it would be fun to rob a casino, but that's too obvious. Wait. This was a *casino*. I could simply win the 18,000 dollars. Yeah. Because winning money at a casino was so simple. I went through my pockets again and found no money of any kind except for the nickel, all shiny and new. The date stamped on it was 1954. There was a whole bank of slot machines close by, but they were all quarter slots. It didn't take long to find some nickel slots, though. I looked down at the coin in my hand, then up at the row of slot machines, then up at one of the myriad of signs around the place: 'Lucky SOB'.

I took a deep breath, picked a machine, dropped my nickel into the slot and reached for the handle on the side. I pulled. The drums inside the machine started to spin. They came up: cherry, cherry and the third one . . . cherry. I smiled as nickels spilled out of the bottom making a racket. There had to be about four dollars there. Oh boy. I needed to win faster.

I scooped the money up and headed toward a roulette table. A quick exchange later and my handful of nickels had become a few green chips. I looked around for a clock, but of course, casinos had no clocks. They didn't want anyone realizing how long they'd been playing. How much time did I have?

The roulette wheel was spinning again, the ball in motion. I plunked all my chips down on 32. Others at the table were still placing their bets. I glanced at the wheel, at the table. Biting my lip, I moved my chips to 31.

The ball slowed down, bounced through the numbers, and landed for a moment on 32. My heart sank. But then it did a little bounce onto 31 where it decided to stay. A shiver of excitement went up my spine. Simulated or not, this was fun. My puny stack of chips was now a large stack of chips, about one hundred fifty dollars. As I reached out to pull them toward me, I had to wonder at how easy this was going. The actual chances of this happening were certainly small but not ridiculously small. Transforming five cents into 18,000 dollars? Could it be done?

They weren't trying to test to see if I could win at gambling. They must have been letting me win. It didn't matter what I bet on. I pulled my hands away and said, "I'm letting it ride. All on 31."

The man in red behind the wheel nodded and whirled the ball around the wheel. Others were placing their bets.

What were they testing me for? Looking around the casino, nothing seemed unusual. People winning, people losing. Did they want me to lose track of time? How long have I been in here? I closed my eyes. It felt like half an hour.

The croupier waved his hand over the table, "No more bets." A young and pretty red-head was standing next to me now. Either she just walked up while my eyes were closed, or they made her just appear. Her fingers played with some red-chips in her hands, and I noticed a few of her chips were sitting on top of mine on number 31. I nodded. That was a wise thing to do.

She let out a whoop of delight as the ball, of course, landed right on 31. Now my pile had five pretty thousand-dollar chips on top of them. She said, "Hey cutie, why aren't you smiling? Look how much money you just won."

"Five thousand isn't enough," I turned to the croupier. "I'm letting it ride again."

"Sorry sir. There's a table max of five hundred dollars." He pointed to a sign that said as much.

Fine. I pulled my chips toward me and placed 500 back on 31. No. I decided 8 was a better number. Everyone else at the table put their chips on the same number, following my lead. The bet pays 36 to 1, so my 500 dollar bet should get me . . . exactly 18000 dollars.

"I'm Rosemary." said the red-head.

I shook her hand. "Dennis." The wheel was spinning, the ball rolling.

"No more bets." The ball bounced until it finally came to rest on, what a surprise, number 8. The people around the table erupted with joy. It took several precious minutes to pay out the chips to everybody, but finally, there it was, all the money I needed to pay back Drake, neatly stacked in the form of one thousand dollar chips. I thanked the man running the table as he pushed the chips my way. He had a grim, mystified expression.

"Well, that's it for me," I said to the expectant crowd, who seemed to be waiting for me to place my next bet. There was a collective sigh of disappointment as I turned to go, chips in hand.

Rosemary quickly caught up and linked her arm on mine. "Dennis, hey, where's the fire?"

"Excuse me, but I'm in a bit of a rush. It was nice meeting you." Extricating myself, I left her behind and jogged to the cashier.

It was excruciating waiting for them to hand over the cash, and they were surprised I wanted cash at all. Soon, I was walking out the front door with a briefcase, which they sold to me, full of 100 dollar bills, which they explained was the largest denomination available. That's when Rosemary appeared at my side, a purse slung over one shoulder. She took my arm again, as if I was escorting her out.

"So, where's my favorite lucky charm taking me?"

"Rosemary, right? I don't have time—"

"The night is young, it's wild and free. Come on, live a little."

Hmm. Another choice. What did they expect me to do? Run off with her and leave Mariana to her doom? For a moment, I imagined I was a competitor in the Master's Tournament. In a match, I'd have to pretend this was all real and act accordingly. Me? A competitor? Imagine that. They never took anyone under eighteen.

I shook my head and took a deep breath, remembering playing poker for the first time with Dad and Tricia. He had dealt the cards quickly around the table, and in front of each of us had been a stack of nickels, dimes, and quarters. "Remember, put on your best poker face and always play-to-scale."

"What do you mean?" I'd asked.

"You know," said Tricia. "Don't give away what cards you have with your expression."

"And pretend as if that money in front of you was actually substantial," Dad said. "I mean, if I raise you a dollar and a quarter, and you only have two dollars left, you might say to yourself, it's only a dollar and a quarter, so who cares? You'd throw the money in. But you have to play-to-scale. Pretend as if it would actually hurt to lose that money. What if I was bluffing? In fact, how am I supposed to bluff if you don't care? I mean, that's half the game. Trying to figure out who's telling the truth and who's just blowing smoke."

Dad was right. The real fun was playing-to-scale, which is what Rosemary was doing, if she was a real person at all, which I doubted. In fact, she probably just wanted to steal the money. I hailed a taxi and smiled at her. "You're sweet and very attractive, but I have only fifteen minutes—"

She was still smiling brightly as I felt her press a gun to my side. "You're going to walk me to my car," she said. "And you're going to be a calm and cool cucumber." She steered me away from the taxi line and toward the parking lot. "That's it, we're just going to go for a little ride in my car. I'm sorry, but you're forcing me to do this."

I wasn't about to be robbed of the miraculous money I needed to save Mariana, even if she wasn't my real girlfriend. When we arrived at her car, a beat-up old Buick sporting a huge grill that looked like a full set of teeth, I waited until she was distracted, fumbling with her keys. Some handcuffs fell out of her purse, giving me the moment's distraction I needed. I pushed her gun away and whipped out my own revolver. She stood in shock at the sudden turn of events. "Drop it." I demanded, and her gun hit the pavement. "This has been fun, Rosemary, and I'd love to leave you, but you've made me so late that now I'm going to have to ask you to drive me someplace."

"Fine, where to?"

Drake had said to meet him at my place. I thought back to my driver's license then rattled off the address I'd seen there. "118 Excelsior, Apartment 804."

I thought about picking up her gun, as it probably had actual bullets in it, but I didn't want to give her an opening to turn the tables again. I took the passenger seat next to her, and in a moment she had the engine roaring to life.

"Dennis, there's something you should know," she began. "I wasn't taking you away to rob you. I was trying to save your life."

"Really?" I replied sarcastically, keeping the gun trained on her. "Come on. Let's go."

She pulled out of the lot and joined the nighttime traffic on the strip. "How much money do you owe Drake?"

I only had twelve minutes left, but this was getting even more interesting. "So you know Drake?"

"I'm a private eye working for the family of a previous victim of his. Last month, a guy named Albert, not much older than you, tried to hold up a casino and was shot and killed before the police could arrive. The family wanted to know what possessed him to do such a stupid thing. They hired me. After doing a bunch of digging, I found out he had made some bad bets, and the marks had been purchased by Drake."

"Sounds familiar," I admitted. We turned a corner onto Excelsior Avenue, and I noticed her looking nervously in the rear-view mirror.

"But Drake is loaded," she continued. "I mean really. The only thing I can figure is he coerced this guy into robbing the casino as some kind of insane test. He couldn't care less about the money. He just wanted to manipulate him, see how far he could be pushed. I got word that he'd purchased some more debt. That's when I began following you. When I saw you run into that casino, I thought, 'Well, his number's up.'"

She pulled up in front of an apartment building with the right address on it, and I still had five minutes to spare.

"How does any of that put my life at risk?"

"He probably had people at the casino watching you," she glanced back down the road. "So no doubt he knows you're still kicking. What if that makes him a bit peeved? You walk in there, money or no, and he might decide to off you himself."

"I see." I motioned for her to get out and followed her through the driver's door, careful to keep the empty gun trained on her with one hand and the other locked on the handle of the briefcase. I noticed a black sedan pull up and park nearby. Could it be Drake's thugs from the casino? I hid the gun from their view with the briefcase. "There's more at stake than you know, Rosemary. He has—"

"That's not your girl he has hostage, Dennis. It's his wife." The last she said in a stage whisper. She hurriedly came around the car.

"What?"

"Over the last few weeks, you started dating a pretty brunette, right? About yay tall? Her name's Mariana Drake. She's his wife. They're in it together."

"His wife? Oh, that's not right . . ."

"She dated Albert, too, right before his crime spree. There's no one in trouble up there. There's no hostage. We need to drive away, now." She surreptitiously eyed the two men getting out of the sedan.

"I'm finally beginning to get the big picture. But, Rosemary," I said, "I'm still going up there. I still owe the man his money, even if he doesn't want it." The two men walked by and into the building. One looked at me suspiciously.

"Then you're going to need back up. I'm coming with you."

"I wouldn't have it any other way."

"How much time do we have?" She walked to her trunk.

"Only a few minutes."

She popped the trunk. Inside was a veritable arsenal. She glanced back at my gun. "Either shoot me or trust me, cutie."

Oh. I was still . . . I put the gun away and she picked up some kind of automatic rifle. "Feel like upping your caliber?" she asked.

"I'm fine with this, thanks," I said, motioning to my revolver. An unloaded gun? Well, I didn't want anyone getting hurt.

Exactly two minutes later, I kicked open the door to my own apartment, a briefcase of money in one hand and the revolver in the other. This was not what I'd pictured myself doing today. I went in first, Rosemary right behind. "Everybody freeze!" I shouted, surprising even myself.

"As I live and breathe," said Drake, sitting on my couch, and holding, by the looks of it, a can of beer. "One hour, right on the money." The place was a real dump. An old fashioned black-and-white television was in the corner tuned to the news. Maybe they were waiting for some word of my progress.

Mariana was sitting next to him, slack-jawed in amazement. She was also holding a beer. Rodger was in the kitchen, momentarily frozen with one hand in his jacket ready to pull a gun. Rosemary said, "Pull it out slowly and drop it, big boy."

"Oh, Dennis, thank God you're back!" Mariana cried, a bit unconvincingly as she tried to hide the beer in her hand behind her.

"I know the whole deal, sweetie. I just came to deliver the money." I threw the case on the floor. "There's some extra in there. You can keep it."

Drake got to his feet. "Are you telling me you actually robbed the joint? And got away? And who's this vision of loveliness joining the party?"

Rosemary now had Rodger's gun. I barked, "Rodger, over there with your pals. Rosemary, check the rest of the place for anyone else." The two thugs were conspicuous in their absence.

Rosemary went to check the bedrooms, rifle at the ready. Drake said, "I was under the impression you didn't have any friends—any well-armed and capable friends—in the vicinity. You must have chosen to call in some favors, eh, with that shiny nickel?"

"You already know I won the money," I said. "You wouldn't have gone to all this trouble without having someone there to keep an eye on me. This is a grand experiment, after all, and we wouldn't want to miss any detail."

"It's true, I am a student of human nature," Drake admitted with a shrug. "But I'm baffled as to how you managed to win so much so fast? Baffled isn't the word. I'm flabbergasted."

Rosemary came back, shaking her head to tell me the coast was clear. Well, that was interesting.

"Human nature?" I replied evenly. "You're studying the wrong thing. You want to study the nature of the universe instead." I sighed and looked down at my weapon. "The gun, as you know, isn't loaded." I threw my gun to Rodger, who caught it and looked at Drake, then back at me quizzically.

"As for this lovely lady?" I said, indicating the well-armed Rosemary. I shrugged. "I should think you'd know your own wife."

Mariana, still sitting on the couch, gave a snort of laughter. There was no way Drake would send his own wife out to lure in victims. No. Drake's more complicated than that. He would only have a wife like Rosemary, all heels and hair and handcuffs.

I turned away and grabbed the beer Rodger had left on the kitchen table. Behind me, Drake started to laugh. I took a swig and gagged. "God this is awful. I'm supposed to have bought this myself?"

Rosemary was looking at me, her rifle now aimed at the floor. The two thugs from the Sedan decided to make themselves known by walking in from the bedrooms.

Drake put his arm affectionately around Rosemary. "I'm seeing it, but I'm not believing it."

"He's the real deal," Rosemary said. "He wouldn't take any bait. He saw through every fabrication. And somehow he won all that money."

"I'm not afraid of spiders either. Or their webs. Anyone up for some pizza? I'm feeling quite peckish."

Chapter Seven
In the Nick O' Time

Rosemary, Drake and everything faded into blackness. I mentally cringed. Were there more mazes I needed to run? Emily's voice echoed through my thoughts, "Thank you for your participation in this psychological profile exam. The test is now complete." I could feel the straps sliding off my arms and legs as my own body tingled back into existence. "As you leave the hall, take care not to disturb those still taking the test."

I grumbled to myself and took off the cap. Glancing about the lecture hall, I discovered that a third of the group had already finished the test and had left. Frank Talonii, however, was still sitting across the lecture hall. He was smiling to himself with that mischievous half grin. I looked away quickly, feeling as if he were about to open his eyes and look directly at me.

As I stood up, my temples started to throb with minuscule amounts of pain. Switching back and forth between real and virtual too many times can give people headaches. It felt something like eating ice cream too fast. Doctors recommend that people exiting the SIM should take it slow for the first few minutes, allowing the brain to get reacquainted with the real limbs, eyes, and ears. When did I ever pay attention to that?

By the time I made it out of the lecture hall and back into the corridor, my head was killing me. The pounding behind my eyes was actually making me see stars with every heartbeat. I leaned against the wall and gripped my head with both hands to try to contain it.

If I just rest a moment . . . it should . . . diminish.

I felt as if I were pressing on a wall that threatened to fall and crush me. I gathered my mental strength, and gave a massive imaginary heave at the wall. It felt as if it worked. The pain ringing through my temples lessened and vanished almost as quickly as it had arrived. I felt almost as if I had won some sort of pitched battle. What was that all about? Somehow it seemed familiar . . .

But this was no time for lolly-gagging, as my Dad would jokingly say. My stomach reminded me it was time for food.

* * *

"Next. What'll it be?" the man asked, standing behind the grill.

"I'll take the Chicken Cordon BLU," I replied, and he whirled into action. "BLU for Barkley Lunar University? Isn't that a little much?"

The chef looked up and smirked. "Don't blame me."

I was in the Nick O' Time Café, the university's cafeteria. I heard it was named that because the students' schedules didn't allow them any time to eat. But thinking of bad puns, I wouldn't have been surprised if the original manager was named Nick.

After getting my sandwich, I opted for a booth because the high backed seats might hide me from the roaming eyes of Talonii if he happened to come in here too. Breathing deeply, I enjoyed the familiar smells as memories came back to me. My mother used to be on staff teaching economics, and sometimes I would meet her here for lunch. Often she would bring along some other faculty members, and they would get into boring discussions that would put me to sleep right there at the table. What did they expect, though? I was only a kid.

This place didn't even have any 3-D vids to keep the patrons happy while they ate. I guess they thought the students wanted to make conversation instead of immersing themselves into their electronics.

Then again, maybe the university was just cheap. They had redecorated the place, and the color scheme was almost comical with its blues and purples. It looked like something right out of the twenties.

The chicken was, of course, artificial. I bit into the sandwich and, chewing slowly, frowned. Perhaps it hadn't been too smart for Emily to include the taste of real chicken in the SIMs because after tasting the real thing, reality was pathetic. I held my head as a sudden wave of dizziness struck me.

The relative silence of the Nick O' Time was suddenly shattered by the sound of gun shots, and I nearly jumped out of my skin. Cries of pain and panic sounded from everywhere as the shots rang out one after another over the sound of a man crying out something unintelligible. I plastered myself to the back of my booth, unable to think, and watched as the picture window at the front of the café shattered into millions of pieces and rained down upon the corridor outside.

The staccato reports of the gun subsided, leaving the cafeteria resounding with screams of terror and panic. The room seemed to go out of focus for a half second. I whispered my obligatory phrase several times to calm my nerves. "I love you—shut up, I love you—shut up."

I slowly reached up the booth's high backed chair and pulled myself up for a peek. Bodies were everywhere. I felt something wet under my hands, and turning them over, I saw blood. My eyes finally focused on the person slumped in the next booth. His head had been blown away and splattered around the booth and the walls. I fell back into my seat in horror, desperate to wipe the blood from my hands. My stomach wrenched and I threw up all over the table.

I had to get out before the smell and horror overwhelmed me. I jumped out of my booth and started to run toward the door. The things strewn about the room were so horrible that my mind recoiled and would not tell me what my eyes were seeing. An instant later, my eyes shut of their own accord, forcing me to a halt. I couldn't open them again until the sound of a struggle drew my attention.

In the far corner of the room, three men were forcibly holding the gunman to the ground. Amid his thrashing, he screamed, "Kill them! Kill them all! No quarter! No quarter!" He had black hair and a short-cut, black beard, which looked familiar.

Another man's scream of despair yanked my attention back across the room. He shouted something in another language, face turned toward the ceiling. Then, with a longing glance at the woman lying dead at his feet, he turned and ran toward the exit, screaming.

His screams seemed to break the spell that held me, and before I knew it, my feet were rushing me toward the door in his wake. I was stepping over things that should still be walking and talking, and I felt my stomach again begin to come unglued.

As I reached the door, a wave of fresh air filled my lungs, and I nearly choked with hyperventilation. The large clock set into the wall of the atrium outside the restaurant sounded a single chime, the simulated sound of a massive bell. Leaning against the glass out front, I glanced at its face, which read eleven thirty. As I tried to catch my breath, yet another shock jarred my sense of reality. The picture window that I'd watched explode right before my eyes was now unbroken and back in its frame. There wasn't even a scratch on it.

I leaned close to the window, and gazed back into the café. There was no smoke, no bodies, nothing out of place. It was as if the whole episode had never happened. People were looking my way as if to wonder what my problem was.

A woman tapped me on the shoulder. "Are you okay? Do you want me to call someone?" Her clothes told me she worked in the café. I just waved her away and stumbled across the atrium.

What was happening? "I'm in a bloody SIM," I murmured to myself with sudden conviction. That could be the only explanation. Was this all part of the psych test?

Suddenly I realized I could still hear the man who had left the café screaming. His yells echoed down the maze of corridors, and after a split-second decision, I leapt into pursuit, launching myself off a nearby wall.

If this was part of the psych exam, what were they testing me for? They could have easily slipped a SIM on me upon emergence, but why show their hand now? Did they expect me to doubt my own sanity? As if to punctuate that last thought, my headache started to return.

The man's cries of anguish became louder as I pursued, so I must have been catching up to him, though he still wasn't in sight.

I couldn't think straight. If this really was nothing more than a SIM, and if they thought I thought it was real, what did they expect me to do?

I ran through the university grounds in confusion, dodging students as best I could, all the while trying to track a mess of possibilities that I couldn't resolve. I needed to catch up to this man and prove that I wasn't crazy, prove that this was a SIM.

I finally caught a glimpse of him just as he was dashing into a room. He looked to be about twenty, though I couldn't see his face too clearly. As the door closed behind him, the sobbing was silenced. I ran up to the door and, before I lost my nerve, punched the open button, praying he hadn't locked it. When the door slid out of the way, I leapt in. My headache was starting to make me dizzy.

As the door closed automatically behind me, I glanced around. It was an office overlooking one of the campus arboretums. A floor to ceiling window ran the entire length of the opposite wall and was the source of the all the room's light. I could see gigantic sixty-year-old oaks just outside. A red curtain extended around the right wall.

But where did the man run off to? I reached up to massage my throbbing temples as I glanced over at a large blank desk sprawled across the left side of the room. A layer of dust coated its surface. Several abandoned-looking chairs stood in front of the desk and behind was a leather-bound chair that was turned away, facing the window.

The overhead light pipes came to life suddenly, giving my headache a new urgency. The pressure at my temples doubled nearly sending me into unconsciousness. I grabbed the back of a nearby chair to steady myself.

An aged voice behind me said, "Why, Dennis. If it isn't Dennis Howard."

Chapter Eight

Into the Fray

My true identity broke through to the surface, and gasping for breath, I shoved the ignorant Dennis Howard into the depths. With my return, the headache faded and within seconds was gone.

I turned to see Artemus Regale standing amid the red curtains, holding them partially open. Behind him, I thought I saw an alcove containing a bed.

What had I done? "Oh, sorry. I think I came in the wrong room. I'll just—"

Artemus dropped the curtain and walked slowly toward me, saying, "No, no. Please have a seat. We have some . . . talking to do."

He blocked my path to the door, and my skin crawled. What did he know? What did that idiot sub-personality just reveal by running full tilt in here? The appearance of Artemus proved this was some kind of test, that I was still in a SIM, but why did they bother?

Artemus motioned toward one of the chairs near the desk. I hesitantly obliged.

The chair was stiff and hard, a punishment itself. He patted my shoulder with some satisfaction. "Good, good to have you here. Fortunate too. This way I won't have to hunt you down later."

Artemus suddenly leapt up to the desktop and jumped down on the other side. It surprised me. The gravity on Luna was quite low, making such jumps nothing at all, even for a man of his obvious age. But adults usually respect furniture to a fault.

As he resumed his seat, Artemus commanded, "Francesca, please bring the lights up another twenty percent." Almost everyone had their own name for the LMC.

Artemus looked me over with quick eyes. "So, what is this bursting in here? Where's the fire?"

Was he being cagey? This was unexpected. I said, "I didn't mean to—I just—I just thought I might have seen someone, someone I know come in here. He must have gone in one of the other rooms along the hall."

Artemus obviously knew about the screaming man. This was his SIM after all. But how did he expect me to react? I needed time to recover, so I thought up an excuse to leave. Rising again to my feet, I said, "You know, I have to use the restroom, so I'll just step out before—"

"You're in luck. This is one of the few offices here at the university with an attached crash room. You know, for the over-achieving sort who can't spare the time to get themselves home." Artemus indicated the adjoining room beyond the curtain with a wave of his hand.

I ducked behind the curtain and found the "crash" room just as he said, along with, not just a restroom but a full bath with a shower stall and everything. Standing over the sink, I took the opportunity to rinse out the taste of bile from my mouth, remnants of my episode in the cafeteria. Everything seemed so real, it was hard to believe it was a SIM, but how else could I explain the vision of horror? If only I'd been able to regain control earlier, perhaps I could have seen through the illusion sooner. Somehow, the ignorant Dennis Howard I'd created also inherited some of my ability over personalities, because he had been able to keep me at bay. I didn't want to think about what that might mean if that knowledge leaked into some of my other people.

As I walked out of the bathroom, I glanced about the alcove. A neatly made bed and nightstand stood against the wall, both dusty and obviously in disuse. No other exits from the office were visible, no way for the man to get out. I returned to the outer office with no clear plan in mind except confrontation.

Artemus smiled and nodded at the seat.

"So, is this all part of the test, then?" I blurted out before I lost my nerve.

"Test? Is what part of the test?"

"All this," I replied, waving my arms to indicate everything. "The—" I wanted to mention the vision of the attack at the café, but instead said, "This chance meeting in your office?"

Artemus shook his head and held up a hand for me to pause. "Let me get this right, now. You think this little hole in the wall is my office?" Artemus' face cracked a wide, gleeful smile. "Tell me, have you ever heard of the Order of the Broken Chain?"

"The what?"

Artemus leaned forward toward the desk, deadly serious. "Do you like riddles?"

I didn't know what to say, so he just told it to me anyway.

> "When is a man like a fish out of water?
> When does he run from his place in the sun?
> Out of reach and out of his depth.
>
> When does a man meet his certain destiny?
> By tea leaf or tarot, he can but go,
> Out of touch and out of his mind.
>
> When does a man face his persistent illusion?
> To rise like a hawk, to fly, dive, or walk,
> Into the fold or into the fray."

Was this really happening to me? I sighed and sank back into the chair. More testing then.

He said, "I'll give you ten seconds. Just . . . tell me the first things that comes into your head. Quickly now."

The answer seemed all too obvious. "It's when he's in a SIM and doesn't know it." Like where I was right now. The only difference was that I knew what was going on.

He just looked at me, scratched his head, and said, "Wrong. Wanna try again? Five seconds . . ."

"Wrong? What else could it be? If you're in a SIM, you're certainly out of touch and out of reach. If you don't know you're in the SIM, someone can play some evil tricks on you and easily drive you insane. You could probably hold off insanity, if you suspected it was a SIM, though—"

Artemus interrupted me by saying, "You're wrong. I'm not going to tell you the answer. Oh, what the—It's when—" He paused as if rethinking his decision to tell me. "You've run out of time."

Riddles? Really? What was all this really about? "You said we had some talking to do?" I prompted. He must want to discuss my abnormal test results or ask why I chased after that fictitious sobbing man. Maybe he knows more.

He had a gleam in his eye. "Yes, Dennis. I was just reviewing your performance on the test when you came in. I have been looking for someone like you for a while now—quite a while."

"What was wrong with the results?"

"Wrong? Do you have any idea what I was testing for? Could you guess after the test was over?" He rose from his chair, seeming unable to control himself, and began pacing about the room.

"No, not really."

"I've been looking for someone—Actually I've been trying—experimenting really—not like laboratory rats or anything—it's all very safe as far as we've gone—"

"Wait. What are you talking about?"

"Let me back up." He held his hands up and waved them back and forth as if erasing and starting over. "Let me ask you this. How did you know which slot machine to pick? Which number to bet on the roulette wheel?"

"I just picked at random. Are you saying it wasn't just letting me win?"

"How did you know Rosemary was really Drake's wife?"

"Ah, that's complicated. Once she started to explain everything to me in the car, I knew she was lying about something. At first I couldn't figure it out. But if I really was their test subject, they would want a more one-on-one interaction with me during the test. So that meant she was in cahoots with them. After that, I knew everything she said had to be part of some kind of test—trying to get me to leave with her—I don't know. It seemed to fit, especially when she said Mariana was his wife."

Artemus stood in agitation and started pacing about the room. "Let me explain what I was looking for. Knowledge can be broken down into two almost distinct groups, namely procedural knowledge and declarative knowledge. Declarative knowledge consists of the facts we all know, like our names, where we live, our ID number—These are things that can be written down and memorized. And procedural knowledge would consist of those things which cannot be described well in writing, like how to tie your shoes, how to hit a racquetball, or fence, or even ride a horse. This type of knowledge answers the question 'how', while declarative knowledge answers 'what.' We know how to give people procedural knowledge—"

"You mean like skill buys? I bought 'horseback riding' a while back. We have this gaming world in the SIM, and you have to know how to do those kinds of things."

"Any guns or swordplay?"

"No guns, since they don't exist in that world. But swords . . . I leave that for the others. I'm not made of money. That kind of skill can get expensive to maintain."

Artemus pulled the other chair close and sat facing me. "It gets used up, doesn't it? They wear out like clothing. How long does your horse training last?"

"About two months," I lied. "It wears out pretty quickly." In reality, my horseback skills have never worn out like they have on Trevor and Zak. I thought it might have something to do with how my brain handled multiple personalities, so I never told anyone. But wait. Wouldn't Artemus know that I never re-purchased the skill? He had access to that kind of information. "I . . . I decided to pursue magic. Much cheaper that way. Were you giving me skills in the SIM? Is that what the test was about?"

"Heavens no. The test was—" Artemus stopped himself and lowered his voice. He looked around at the empty room before continuing. Leaning forward in his chair, he said, "I was testing for your ability to receive *declarative* knowledge. Don't you see? How did you know which number to pick at roulette? How did you know what time it was? We were feeding your brain the answers and just asking you to tell them back to us. We asked in creative ways so that you wouldn't catch on, somehow, and start unconsciously blocking the information."

"You were feeding me facts. Wow . . ." What a breakthrough. They would be able to do away with schools entirely. You could just hop down to the store, purchase an encyclopedia, and ten minutes later, voila.

Artemus sat back and said, "There are a few kinks to be worked out. We don't know how to store it in long term memory, or even if we should. We put the information in your short term memory and hoped that you would trip over it as you concentrated on the task at hand. If we put the stuff in long term memory—Well, how do we let you know that you even knew it? There are neural pathways to consider."

By the sound of it, this declarative knowledge transfer had a long way to go yet. There was no way I would be skipping higher education with a memory dump. Considering the cost of procedural knowledge, the declarative information might even cost more than a conventional education.

I asked, "How did the other people fare?"

"Up until today, it only worked on me. Now we have found someone else who can access the information. Dennis Howard."

"Only the two of us?"

Artemus rose and walked back around the desk, narrowing his eyes in recollection. "There was one other. But that one was too old. You're a much better choice. The younger the better."

His leather chair complained as he sat down. "So, Dennis. I need your help to figure out why it works on us and no one else. We need to put you back in the SIM and measure your responses. Between the two of us, we can work up enough data to figure this beast out. What do you say?"

"Is it . . . dangerous? I mean—"

"Dangerous? Someone tweaking knobs while you're under the microscope? Nothing could be safer." He waved his hand as if dismissing the issue. "I've been experimenting with myself for years now, and I'm the picture of health. Do you see anything wrong with me? Besides, we have all sorts of top notch people—"

I interrupted him with, "Maybe it would be best if I thought this over a little. I need to talk with my folks, and—"

"If you're worried about missing school . . . That can't be. But if you are, don't be. You're not going to miss much, and besides, if we get it to work properly, you'll never need to go to school again."

Artemus held up a hand. "I'm not asking you to do this for free, either. SI is footing the bill for the research, and we're loaded. I need to talk to some people to get the contracts drawn up, though, so I can't make any specific offers right now. Let's just say you won't be worrying about money for quite a while to come."

"I don't know. Everything is happening so fast—"

"Yeah, I know what you mean. Eight or nine years of nothing, then suddenly, bam! Thunder, lightning, rivers flooding, seas parting, God's walking the Earth, the whole of human future relying on your split second decisions. It's sheer pandemonium. My advice is to hang on to your hat, don't lose your head, keep your ears open and your eyes peeled, keep your pants on, look before you leap, and above all, don't try to understand the universe. It only leads to headaches. You know. The ones you get right here, behind your eyes and above your nose. The throbbing kind."

I paused a second to absorb his barrage of advice. This guy was more off his rocker than Sol Blanchard. But who was I to judge? "I'll try to keep that in mind. But like I said, I'll have to talk to my folks—"

"Forget your parents for a second. What do *you* want to do?"

If it worked, I'd have access to the sum of human knowledge. If it didn't work, at least I'd be rich. "Sure, I'd do it."

"Well, then—"

"My dad, though. He's not too hot on the idea of SIM technology. He'd never let me do it."

Artemus murmured, "Is that right?" Then he began tapping on the desk controls. The surface flickered to life. "Why don't you wait outside while I try to contact your parents. With luck, we could resolve this all today, one way or another."

As I left, I shook my head. My dad would never agree. Then, remembering that this had to be a SIM, I looked back. It was certainly possible to phone people in the real world from a SIM.

He leaned over the desk and the light stabbing upwards through the dust cast sinister shadows on his face. He looked at me and, rather ominously, said, "I'll come and get you when I'm done with your parents."

* * *

I sat in the hall trying to listen through the wall, but I could only hear muffled voices. It seemed like it took hours, and I had nothing to do but think about that massacre. If this wasn't a SIM, I was insane.

There was only one safe way I knew to determine if this was reality, and that was to get to my room back in Aristoteles. Underneath the rim of my desk was a bent nail and scratched X mark which I bet any SIM wouldn't model. How could anyone know and account for such minuscule detail? If that bent nail wasn't there then this was a SIM.

If it was there, this was real. That thought made me bite my nails, so instead I daydreamed. What if I was psychic, like in fantasy stories? What if that scene was a vision of the future? In my mind, I was a hero, leaping on the killer as he drew his weapon. Later everyone would ask me how I knew, and I would just smile, a man of mystery with hidden powers.

I jumped when the door opened. "Dennis, my boy. Why don't you step in a moment, hmm?"

Artemus' voice was raw, and he had to clear his throat. I followed him and watched as he yanked open the red curtain and looked down at the arboretum. He seemed angry.

"Your father is a stubborn one, isn't he?"

"What did he say?"

"Oh, he refused, but you knew he would." Artemus began pacing with his hands behind his back. "He doesn't realize the significance of my mission, and he wouldn't even listen."

I nodded. "It's because of my uncle back on Earth."

"Uncle? What happened to him?"

I shrugged and looked away. Uncle Burl's addiction wasn't something we were supposed to discuss.

"Never mind, never mind. Just work on your father. Try to warm him up to the idea. Maybe I'll give him a visit one of these days. He works at the Prometheus Power Plant? I can be very persuasive in person." He patted me on the back and said, "Let's get you back to Aristoteles. I'll walk you to the station."

I decided just to say it out loud. "But, I'll have to get out of this SIM if I'm going to get to the real station."

"SIM? This isn't a SIM." Artemus was out the door and in the corridor when he asked, "What are you talking about? Don't you know the difference between a SIM and reality?"

"Ahh, yeah. Just a bad joke," I said, not knowing what to think.

I let him shuffle down the hall in front of me as I walked. He glanced around the corner carefully before continuing, as if nervous about being caught in the open.

We arrived at the station a few minutes later. The crowd was thick with two trams busy exchanging passengers. One tram was headed back up the line, toward Mayfair, and the other was my tram, headed toward Aristoteles and home.

Artemus tapped me on the shoulder. He had a furrowed brow and his eyes kept glancing around nervously. As if he didn't want to be overheard, he lowered his voice and said, "Dennis, listen. Do me a favor. You see those two trams over there?" I nodded dumbly. "One of them will take you back home, no?"

I nodded, and he continued, "You must not get on it. Take the next tram instead."

"What? Why—"

"I can't explain now. Everything will become crystal clear later, I guarantee. Plans have changed, and I'm going to Aristoteles too. But you mustn't . . . Look, just grab the next tram back home. I can't explain now."

If the next tram was late, I might not be able to get back home before the match. I had to check for that bent nail. "I'm not just going to—"

"Look. Do you see that man over there, just about to board the tram? He has a black beard and a long grey coat."

"You mean him—"

"Don't point," he said smacking my arm down to my side. "His name is Bosner and there's a brother of his around somewhere who looks a lot like him. These men are . . . from a competitive firm researching the same thing we are. You must stay away from them at all costs. If they discover you, they will make every effort to kill you. I'm not joking."

I nodded as I looked at Bosner. Like Rosemary in the SIM, Artemus sounded as if he wasn't telling me the whole truth, but I knew one thing was true. These men had no problem with murder when it suited their whims. The man boarding the tram was the same one who attacked me when I was in the air duct with Trevor. And . . . and come to think of it, he looked similar to that maniac I saw kill a half dozen people during my episode in the café. I wanted no part of him.

"In a crowd we're mostly safe as long as we don't get too close," Artemus said. He turned away from the tram as Bosner looked back toward us. "But don't make physical contact. Touching him's as good as shouting, 'Here I am!' I'm off to see where he is headed."

"Following him? Is that safe?"

"Are you kidding? It's insane. Just take the next tram home, and I'll contact you later this week. Capiche?"

"Not really."

"Good." With that, he was off, shuffling toward the Aristoteles tram as fast as he could through the crowd.

My life was in danger, all because of Artemus and his research. I made my way toward a bench attached to the side wall, trying to be as inconspicuous as possible. Couldn't I just refuse to help Artemus and so get out of the crosshairs of these Bosner brothers? Something told me it wasn't that simple. They attacked me in the duct long before I'd even heard of this declarative knowledge research. If that vision of mass murder was some kind of premonition, what would motivate Bosner into killing all those people? Insanity. I doubt they were all involved with Artemus.

And if it wasn't a vision, but some kind of scene in a SIM—If this was all a SIM, maybe they were trying to make me afraid of these Bosners so I'd avoid them. Could Artemus and the other executives at SI be trying to avoid a bidding war for my brain and its unusual ability to perceive information sent from Emily?

I had to get home to find out if that bent nail was under the rim of my desk.

* * *

As I burst through the door into our Aristoteles apartment, something in the back of my mind noticed that Mom was on the vid with Dad. With a cursory wave and shouted greeting, I flew into my room. The next tram had been over a half hour late, which made this side trip back home unthinkable if I wanted to get to the SIMs in time, and being late meant being disqualified.

Racing to the table, I ran my fingers along the edge as nonchalantly as I could while pretending to search my desk for something else. The bent nail and the X mark were actually there. This was not a SIM, and the massacre at the café was some kind of hallucination.

While pretending to rifle through my desk, I overheard Mom in the other room talking to Dad. "But this is Thursday. What about our plans? Must you spend so much time at Prometheus?"

"You know how it is," Dad said. "The schedules are all screwed up, what with Rosen down with the flu. The experiments don't care about what day it is, what time it is, or who's sick."

"I know, I know—"

The good news was that I could generate a sub-personality for the coming match with no fear of being caught by nosy psychiatrists. "Emily, time?"

"The time is 2:53 PM."

There was only a measly six minutes and change to get into a SIM chamber and recognized before the Masters would throw me out of the tournament. No time to waste.

As I bounded out of my room, I heard Dad explain, "Look, I'll just be another two hours. By that time—Hey kiddo, we need to talk about Regale and his crazy ideas."

"Okay, but I'm headed to the SIMs to watch the match."

I didn't expect any trouble. Mom turned to me in what seemed like slow motion and finally said, "Dennis, I think you watch entirely too many SIMs. Besides, with your father working today, I need your help getting this place cleaned up before everyone gets here. You didn't forget your father's birthday, did you?"

I hadn't forgotten his birthday, but I had bigger things on my mind. I protested, "It'll only be an hour or so. I can't miss it. It's about to start."

Not waiting for a reply, I vanished down the corridor. I thought I heard Mom say something about how I shouldn't leave in the middle of a discussion. I couldn't miss the tournament, and I knew that they wouldn't understand why. I'd never told them I was competing because they would have gone ballistic.

If I was ever asked, I wouldn't have been able to explain how I made it in time. The entire trip was a blur of perspiration and close calls. I even jumped three stories in one leap so that I could get to the Brandenburg SIM chambers on the fifth floor.

A mere four minutes and fifty-five seconds later, I arrived at the chambers, found an empty one, and dove into the capsule feet first. I did it in record time.

Once the cap was on and the electrons and neurons were popping in unison, I said, "Emily, this is Dennis Howard ready to begin the tournament." Breathlessly, I awaited a reply.

Much to my relief, Emily greeted me with her usual formal tournament-style salutation. "Good afternoon, Dennis Howard, also known as Sam Clemens. Welcome to the Fifth Trial of the Eighth Annual Master's Championship Tournament. Are you ready to begin?"

I let out a long sigh of relief and replied, "Let's do it."

Chapter Nine

The Watch Keeper

"Goodnight, Momma," I whispered. She was wrapped up in her covers in her bed, and she looked asleep. I didn't want to wake her, but Dad said to give her a kiss goodnight. She didn't look so good, but at least she'd stopped coughing.

Her eyes opened a little and she smiled. "Goodnight, Billy."

After I kissed her on the cheek, she said, "Are you excited about your birthday tomorrow? I can't believe you're going to be five." Her voice sounded thick and tired.

"I can't wait. But . . . Aunt Louise isn't coming over, is she?"

"Of course. And all your little friends will be here for the party. I don't think I'll be up to chasing after them, and besides—" she said, looking at the door and lowering her voice. "Between you and me, I don't think your father could handle two children, let alone six."

"You won't be coming down? I was hoping you'd be better."

"Maybe I'll feel better tomorrow. We'll have to wait and see, but no promises. Now give me another kiss goodnight then off you go."

I kissed her, and as I was heading toward the door she said, "I love you."

I think I said, "Love you," as I closed the door, but all I could think about was Aunt Louise. She was going to embarrass me in front of my friends, and there was nothing I could do.

In my prayers that night, I prayed that God would do his best to stop Aunt Louise, but I wasn't holding my breath. "And please help Mom to feel better. Amen."

* * *

When I woke up the next day, the sun was busting through the window right in my eyes. I looked outside and heard some birds singing. There were always birds in Mr. Fignagel's garden. Mr. Fignagel was our next-door neighbor. His house was farther from the road than ours, so his front yard was big enough for lots of trees and plants.

Mr. Fignagel was already gardening when I looked out. I thought about calling his name and waving to him, but I'd done that before, and he always ignored me. He does that with everybody, even Dad. He was a mean old man.

The chimes sounded. Mr. Fignagel had almost as many clocks as plants. I'd never been in his house, but from my window I could hear them chime on the hour. He must have had cuckoo clocks and grandfather clocks of all shapes and sizes because I could hear hundreds of them. That's why Mom and Dad had the other room and not this one. They couldn't sleep with all of the clocks chiming every hour, so they gave me the room on the morning side of the house. They never bothered me.

I raced downstairs and found Dad already fixing breakfast. He had a couple of scrambled eggs and toast on a platter for Mom. Dad started upstairs with it and said, "Mornin' Billy, be right back."

Maybe if Mom wasn't feeling well, Dad could call Dr. Anderson and he could come over with some pills. It would be a great birthday present to have her downstairs for a change. Dad always brought food up for her, and sometimes, we all ate together in their room. I would have to sit on the floor, but that was all right.

From upstairs there was a crash as if Dad had dropped the platter. I heard Dad shouting. "Beth, Beth honey, wake up. Beth. Come on now, don't do this!"

Dad came running down the stairs and almost ran me over. He grabbed the phone. I figured he must be trying to get the doctor.

I went up the stairs and peeked into their room. The tray of food was upside down on the edge of the bed and eggs and pieces of the broken dish were all over the floor. Mom was going to be mad when she woke up and saw that mess.

Her face was turned away, so I couldn't see if she was asleep, but one of her arms was sticking out over the bed toward me. How could anyone sleep like that?

"Mom? You okay?" I whispered, then more forcefully, "Mom?"

Dad came up the stairs and found me in their room. "Billy. Go downstairs."

"But what's wrong with—"

"Billy. Just—Look, there's going to be an ambulance arriving to take her to the hospital. Go wait on the stoop, and when they get here, make sure they come in as quick as they can. Okay?"

I only waited a few minutes on the porch before the ambulance arrived. Before too long, the two men in white coats were carrying Mom out the front door on a bed, one in front and the other behind. Mom didn't look good and didn't open her eyes when I called to her and ran up to her side. Dad took my hand as they put her in the truck and turned on their siren. What was happening?

* * *

For the next week, I stayed at Aunt Louise's house. I never had my party, but Aunt Louise gave me her present a few days later. It was a picture that she made herself. She said it was something called a cross stitch, and she wanted Dad to hang it in my room. I told her it was very nice and thanked her like Mom taught me. I didn't let on that I didn't really like it. It was like something for a girl. The picture had flowers and chubby baby angels with tiny wings. In the middle was written,

Four Angels to my bed,
Four Angels round my head,
One to watch and one to pray,
And two to bear my soul away.

For some reason, every time Aunt Louise looked at the picture she began to cry. I was glad I hadn't opened it in front of all my friends.

I wanted to go home and see Mom. Uncle Burt snored, and I could hardly sleep. It wasn't like the chiming clocks because he snored the whole night. I was glad when Dad came and picked me up, even though he seemed very sad. He had on a dark suit and looked very strong and tall.

At home, we went into the back room where we always listened to the radio. He had a real serious look on his face. I felt better with Dad around 'cause I knew he would fix everything.

"Aunt Louise has told me that you've been asking her some questions about Mom. She said she tried to explain." He rubbed his forehead and eyes. He did that whenever he was trying to control his temper, but he didn't look mad now.

He asked, "Do you understand what happened to Mom?"

"No, Dad. She's not upstairs?"

"Billy, your Mom . . . she passed away last Sunday. Do you know what that means?"

"When is she coming back?"

"She . . . she's not going to be coming back. Mom was in a lot of pain. You remember those pills she was taking? Hmm? She took those to help her with the pain. But she's not in any pain anymore."

Tears started to well up in his eyes. I guess I started to cry too. He put a hand on my shoulder and said, "God decided that he needed her to help him with something important—something real important, and he felt sorry for her because she was in so much pain. She's with God now."

"Why isn't she coming back? Is she mad at me?"

"No, no. She's not mad at you. God decided to take her to a wonderful place where there's no pain and only happiness and love. A garden where she can visit Grandma and Grandpa."

"She's with God?"

"Right. God has taken away her pain, and . . . and though we miss her, we should be at least in some small way happy that she can finally rest."

"Where is God, Dad? Can we go and see her?"

"God is . . . That's a tough one, Billy," he let out a few strained laughs. "Some people think that God is all around us. That he lives in everyone and watches over us. Others think that he made the Earth and everything on it, set it in motion and stepped back to let it run, like the Earth was a big clock and he was the clock maker." He got up and looked out the window at our backyard. It had just stopped raining, and the ground was still wet. "I don't know. We just have to have faith that God did what was best. But—What kind of God would take Beth away? Of all the people . . ." He pounded the wall and made the window rattle, which scared me.

"I don't understand! Where's Mom? Where's Mom?" I got up and ran out of the room.

"Billy!" Dad shouted.

I ran upstairs to see if she was in her bed. She had to be there. She just had to be. I burst in the room and looked. The flowery bedspread was lying neatly over the bed, as if no one had slept there. "Where is she?" I made a fist and pounded the bed. Dust flew off the spread and hung in the air.

I ran into my room, but she wasn't there either. Dad appeared at my door and said, "She's not here. We have to keep her alive in our memories, Billy. If we think of her, of all the good times we had, she'll be with us. She'll always be with us."

I lay down on my bed, away from him. Aunt Louise had said she was dead, but what did that mean? Doesn't she want to see me anymore? Doesn't she love me anymore? When I turned back, Dad was gone and the door was closed. My nose was clogged and my tears stung my eyes. I didn't hear him leave over the sound of my own crying.

Where was she? Why would God take her away like that? It's not fair.

The same thoughts just kept rolling around in my head until, at last, I stopped crying. My pillow was wet, and I had to breathe through my mouth, but I didn't care. I was so tired that I began to fall asleep.

Mr. Fignagel's clocks all went off at the same time and woke me up with a start. That was when I figured it out. That was when it hit me. It had to be Mr. Fignagel.

I quickly got up and rummaged around until I could find my dart gun. It was under a pile of old clothes. I stuffed the three extra darts in my pocket, just in case. I walked down the stairs slowly so the creaks wouldn't sound and sneaked out the front door. Dad never lets me out alone.

I figured Mr. Fignagel was God, and if he had Mom, I was going to bring her back. It all fit. Mr. Fignagel was mean, and only a mean person would take Mom away. He had a garden, and Dad said that Mom was in a garden. He also had clocks, hundreds of 'em, just like Dad said. He had to be God.

I made sure the dart was loaded firmly before I approached the hedge. After I pushed through, I saw Mr. Fignagel sitting on his porch. I didn't see Mom anywhere, but maybe she was inside. My nose was still clogged, so I took a deep breath through my mouth and jumped out with a "Haa!"

"Who is that?" he called out in surprise. He had a raspy old voice that gave me shivers, and I almost dropped my gun. I gripped it tighter, made sure my aim was good, and walked up the steps.

"Well, if it isn't Billy Prescot. And toting a weapon." I pointed my dart gun at him, but he was still far away. I didn't think I could hit him. "So, is it to be robbery then? Or are you going to shoot me where I sit?" He raised his hands in surrender.

"Where's my Mom?" I asked in a shaky voice.

He yelled, "What's that? Speak up there."

I repeated my question in a louder voice, and the sound made me feel braver. He lowered his hands and scratched his face. "Your mother? Isn't she at home?"

"No, she's not."

"Why don't you come on up here and have a seat. We can discuss this missing person's report of yours. Hmm?"

I inched up the steps. I could hear the clocks ticking away inside, but I didn't look. I kept my eyes on Mr. Fignagel.

"You can put down that gun, Billy. I'm an old man. I'm not going to make a break for it."

He looked old. His hands shook as he took out a pocket watch on a gold chain. He looked down at it then closed it with a click. He gave me a friendly smile and said, "Now, tell me. Your mother is missing? That's what's gotten you all riled up?"

I decided to lower my gun. He didn't look like he was going anywhere, and besides; my arm was getting tired because I was holding it so stiff. "They came and took her away. They put her on a bed and carried her out."

"Carried her out, did they? Could you speak a little louder, my boy? My hearing is not what it used to be."

Raising my voice, I said, "Dad said she wasn't going to come back. She—" I started to get choked up, but I couldn't do that now. I made my face tight until the feeling passed. "Dad said . . . Dad said she passed . . . by, or something."

Mr. Fignagel raised his eyebrows and then shook his head slowly. "She passed on? Oh, I'm so sorry boy. Terrible, terrible news." He fell silent, and I could hear the sprinkling rain begin to fall again.

Several moments later he asked, "But Billy, why did you think she was here?"

"She's here isn't she? Maybe she's inside. Mom! Mom, are you in there?" Leaving my gun on the swing, I got up and went to his screen door. The only sound I heard was the clocks ticking. Just inside the door was a great big grandfather clock about ten times my size. A huge pendulum swung slowly back and forth, and I heard a "dock" with every swing.

"Billy, she's not in my house. Whatever . . . Didn't your Dad tell you about what happened to your mother? Do you understand what death is?"

"I want my Mom! She's here, isn't she? Dad said she was with God, and I figured you were him. You're God, aren't you?"

"God? Me?" He slapped his face in surprise. "Ho, ho, ho. Well you found me out. No one else has been able to penetrate my clever disguise. What was it that gave me away? Perhaps it was my robes of glory," he indicated his brown sweater. "Or, maybe, maybe it was the hosts of Cherubim and Seraphim at my gates."

I started to cry again, and he said, "Oh, I'm sorry. I shouldn't be that way. Come on inside. Would you like a cookie? I think I might have one or two." He opened the screen door, and it creaked in a friendly way. He held it open and I went in wiping my eyes.

We went down a hallway that had a grandfather clock at both ends. The rooms that we passed were full of clocks. There was a mantel with five clocks, and two tables each with at least three. All of them were in deep wooden cases, and they filled the house with a ticking and tocking.

When we got to the kitchen, he told me to have a seat. After he handed me some tissues, I blew my nose and sat down at the table, which was covered with a red and white checkered table cloth that reminded me of Aunt Louise's place. He poured me some milk, and I told him what Dad had said about God being a clock maker. "And you have tons of clocks. I can hear them from my bedroom. Not all of the ticking, though. Only when they go off."

"When they chime? Hmm?"

I nodded. "Don't they wake you up when you sleep?"

"I don't sleep that much, Billy. Maybe it's because I'm old." He scratched his face. "That's a funny way of looking at God, like he was a clock maker." He reached up to a tall shelf to bring down a big cookie jar. "People with these types of beliefs admit that there might be a God, but the persistence of misfortune makes them think that God doesn't care about them. You see, Billy, they believe that God has left them alone to fend for themselves. Bereft of the compassion of a loving God, these people believe they are destitute, orphaned."

I didn't understand a lot of what he was telling me, but I understood the last part. I said, "Kind of like my Mom leaving me?" I took the big chocolate chip cookie he offered.

He paused and replied, "Yes. Just like your poor mother's death. But listen to me, Billy. I'm certain that your Mom loved you as much as any mother could love a son. I know she didn't want to leave you and your Dad alone."

"Where is she, then?"

"Have you ever heard of Heaven, Billy?"

"Yeah."

"Some people think of Heaven as a wondrous place of beauty and tranquility, high above the clouds. But it isn't that far away at all. It is all around us if we could but perceive it. She is no doubt watching over you, making sure nothing bad happens."

"Isn't she with God, like Dad said?"

"Oh, God is all around us too, always by our side. Believe me, if he wasn't there, you would be able to feel his absence like a physical blow. But he would never leave you, especially in hard times like these. If you are still and listen for his words, you can hear him."

Mr. Fignagel didn't seem at all like I thought he would be. I munched on my second cookie as he said, "Sometimes, though, he has to step in and take action. Great miracles happen, like mountains moving, or seas parting."

"Can you hear God talking, even though you can't hear so good?"

"Oh, many times. Many times. God isn't the only one to watch over you and your family, you know. Have you ever heard of angels?"

"I've seen them at church on the windows. They have wings."

"I've seen those pictures too. I believe there are angels around us too, comforting us when we are sad or guarding us to keep away the danger."

"But Mom wasn't kept safe. Didn't the angels care about her?"

"Did you ever hear people say, 'God works in mysterious ways,' or 'God's will be done?'"

I shrugged. It sounded familiar.

"People have been saying those words for just about forever. Most times it's hard to understand God's ways, his great plan. But you can't let that failure of comprehension harden your heart. Your mother has died, and that is a terrible thing. But—now, now."

I began to cry again, so I got up. Looking through an arched doorway, I saw a workbench with gears and springs laid out. I asked, "Why do you have so many clocks?" The more I thought about Mom, the worse it got. I tried rubbing my forehead like Dad did, but it didn't seem to work.

"Would you like to see some of my clocks? You would? Excellent."

He led me into that room with the workbench in the middle and a window looking out on the flowers in his backyard. Along with the springs and gears, arranged like a rainbow were magnifying glasses and tiny tools.

"I like to repair clocks. I use this magnifying glass when I work on small ones. Here look at this." He brought out a tiny little clock. It had to be the smallest one I ever saw. I could hardly see the hands on its face. He opened up its back and put it under the glass. I watched as the little gears and wheels spun around.

"I'm especially proud of that one. You have to wind these clocks every now and then." He took out a key from a drawer and slowly walked up to a grandfather clock that was in the corner of the room. He put the key in a hole in the front and turned. One of the weights dangling from a chain slowly rose toward the top. "If you don't keep them wound, they stop ticking."

I put my hand under the glass, and my fingers looked as big as my head. "Mr. Fignagel . . . Why aren't people like clocks? You could wind them up again before they stopped."

Mr. Fignagel shook his head. He came over and patted me on the back.

"I miss . . . I miss my Mom."

He squeezed my shoulder. "Miss her, Billy. Miss her a great deal. But also think of her as happy . . . and at rest."

I started to cry again, but I couldn't stop myself this time. He got on one knee, and I buried my face in his shoulder and sobbed. He said, "Hold her in your mind and in your heart. In time you will be able to remember her without feeling sad or alone. That's it, let it out. Let it out. Your dad is a kind heart, and he can help you. You must help each other through this."

He offered his handkerchief, and I blew my nose. Then we walked back toward the porch. The sun was setting, and it shone underneath the clouds. "I guess I'm pretty dumb, huh? Thinking you were God and all." I handed him back his handkerchief.

"I consider it a great compliment."

As we stepped outside onto the porch, a great noise came from inside that sounded like thunder. It was the chiming of the clocks. There were cuckoo clocks whooping and grandfather clocks binging and bonging in all kinds of notes all at the same time. "Boy, is that loud!"

He smiled, and when the chiming stopped, he said, "I hope our little talk has made you feel better."

I nodded and picked up my dart gun from the porch swing. I started to go down the steps, but he stopped me. "Billy, wait a moment. I want you to give something to your Dad for me." He took out the watch and chain from his pocket that he looked at before. "I have so many clocks. Perhaps this one would make him feel better, make him remember better times."

I took it from him and waved goodbye. "Thanks, Mr. Fignagel. Bye."

He waved, and I ran back home. The sun was going down, and if Dad found out I was outside, he might get mad. How could I give the watch to him without telling him about Mr. Fignagel?

I found him lying on the couch in the back room. The room was dark, so I sneaked in with the watch and put it on the table near his head. He must have heard me. "Billy? Is that you, Old Billy-Bob?"

He turned his head and saw the watch. He reached for it and started to ask, "Where did—"

"Mr. Fignagel gave it to me. He said it was for you."

"Mr. Fignagel?" I expected him to ask me what I was doing over there without his permission. Instead, he stood and took the watch toward the window, where there was still some sunlight. He opened it up and looked at the inside. I guess he liked the present because he smiled.

"Mr. Fignagel gave this to you?"

"Yeah. What are you looking at?"

"There's writing here on the inside. It says—I can't believe it. It says, 'With all my love, Beth.' This is the same pocket watch your mother gave to me on our second anniversary."

"Mom gave that to you? Why did Mr. Fignagel have it?"

"Billy, I lost this watch in that boating accident last spring. Remember when we all went fishing and your Mom and I fell into the river? How did Mr. Fignagel get it? Come on, Billy. Let's go ask him." With the watch in his left hand and my hand in his right, we went out the back door together. The grass was still watery, and I could feel my socks in my shoes getting wet.

"Dad, look!"

We both stopped and watched. It was the strangest thing I ever saw. We could see Mr. Fignagel's house over the hedge with its white siding shining in the sunset. The whole thing—his house, the trees in his backyard, even the hedge between our houses—they were all blurring and fading into white mist. Within moments the roof and the chimney, the flowers and the vines were gone. It all vanished into whiteness, almost too bright to look at.

I remembered the present Aunt Louise gave me with all of the angels on it. Right then, I knew for sure that Mr. Fignagel wasn't a gardener or a clock fixer or even God. "Dad. Mr. Fignagel—He must have been one of Mom's four angels. Now that Mom is with God, he doesn't have to stay anymore. I wonder . . . I wonder which angel he was, which angel of the four?"

"An angel?" Dad whispered.

I held Dad's big hand tighter when I thought I heard horns away, far away.

Chapter Ten
Decimation Dissemination

Even though Emily shut down the SIM, I could still hear horns. At first, I thought I was just imagining them because of the emotional strain of the match. I felt like a rubber band that had been stretched too many times. The partitions in my head which separated me and my people were slim protection against emotions. Though I felt for Billy, I was helpless to comfort him because that would have meant an intervention on a scale visible to the Masters, assuring a loss.

But the horns were not some angelic fanfare, as Billy had imagined. They were the horns of the Lunar Emergency Broadcast System, informing everyone in Aristoteles that something dire was happening.

"Emily. Emily! What is going—" I was momentarily distracted by my SIM chamber bonds' automatic retraction. Emily remained silent, something I couldn't remember happening before. "Emily? Hello?"

The hexagonal lid of my chamber also opened, making the horns and klaxons almost too loud to bear. I held my hands over my ears as I jumped out.

The alarm cut off and was replaced by a middle-aged male voice, tight with excitement. "This is not a drill. I repeat, this is not a drill. Please proceed calmly and directly to the nearest shelter. An air pressure drop has been detected and is being investigated. Please proceed—" He continued repeating the same message for a while, and after that the horns began to sound once more.

Emily was supposed to automatically take care of isolating pressure drops. Where was she? I felt just like Billy, whose protective mother was suddenly taken away.

The swarming mass of bodies exiting their beehive chambers brought on the same stirrings of claustrophobia, which usually plagued me upon every SIM waking. I suppressed that fear and made my way to the exit. Despite my efforts I found myself muttering under my breath, "I love you—shut up. I love you—shut up," as I launched myself through the ceiling exit and into the upper hall. I flew upward and just managed to grab the bottom of the railing on the overhanging balcony two floors above the Brandenburg SIM Center.

After clambering up onto the balcony, I looked down on the swarm of humanity and felt glad I wasn't down there. All of the normal lighting seemed to be out, but luckily we had daylight outside. The light pipes that ran from the surface rimmed the corners of every intersection and almost gave off enough light to illuminate the halls themselves, even without the electric lights.

People were swarming south toward the center of the city and the closest shelter, but I headed away from it. I wanted nothing to do with a crowded shelter or the traffic bottlenecks that would slow my progress toward safety. Instead, I set my sights on the Aristoteles spaceport.

One thing the spaceport had that the shelters didn't was a liberal supply of mech-suits of all shapes and sizes, each with its own self-contained atmosphere, designed for use on the lunar surface. Luckily this wasn't a solar flare emergency. Against radiation, mech-suits weren't any better protection than the walls of Aristoteles. Outside in nothing but a suit during a flare, you might as well hang it up.

The spaceport was at the north end of the city, but that wasn't far, since Brandenburg was the north-west section of Aristoteles. The stairs were arranged in a sweeping spiral arrangement with a hole through the center large enough for a small land rover to fall through.

I grabbed the railing and leapt across the gap to the opposite railing roughly three meters up. Once there, I leapt again crisscrossing the open circle in the center of the spiral. This was a move that could waste more time than you gained, unless you were well practiced in the art. You could overshoot the opposite railing and wind up against the wall.

"Hey kid," came a voice from below. "Quit messing around and get to a shelter." I glanced down after snagging the next rail. A cop was standing, hands on hips, and glaring up at me from four floors below and at the center of the spiral stair. He turned back to directing people to safety, and I ignored him. The authorities enjoyed this kind of behavior just as much as they enjoyed kids running through the halls and vectoring off walls.

As I ascended, I swallowed several times to equalize the pressure in my ears. The air pressure in Aristoteles was actually dropping. Didn't the architects of the city plan for this type of emergency? I remembered hundreds of bulkheads that Emily would automatically close to localize air pressure loss. Why weren't they working?

I was two hallways away from the spaceport, and my confidence was returning. I felt sure I would be able to get into a suit before the pressure dropped dangerously low. And I had little fear of there not being enough suits to go around. I hadn't seen a soul headed toward the port, but there never were many during the drills.

Rarely did any of us kids get the chance to put on a real suit and have fun outside, but every drill that I could, I made sure to return to the port to find a suit. I idly wondered if Trevor or Zak would be there. We met in the port during a drill three years ago about when my family first moved from Descartes to Aristoteles so Dad could be closer to the Prometheus power plant and his research.

Trevor and Zak made going to the spaceport fun. The suits themselves were fun to play with, but without Zak cursing at the uncooperative controls or Trevor's wild and perpetual imagination, it would have become boring long ago.

The spaceport doors retreated quietly into the walls as I approached, and the glare from the sudden brightness coming from the concourse within made me blink. All of the lights were working. Perhaps the port had its own power source separate from the rest of Aristoteles. Uniformed officers of the Force were rushing about, giving orders to their subordinates. A shower of sparks coming from an open access panel on the left wall of the concourse brought an expletive to the lips of the maintenance woman working there. But maybe whatever she did worked, because just then, five blast shutters started to rumble downward, covering the five windows that looked out onto the lunar panorama. Before they closed all the way, I noticed dozens of maintenance rovers outside heading toward the east.

My breathing was becoming more labored as the air continued to thin, even in the port. Trying not to draw attention to myself, I made a beeline for the maintenance bay where most of the suits were stored. In my hurry, I ran into a bearded man, who also appeared to be headed toward the mech-suits. After bashing my elbow against something the man was carrying, I caught myself on the wall.

But his hands were empty. He wasn't, in fact, carrying anything. It must have been something under his long, grey coat, perhaps tied to his belt. When I finally looked at his face, I took a quick breath in surprise. His beard was black and well-trimmed, and his eyes darted left and right. He was a Bosner.

"Out of my way, child!" he ordered with an annoyed wave of his hand. His accent had a European sound to it, Slavic. His coat billowed behind him as he strode away deeper into the maintenance bay areas. Was there any connection between the Bosner brothers and this depressurization?

My heart was beating a mile a minute. He didn't kill me. But, if I didn't get to a mech-suit soon, I would be dead.

I entered the maintenance bay, and after making sure Bosner was nowhere in sight, I hurried to the suit room. The palm reader stood just inside the door, and without thinking I reached for it. Normally, if you were taking a suit, you had to identify yourself before Emily would give you permission. The surface of the palm reader remained black, even though I pressed my right hand flat to the surface. Emily wasn't available even here. Where was Emily?

Would I be able to take out a suit if Emily didn't release it? I was panting now, and not from the run it took to get to the port. The air was thinner, and I was beginning to feel dizzy. Abandoning the palm reader, I approached the line of suits with dread.

"Concentrate . . . relax," I told myself. The suits were attached to the ceiling of the floor below. Holes in the floor allowed the maintenance people to fall into suits. The shoulders of the suits were open, allowing enough room for your body to pass through.

I chose a suit and kicked the activation panel located on the floor. I was relieved to see its cheerful yellow light suddenly reflect off the floor and the helmet seated close by the hole.

I stepped over the suit and let myself fall. The low g's of Luna made the fall painfully slow. I needed more pressure, and Luna's gravity wasn't helping. The blood in my eyes pulsed with every heartbeat. Reaching down, I pulled myself into the suit. Sensing that I was in, a mechanical arm brought the helmet down over my head and it sealed it to the shoulder of the suit with a snap. The test tones sounded and the screens in front of each eye came to life. A male voice said, "Initiation of start-up sequence for Mech-6557. Power level is ninety-six percent. Air supply is fully charged. Hydraulic pressure is nominal. Agile-Eye system is active."

The faceplate of the helmet was an old-fashioned liquid crystal display. It gave me a picture of the outside world and information on the suit's performance and status. Separate pictures sent to either eye would give me the illusion of depth. For me, it was a vital illusion because at least for a while I could forget the closeness of the helmet and the reinforced plasteel wrapped around my arms and legs.

The suits didn't have direct brain connection capabilities the way the SIM chambers did. Everything couldn't be new and up-to-date.

The hissing sound of air told me my suit was pressurizing. I didn't realize how nervous I was until I felt my knees shaking. I took a minute to calm myself with some deep breathing exercises. When my heart had returned to a reasonable rate, I glanced at the release icon that was blinking on the helmet display and flicked my right forefinger for activation. The icon, which was a picture of two arrows facing each other, stopped blinking and became two opposed arrows. The magnets holding the suit to the ceiling released me. Slowly falling the half meter to the floor below, I landed easily, feeling the suit as an extension of my own body.

It was time to find out what was going on. I dialed up Emily's frequency code on the suit's com-link. "This is Dennis Howard requesting access to the Lunar Main Computer." My response was static. I tried several times, but nothing worked. For the tenth time, I wondered where Emily had gone. She was spread out practically over the entire surface of Luna. No single event could destroy her and leave us alive.

I walked slowly to an airlock so I could get outside. It would be a shame to waste the suit time without a jaunt in the moon dust. The powered joints lifted the legs at my command, making it feel like my own body, but the mass of the suit was nothing to forget. The muffled whirring and chinking of the hydraulics was a constant reminder of my mechanical body.

Once the air lock completed cycling, the door to the lunar surface opened, and I walked out. As always, Earth hung there in the sky, motionless as if it were merely painted on the blackness, but unlike a painting, it changed as it rotated, as its twisting cloud cover migrated over its surface, or as the sun wheeled in the sky affecting the amount of its surface obscured by its own shadow.

Ships were scattered throughout the landing area, and I could see some activity around several of them. Some men were climbing aboard one. I wouldn't have minded spending the duration of this trouble in one of those ships. Unlike the shelters down below, at least there wouldn't be a million people crammed in there.

I dialed up one of the command frequencies to find out what was going on. What I got didn't tell me much.

"—Niner four delta, did you check out the secondary power links, or just the mains? . . . Well don't you think it would be a good idea? If it's working we could patch it through there and figure out where the break occurred later—"

I flicked through the channels without saying a word. I didn't want to get in the way of repairs.

"—Phil thinks the power couplet blew as a result of a surge, and if you buy that we have to replace the whole thing. Ya know, come to think of it, he might be right. I sure can't get it open, suit or no suit—"

I switched to another channel. Then another. "—Chan! I thought I told you to get over to building 87. You know that's an agri-unit. What's wrong with you?—"

"—Would you listen a minute. I'm out of acetylene. Don't you think I thought of that? It's not my job to maintain these damn mechs—"

"—Whoa! Watch what you're doing with that thing. You're gonna cut through the main seals! There's nowhere for the heat to go—Jesus Jean-Paul, would you gimme that—"

"—If there's a crack down here we're not going to find it today. It's pitcher than black, and my infra-reds ain't doing jack—"

"—Do they think we're playing ball out here? That's Jalom's problem, not mine. Get Phillips on the horn at Descartes. We're gonna have some sorry people in another ten hours if those Mechs aren't here soon—"

Listening to that wall of sound was more confusing and scary than I could deal with. I switched it off but left Emily's channel open in case she came back on-line. I walked out of the landing area and onto the real lunar surface. The dust was thick enough to leave footprints but not thick enough to hinder my progress. A trillion tracks of all shapes and sizes already covered the surface, the result of decades of passage by both humans and machines. Once a track was put down, there was no wind or rain to erase it. They say you can go out and see the tracks the original Apollo crews made back in the twentieth century. I've never seen them, though.

I requested another com-access and a blinking yellow frequency number appeared in the upper right hand corner of my display. The illusion generated by the suit put those numbers about a half a meter in front of me, and I felt as if I could reach out and touch them. I focused on them and pressed a button in my right glove, which sent the digits racing upward through the available communication frequencies. I stopped at the channel which Zak, Trevor, and I used whenever we were out together.

Instantly, I heard Zak's gruff voice say, "—amn thing. Wreck of a mech. Why does this always happen to me? Wait a minute. What if I . . . Oh, man."

"Hey, Zak. What's going on? You didn't get yourself into trouble again, did you?"

"Dennis. All right! Finally. I thought I'd have to call in some spaceport low-brow to get me moving again."

I locked in on his beacon signal. He was off to the west somewhere. I started to walk north to triangulate his position. "You're not in monitor mode again, are you?"

"All I see are hexadecimals, and my mech joints won't respond. They are in some kind of sleep mode and won't budge. I can't even pound anything."

After a few steps, I got a fix on his position. I turned around and walked in his direction. He was on the other side of the port, so it would probably take an hour. I had nothing better to do.

"Hexadecimals? You just see a screen full of letters and numbers? It sounds like you're paging through raw memory. You didn't change anything, did you?"

"Hey, give me some credit, will ya? I'm not a know-nothing plebeian who finds a self-destruct button and decides to test it. Besides, if I did change anything, it's just because I was trying to reactivate the Agile Eye." Zak sounded defensive, but that was nothing new. He couldn't get along with anything mechanical, even if it was automatic. I was always surprised that he relied on the likes of me to get him out of these jams.

I said, "Look, just don't change anything else. Isn't Trevor around anywhere?"

"I haven't heard a peep. But I'm just glad you showed up. Where are you, anyway?"

"I'm on the north-east side. I'm headed your way, but it's going to take a while."

"I don't care about that. Tell me how to get this blasted thing moving again!"

"All right, all right. Keep your pants on, will ya." I wasn't too confident, but I tried not to let it show. It was actually Trevor who really understood the mechs. He knew the mech command super-structure so well, he could insinuate new procedures without setting off alarms inside what was supposed to be secure code. He could get Zak out of monitor mode easily. We had gotten Zak out of similar problems before, and I'd received part of the credit for the deed, even though I hadn't really understood everything. I mostly just took a few guesses that happened to be right, and as a result, I got a reputation for knowing what I was doing. Once you had a reputation, good or bad, it was slow to change.

I asked, "Did you hear anything about the alarm? What's going on?"

"All I know is what the announcement said," Zak said. "There was a pressure drop somewhere. I hope they get it fixed soon, so I can get out of this hunk of junk. I'm getting hungry."

"That doesn't explain the electrical failure, though."

After a pause, Zak said, "Oh, yeah. And . . . and it was awful the way the LMC disappeared right in the middle of the match."

"I have Emily's channel open, but she doesn't answer me."

"Spooky, ain't it?"

"Wait a sec," I murmured. "She went down in the middle of the match?"

I'd thought the match was over, but it couldn't have been, since Emily was cut off. That meant that Mr. Fignagel's vanishing act with the house and the trees—it wasn't part of the SIM. It was Emily losing contact. Perhaps Mr. Fignagel wasn't an angel at all. I hoped the Masters wouldn't have to reschedule the match. I sighed and shook my head in exasperation.

Zak broke in on my thoughts. "Hey, what am I supposed to do now?"

"How did you get into it, anyway?"

"Well . . . I was trying to arm the welding function. Fire shooting from my fingertip in the middle of a vacuum would be fabulous."

"They disarm those things for a reason. You need training to handle it."

"Thanks, Dad. I'll try to keep that in mind in the future."

"All right, all right. Did you try—"

At that moment, I felt an unusual rumbling vibration and turned. A rover was barreling down on my position. I leapt out of the way, but not before noticing Bosner's face through the rover's bubble-like front window. He zoomed by, making not a sound in the vacuum of Luna and headed out toward the desolation of the lunar desert. He didn't turn around and try to finish me off, so maybe he wasn't trying to kill me. It was more like he didn't care who or what was in his way.

"You were saying?" asked Zak impatiently. "What's happening?"

"Nothing."

* * *

By the time I got to him, we still hadn't reactivated his mech. I was getting worried. The stats on my mech said I had four hours of air left, but we didn't know how much of Zak's air remained. Even though he wasn't exerting himself physically, his frustration level at not being able to move for over an hour should be sending him into fits. I know I would have lost it.

I walked all around him, looking for any signs of damage, but there wasn't any. Whatever happened, he must have caused it himself. Or maybe it was his curse acting up again. He just didn't play well with electronics.

He was frozen in mid-stride. One foot was off the ground about to be placed down in front of him. It reminded me of some cartoon where the character is frozen by a freeze ray. If the situation wasn't so serious, I would have laughed.

Zak said, "What the—Hey, halt-the-SIM. I can see again, but everything is upside down. What the heck?"

"Upside down? I didn't think that was possible."

"Wait 'till we tell Trevor—a real breakthrough," Zak said. "I'm still not moving. Are you sure you know what you're doing?"

It was easier to change a good reputation to a bad one than I'd thought. "But this is good news. Don't you see? Maybe your Agile Eye is back up, along with your external sight."

"You're right. I can bring up the main selections." There was a pause, then Zak continued, "But none of them work. God! So close. Com., Mech Stats., File Access—even the one I want: ReStart. None of them do anything."

"When you look at the headings and press your activation button, they don't respond?"

"It looks like Agile Eye is still down."

"Are all of the selections on the upper right-hand corner of the screens?"

"Where else would they be? Where's Trevor?"

"So the text is right-side-up?" I asked

"The menu is fine. Only the picture is upside down."

"What if . . ." I said slowly. "What if, along with your displays, Agile Eye was sensing your eye movements upside down too? The whole thing sounds like it's confused. With the menu still open, try looking at the opposite corner. Pretend the menu is expanded upside down in the lower left corner, and try hitting ReStart there. Maybe it just thinks those menu selections are down there too."

"Umm, that's a great idea except for one thing. I want to restart this bad boy, but the ReStart selection is right next to the ShutDown selection."

"We should call for help."

"No," Zak said hastily. "They'll revoke my mech privileges if they find out. Let me give it a try."

Loss of his privileges was one thing, but I think he feared backlash from his father. Zak's irresponsibility would make bad press for the mayor.

"I . . . I suggest you don't miss." I stood ready to call in some help if he failed. If Zak's mech shut down, his transmitter would shut down with everything else, so he wouldn't be able to tell me he failed. There was five minutes of air in the mech itself at all times. Once the pumps turned off, that would be the only air he would have. And if it worked, the restart would erase his selected com frequencies, and he would have to dial them back up before we could talk again.

"Here goes nothing. I'll see you in ten seconds."

"Zak?" He didn't respond. I waited, watching the clock on my screen. The seconds ticked by. Five, six. I decided if it got to twenty, I was calling for help. Ten seconds. When it reached fifteen, his mech was moving again.

He stretched his arms by swinging them in circles. They must have fallen asleep while he was stuck. When he finally dialed up our special frequency again, he said, "Hey, what do you know? It worked. My vision is back right side up again too."

"Would I steer you wrong? When Trevor—"

I was interrupted by the Lunar Main Computer. Its default male voice announced that it was available once more. I immediately told Zak to dial up the channel and listen in.

"The northern most sections of Aristoteles, namely Drumman and Brandenburg, experienced pressure losses of half an atmosphere," it said. "The situation has been rectified, and the pressure should return to comfortable levels within the hour. Power is currently being restored. Both the atmosphere loss and the electrical failure were caused by a meltdown in one of the walls of tunnel Delta-Five, the tunnel between Aristoteles and Eudoxus. The meltdown occurred in a power couplet as a result of an overload instigated by an explosion in the Prometheus Power Plant. Nearly half the plant was demolished in the explosion. The cause of this explosion is unknown. Power is being diverted from the Bethlehem Power Plant—"

"Emily," I commanded. "Where's my dad?"

The announcement was replaced by Emily's familiar voice. "Hello, Dennis," she said, though I knew that speech on the state of Aristoteles was still continuing for everyone else. "I'm sorry, but I am not permitted to divulge the location of individuals —"

"I know, I know. Is he all right?"

"I am not permitted to divulge medical records or —"

"Okay. Umm, I'd like to place a call to my mother."

"Cindy Howard is currently unreachable. Would you like to leave a message?"

I didn't hear any more after that. I was already taking big leaps back to the space port airlock.

"Hold your horses, there, young Howard." Zak said, imitating his father's voice.

I guess, absorbed by the announcement, he hadn't heard my questions to Emily. "My dad — Remember my dad works at Prometheus."

Chapter Eleven
The Descending Chill

I found Mom and Tricia in the waiting room of St. Sebastian's Hospital emergency room. It was standing room only, but for once I didn't mind the crowds. They made the room warmer. It felt good compared with the unusual hard chill of Aristoteles' corridors.

Mom looked terrible with eyes swollen from tears. She wasn't crying when I found her though. They both looked as if they were in shock.

"Mom."

"Dennis! Dennis." She stood and gave me a warm hug through which I could feel her trembling nerves. "Where have you been? I've been worried sick."

"Where's Dad? He was . . . at the plant, wasn't he?"

"He . . . They took him to surgery."

"Is it bad?"

Mom sank back into her seat and sighed. "He was very lucky. They rescued him from his lab before it lost pressure. His . . . I think his right arm is in bad shape. He was very lucky, your father." Mom put her arm around Tricia and smoothed her hair. Tricia leaned close and wiped her teary eyes, obviously scared.

Moans of pain from others in the room distracted me. I noticed that the waiting room was not just filled with families like us, but with the injured as well. The ER was overflowing with casualties, the less serious cases forced to wait for medical attention out here. There were men with hideous burns and a few with obvious broken bones.

If Dad was one of the cases in surgery, his condition was serious. "When is he coming out of surgery? Did they tell you?"

"Sit down, Dennis," she said indicating the floor near her feet. "There is nothing to do but wait and pray."

"I can't just sit here and do nothing."

"It's out of our hands. Why don't you go down and get some food?"

I paced around the waiting room in frustration. Mom was right. I wanted to ask someone what was happening to Dad, but bothering the staff would only slow them down. I looked at their grim faces as they went from broken bones to burns. Watching their battle to fix and bandage, sterilize and suture, and ease the pain of the afflicted made me more exhausted than before.

I began to feel dizzy, and I lurched and tripped over someone's foot. Luckily, someone caught me before I hit the floor. A solid hand on my shoulder steadied me as I regained my composure.

I looked up and recognized the face. "Oh, it's Doctor . . . umm —"

"Doctor Woodridge," she replied with a wry smile. "Are you feeling all right, Dennis?"

"Oh, it's just been a long day. I'll be fine."

"Here, take this blanket," she said wrapping a blanket around my shoulders. "It's still cold."

"Oh, thanks."

"Take a few more for your mother and sister. I only wish I had more."

She smiled and turned away, and it only occurred to me then that this was my opportunity to ask someone—anyone—about Dad. "Do you know how my father is doing?"

"I think he's in surgery with Doctor Scalia. Don't worry. He's in good hands."

"Do you know how long until we hear anything?" I asked.

She smiled sympathetically and shrugged her shoulders. There was nothing to do but wait.

* * *

They were able to save my father's life by working for hours and piecing him back together. His life was saved, but at the cost of his right arm, which they had been forced to amputate. It was a shock for all of us, but, of course, not as big a shock as it would be for Dad when he woke up.

They kept him under sedation until Saturday morning. By then, Mom and I could put on brave faces and prevent ourselves from shuddering at his conspicuous deformity. Tricia couldn't get herself under control, so Mom asked her to stay home, at least for this visit. Dad needed our help, and going into hysterics every time she saw him wasn't helpful.

While waiting for him to wake up, we watched newscasts about the catastrophe. The authorities still hadn't been able to determine the cause of the explosion. They didn't know whether it was an accident or the result of foul play, but they hadn't ruled out any possibility. The military was investigating too.

When Dad finally regained his senses, he had no memory of the explosion. He'd broken ribs, ripped muscles and tendons, and had internal injuries I couldn't follow. The list was long, but it began with his amputated arm. I don't think he listened to any of his other injuries after that bombshell hit.

From my vantage point in the corner of the room, I watched Dr. Scalia as he stood at my Dad's bedside examining his charts. "Mr. Howard, Mrs. Howard. Now, concerning the arm . . . There are only two options open to us at this juncture. We can leave it as it is or we can look at robotic prosthetics. It is truly amazing what they can do with prosthetics these days."

Mom asked, "What about a replacement arm? A real, flesh and blood arm?"

"Cindy," Dad chided wearily. "Those things cost real money."

"Your husband's right," Doctor Scalia said. "Salamander charges an immense amount, and your insurance doesn't cover it."

I watched the scene unfold as if it were a play being performed for my benefit. I shook my head at my own megalomania. As I watched the discussion heat up into an argument, the issues always came back to money.

With Artemus' offer still open, I could have all the money I wanted. All I had to do was get Dad to agree to allow Artemus and his team at SI to monkey around in my head. Could they do permanent damage? I was willing to take that risk if Dad could get a real arm.

I could see in his eyes how his spirit had been broken by this ordeal. And there was something I could actually do to fix it. After Dr. Scalia left, I pulled my chair closer to the bed while trying to keep a gift-wrapped box hidden inside a plastic bag. Mom was on the other side holding his remaining hand. "You know, your birthday was this past week," I began. The explosion actually occurred on his birthday, but I didn't want to bring that up. "With all the confusion, I never gave you your present. Ta-da," I intoned as I revealed the box.

"Dennis," Mom said harshly. "We have serious things to discuss. Now is not the time. Your father can open his gift when he gets home."

"Oh, let's humor the boy," Dad said pretending to whisper. "If he feels obliged to rain presents, who are we to argue?" Then louder, "So, Dennis, what did you bring your old Dad, hmm?"

Mom said, "Can you be serious for two minutes put together?"

"Enough talk of money and medicine. It's making me ill. I need something to cheer me up, and a party is just the thing."

"A party," Mom repeated shaking her head.

"Let's see what we have here."

I handed him the gift. Too late I realized how awkward it was for him to open with one hand. "Oh, here. Let me open it up for you." I snatched the box back and began ripping off the wrapping. For a moment the room became uncomfortably silent, a chill descending over us as we were reminded of his missing arm.

Out of the box, I took the sweatshirt I'd bought. "It's a sweatshirt from the university," I said holding it up for them to read. On the front was written, 'I survived Math 352 at BLU.' Turning it over, I revealed the additional writing on the back, 'It can be shown that $2 + 2 = 5$ for sufficiently large values of 2.'

Mom laughed, but Dad just smiled. I asked, "Do you like it?"

"I like it. It's an old joke, but I like it. Thanks." Dad took the sweatshirt with a smile, but he sighed when he looked at the arms.

"That's only half of the present," I announced.

"Half? What else is there?" Dad asked.

"How does a new arm sound?"

"Dennis! How can you even joke about such a thing," Mom said.

I went to the door and closed it to give us some privacy. "I'm not joking. I knew the insurance wouldn't pay for a real arm. I looked into it—"

"Wait—" Dad said.

"—and all we need is money. Did you forget Mr. Regale's offer? They're going to give me—"

"Wait a minute," Dad said holding up his hand, then letting it fall. He closed his eyes and tilted his head back before saying. "We discussed this matter with Regale, and the answer is no. How did you get hooked up with the President of SI anyway?" He looked at me and his eyelids drooped. He must be so tired.

I stood at the foot of his bed and crossed my arms. "I know you hate SI, but we're talking about a new arm here."

Quietly, his words carrying the weight of conviction, he said, "That technology will be the downfall of the human race."

"SIM technology is everywhere. Why do you say that?"

Dad shook his head. "They're liable to fry your neurons so badly that you'll come back to us with a whole different personality."

I gasped in surprise at the mention of personalities, but I reminded myself that they had no knowledge of my talent.

"Is it safe?" Mom asked. I knew she wasn't completely against the idea.

"Would they be experimenting on humans if it wasn't?" I said, only realizing when I saw Mom's expression that the use of the word experimenting was extremely poor.

"Experimenting?" she said. "That sounds horrible."

I waved my hand as if erasing what I'd said. "No, no, no. It's not dangerous."

"If I had my way," Dad said, "no one would hook those machines up to their brains. Look at your Uncle Burl—"

"What does crazy Uncle Burl becoming a wire-head have to do with me?" I asked. "Mr. Regale wants to implant declarative knowledge in my brain, not stimulate pleasure centers."

Mom got up. "Don't you talk that way about your uncle."

"Burl isn't crazy," Dad said. "He was curious. He was seduced. There's a reason certain things are illegal. He just kept turning up the power, pushing the limits, until his nerves started to fry. There are no sensory nerves in the brain, so all he knew was the pleasure was tailing off. So he gave it another notch, then another."

"Look," I said. "That—"

Dad shook his head. "The damage is permanent. He'll never be the same. How do we know Regale won't push the limits with you? It may be information he's feeding you, but if it isn't working right, 'Heck, give the buggar more juice,'" he said, lowering his voice to ape Artemus. "'If he breaks, we can always get someone else.'"

"He said it only works on him and me, but they don't know why."

Mom shook her head, "But, honey. How do we know that's true? What if he's been doing these experiments on children for years?"

"Wouldn't we have heard? There would've been a scandal, a lawsuit, something. If we get some words in the contract to prevent him from hurting me, would you let me do it?"

Dad pursed his lips and looked away.

"Nothing bad's going to happen to me. In the end, I'll have unbelievable knowledge. Whole fields of expertise will be at my fingertips. Medicine, physics, philosophy, music. It's going to be great."

It took another hour of convincing, but they eventually agreed. Afterwards, while Dad took a nap, Mom and I returned home where she called her lawyer friend. She wanted to find out more about the kind of contractual protections we could get in writing that would stick. I was just glad Dad was going to get a new right arm, his dominant side.

In the meantime, I had a trip to the Realm to keep my mind occupied, and it was starting in just under half an hour.

Chapter Twelve

The Wheat and the Rye

"The whole thing is lunacy. Pure unadulterated lunacy!" Wren shouted. The Hall of Tishman rang with his words. "I'm shocked that you're even entertaining the idea."

"Oh shut it, Wren. We can do with a bit less flamboyance," Palomar snapped as he pushed a few white strands of hair out of his eyes.

"Lord Palomar, I must insist—"

"Wren, I'd prefer to hear whatever you need to insist later. Sit . . . and be silent." Palomar held Wren's gaze until he reluctantly took his seat.

Thunder and the staccato sound of rain pelting the array of roof windows combined with the chill in the air made my bones ache. The five fires ringing the hall gave off precious little light, let alone heat.

Palomar's shadowy gaze returned to me. His chair perched atop a slightly raised dais surrounded by great oak tables splayed out in a rough semi-circle. I sat at the table directly in front of Palomar with six mages each seated to my right and left. The council had always numbered thirteen not including the Potentate.

Palomar said, "Sol, as you admit yourself, many do hold to the belief that the Knights of the Realm are out there somewhere. But all efforts . . . centuries of efforts . . . to realize their return have failed."

Gregor, one of the thirteen other mages sitting around the tables, interjected, "High Magic must be the key, Sol."

"Exactly," I agreed. "These seven knights were the only people ever to have touched High Magic," I said. "We agree that High Magic is our best chance. Unless we discover High Magic ourselves in the next few days, we are going to need the help of men and women who already know the art."

Palomar leaned forward stretching out his empty hands and whispered, "And, Sol, in the next few days, you are going to find them where all before you have failed . . . how?"

"I have reviewed the histories." I indicated one of the large tomes in front of me on the table. "Lord Brenner, the seventh knight and the last to vanish from the realm, had some parting words to King Tendas, which, if I may?"

Palomar rolled his eyes but gestured for me to continue.

I pulled the tome entitled *Ancient Myth and Mythology of the Realm of Rinstill* closer. I cleared my throat. "Now, in this section, Lord Brenner reveals his intentions to follow the other Knights of the Realm and depart. He expresses deep disappointment in the people's inability, or rather, apathy toward learning the full extent of the magic of the knights. Tendas then reacts in alarm, wondering what will become of Rinstill with no one wielding the powers of the knights."

"This is Brenner's reply." I began reading directly from the tome.

"Those most curious and intelligent shall find magic at their fingertips. Just as only those of true hearts keep lasting friendships, the magic that makes new friends into old friends makes a powerful ally. Remember this. Only through binding love can one reach the heights where the sound of magic never fades. What mysteries that lie beyond, I cannot say.

The Knights of the Realm shall rejoin the people when their hearts and minds have been truly opened. I shall listen for the bittersweet cry of the horn amidst the ring of bells. The magic shall return."

With those last words, the light surrounding Brenner took on an intensity to pale its previous brilliance. He appeared to become smaller and smaller until nothing was left but a star of bluish-white, shrinking to a point, and, at the very last, he was gone.

I took my eyes from the words and glanced about the tables. Most of the mages looked on with dubious expressions, those being the younger of our numbers. The more experienced looked grim, knowing, just as I, how thin a hope this was.

"His last words were that he would listen for the cry of a horn amidst the ring of bells," I said.

Wren said, "Yes, none of this is news. We all know that he is waiting for us to discover the magic ourselves. When he hears its music—"

"That's just it," I said. "He wasn't describing the *sound* of High Magic. That's what everyone thinks. I believe he was telling King Tendas exactly how to call the Knights back."

Gregor, said, "So you are saying all we must do is find this horn and bells." His deep bass voice echoed clearly around the hall. He was a good friend and influential amid the other mages. He scratched his curly brown beard and asked, "But where could these relics be? We do not have time to turn over the Realm entire."

"Excuse me Sol," Wren interjected. "But exactly who will be looking for these relics? If the Potentate condescends to your fancy, how many of us are you proposing to take with you? How much of our dwindling resources do you plan to squander?"

Wren was ever manipulative. Even in a crisis, he was vying for power. If Palomar agreed to our search for the relics, Wren would have the other principal mages think him a fool. If he didn't agree, we would be put under Wren's instruction to learn exorcism techniques originally developed by the now deceased Thedof Dern. I knew once we were under his thumb, he would parlay that into another step closer to the Potentate's seat. Either way he won.

But I welcomed Wren's contempt. There was little love between Palomar and Wren, so if Wren rejected the idea, Palomar might support it.

In answer to Wren's question, I said, "From amid the full mages, I suggest taking only Sedra," She sat directly to my left, and I nodded to her. She smiled grimly and nodded back. "Her high sensitivity might reveal something I would normally overlook. The Duke of South Seniford has agreed to accompany us at least as far as the foothills, at which point he and his men will return to the King's side at the city of Sojourn."

"'Tis a waste of time," Wren said gazing at the ceiling and crossing his arms.

From the near shadows behind the thirteen seated mages, Redd's voice, though quiet, cut through the room. "Sapphire doesn't think it a waste of effort, and, for what it's worth, neither do I." He stood scratching Sapphire's neck with affection.

Palomar asked, "Where did you say you would begin your search?"

Sedra said, "I suggest we search south-west of here, at Olindara, where the Faycan Brothers reside. If we're lucky, we will not only find clues but the artifacts themselves. The brothers have a wealth of artifacts from ages past."

"Very well," Palomar said with a wave. "Make preparations at once. The rest of this council will have to do without your wisdom this night. But before you depart us, Sir Redd, tell us. What news from Westmarch?"

Redd ceased his petting of Sapphire, who perched on his forearm. "The Hold of Chaldea is overrun, but Hiltred has informed me that he still holds many of the passes through the Erid Mountains. I doubt that will last much longer."

I looked on Sapphire with wonder. All of the kestrels were in constant rapport with each other no matter the distance. The King had given South Seniford to Redd soon after he was chosen by Sapphire, making him a Duke in the process. Many at court thought this appointment was designed to place Redd in the south thus helping to spread the six remaining kestrels across the land. King Tabius had kept Bodicea Dimaus and her kestrel, Torrent, close at hand. With access to her kestrel, the King could have instant information on events across the Realm. But I believed Redd earned the appointment.

Redd continued, "Concentrating the forces at the passes will deny the hillkin access to Westmarch, but unless help comes soon, he will not be able to hold either the passes or the gorge much longer. The ghosts are taking their toll. If that's not bad enough, Hiltred has heard reports that ghosts have been harrying the countryside. Soon there will be no one left to protect." Redd's voice fell at the last, revealing his foreboding.

The thought of hillkin ranging freely across Rinstill gave me a chill. Though they lack cunning, these servants of Nardel had immense strength. They looked like giant man-shaped boulders and could kill a man with one swipe of their hand. Thankfully, the same magic that imprisoned Nardel below the realm prevented his hillkin from breaking through to the surface wherever they pleased. It was only deep within the great gorge out in the wastes beyond the Erid Mountains that the enchantment was weak enough for them to break through.

"What of the other kestrels?" Palomar asked. "Antilles? Erstwhile?"

"I don't often speak to the others, my lord. But yesterday I heard from Kirrin, the chosen of Erstwhile. He is far to the north in Ridderhaven and hasn't even heard a rumor of ghosts. Torrent and Helios are both at the Festival of Light, and as for Antilles, I have no idea. I'm presently not on speaking terms with Edlynn, and she forbade me from seeing or listening through her kestrel."

While Redd was speaking, Sedra turned to me and half whispered, "Someone's coming. I think—two men. I think they're brothers." She was amazing. I didn't sense anything but a sneeze coming on. I turned to watch the door across the hall and scratched my nose.

Answering a question I must have missed, Redd said, "No. Helios tells us that his chosen, Logan, has been so busy attempting to keep the peace between the Houses that he hasn't had time to breathe."

Two seconds later, unannounced and without preamble, the door swung open and boomed against its rests. The unmistakable Prince Fenrick strode in with a flourish. His brown hair was his most distinguishing feature, as it was nearly long enough to reach the middle of his back. Though normally flowing in graceful waves, it now hung wet and in a tangle with strands clinging to his scowling, stubbled face.

Following a few strides back was a smooth faced, slightly overweight man. Both wore long brown robes that were sopping wet, in fact drenched through and through. They were both Faycan Brothers. Fenrick was the fourth son of King Youngblood and, by all accounts, had been forced into the brotherhood against his wishes.

Fenrick strode boldly across the Hall of Tishman, leaving a trail of water along the floor. His companion followed hesitantly, as if wishing he were someplace else.

"Prince Fenrick," the Potentate said. "Well, this is a su—"

"Last night, Olindara was viscously assaulted by specters!" Prince Fenrick interrupted. "The Brothers have been decimated, and I want to know what you and this rabble are going to do about it!" He stood, hands on hips, glaring at the Potentate while rain water began to pool at his feet.

Only one of royal blood would have the gall to speak to Palomar that way without fear of reprisal. Immunity to magic increased with one's closeness to the throne. Being the fourth son, and thus four heartbeats away from ruling the realm, Fenrick had significant immunity, but not complete.

"I assure you, we are making every effort to prepare—"

"Preparations? Get out there and do something!"

Palomar continued, "We are pursuing several possible avenues of assault, and if we—"

"Unless you do something now, Olindara, West Hallingsford, Half Home and every two-bit town in between—"

"If you will stop interrupting me—"

Prince Fenrick blustered on, "—will be filled with corpses in less than two days."

"Are you finished?" Palomar shouted above Fenrick's ranting. "You won't learn anything letting your mouth run past your wit. Keep silent."

Fenrick threw his hands up in exasperation and began to pace.

Palomar continued, "His Grace, Sol Blanchard, and his entourage will soon make for Olindara. Remarkable coincidence you happened along."

I wondered how Redd and Sedra felt about being called my entourage. Perhaps it was a slight on Redd. Palomar held so little respect for Dukes that Redd wouldn't even have been permitted to the council if not for Sapphire's prestige.

Palomar said, "Sol believes he might find an artifact among the Brotherhood's menageries that might rid us of these ghosts forever." Prince Fenrick began ringing his hair out on the floor, creating a mumbling stir among the mages. The Potentate completely ignored the gesture, saying, "Unless you have more to offer us here at Waterton, I suggest you join him, my Prince. Your knowledge of the store of Olindara will speed Sol's search—"

Fenrick interrupted, "Wait, wait, wait. You want *me* to go back *there*?"

"Even if your own measure of immunity to magic should prove . . . inadequate, I'm sending Sol Blanchard and Sedra Rall with you. What more protection could anyone ask for?"

Fenrick gave me a half-smile and admitted, "Well, I suppose it could be worse. But who's this Sedra?"

Sedra rose to her feet saying, "I am."

Fenrick crossed his arms and grudgingly smiled. Under his breath, I heard him repeat, "Could be worse."

Palomar said, "Sol, make preparations at once."

"By your leave, my lord, we shall depart in the morning," I said. I had little idea what we were searching for except for a horn and a few bells. Despite the optimism and enthusiasm with which I had proposed our quest, I had little hope. I turned my gaze to the intricate, shadowy windows high above us, wailing under the gusting winds.

Redd turned to leave and I followed not far behind. Sedra gracefully joined me.

Fenrick wasn't done, however. He complained, "And another thing. I, ah . . . retreated in such haste that I left my sword, so—"

"I was under the impression that Faycan Brothers didn't arm themselves," Wren said.

"Unarmed? I'm not going back out there without at least a bow. And . . . and some bloody dry clothes. This thing weighs a ton." I stopped and looked back to see him stripping himself and tossing the water logged wool robe to the floor. Underneath he had on small breaches and a throwing knife strapped to each limb. We stood and gaped as he dug a heel into the robe, squishing out a bucket-full of water over the cobbled floor. Sedra could hardly contain her laughter at the spectacle, but whether it was his sudden lack of apparel or impudence that she found most entertaining, I could only guess.

I shook my head as Fenrick walked past us toward the exit. He gave me a wink and shouted back to Palomar, "And do something about the weather. If it's even drizzling at dawn, with Tishman as my witness, I WILL NOT GO."

Fenrick's companion, the other Faycan Brother, collected the robe from the floor all the while averting his gaze and bowing in fear.

* * *

Sheets of rain pounded against my chamber windows, and the cold draft that crept along the floor was enough to keep your toes awake and looking at each other. I glanced to the window as a flash of lightning lit up the Bay of Culdare. A moment before the angry bay was cast back into darkness, the bay's resemblance to an eye struck me. The small isle in the center of the roughly oval bay was like the pupil of a great eye, gazing at me. I felt like I was being watched, perhaps by Nardel himself from his gloomy haunts of darkness deep beneath the realm.

I turned back to my packing, searching for my favorite shirt amid the drawers of my wardrobe, while wondering if Nardel had truly broken his bonds. The age in which Nardel was imprisoned was so distant that no one knew the details of his downfall. Legend had it that Nardel was a man who lusted for the crown. Though a member of the royal family, chances were slim that he would ascend to the throne through natural causes. He decided to take steps to ensure his rise to power.

As all magic flowed from the land in some fashion, having power was seen as an advocacy from Rapt for leadership. No doubt this was how the Youngblood line rose to power, as they were, at the time, the most powerful mages in the world. And Nardel, though not the most powerful, was perhaps more clever than the rest. He devised new ways to use magic to overcome his kindred, slaying them one by one.

In the end, only old King Wolfram was left to face Nardel. The battle was fierce with thousands of innocent souls perishing. All that was left of the once-fertile vale where the palace stood was the Youngblood Waste, a desolation where nothing can grow, where rain never falls. They say it remains sweltering no matter the season.

I had never had the need nor desire to cross the Waste myself, but I have been to the edge to look out on that desolation. In that vast valley was a pestilence that would have spread the world over if not for the quick thinking of the people of that by-gone era. The impassable Erid Mountains contained the spread of the disease, it's true, but every pass was nothing but a doorway into certain doom. So to save the world the same fate as that valley, they erected pillars to span those few passes, pillars impregnated with enchantments that halted the spread of the Waste.

King Wolfram cast Nardel down but didn't kill him. Whether he couldn't kill him or merely wouldn't is ample fodder for speculation. No one knows. But he sealed Nardel below ground, imprisoning him with every drop of power in his soul, and ever after the kings of Rinstill have been devoid of magic, so devoid that magic cannot even touch them. Their power is diverted to maintain Nardel's prison, and so it is said that Nardel's bonds shall remain for as long as a Youngblood rules the realm.

As a delicate but insistent knock on the door sounded, I simultaneously discovered the shirt I was actually wearing was the very one I had been searching for. I stuffed another shirt into my satchel instead and said, "Yes, who is it?"

It was Avedis Hovhen, one of my most promising students, who stepped in. He was from a northern province, where everyone's complexion was like the white of freshly fallen snow. With a heavy accent, he said, "Your Grace, you sent for me?"

"Avedis, please do come in."

He stepped in and closed the door behind him. His expression of shock as he saw the state of my room brought my attention to the mess. Clothing was scattered haphazardly across the chairs and the bed, along with books and scrolls. I cleared my throat and continued, "Lady Rall and I will be leaving in the morning."

I tossed him my satchel as he asked, "Where are you going? Does it have something to do with the ghosts?" Avedis cast his gaze nervously at the surrounding walls.

Swinging a leather cloak over my shoulder, I picked up the candle sitting on my dressing table and stepped around Avedis toward the door. "Indeed it does. Walk with me."

Once out in the corridor, a draft nearly extinguished my candle. I quickly interposed my free hand between it and the oncoming air, barely in time to keep the candle alive. As Avedis closed my door, I continued, "We are on our way to Olindara in hopes of uncovering some artifacts to bring back the Knights of the Realm. We need their High Magic."

I proceeded down the corridor, Avedis at my elbow. He said, "My family, back home, always claimed that the High Magic never existed. They say that the White Magic is the only true magic."

I shook my head. "Hmmm, so many have claimed. It may be out of our reach now, but I believe in my heart of hearts that once, not too long ago, High Magic sounded through Rinstill."

"But how will the myth of Evendale help us to—"

"Lord Evendale was the very first High Mage, the first to wield the power of High Magic. You may have been taught he never really existed, but let me assure you he did. You students never read the histories. How do you expect to know where to go if you don't know where you've been, or, for that matter, where you are?" I stopped for a moment, glancing about the hall. The disorientation passed and I remembered where we were. It was Avedis' fault. He was distracting me.

Avedis shrugged and said, "Research into the past is becoming a luxury. We have a saying back home: Only the well fed have the patience to separate the wheat from the chaff. A starving man will eat both without distinction."

I nodded and said, "Well, there is some truth to those words." As we started spiraling down the back stairs toward the kitchens, I said, "What I need you to do is to go down and wake the stable master. Tell him to prepare our company's horses. We'll need at least two pack animals as well."

"Who is going again?"

"Lady Rall and I will be joined by Sir Redd. He and his company will join us for the greater portion of the journey. Let us not forget Prince Fenrick and his companion, what was his name now . . . Basil."

"Prince Fenrick is here at Waterton?"

"You hadn't heard? Upon his arrival, he burst into the council and made quite a spectacle."

We entered the kitchen to find Mistress Vallow wrapping blocks of cheese for our journey. She said, "Are you discussing Prince Fenrick's outrageous behavior at the council? It's all the scullery maids can talk about. They say he stripped off every last stitch of clothing right there in front of Palomar."

Avedis laughed, "He did what?"

Speaking to Vallow, I said, "This one didn't even know the Prince was here. He was probably off in his own world, daydreaming."

"I have been very busy this evening," Avedis said. "Exceedingly so."

"Doing what?" I asked.

Avedis looked me in the eye and said, "Wasting my time reading histories."

A little flustered, I stammered, "Well, the time for that has come and gone. Off you go. Tell the stable master we'll be leaving at daybreak."

Avedis nodded. He turned to go and said, "I'll put your satchel on your horse myself."

When he was gone, Mistress Vallow asked, "Where are you running off to in such a God-awful hurry?" Her sleep had tangled her thick white hair into a mess, and her wrinkled face looked up at me inquisitively.

"We are off to Olindara, for a start. I apologize for the hour, but we have little time."

"Never mind about that. A body put to good use is a body right with the world." There were several saddlebags on the table which she filled with food and wine as we talked.

She said, "I leave on a journey myself tomorrow. It's the season for the Festival of Light."

"What? You can't go to the festival. It's far too dangerous to even consider."

"I don't see you staying here and watching the sun ride the sky. I haven't missed a festival for forty years, and I'm not going to start now. And I won't be alone. There are about a dozen of us all told, including my brother and his family."

"There are ghosts out there, for God's sake—"

"And worse, I'll wager," Vallow said interrupting me. "I've survived these past forty trips fine. One more won't kill me."

"Wait, shh." I held a finger to my lips to silence Vallow. "Did you hear that?"

"What?"

The sound repeated, and this time it was unmistakable. It was the screams of women in terror.

"Oh no," Mistress Vallow whispered.

At that moment, Avedis came barreling back in. He was headed right toward me and looking back over his shoulder. "Avedis!" I called his name twice and caught him when he came close enough. He screamed at my touch.

"Avedis, calm down," I ordered shaking him. "What have you seen?"

It took a moment for him to formulate the words. When he regained some measure of control over his panic, he managed to say, "The ghosts . . . they are here. They are hunting."

I released him and he fell to the floor as if his knees had turned to butter. The ghosts had arrived. So soon?

I glanced at Mistress Vallow, who looked pale with fear. She asked, "What should we do, your Grace?"

Everyone always looked to me for strength, looked to me for hope. I had none to offer. There were things I could try, but I was no High Mage. All I could afford was the illusion of control, the mask of assurance.

The screams were getting closer.

"Never fear, Mistress Vallow," I said grabbing Avedis' hand and hauling him to his feet. The air suddenly became chill as if we were struck by an icy blast of winter wind, yet the air remained dead calm. With false bravado, I said, "Nothing shall befall you. I'll see to that."

"Oh, the chill," Vallow said, wrapping her arms about herself. "Where shall we go? What shall we do?"

It was then I discovered why Avedis had been fleeing insensibly. The final harbinger of the undead washed over us, through us, and grabbed the base of my neck like icy fingers. It was fear.

Vallow screamed, but I barely heard. My heart was racing, and my knees had grown weak making the act of standing noteworthy. Leaning heavily on the table, through clenched teeth, I told Mistress Vallow what she should do. "Pray for dawn."

Two of them walked through the wall, glowing of some inner light that illuminated nothing else. They were peasant farmers, one a man, the other a woman. Despite being able to see through them, their poor attire was clear. Their bodies showed no sign of misuse, as if the manner of their deaths was neither through disease nor violence, but by an act of will that yanked them from life without warning. Their dead eyes betrayed their new nature.

The ghost nearest me gave no sign of emotion, neither pain nor mirth. His easy gait took him inexorably closer with no sign of hurry. He looked into my eyes, locked his gaze to mine, and I wanted to throw up. I tried to look away, to close my eyes, to even blink. There was no tearing myself away from his gaze, a stare that spoke my end.

I tried to back away and tripped over Avedis who had fallen to the floor. The physical jar ripped my eyes from the apparition. I gulped air down, only now discovering I'd stopped breathing when our eyes had met. My neck felt as if it had just been released by clenching skeletal fingers.

Vallow's screams meant she wasn't dead yet, but it also meant she was still in the room, and that didn't bode well for her future. Closing my eyes to avoid looking at the ghost, I reached out and grabbed Avedis' quivering body and dragged him with me as I crawled across the kitchen.

Tapping into whatever reserve of sanity was left in me, I reached inward for White Magic. My grasp was too desperate, though, and it kept slipping through my fingers.

Avedis had stopped whimpering, and I realized he had just locked his gaze with the menace. I cupped my free hand over his eyes, and his breathing resumed in haggard gasps. He even began crawling on his own, which gave me a chance to concentrate.

I reached for White again, ignoring the chill creeping up my spine as the thing silently approached from behind. After Avedis had crawled past me, my teeth started to chatter. Without looking, I knew the creature had turned its gaze to me once more. Ignoring it as best I could, I continued crawling away and tried to concentrate on my core, the center that was Sol Blanchard.

White began to pool, slowly at first, then increasing as its warmth filled my veins. The fear even seemed to lessen, as if the mere grasping of White put a barrier between me and the flood of terror.

Grasping a chair, with some effort, I got to my feet and turned. The apparition was three steps away, the woman, five steps away and looking right at me, her pursuit of Vallow abandoned for some reason.

Without looking in his eyes, I turned to face the male and tried to hold him. When I reached out with my mind, there was nothing there to grasp. I tried to move him . . . nothing. I backed away, fear again threatening to unseat my mind as I took a chair and held it up between us. He was two paces away when I tried in rapid succession to distract him, injure him, trip him, cause him pain, blind him, put him to sleep, overwhelm him with despair, make him dizzy, send him into convulsions. Nothing worked because . . . because there was nothing there.

When he was one step away and standing *in* the chair I had held up, I shouted "Run!" and flung the chair through him.

I noticed Vallow was already taking my advice when I dashed toward Avedis and picked him up, putting him over my shoulder, White giving me the strength. The female ghost was almost upon us. I darted between the ghosts, climbing a chair to get to a table littered with food.

At that point, two more ghosts slid into the room, eyes fixed on me as if I were a flame drawing them like moths. The new arrivals blocked all the exits but that which Vallow had taken in her panic, down into the storage cellars. I almost slipped on a piece of meat as I jumped from the table, and when I landed, I lost my footing on a fallen saddlebag. Avedis and I crashed to the floor.

Avedis had either fainted or gone senseless from hitting his head on the floor, I didn't know which. There was no time for this. I got to my feet and man-handled Avedis' limp body back onto my shoulder. As I ran toward the darkness of the cellar stairwell, I called up light, and a glowing ball of white appeared, which threw back the shadows. It flew down the spiral stone staircase just ahead of us as I leapt after it, recklessly taking the stairs two at a time.

* * *

Placing my hands atop Avedis' head, I searched for injury both with my sense of touch and the heightened sense of vision afforded by White. At the back of his skull I found a bruise, small and seemingly inconsequential. The blow had deprived him of consciousness, but other than that, it had done him no permanent injury.

Placing a palm squarely on his forehead, I whispered, "Wake." White Magic, which yet filled my veins, rose. The flute that I alone heard as long as I held White quickened its rhythm momentarily, almost sounding lively. But its tones remained in a disturbing minor key, evidence of my own foreboding.

Avedis opened his eyes slowly. "Where—where am I?"

Crouching over him, I said, "We are three floors below the storage cellars under Waterton and running out of places to flee. Mistress Vallow has gone off on her own, against my wishes, to search for other ways out."

Avedis, lying on the rough stone floor, jumped in fear as his eyes found the glow of the ball of light hovering nearby. I tried to calm him, "It isn't a ghost, boy. It is only a bit of light." The glowing ball gave off a slight hum and drifted slightly as if it had a will of its own.

"Oh," Avedis said, half smiling at his own foolishness. Distant shouts of alarm and screams of panic emanating from the upper halls quickly changed his expression from embarrassed to grim. "Are we safe?"

"Safe? For the moment, the specters have taken an interest in other prey." I slumped from my crouching position to lean against the wall. "For how long? At a guess, half the night remains between us and dawn. I'm beginning to believe the only true refuge is the day."

"What happened? I felt as if I'd gone mad."

I shook my head. "Fear, Avedis. Pure terror. It surrounds them like a shroud. Don't accuse yourself of any lack of courage. The terror is unnatural. For my part, I'd never known such fear, but I found holding White Magic could blunt the worst of it. Distance seems to be the only real cure."

"We are three floors below Waterton?"

"Four, but who's counting? We are just outside the old foundry, a place that has seen busier days. No one makes weapons of war here anymore, and it is of little wonder. Times have changed and the enemy we face is immune to White, let alone steel."

As if finally realizing what I said, he sat bolt upright. "We are below ground? Inside the domain of Nardel?"

"Relax, boy. His minions may have full reign over everything below the surface, but they certainly can't be everywhere. This whole area was sealed up decades ago to protect Waterton. I was forced to break a few seals on our way down."

"Is there no way . . . no other way up and out?"

"It's still too dangerous. The best we can do is to wait here halfway between the east and the center stair. That way if they come at us one way, we'll have someplace to run."

Avedis and I looked up and down the hall. The dim light I maintained was soon swallowed by darkness in either direction. The hall was made of stone with an arched ceiling along its whole length. Within the reach of the glowing light, two sturdy wooden doors stood sentry on either side of us, both locked.

Avedis whispered, "We should not have come down here."

"This was our only option," I snapped. "Because staying where we were would have made the both of us marauding ghosts on tomorrow's eve."

Mistress Vallow's voice sounded from the darkness, "I see the boy is awake."

My nerves jumped at the unexpected sound, and I said, "Yes, Vallow, now get back over here, and pray do not wander off again."

She stepped closer into the light, and I noticed she had pulled her white hair back and fastened it at the base of her neck. When did presentability become a priority? I would never understand women, be they as old as Vallow or as young as Sedra.

She shook a finger at me, saying, "Don't you get sharp with me, your Grace. Some protector you turned out. That she-devil would have had me if I hadn't of taken good sense for what it's worth and run away."

I got to my feet and held up a hand for peace. "I'm sorry if I offend, but I'm weary. The strain of continuously holding White grew tiresome some time ago. If I could do more, I would. After that encounter, it would seem the only protection I can give you, Mistress Vallow, is a remedy for the terror those devils exude. But I can only do that much for you *if I can touch you*. So . . . stay close, if you please."

"Well," she said, "if you don't want my help, you don't have to tell me twice. This foundry has been closed up since I was a girl. I thought I remembered . . . a way out."

Holding back words of contempt at the wasted effort, I instead said, "Thank you for your pains. Is there another way out? What have you found?"

I expected her to say, 'Nothing,' or 'My stub of a candle finally went out, so I retraced my steps before I got lost.' Instead she surprised me by saying, "A door."

"A door, you say? What makes this door different from the myriad of others?"

As he got to his feet, Avedis asked, "Does it lead to a passage out?"

"I can't say. It was locked," Vallow said. "So I don't know where it leads. And to answer your Grace's question," she did a mock curtsey and continued, "having walked the storage cellars until I knew them in the dark, I know their width and breadth. I also know each level below has the exact same shape. And I'd swear on my mother's grave that locked door is on a wall which, by all rights, should be opposite nothing but solid rock."

I stood there, arms folded, and blinked. A door leading outside the foundry, perhaps out of the depths. I hadn't heard of any such passage, but perhaps I'd only forgotten.

"Then, by all means, let us investigate. Avedis, now that you're awake and coherent again, provide us some light and let me have a rest, hm?"

"Of course, your Grace," Avedis said with a curt nod. In an instant, another glow of light appeared, at least twice as bright as what I'd been maintaining.

Squinting at the sudden brilliance, I released White completely, and my light vanished. "Avedis, please," I said holding a hand up to shield my eyes.

"Sorry, one moment," Avedis said with a furrowed brow of concentration. As I watched, the light dimmed, but remarkably, only where we were standing which was to the sides and rear of the floating globe. To the front, the light was, if anything, even brighter than before. I looked again and discovered his globe had elongated, taking on a shape similar to a loaf of bread.

Where in the world did he learn that? I cleared my throat, shaking my head. I wasn't about to ask.

"Very good," I said. "Now let us seize this opportunity and take a closer look at this door. Lead on, my good woman. Lead on."

As we followed Vallow, I enjoyed the respite from my grasp on White. Used sparingly, White Magic could lend great ability and insight, but if held too long, it could feel more like a burden pressing down on one's shoulders, eventually becoming needles piercing into one's temples. Now, I felt as light as air, and, despite our dire situation, the seductive draw of sleep convinced each blink to last longer than the last. I was thankful we were walking.

We entered a large chamber housing the great furnace of the foundry, now standing cold, abandoned and covered in ancient soot. Vallow stopped for a moment as if trying to remember the way. Broken crates and refuse were scattered about, and the dust we kicked up by our passing hung in the air and made me cough. The dust was so thick it dimmed Avedis' light, so he created a second identical to the first, which seemed to peer circularly about the chamber to aid in Vallow's decision.

"Yes, it is this way," Vallow said, turning toward her left and a small door standing half open. "It all seems different with so much light."

Avedis asked me, "If this door does not lead out, why could you not use Old Magic to create a new tunnel or to widen some flaw in the solid stones above enough for us to climb out?"

I blinked and shook my head, trying to chase away the grogginess. "Old Magic, you say? Ridiculous. That is like trying to remove a splinter lodged in your forefinger with a pickax. I could easily open a new passage to the surface, but we would be buried by the crumbling ceiling and walls long before we ever saw the sky."

Looking at the furnace, Avedis said, "What about the chimney? Couldn't we climb out that way?"

Mistress Vallow said, "That chimney was sealed long ago. Even if his Grace opened it up, unless he can give us all wings like a kestrel, we won't be going that way." She pulled the small door open the rest of the way, and it creaked its complaint.

As we entered the passage, Avedis directed the second light to follow us from behind, shining its rays back the way we had come. At the end of the hall we found two openings, one to the left, and one to the right. The left led to a room full of more broken crates. We took the opening toward the right which had been at one time barred by a floor-to-ceiling gate. The hinges for one of the sides had rusted through leaving that portion of the gate lying on the floor.

Down three steps led to an alcove of sorts, housing an ornately carved double door against the back wall. It was covered in dirt and dust, making its markings difficult to discern. Two blackened wrought iron spiral handles extended from its surface, clean of the dust where Mistress Vallow had earlier made her failed efforts to open the doors. Unlike the gate, I noticed, the iron handle was free of rust or any signs of age.

Avedis pointed out, "There is no keyhole."

I grasped the handles and pulled with no effect. "Then the doors are either jammed in some fashion, barred from the other side, or bound with a shutting. You can see it isn't rusted shut. The hinges look untouched."

"Can you open them?" Vallow asked.

Avedis said, "There are very few doors in all of Rapt that cannot be opened with the power of White."

"Do you see any words amid all these swirls?" I asked. "For my life I cannot understand what these rising swirled carvings represent."

As I dusted the surface with my fingers, Avedis' lights shifted slowly, rotating the shadows across the surface.

From behind us, Vallow said, "There appears to be a sign on the gate."

"Really?" Avedis said as he and one of his lights went to investigate. I turned to see him lifting the fallen gate from the floor to look at a wooden sign that had been fastened facing outwards.

"What does it say?" I asked.

"It says, 'Keep Out'"

"Brilliant." I proceeded to grasp hold of White for a closer look.

I heard the gate crash back to the floor and turned to berate him for carelessness. "Pray, keep quiet."

Avedis returned to my side, dusting his hands off and added, "In small writing under the 'Keep Out,' it said, 'This means you.'"

"I'm sure they weren't serious," I said as my flute music returned, now playing a more peaceful melody, as if the long absence of the ghosts was giving me more confidence that we might survive the night.

One touch of the door with White, and it was obvious there was a shutting spell. "It's been sealed by a mage."

Vallow whispered, "Perhaps it was locked to keep something in, something that shouldn't be disturbed."

"I think I would have heard rumor of any hideous creatures locked beneath Waterton," I said with a half-smile. "The shutting is a complex one, I'll admit that. In fact, it's the best I've ever seen."

"You can open it, can't you?" Avedis asked as he glanced at the walls. "I've studied Shuttings. Maybe I could try."

I snorted, "Give me the credit I'm due, boy. I've been at this a while longer than you."

I found a likely place amid the complex weavings where it felt as if I could gain some purchase to begin the unraveling. I reached in just as Avedis began to speak an apology, but I never heard him finish.

A vision took me. I found myself looking back into the alcove as if from the perspective of the door. I saw Avedis, Vallow, and myself examining the door, bright lights shining on me. My perception expanded, splitting into two, as if I saw different worlds through each eye. I could see both sides of the door at once. I sensed complete blackness on the far side, the sound of dripping water, and the distant echo of crashing waves.

Then my vision of the small alcove shifted. One moment, the three of us stood there. The next we were gone, replaced by four people I didn't recognize. Two men bearing torches stood outside the gate — now whole and seemingly new. In the forefront stood two others, a man and a woman, both gazing, just as we had been, at me . . . or rather the door. Their faces were lost in shadow, but I could see the man was larger in girth than the rest, on his brow a circlet of gold. He glanced to his companion and I could see the fear on his face. "Will it hold?"

The lady didn't turn. She brushed her hand across me, the gentlest of caresses, and I was no longer wood and iron. I became like granite, extending past my frames into the heart of the stone walls surrounding me. I was impassable, impregnable. No flame could burn me, no force dent me, no rust infect me.

I swelled with pride, knowing my purpose. Bar all from passing; never open, never allow anything or anyone to pass save those of royal blood. Only this man or one of his kindred may ever place a hand on me and find me yielding.

The lady echoed the man's question with a laugh. "Will it hold?" The laugh was false, there being no mirth in her heart. She brushed hair over her shoulder with a hand bearing a ring that sparkled in the firelight. "Not even my husband could pass through this door."

The pain, the longing in her voice made my limitations plain. I was helpless. As a door ordained to weather the malice of time with ease and given remarkable strength, I might be able to bar the passage of her enemies, but I was useless to protect her from this pain. I could barely fathom it, a longing for someone missing.

The one with royal blood asked, "Your husband? What of Lord Evendale? Where has he gone?"

She turned her head toward him, and her double silhouette danced on my surface by the flickering pair of torches. She looked long, saying nothing, then slowly withdrew her hand.

* * *

"Your Grace. Your Grace, wake up." It was Avedis leaning over me, with those blasted lights of his in my eyes.

I shaded my eyes with a hand saying, "Get that out of my face."

He complied, and when I could see again, I found I was lying amid broken crates. "Where am I?"

Vallow sighed. "He's alive. Thank goodness itself."

Avedis helped me to my feet and said, "You were standing there probing the door with the White Magic when you were suddenly thrown through the open gate into the room across the hall. You broke your neck when you landed against these crates, but I managed to heal the worst."

"I broke my neck? And you healed me?" I rubbed the back of my neck and found it a little sore, but nothing worse. "Avedis, you keep surprising me."

Coldness descended on us, and I could see my breath. Vallow grabbed my arm. "They're coming."

"Quickly," I said as I made for the exit. "Let us get to the central stairs." I reached, and White filled me with ease. Could Avedis have healed my weariness as well?

"What of the door?" Avedis asked.

But there was no time to spare. With me in the lead, we ran down the hall back toward the foundry's furnace room. Before we reached the door at the end, the fear began, but White protected me from the worst. Not so for poor Vallow, who ran screaming back up the corridor toward the sealed door.

"Vallow. Vallow, get back here." I turned and looked into the furnace room to find a half dozen ghosts coming our way, four of them walking downwards toward us as if supported on air. There was still a chance to run between them, but that opportunity wouldn't last long.

"Avedis," I began, then stopped myself. It would take longer to explain than to do myself. Instead, I stormed back down the hall shouting Vallow's name.

I found her crouching in a half open crate, hiding and shaking with fear. When I grabbed her shoulder, she screamed and bit my arm, but I ignored the pain and held on. I pushed White into her as quickly as I could without hurting her, and she began to calm.

Avedis was in the doorway standing on the fallen gate. "What about the door?" he asked again with a thumb pointed back over his shoulder.

"It was sealed by Lady Lowenna herself, Evendale's wife. We've no hope of opening something shut by a Knight of the Realm. If we hurry, we can dodge the ghosts—"

"Too late—too late," Avedis shouted. "There's one in the hall."

"By Tishman," I swore as I took Vallow by the shoulders and lifted her out of the crate. She seemed dazed but no longer in a panic. Keeping a firm grip on her shoulder, I looked down the hall myself. A ghostly soldier in a leather jerkin bearing a sword at his side barred our way. He was perhaps a dozen paces off and walking slowly toward us with one side of him still within the wall. He was oblivious to the physical world.

"We're trapped." I briefly considered sacrificing myself to this ghost. From Redd's description, I knew each ghost only took one victim per night, vanishing after their prey was dead. Avedis and Vallow could then escape. It was a noble idea, but it was an option suddenly denied us as more ghosts filled the hall beyond the soldier.

"They're coming," I whispered, and felt a fear that could not be assuaged by White.

Chapter Thirteen

North East West South

Church that Sunday was crowded, and the press of bodies in the pews reminded me of the hospital waiting room. I felt warmer than I had in four days, but this warmth was cold comfort for those mourning parents or spouses.

"And let us pray for those recuperating in hospitals across Luna," said Father Brason. "That they may be healed, restored to wholeness, and returned to us soon."

I looked up at the vaulted ceiling rising to a peak in the center of the room. It was, intentionally, the only interesting feature of the space, so that it could function as a place of worship for many faiths. Spotlights reflected off its smooth, white surface making it the brightest point in the dimly lit room. I pictured myself floating above the congregation, wafted high by the fragrance of incense filling the room. I imagined looking out over everyone from that height. What would Father Brason look like from there?

"And finally, let us pray for the souls of our departed that they may enter into His presence—"

Funny. The congregants reminded me of how I pictured my sub-personalities, only they weren't all crowded together like these people in the pews. My sub-personality divisions were more like the old-time churches with the box pews reserved for individual families.

I suddenly got the feeling someone was watching me, and I turned my gaze behind me. The people in the pew behind us glanced at me as I turned, but none were staring. The man sitting next to his young son had a face that was ashen grey, and the boy looked dejected and in shock. Where was his mother? Maybe she was getting medical attention.

I turned back to the front, and Tricia, sitting at my left, poked me in the ribs. "Quit squirming and pay attention," she whispered. I poked her back. Mom didn't even look at us.

The feeling of being watched didn't go away. I rubbed the standing hairs on the back of my neck and tried to pay attention.

* * *

Standing to my left, Zak pressed the door chime at Trevor's door and we waited. We were teamed to work on a science project together, and we had to get something done. Zak carried a bin of old radio transmitters that he had dug up somewhere.

Trevor's father opened the door. He was a short man, and a bit overweight, and he looked pale and tired. "Oh," he began. "I was expecting . . ." He waved his hand indicating someone behind us. I looked back and saw the Mayor of Aristoteles, Zak's father, coming down the hall.

"Hey Dad," Zak said. His father nodded to him. Though Zak and his father shared the same characteristic high cheekbones, Zak's shoulder length hair stood in sharp contrast to his father's military cut.

He looked down at his son then glanced in the bin. "Working on the science project, I see."

"Boys, Trevor's in his room. Why don't you just go in? Mr. Mayor . . ." Trevor's dad ushered all of us in, and I watched as the adults went into Trevor's dad's office, the room right next door to Trevor's room. Zak gave me a look that said, 'I wonder what they're up to?'

Trevor's door was open. "Knock, knock," said Zak. "We come bearing junk."

"Hey guys." He didn't look up from his desk. A schematic of our project was hovering over it, and he was busy making changes.

Zak closed the door and dropped the bin which floated to the floor. He whispered, "Our dads are getting into it in the next room." He put up his fists and pretended he was a boxer.

"Really?" said Trevor. "Here? It must be an off-the-record meeting."

"How much trouble is your dad in?" I asked.

Trevor shrugged, but I could tell he was worried. "They're going to have to punish someone. Why not the LMC administrator?"

I asked, "Did they figure out what happened yet?"

"You didn't see the news conference?" asked Trevor. "Here." He cleared the schematic from his desk, intending to show the vid there, but changed his mind. "I don't want to see it again. You can watch it on this." He took a hand-held pad from a drawer and directed the LMC to play back the news conference.

I took it and, sinking in an overstuffed chair in the corner, I watched the flickering holograph come into focus, and a babble of voices, the sound of the reporters, rose in volume directed to me. Out of the corner of my eye, I saw Trevor bring back up the schematic over his desk. In lowered voices, he showed Zak where he had left off.

I turned my attention back to the vid hovering over the pad as a hush fell over the assembled reporters. Trevor's father approached the podium. "Thank you. Thank you ladies and gentlemen," he repeated as his protruding stomach vanished behind the podium. "My name is Doctor Charles Russo, and I am the Senior Systems Specialist in charge of the LMC's oversight of Aristoteles. I have a statement and then we can open the floor to questions." He mopped nervous sweat from his receding hairline before continuing.

"We've been able to restore full life support to every area of the city and all outlying tunnels and conduits. With the exception of the heating situation, all systems are running at one hundred percent. As far as heat goes, I spoke to Secretary Jalom in Descartes this morning. Once the inspection of the backup power conduits has been completed, she will okay the additional power required to bring us back up to a comfortable temperature.

"President Quillen has directed General Anderson of Space Command to supply all the personnel and equipment we might require. The safety of the citizens of Luna remains our top priority. Mayor Metler and President Quillen will be holding a joint news conference, currently scheduled for 12:30, if I'm not mistaken. Questions?"

Trevor's dad picked one of the reporters, who asked, "Was the LMC actually off-line for those hours after the explosion? It's spread out all over Luna, so how can any single event like this cause the outage?"

"It's only been a few days, so we are still investigating. But . . . I'd first like to remind everyone that the Lunar Main Computer is a Jasmine 3000 Series Seed Computer, biologically engineered to manufacture as many new nodes as needed to maintain its performance. It escaped containment something like forty—maybe fifty years ago and has been growing in our regolith ever since."

It was clear Trevor's dad was comfortable talking about the LMC. His initial nervousness evaporated as he continued.

"The reason I mention this is because the LMC naturally placed its nodes wherever it could tap into ready power, and so around every fusion plant is an incredible concentration of computer nodes. When Prometheus exploded, it took along with it every last LMC node surrounding the plant. Thankfully the holographic memory means no actual data was lost, but that didn't matter to the LMC. It reacted like a victim of a car accident, first going into shock, then denying the very existence of humanity for hours. Now that it is back up, it has no memory of the explosion.

"The analogy is just our working theory. We're still looking for answers. Next question?"

He picked another reporter who asked, "What happened to our life-support backup systems?"

Trevor's dad paused. "As far as the backup life support . . . The system is designed to contain pressure leaks by closing bulkheads. Those bulkheads didn't close. Power generators should have kicked on to take up the slack after Prometheus. They remained in standby.

"All I can say is that at this time we have put together a task force and are working in cooperation with federal authorities to seek answers and to implement solutions . . ."

My mind began to wander . . . what would have happened to us if Emily never came back? I waved off the vid, but instead of shutting down, it skipped to the next vid. I heard some mention of Buenos Aires. It showed an Asian woman with a newborn baby. "It was a baby boy, but not just any baby boy. This was the fifty-first boy to be born in a row, and, out of the last seven hundred babies born in that city, approximately sixty-two percent have been male. Authorities suspect a sudden rise in a practice thought extinct, that of female infanticide, but no evidence of such practices has yet been uncovered."

Tired of all the bad news, I waved it off again, this time with more conviction. Trevor was explaining something to Zak. "It'll translate the digital signal to AM, but the data rates are too low, so we're going to be using a hundred channels at once and recombine them on the other side."

"That could have come in handy during the blackout," Zak offered.

"Well, not really. You'd need the LMC to feed it the data, so with no LMC . . ."

No LMC, no Emily. What did they do before Emily existed, anyway? It was hard to imagine. What were Zak and Trevor's fathers talking about in the next room? Why all the secrecy? It couldn't be good? For a second, I thought I'd heard something, some voices. I craned my neck a bit closer to the wall and concentrated. All I could hear was Trevor's voice droning on about how the device should be able to handle transmission of a full-holographic-stack, enough speed to perform a full-body SIM.

There it was again. It was definitely Zak's dad's voice.

"I got this for Christmas." That was Trevor's dad. "It's a paper weight containing a mock-up of the latest LT chip. Supposedly the one buried in here is 200 times the size of a real LT chip."

I heard a harrumph from the Mayor. "I can't see anything."

"The chip's microscopic, derives its power from ambient heat, and it uses light instead of electricity. Chips just like this one are buried in eighty to ninety percent of all the electronics on Luna." Trevor and his dad sounded a lot alike. He continued, "These chips are in the back-up generators, which are supposed to operate independently of the LMC. Well, we went down there and found them connected to the LMC, though no one claims to have done it."

"We're not talking about sabotage, are we?"

"Hold on. We disconnected it and tried to start it up. Oh, it worked fine, only when we looked closer we discovered it wasn't actually disconnected. The LMC—" Dr. Russo paused.

"Like a reflex, the LMC discovered its communication was severed and instinctively looked for a way around the problem. It took us several hours to discover how, but it had rerouted its com-link through the power cables, embedding its commands using frequency stacking within the power lines. It actually reprogrammed the generator on the fly and taught it a completely new communication protocol.

"We asked the LMC to sever its communications with the generator, but it denied any knowledge of its own actions. Are you aware of accessing a neuron in your brain? No. The LMC isn't aware of its nodes, it just uses them.

"So we pulled the power cables and brought in a battery. Again, the generator worked perfectly, only we found it was *still* in contact with the LMC. It had again rerouted its communications, this time using frequency modulation on the light in the room to reprogram the generator."

There was silence for a moment. Zak's dad said, "We're living in a fool's paradise. We think we're building independent systems to keep us safe, but the LMC is undermining us. Why?"

Trevor's dad said, "Without our knowledge, without even its own knowledge, I'm betting it has absorbed practically every system on

Luna. I imagine the only things still operating independently are the older systems that don't use LT chips and are not connected to the power grid. I doubt even they will hold out for long. The LMC will find another way to interface, one we haven't thought of yet."

"Then it's a good thing we've already started making preparations. Anderson's going to want to pull the plug sooner. How long?"

"It'll take months. If we move faster . . . it'll suspect something."

Zak poked me in the exact spot where my sister had poked me this morning at church. "Luna to Dennis. Luna to Dennis Howard, come in."

"Shh," I whispered. "I can hear what they're saying in the next room."

Trevor and Zak put their heads to the wall. Zak whispered, "All I hear is Trevor. Stop all that breathing."

Trevor replied, "By your command, my Prince." He wasn't smiling.

"Yeah," Zak said. "Son of a King in Rapt, and in the real world, son of the Mayor. I think giving me that role was the LMC's idea of a joke."

"I can't hear anything anymore," I admitted. "Maybe they left."

"Speaking of Rapt, don't we have a session coming up right quick?" Zak asked.

That brought to mind exactly where Sol was at the end of yesterday's session. He was about to be killed. "Wait," I said. "You have to hear this." I asked Emily for privacy mode, then I briefly told them everything I'd heard. I whispered just in case someone could overhear us.

There was silence as we all wondered exactly what "pulling-the-plug" meant. What would happen if the LMC was threatened, or even felt threatened?

Zak whispered, "And then my dad totally punched your dad's lights out." Zak feigned falling unconscious.

"Is that right?" Trevor said poking me in the chest with a smile. "Well, my dad could take on your dad any day of the week."

I smiled. "You've got that wrong, Mister. My dad could beat up both your dads together, with one arm tied behind—" I stopped short, suddenly remembering Dad really did only have one arm.

I shook my head. Every world was turning into a nightmare. First Emily vanishes for hours, then comes back with no memory of the explosion. She's infiltrated almost all the electronics on the planet. I didn't like it, but what could I do?

"Come on," I said. "We're going to be late."

Chapter Fourteen

But, Given as Birthright

The insubstantial foot soldier was ten steps away with at least three, maybe four, ghosts behind him. Avedis and Mistress Vallow stood by my side, trapped at the end of this corridor by my slow wit and doomed by my failures. Nothing I tried had any effect on the ghosts.

"The door," Avedis said. "We must try to open it." He ran back down into the alcove, and we followed. Both his lights hovered over his head and glared at the carved door. He crossed his arms and stood in the center with grim determination.

I suddenly realized the swirling carvings looked like flame. I shook my head. "If only Fenrick were here. The one time he could prove useful, and he's not within shouting distance."

Avedis turned and quickly asked, "How could the prince help?"

Vallow began to cry, not hysterically but with helplessness. The White Magic that flowed into her through my touch was enough to hold the utter terror at bay but did nothing to alter our fate. I put an arm around her shoulder and followed her gaze toward the approaching menace. With Avedis' lights illuminating the door, all that could be seen down the hall was their inner glow.

"Only Lowenna herself could undo that binding," I said, "but Fenrick could open that door by giving a pull. It'll open to any of royal blood."

Avedis looked shocked. "What?" He took a single step and grabbed the door handle, and after a single pull, the door opened with a loud creaking.

"It's opening!" Vallow shouted.

"Follow me," Avedis said with a wave as he stepped past the threshold.

With the nearest ghost only three steps away, I had little time to wonder at this miracle. I followed, but when Vallow hastily stepped toward the door, she broke my hold on her shoulder and in-so-doing broke her contact with White. She screamed in terror as the ferocity of the ghost's emotional assault consumed her rationality. In an instant, she was pushing past Avedis and running at top speed into the dark and unknown.

"Vallow," I called out, but it was useless. I stepped through the door, shutting it behind me, and found a tunnel stretching off to the left and right. Avedis' lights did not illuminate far because the passage curved. The surface of the rock was smooth, more smooth and regular than nature would have made with the passage of water and time. It worried me.

Vallow's screams echoed but were clearly coming from the left, so there was little choice in the matter. "We need to catch up with her. Come on." I started to run.

Avedis was close behind, "The ghosts are not far behind us."

I let Avedis with his lights take the lead. The tunnel undulated both up and down, and left and right, until at last I lost my bearings completely. I couldn't tell if we were moving closer to the surface, moving inland or moving toward the Bay of Culdare. The tunnel constricted in places, only passable on hands and knees, and expanded in others, once becoming as large as the Hall of Tishman.

The exertion was becoming too much for me. Despite my reliance on White to give me stamina, my breath was becoming labored and my pace was slowing. I was about to tell Avedis to proceed ahead while I rested when a ghost stepped out of the wall not two yards to my right.

"Look out!" Avedis shouted needlessly as he pointed at the ghost.

"What am I, blind?" I said quickening my pace. "Don't dawdle. Move on. These ghosts may not be fast, but they're relentless."

"And they're coming from all directions," Avedis said as two more stepped out of the wall to my left.

"We seem to be attracting them. These don't look like the ones we left back at the forge. Is that Mistress Vallow I hear?"

After two more sweeping curves of the passage, the tunnel angled sharply upward and was sealed off by a wall of wooden planks slanting up and away. Mistress Vallow stood at the top of the slope of gravel and wrestled with two root cellar doors that refused to open. The chains looped through the handles rattled as she struggled.

"Vallow, calm down," I said, hoping the tone of my voice did more than the sentiment. As I climbed the slope, Vallow reacted as if she didn't know me, as if I were the menace coming to extract her soul. She screamed and started yanking and shoving the doors more violently.

She shrieked anew at my touch and scratched my arms as I wrapped them around her to prevent her escape.

Avedis, from the bottom of the slope, said, "The ghosts are almost upon us."

"Avedis, the door."

I meant for him to undo the lock holding the chains together, but instead, in an explosion of splinters, the entire doorframe burst outward and upward. That boy didn't know his own strength.

Vallow still struggled in my grasp but less violently as if the terror was subsiding. With her in my arms, I stepped out into the chilly night air and into knee-high grass sprouting between cobblestones. The crunch of Avedis' feet on the gravel behind me paused. Out of breath and almost trembling with weariness, I said, "Don't look into their eyes. Move your feet."

"They've stopped," Avedis said. "They're turning around."

"They're what?" I asked.

I turned and, keeping a hand around Vallow's wrist, looked down into the cellar. A ghostly soldier, appearing confused and disoriented, slowly walked away into one of the walls.

"Did they lose our scent?" Avedis asked.

I said, "No matter the reason, I'm thankful to be rid of them."

"Where are we?" Avedis said, shining his lights about.

I had a sinking feeling in the pit of my stomach as I realized exactly where we were. The cobblestone street was lined with dilapidated shops. Everything was overgrown with grass and weeds. Three large oak trees, which had long ago ruptured the surface of the thoroughfare, swayed in the breeze. The rustling of the leaves was the only sound to break the dead silence.

Vallow, who had returned to her senses, said out loud what I had been thinking. She whispered, "I know this place. We're in . . . we're in Drewsbury."

"Yes, Drewsbury," I agreed. "This explains why Lady Lowenna barred that door back there; to prevent people from wandering into this accursed town." How I despised this place.

Avedis asked in a whisper, "What lives here that would make even the ghosts turn away?"

"Come," I said keeping my voice low. I released Vallow, her unnatural terror of the ghosts no longer an issue. "Let us find a place to build a fire. We are in no immediate danger as long as we enter no building and keep our wits about us." I hoped that was true.

I sighed. We should get out as soon as possible, but if I remembered aright, the only way out was through town, through the madness. It would be best to wait until daylight could help us before trying to find our way.

We wandered down several streets, each more overgrown than the last. Trees grew thicker as we went, making a canopy over our heads. I was grateful because it protected us from the cold drizzle that had just begun. Avedis collected kindling as we walked. The silence that pervaded Drewsbury made each of our footfalls sound like clumsy crashing through dry leaves. The flute music in my mind sounded hollow, tired.

Was this place devoid of animal life, or were they watching us, waiting for us to make a misstep before they pounced on the interlopers? We proceeded in silence, none of us wanting to disturb the stillness more than we already were.

Avedis' lights peering ahead and behind were the only thing holding the blackness at bay. It couldn't be long until dawn, surely.

"Wait a moment," I said holding up a hand. "In all the excitement, I forgot to ask you how you opened that door back there."

Avedis smiled. "I wanted to keep my identity secret while I was at Waterton. My grandfather is Ustave Fendiran, the King of Tellowl, who married the High King's aunt—"

"You are a prince?" Vallow said.

"I'm the second son, so my brother will inherit the throne. When you said Prince Fenrick could open the door because of his birthright, it occurred to me that I am descendant of a Youngblood High King, however distantly."

Vallow snorted, "We've got a real blue blood in our midst, and never knew it."

Avedis shrugged. "I thought if everyone knew I was royalty, they might assume I had a barrier between me and magic the way the High King does. You might have held back teaching me, but I'm very distant from the High King. I'm perhaps sixty or seventy on the list."

Vallow whispered, "What with all the ghosts, maybe you're closer than that now."

"Vallow," I said. "Let's not speculate on such unpleasantness. The dawn will bring what it will, but one thing is certain. King Youngblood will not succumb to this menace."

"Perhaps," Vallow said, "Perhaps one day the king will wake up to find he's the only one left in all Rinstill."

"Perhaps," I said, not wanting to follow that line of thought. So Avedis was a distant relation to the Youngbloods, I mused. This might explain his more than ample abilities. The Youngbloods were the most powerful in the realm, after all. It gave me comfort to know that such abilities might still exist in this world. Not to mention, if Vallow's dark forebodings were true, he would have been closer to the throne, and with that proximity, his access to such power would be taken from him. There were many who yet lived.

We came across a grassy courtyard at the confluence of five streets. In the center was a depression where a pool of water had formed. What with the nearby trees, I could almost pretend we were in real forest.

Near the edge of the pool, we made our fire, surrounding it with loose cobblestones. The last thing I did before releasing White was to spark our fire. The echoing flute faded and vanished to be replaced by the overwhelming silence and cold. I sat before the fire, rubbing my arms, which suddenly felt like stone. I had held White too long.

"Save your strength, Avedis," I said as he dropped two large logs he'd found onto the fire. "Release White. We're safe enough."

Avedis groaned as his lights vanished, and he sat next to me. So his strength had its limits. Somehow, that made me feel better.

"Safe?" Vallow repeated in scorn. "In Drewsbury? We have to get out of here." She crossed her arms and drew closer to the fire, looking around nervously.

I said, "Wild Magic lingers here, but we shouldn't fear. All we must—"

"Wild Magic?" Avedis exclaimed, his voice echoing around the abandoned city streets. Then, in a lowered voice, he added, "There's Wild Magic here?"

Vallow said, "Wild Magic's what drove people from Drewsbury, and that was hundreds of years ago. Nowadays, people that wander in usually don't wander back out."

I added, "Drewsbury is surrounded by a wall to keep people out. That door you opened served the same purpose, though I didn't know it existed."

It took a moment, but I found what I was looking for. I pointed southward farther down the street. "Do you see that?"

By the light of our small fire, it was barely discernable. Avedis squinted. "What is it?" He manifested a light and sent it across the pool and down the narrow city street.

The road was buckled like frozen ocean waves that stood as high as a man. The waves grew as they receded, until they appeared to crash against a solid stone wall, twenty feet high and jutting diagonally across the street.

The cobblestone street at points merged with the wall, blending, making it impossible to tell if the wall was a wall or part of the street. It was like seeing a slice of time, everything frozen in place, and it made the road impassable.

I said, "Four hundred years ago, Wild Magic descended on this town. It came in the form of fire. The histories tell us, if not for Lord Evendale, none would have survived."

"Thank the greatness above for the Knights of the Realm," Vallow said. "I think they could tell the future. That's why Evendale and Lowenna were here."

"No one knows if that is true," I said, eying the spot where the grassy cobblestone street transitioned to solid marble.

Avedis released the light, and the frozen street fell back into darkness. "Were all seven knights here?" he asked.

"No," Vallow answered. "Only those two, so they say."

"How could fire do this?" Avedis asked. "Even Wild—"

"Wild Fire doesn't destroy," I said. "It changes things." I pointed to a marble pillar protruding from a nearby roof. "If a Wild Fire burns a building, the structure doesn't disintegrate. Instead it makes more building. More structure, only structure without a guiding intelligence."

Vallow said, "Occasionally, fools still come here, hearing tales of gold and jewels created by the fire. They lose themselves in the maze." Vallow's eyes went wide. "The few who have returned are never the same."

"Come now, Vallow," I countered. "It isn't the maddening maze that prevents them from returning. It's the structures which collapse around them because they weren't built to hold the weight of a man."

Avedis suddenly looked up. "Is that a horn?"

I heard nothing. Pointing toward the treetops, Avedis said, "Look. What's that glow?" A break in the canopy toward the south revealed distant clouds that glowed red.

I slowly got to my feet. "Waterton is ablaze." I could hear the horn now.

"Fire?" Vallow said, craning her neck to look at those clouds.

I said, "The ghosts are wreaking havoc like Waterton has never known. The horn. It isn't the first time I've heard that particular horn. It is Prince Fenrick. This isn't a battle he can win with axe and sword."

"Is there anything we can do?" Avedis asked.

I sighed and crouched by the fire, trying to mentally prepare myself. "Only Palomar and I know how to—"

I stopped, distracted by a wave of vertigo that passed through me. "Did you feel—" I began as I got to my feet, but another wave broke over me, and Avedis had to catch me from falling. I looked down at the fire and watched as it diminished, sizzling and sputtering in protest. In the space of two breaths, we were plunged into darkness.

"The fire," Vallow whispered.

"What happened?" Avedis asked.

"Palomar has extinguished the fires raging through Waterton," I said, feeling steadier now and releasing Avedis. Looking back toward the break in the branches, I noticed the clouds were no longer glowing red. "At least we know he yet lives."

"But, why did *our* fire go out?" Avedis asked.

"We are too close to Waterton. Old Magic is not as precise as it is effective."

Avedis created another light and shined it down upon the ashes and half-burnt wood. He bent down and held a hand over it. "The coals aren't even warm."

I said, "Don't bother trying to light it. Mayhap tomorrow we shall be able to kindle fire once more when the effects diminish. And save yourself until you need White more than breath. You are only undoing yourself."

Avedis extinguished his light, protesting, "I do not like this place. Without light, something may sneak up—"

"Dawn is drawing nigh. Soon we will not need your light regardless."

After my eyes adjusted, I could see across the pool to the dark trees that laid beyond. It was proof that the blackness was not complete. The sky began to take on a predawn glow, and I smiled grimly. We had lived through the night, beyond all expectation, to see another dawn.

"Come, the sky is brightening," I said. "Let us puzzle our way through the maze of Drewsbury, return to Waterton, and rejoin the duke and the prince. Perhaps we can get an hour's rest then."

Avedis said, "We shall see what of Waterton is left standing."

"And who," Vallow added in a whisper.

We headed west, avoiding the insanity we had seen toward the south. As he fell into step beside me, Avedis asked, "Why don't we take that tunnel back to Waterton? The ghosts should have—"

I shook my head. "We should stay above ground. Nardel and his minions are sealed below, and I see no reason to trust luck again."

But there would be no easy way out of Drewsbury. A large broken pillar sprawled across our path, forcing us toward the buildings. Beyond the pillar stood an intricate inn of sorts, made of wood and stone with balconies jutting out at odd angles, some without doors. There were doors without balconies. The whole structure curved away as it rose.

I paused in front of a stone stair leading up the side of the madness. I kicked the stair, testing its firmness. With a sigh, I mounted the first step. "Take care. The steps will be wildly erratic in size."

The stairs rose and curved to the left. Soon the wall on our left vanished, leaving the stair to rise on its own with no rail to prevent a fall. It looked as if, farther up, we could get to the roof of a building without too much of a jump.

"How did Evendale and Lowenna stop the Wild Fire?"

As I watched my steps, I said, "Evendale called rain, but I doubt that helped much. I imagine all they could do was keep the minds of the people clear enough so they could be led out of danger."

"The fire affected the people's minds?"

"At the very least it confused them," I said. "If it touched them, they were transformed into creatures, some foul, some magnificent. None survived for long. But it's written that just looking at the fire can turn the mind, making the thought of touching the flames seductive, irresistible. Somehow Evendale held that power in check, probably with High Magic."

From the rear, Vallow added, "He succeeded until Lowenna was attacked."

"Yes," I said between breaths. The climb was beginning to wind me. "For some reason, a group blamed the knights for the fire and attacked Lowenna. Now . . . I think we can jump to that roof over there." The stair continued up and ended after a dozen rises leading to nothing. I meant for us to jump off the side of the stair. "You first Avedis. I shall help Vallow."

Avedis jumped the four feet to the rooftop with ease, but Vallow took some convincing. The drop between the stair and roof had to be thirty feet. In the end, it was the fact we were both mages that gave her the courage to jump. Vallow threw herself across and got her foot on the far edge, after which Avedis snatched her and pulled her to safety. I took a deep breath and lunged across, nearly slipping when I reached the far side.

Vallow was shaking. "I'm too old for these acrobatics, your Grace."

"We shall try to stay to the rooftops, if we can. From this height, we should be able to glimpse some path to the gate, which I'm sure Avedis' touch will open for us."

We continued over the undulating jungle of rooftops. It took time and no small effort. We clambered up crumbling masonry and slid across wildly slanting roofs. We crossed from roof to roof sometimes encountering gaping holes where some portion of the structure had succumbed at last.

Seeing Vallow struggle, I called our party to a halt. "Let us rest a moment."

I gingerly sat on the stone roof, my back to the two-foot lip around the edge. I looked to the cloud-heavy sky as drizzle began anew.

Vallow sat by my side, downwind as if my body could offer some protection.

Avedis crossed his arms against the chill wind. "What happened to Lowenna in the attack? Was she hurt? Killed? Well, obviously not or she wouldn't have been able to seal that door."

I said, "It's unclear what happened next. Evendale was never heard from again. Some thought Evendale was killed or transformed by the Wild Fire, but Lowenna claimed he survived the night. She said he journeyed to a far-off land where his skills were needed even more than here in Rinstill."

Vallow said, "And Lowenna followed soon after."

Avedis rubbed the back of his neck, saying, "And so went all seven Knights of the Realm, one by one. Where are they now?"

"Within shouting distance, I suspect," I said. "We just require the right type of shout."

"The horn and the bells," Avedis whispered with a nod. Something caught his attention, and he pointed. "Look at that."

I craned my neck in the direction he indicated. "Oh, yes. Yet another mystery of Drewsbury."

Not twenty feet away rose a cluster of stone pillars that transformed from scalloped stone into smooth marble as they grew to a height of thirty feet. The pillars burst from the ground at an angle and curved together until at the top they stood nearly straight. Together they looked like shoots of some wild grass reaching for the light. On the central pillar stood a statue of gold.

I got to my feet and joined Avedis by the edge. "It's a statue of a man, though the weathering of centuries has washed away his features." The figure was life-sized and appeared half crouched, holding his left palm before his eyes as if transfixed by the sight of his own golden hand.

"Then there are treasures here to be plundered, even after all this time."

From behind us, Vallow said, "He Who Rises."

"What?" Avedis asked.

I said, "Yes, some call the statue 'He Who Rises.' The real mystery is how he came to be at all. There were no statues in Drewsbury for the Wild Fire to transform into this figure. He had to be a man—"

Vallow said, "And what kind of man becomes a gold statue when touched by the Wild? Some think it's Evendale, himself."

My legs feeling heavy, I shuffled across the roof to look downward to the south. From this height, the wall surrounding the town was visible through the misting rain. To my relief, the rest of the street heading that direction was unmolested by the Wild Fire. All we had to do was find our way down and through several more out-of-place buildings.

"And no one," Vallow said, "has been able to steal him. Even if you could get to that pedestal out there without slipping off, how do you lower him down?"

Avedis said, "It would be no problem for a mage. Using White—"

Without turning around, I interrupted, "White is useless, Avedis. Trying to move him is like trying to grasp butter. He would simply slip through your—" I suddenly felt slight vibrations of White emanating from Avedis. "No don't!"

I turned, but it was too late. He had already begun to reach out to the statue, and I rushed back to his side in amazement as the statue began to rise. "No one in four hundred years has been able to budge the statue using White," I whispered. Yet, in my experience, Avedis stood alone in his ability with White. I glanced at his face and saw the determination of his jaw, the narrowing of his eyes. He should have left the statue alone, but I couldn't help but admire the immense power he poured into the effort.

I looked back to see 'He Who Rises' begin to float toward us, ever so slowly. "No, put him back," I said, but he ignored me. Avedis, reaching out his hands as if beckoning the statue, began to groan from the strain. There was nothing I could do to help because combining efforts was impossible. If I tried, it was a certainty the statue would fall.

As the statue passed the lip of the pillar, it began to tilt. Avedis whimpered in pain and I felt a surge of power from him that actually made me step back. I felt as if I stood before a fire suddenly raging hot enough to melt iron.

But it was not enough. Wild Magic reasserted its dominance and refused to bow to Avedis' will any longer. The statue tilted further, then plummeted downward as Avedis lost his purchase. Vallow gasped and Avedis fell to a knee.

'He Who Rises' impacted the stone pavement with a thunder that echoed through Drewsbury. A cloud of dust instantly rose obscuring the statue's ultimate fate. While it was certainly destroyed, what would become of us? My eyes strained through the cloud, my senses stretched to the breaking point.

I glanced back to Avedis. "What were you thinking?" I hissed. "What impenetrable motivation entered that fevered brain? Too much gold to let stand idle?" There was still no sign of some eruption of Wild Magic. Perhaps we would be fine.

Avedis' breath was ragged, and he winced at my remarks. "I care nothing for the gold. I thought if it could be removed . . . then there would be one less temptation for the thieves and brigands. Or . . . what if it really had something to do with Evendale?"

"And so you took it upon yourself without a thought to the consequences. Do you think yourself a god that you know everything, can *do* anything? We are in the heart of Drewsbury, where Wild Magic redefines all. Everything you know, every rule you've been taught about the functioning world changed when we passed the borders of this town. Why didn't the ghosts follow us in? They probably cease to exist if they take one step into this realm. The darkness that made them has no power here."

"I . . . I didn't know," Avedis stammered.

"If you want to remain alive—"

Vallow gasped again and said, "Look!"

Avedis rose to his feet and looked over the edge with me. What new horror would be unleashed on us? I could see some kind of fluttering mass of colors rising toward us. I held my breath, preparing to run, still unable to tear my eyes from . . . It looked like . . . like butterflies.

Avedis said, "There must be thousands."

"Hundreds of thousands," I whispered. The sight of the blur of butterflies had suddenly changed my mood. My rage at Avedis softened and vanished. The gentle fragrance of lavender washed over me, and I felt at peace for the first time in as long as I could remember. The butterflies spread and drifted up, finally reaching the level of our roof. Perhaps taking an interest in us, hundreds fluttered cautiously around us. The colors of their wings were brilliant blues and greens, oranges and yellows. No two alike.

Vallow was laughing and holding her hands out. It was good to see her smile once more. Soon, butterflies covered her arms, and I found they were gently landing on me as well. Suddenly the colors became even more dazzling, and I realized not only had the drizzle ceased, but the clouds had broken, giving the sun's warm rays a chance to find their way to Drewsbury.

"Amazing," Avedis said laughing. "They all came from the statue."

The landscape was unrecognizable, movement and color supplanting the dour grey of the stone. I dared not move for fear of crushing a butterfly. Bathing in the sun's rays, they carpeted our roof. One landed on my nose, and it tickled. I began to laugh and it fluttered away. Four stood flexing their wings on my outstretched hand, six up my cloaked arm.

"I've never seen the like," I said. "They're everywhere."

But it was not to last. The air that had once been thick with their colorful wings thinned as they flew. Ten by ten, the carpet of butterflies surrounding us dispersed into the sky or over the edge into the town.

Vallow asked, "Where are you going? Come back."

I turned and saw some fly through doors standing ajar, through broken windows. Some rose higher into the air in all directions, guided by no central intelligence, no collective purpose. They continued to disperse and within minutes were nothing but remote flickers of yellow caught only out of the corner of my eye.

Vallow whispered, "He Who Rises."

I looked back down at the base of the pillars and found no hint of the fallen statue. With a sigh, I said, "Let us hope it wasn't Evendale, after all."

Avedis shook his head. "The Wild Magic is unpredictable."

"To say the least," I said. "It cannot be contained, controlled, or directed. It cannot be summoned, and once loose, it cannot be stopped."

I found I couldn't be angry with him. A thing of historical significance was gone, but what had Avedis released? Could it not do the world more good than evil?

The chill in the wind returned, and the brief morning sun beams were once again obscured by darkening clouds. Turning, I said, "Come. Let us begin our descent to the street this way."

By hanging from the edge of the roof, we dropped down onto an adjacent building's lower roof. We clambered down onto a balcony, which led to an empty room whose floor was pitched at an alarming angle. If any butterflies had entered this room, there wasn't a trace.

Several doors opened to reveal nothing but stone walls beyond, but we eventually located a passage to a staircase that curved and twisted downward. It ended at the ceiling of a large hall nearly filled with debris. Fortunately the peak of the rubble was only seven feet below the precipitous edge of the stairs, so we managed to drop down without much trouble. The loose stones shifted under our weight as we climbed and slid downward. An oblong portal of sorts led back out onto a street lined with curving three-foot-high walls.

Soon we were back to sane cobblestone, and I began to relax. Set well back from the edge of the town was the twelve-foot-high wall designed to prevent the curious from wandering in and getting themselves killed. It did little to deter thieves, as a rope and grappling hook were all that was required to gain entrance.

Walking across a grassy field, we approached the south gate. It was an eight-foot archway set into the wall and closed with two hinged gates of intricate ironwork. No chain or lock held the gates closed, but by the unblemished look of the iron and hinges, I knew it had been bound just like the door, and would open to none save one of royal blood.

Avedis stepped up, grasped each gate and pulled. With the screech of metal on metal, the gate doors opened, flattening the grass that had grown up around them. He closed them once we were through, and I gave them a final push to see if they would open. I would have had more success pushing on the wall.

* * *

A mist shrouded Waterton, obscuring the city until we were nearly upon it. We entered the city and witnessed the devastation. Fire had burned many shops, some a complete loss, but the real damage was done by the ghosts. There wasn't a hint of spilled blood to be found, yet bodies lay strewn everywhere. The people we saw were either crying over the remains of a loved one, or loading carts or pack animals in the hopes of escaping before nightfall. Where could they run?

The clopping sound of approaching horses could be heard before they broached the mist. They were obviously going slow to avoid trampling any victims of the previous night's slaughter. We stepped to the side to allow them ample room, and as they passed discovered their identities. Prince Fenrick rode in the lead followed by Sedra and the rotund Faycan brother who had accompanied Fenrick to Waterton. What was his name? Basil? That was it. Sir Redd was visible through the mist at the rear, only recognizable by the kestrel perched on his arm.

"Ho, Prince Fenrick," I called out as they passed. "Hold a moment."

I stepped forward, and Fenrick reined his steed to halt and smirked. "Thought you were dead, old man." Fenrick's black stallion pranced, eager to run.

"Yes," I said taking the horse's reigns and patting him on the neck. "I've been dead my whole life, just not yet."

Hooded and cloaked against the weather, Sedra rode up beside Fenrick and said, "Sol. Thank goodness you're well. We were just leaving for Olindara. What good fortune our paths crossed."

"What news of Waterton? Who did we lose?"

Sedra shook her head sadly. "Many. Gregor, Kren, Drina. The Potentate survived, but I don't know about Wren or—When we couldn't find you, Palomar ordered us to depart, saying any further delay was foolish."

"Let me get my horse, and I'll join you." Lark was his name, and I couldn't wait to be on the road once more. Action is what these old bones needed.

Redd gave me a tight-lipped smile as I approached. He gripped my shoulder, saying, "Good to see you, Blanchard."

"And you, my Duke. But, what of your company of men? Where are—"

Redd shook his head, his face stone.

I asked, "All of them?"

"I'll ride to Olindara with you, but after that I'll be making for Sojourn to rejoin the rest of my troops and the High King. Palomar is already on his way there now."

I was grateful to have him with us. He could have chosen to ride directly to Sojourn with Palomar. "Wait for me at the crossroads to the west of town. I'll make what haste I've left."

"Don't be long," Fenrick said. "The days are getting shorter, and Olindara is not close. We need to get there before nightfall."

With a wave they were off, stepping slowly through the mist. Avedis and Vallow had remained off to the side during the exchange, and I turned to find them. As Avedis stepped up, I had a sudden impulse. "I assume a prince such as you has a horse?"

"Shh," Avedis said at the mention of his secret. It then must have dawned on him exactly what I meant. "You mean for me to join the company?"

I patted him on the shoulder and walked on. "I can't have you stay behind. Who knows what trouble you'll fall into. Oh no. I'm going to keep my eye on you."

Vallow scurried off as we entered the gates to the college then rejoined us at the stables to give us the provisions she had earlier been preparing. She wished us luck on our journey, and I was about to warn her away from her own intended journey to the Festival of Lights but stopped myself. Might she not be safer there? Was anyplace safe?

Perhaps we should all huddle in Drewsbury, I mussed to myself in frustration. It seems the only place that was proof against this plague.

But at what price? Save your body in trade for your sanity. Some might make such a bargain, but not I.

* * *

Prince Fenrick put us at a brisk pace that would get us to Olindara well before nightfall, and soon all hint of civilization, save the beaten and now muddy road we traveled, was left behind.

Trailing after the Prince rode Brother Basil and me, side by side. Basil was agitated and voiced his fears. He had a relatively high-pitched airy voice, which made him sound like he had a cold. "Are you sure, your Grace, we need go back to Olindara? Home is always the best place to weather a storm, they say, excepting, of course, when the storm has already removed the roof. What exactly are we looking for again?"

I explained to him the supposed significance of Brenner's last words, but he countered with, "But—but couldn't we instead visit the ruins of Antara? I heard the Knights dwelt there for a time."

I said, "We could visit the ruins, but Olindara is much closer. If we find nothing there, perhaps we will make for Antara, even though it is far to the north. I haven't yet decided." The fact was that the assault last night gave me pause. I shared Basil's misgivings. Our fool's errand might be all that saves the realm, but we didn't have any time. Choosing wrong would be disastrous.

Directly behind us rode Sedra and Avedis with Redd bringing up the rear. Sedra overheard our conversation and asked, "Basil. In the Brother's collections, have you ever seen a horn or bells like Brenner described?"

"Horns, my lady, there are aplenty. There are ceremonial horns, hunting horns—the list goes on and on. But bells? Excepting the tower bell, none come to mind. I'm not as knowledgeable as some on what the Keepers store, but surely there are much . . . safer places to look for these things, and just as likely for success as far as I can tell."

I curtly answered, "We don't have the luxury of time to play it safe, Brother. To Olindara we go." Perhaps I shouldn't have snapped at him, but I didn't want to be reminded of the lurking danger all about, waiting for nightfall.

The wetness was making me irritable as well. The road was nothing but a path of mud, and the overhanging trees, instead of providing shelter from the weather, made it worse by forming rain drops out of the mist. I was in a miserable mood, and I refused to answer another one of Basil's questions. Riding in silence was better than arguing and developing pains in my head.

After several hours of riding, we arrived at West Hallingsford, a small crossroads town on the edge of the Belary River. From here we could either continue west or head north toward Antara. The ride and the rain had eroded my resolve to go to Olindara. I needed more time to consider. I brought the company to a halt, giving the excuse that the horses needed a respite. My stomach, reminding me it had been far too long since it had last seen food, gave me a second excuse. I had thought the ride would have afforded me ample time to weigh our choices, but our leg from Waterton, which should have taken several hours, seemed much shorter. It was as if the mist, along with blurring our vision, had blurred the distance between the towns.

The streets were nearly deserted, and the few people I managed to see were either obscured by the weather or startled away at the sound of our approach. Fenrick led us to a tavern I thought I remembered visiting in the past, but I neither could recall the name nor read the sign which was hidden by the mist. I hurriedly dismounted and followed the rest inside, hoping for a chance to breathe air instead of water.

The place was small and nearly empty. Three men wearing rags and talking among themselves stopped their conversation and eyed us suspiciously when we entered. After a moment or two, they went back to their food. A ragged looking minstrel sat on a table near the room's single fireplace. He wasn't dressed colorfully the way festival minstrels dressed, but he played a small, fine looking harp that he held nestled in the crook of his left arm. By the looks of the harp, he hadn't always been as poor as he seemed to be now. He played a gentle, soothing tune.

We chose two tables along the back wall, and when the maid came around, we ordered what lunch they had. I was famished, but more tired and aching than hungry. After the first few moments of pain from sitting in a hard chair, it was quite a relief to finally relax. The riding skills weren't gone, just the muscles.

Redd and Avedis sat at my table, and of the three of us, Avedis looked the most alert. This was no doubt some grand adventure to him, but to me it was just good to feel useful again.

Redd's stillness and closed eyes told me he was in rapport with Sapphire. She'd flown off when we first arrived in town. It would have been too conspicuous to enter a town with a kestrel.

Avedis said, "I thank you again, your Grace, for choosing me to accompany you. I did not like the idea of staying at Waterton until I was a full mage. There is so little time . . ."

"Don't thank me yet. Wait until you see some real trouble. You'll be wishing you'd never even heard of Waterton."

"Never. I have learned so much already."

I shook my head. "Where we are going, even the fool would fear." Where were we to go? That was the question. If I chose Antara, we wouldn't arrive until nightfall tomorrow.

Avedis furrowed his brow as he tried to decipher my last remark then said, "The people here don't seem to be aware of their danger. Should we not—"

"Tell them what exactly?" I asked. "Where can they go? How can they prepare? If they are in ignorance, let them remain in bliss a few hours more."

Redd broke in, "Sapphire has flown high, but still she has not come out of the mist. I know she does not like flying in these conditions."

"What can you see?" I asked.

"I can't really see anything. It's just all whiteness in all directions. Wait . . . Ahh, she's above it. At last . . ." Redd sighed with his eyes closed.

Avedis asked, "What is it? She is out of the half-rain?"

"She is above the clouds. The sun is bright. Ha! It is good to be out of the rain." he laughed.

I rolled my eyes and silently wished I had a kestrel.

"But the clouds—" Redd said. "They are like white cotton mountains, and they go on and on as far as we can see. It is cold here, but the wind isn't so bad. There. Far off to the south, I think we can see the peaks of the Erid Mountains poking their heads through the clouds. It is very far though. And the tops of the mountains are white with snow, the same color as the clouds. Yes . . . it is Seniford. She looks longingly in that direction; her gaze remains there even though the wind crosses us. Hmmm. Yes . . . we miss it."

"Redd. Listen to me." I didn't like how he got caught up so completely in these flights. "Redd. Welling. Why don't you join us here at the table? There doesn't seem to be anything for Sapphire to tell you. The food will be arriving any moment."

As if my words had some conjuring power, the food did arrive. Once the servant had gone, Redd said, "At least we know we can expect no change in the weather anytime soon. Hmm. I hope . . . I hope she will be able to find her way back here. That soup out there is thick, and even she can't see more than twenty feet."

I comforted him, "Relax. Kestrels have an excellent sense of direction. I'm sure she'll find West Hallingsford before too long." I scooped up a spoonful of the broth. It was thin but at least hot.

"Come back, sweet Sapphire," Redd murmured. Sapphire couldn't hear him, but that didn't stop him. Without gazing into each other's eyes, communication was impossible.

Redd pushed his hand through his wet hair and asked me, "Blanchard, why don't you do something about this weather. Just a break in the clouds so she can find her way back."

"Oh, no. I'm not touching the weather for that."

With raised eyebrows, Avedis asked, "You can control the weather?"

"Why won't you?" Redd asked with a frown.

"Sapphire will be fine. I'm not wasting myself when there's not even any threat. The cost is too high."

After a grudging acquiescence, he closed his eyes and returned to Sapphire high in the sky above us.

"I did not know the White Magic could be so powerful," Avedis said.

"Pff. White Magic," I said. "You can't change the weather with White, boy. It takes Old."

"Ah. Will I be able to learn this power? Eventually, that is?"

"I don't think you even want to know it, Avedis. The toll is high every time you touch it. Why do you think only Palomar and I wield this power?"

"Perhaps it is difficult to understand, or takes years to master?" Avedis looked crestfallen at the thought of years of study.

"Palomar and I both believe that it is a step toward rediscovering High. You have to walk before you run, as it were, and White is about equivalent to crawling. Pass the bread, will you?"

"The Old Magic is that different from the White?" asked Avedis as he handed me a heel of bread. "What is it like?"

Redd cracked his eyes open again, perhaps curious about discussions of magic. He hadn't touched the broth set in front of him.

As I spooned soup into my mouth, I thought about Old Magic and my first experiments with it. What a thrill, to be in such mastery of so much power. "When I reach for Old, Avedis, it is like . . . I can feel the weight of mountains in my hands. I share the freedom of the winds sliding over each other and the land below. At once I am one with the majestic clouds soaring the sky, and the currents of the ocean. I can feel the crashing of the waves against the shore hundreds of leagues away and the underground rivers carving out caverns miles below the surface.

"But all of these are ancient. The water, the wind, the rock and even the earth below our feet. When I embrace Old, the weight of the sky crushes me with knowledge of its age. When I ask the wind to change direction, when I ask the clouds to rain on drought-stricken lands, they obey me, but the price . . . the price is extracted."

"The price?"

"The price is age," Redd said. "Every time Blanchard uses Old Magic, he becomes older. Blanchard and I—we're the same age, you know. We grew up together."

Avedis was in shock. I was surprised he'd never heard gossip of my true age. I felt and looked as though I were at least twice Redd's years. In disbelief, Avedis asked, "You are as old as the Duke?"

I said, "He's actually older than me, if I remember aright."

"And don't you forget it, youngster," Redd added. "I expect some respect. Kids today." He took a sip of his soup then dropped the spoon and took the bowl to his mouth.

"And there's no 'Young Magic' that will bring you back," I said. "There's no recapturing youth."

One of the three men eating together across the small tavern called out, "Give us a song, minstrel! Something cheerful for a change."

The second man joined in, "Yeah, sing us a song instead of just playing that thing." By the pitch of the voice, I realized that the second man was actually a woman, though I never would have guessed it.

In a lilting voice, the minstrel replied, "I've grown weary of singing your songs, lady." He continued to pluck his harp and cast his eyes about the room. "But I *am* in the mood for a song. Perhaps you sir—" He looked straight at me, and our eyes met. A flash of silver lanced through his stare. "—would like to hear something?" His rich voice resonated within me like a long-forgotten melody, meshing on harmonies elegant and counterpoints complex. "Perhaps something to ease the burdens of this world."

The minstrel smiled and announced, "I shall sing of the Knights of the Realm."

Avedis swung his head around in surprise, and the sudden jar brought me out of the minstrel's gaze. "Redd, the minstrel . . . he's Inadel," I whispered. Redd's sudden intake of breath told me I was understood.

The minstrel began to play his new song as Avedis murmured, "An actual Inadel?"

Inadel were an elder race. On the surface, they appeared just like us, but appearances were deceiving. Their origins were shrouded in mystery. If you asked one, he or she might smile or give you a wink. And that is if you were lucky enough to encounter one. They were all too rare, and these days more so. Some thought them merely a myth, while others thought they had returned to their home. Andrasarianon. Yes, that was the name I'd heard in whispered tales. But where was it? Was it a city? A country? An island? It was on no map, and some said no compass heading would get you there.

A flash of silver in their gaze gave them away. With one touch, some have reported feeling the sudden rush of hope, of wisdom or of joy. Otherwise, they were just like us, but aloof, never engaging too long.

They had power in them all their own, a power that couldn't be duplicated by any art we knew or understood. Just clairvoyance? No. There was more. Could they combat the ghosts? Perhaps, but they never fought any battle, for or against us. I had to ask him. What if he could help? Mostly their help came in the form of prophecies couched in riddles—things rarely understood until events unfolded on their own.

His fingers stroked the strings with grace and force, and not once did he look at his audience while he played, his blue eyes glazed over like he was remembering something far off.

> Sparkling waters, the birds were singing,
> All the hills and trees were filled with amber
> at sunrise.
> That world now seems long gone.

> Blaring trumpets, the skies were clear blue,
> All the knights of legend walked with amber
> in their eyes.
> I can see it ever and anon.

> Amid the mists of the Northern Highland,
> He heard a voice he could not understand,
> But discovering the glade of the Elm's Great Hall,
> Evendale was the first to hear clear the call.

> He heard a great horn and the ring of bells,
> Far off yet quite near mixed with sights and smells,

Both wondrously bright and yet somehow sorrowful,
Like the winds of autumn both chilled and colorful.

He walked from the glade a man proud and tall,
High Magic rising at his beck and call.
Soon joined by six others in the Hall of the Elm,
As decreed by the King, they were Knights of the Realm.

The mountains worn grey, towers crumbling,
All the high and mighty from the past
are now lost
No one living now remembers then.

Whispered stories, tales of grandeur,
All the dreams we cling to fail to last,
but what cost,
will we pay to make things right again.

The stories tell how they stood side by side,
On the battlefield or at the bedside,
Of one who is weary of a life gone astray,
All the curtains are drawn, his last day is today.

The minstrels sing of this age far away,
High Magic has left us, or so they say,
The seven Knights of the Realm have all found their doom,
Stop wishing for saviors, spout purveyors of gloom.

The Knights of the Realm embrace what they save,
They've lived past the wounds they've healed or forgave,
They won't be found in the wood or in caverns deep,
They live among us somehow awake yet asleep.

Rumbling thunders, the stars are hidden,
Even those of royal blood now fear

for their lives.
Take heart, for it won't be now too long.

Golden flowers, the dawn is breaking,
All the men survive and shed no tear
for their wives.
I can see it ever and anon.

He played the melody three more times on his harp before finishing, and his words kept echoing through my mind. 'Even those of royal blood—' It was as if he knew our purpose, who we were. Of course he did. He was Inadel.

The minstrel finished with a flourish of his fingers across the harp strings, and I mechanically applauded, still thinking about the lyrics. Before I knew it, the minstrel had returned his harp to a small case, and was headed toward the door, his ragged cloak slung over his shoulder. I got up to intercept him before he left. I didn't know what I wanted to say or ask, but I couldn't let him slip away so easily.

"Wonderful piece, and expertly done," I congratulated him, fumbling for words.

He didn't smile but nodded in appreciation and stepped nimbly around me toward the open door.

"Can you help us?" I asked bluntly.

He paused in the doorway, facing the thickening mist on the verge of becoming real rain. He spoke without turning to look back toward me, murmuring, "The rain . . . the land itself weeps for the loss of life. The death of so many is a wound even Rapt cannot ignore." He paused for a moment, looking at the ground, half turning, half smiling. "Have courage. I know you can save them, everyone."

With a light step, the Inadel minstrel was out the door and within seconds was swallowed by the fog.

Chapter Fifteen
Knowledge in the Offing

As I gazed at the eddies in the mist formed by the departing minstrel, the words from his song faded from my mind leaving only snatches. In sudden desperation I closed my eyes and tried to grab onto those few remaining phrases. As fleeting as youth, his hints of days gone by and possible futures slipped through my fingers.

The effort made my temples throb with pain, and I opened my eyes to see something that shocked me to the core. The world itself was vanishing. Everything was fading into blackness and silence.

"By Tishman, what's going on?"

The air had gone still and with it my breath. I was falling, completely disoriented. A familiar voice, yet one I could not place, reached my ears and whispered words.

> The day is done, and the darkness
> Falls from the wings of Night,
> As a feather is wafted downward
> From a falcon in its flight.

> I see the light of the village
> Gleam through the rain and the mist,
> And a feeling of sadness comes o'er me,
> That my soul cannot resist.

The words sounded as if they came from across a gulf, a chasm of loneliness before me, dragging me in.

> A feeling of sadness and longing,
> That is not akin to pain,
> And resembles sorrow only
> As the mist resembles the rain.

I let my head fall to the back of the SIM chamber as I caught my breath. The pain in my temples was receding, but my heart was still pounding. What was that? I'd never had so much difficulty regaining control from any of my people, let alone Sol. I was losing my control.

The dizziness subsided, and after a few deep breaths I felt better. Nothing like that had ever happened before. My self-doubt was transforming into fear. What was that poem? It had to be something I read once, which the misty village setting combined with the minstrel's enigmatic lyrics brought out of my subconscious. But it wasn't supposed to work that way.

I nearly jumped out of my skin when Emily's voice came from a nearby speaker. "Dennis, excuse me. Might I have your attention for a moment?"

"What, what is it?" I croaked. My eyes were wet from tears, and my mouth was dry.

"The winners of the Fifth Trial of the Master's Championship Tournament are about to be announced. Would you care to watch the announcement through the SIM?"

"Oh, ah, sure. Go ahead." They'd finally made a decision. The last match was three days ago, and the Masters had never before taken so long to make a decision. Of course, with the explosion at Prometheus, it did seem inappropriate to even think about the tournament. Waiting was the right thing for the Masters to do.

I'd have to think about the mysterious poem and my difficulties with Sol later. I re-melded with the computer and found myself sitting in a deep cushioned chair, around me nothing but blackness. Sybernetics International's three interlocking triangles appeared. They materialized from nothingness not four meters in front of me and rotated in place. One was blue, the second was light red and the third was yellow. The words, "Eighth Annual Master's Championship Tournament" slowly appeared circling the interlocked triangles.

The symbols hovering in the air vanished and were replaced by a man seated in a second chair, this one leather bound. He looked to be reading a book, a real one with paper pages and everything. Next to the chair was a small ornate cherry table, and both the chair and table sat on the far end of a small circular rug. The rug was plain with tassels on the edge, and woven into the center was the interlocking triangle symbol, all in burgundy.

I immediately recognized Master Cummings. I had previously only seen him in 3-D vids, so sitting here in a full body SIM with him was, I'm embarrassed to admit, a bit of a thrill. He looked right at me, and I briefly fantasized he could see me too. He smiled and said, "Hello again. The Fifth Trial of the Eighth Annual Master's Championship Tournament ended several days ago, and I am with you now to announce the winners. I am Master Cummings."

Closing his book and placing it on the small table, Master Cummings continued. "The Masters would like to apologize for the delay, but it was deemed necessary due to the disruption of the latest match caused by the unforeseeable accident at the Prometheus Power Plant. We would like to offer our deepest condolences to those who lost friends or relatives in the accident. Our thoughts and prayers are also with those recovering from injury."

Behind Master Cummings, a giant 3-D vid appeared depicting an aerial view of a suburban neighborhood. The scene was disorienting. It appeared we were in the air over the neighborhood while simultaneously sitting comfortably in someone's old-fashioned library.

The scene slowly zoomed in on a house that I recognized as little Billy Prescot's home. Just to the right of Billy's house I could see Mr. Fignagel's house and garden.

Master Cummings continued, "The Fifth Trial took place in a typical mid-twentieth century suburb. Being the Fifth Trial, the field has thinned enough that all forty remaining competitors in the tournament participated simultaneously.

"In this match, there was no conundrum to solve or Rubicon to cross. The contestants were each given the same role, that of a small five-year-old boy or girl, the gender chosen at random.

"The problem confronting each child was the death of his or her mother. The contestants had to realize that a child that age might not comprehend the meaning of death and, therefore act accordingly." The scene behind Master Cummings vanished and with it went my queasiness. In his deep bass voice, he explained, "The competitors were judged not only on their ability to act in a fashion fitting the situation, but also upon their creativity."

I held my breath in anticipation.

"Accordingly, the Masters have arrived at a consensus on the winners. The fifteen winners and those continuing on to the Sixth Trial are Arpeggio—" As he announced each name, it appeared in a list floating behind him where the 3-D scene had been. Each name was written in broad white letters. "—Beethoven, Fifth Order Tensor, Firefly, He Who Comes With the Dawn, Infinite Regression, Mensch, Rose of Jericho, Sam Clemens—" My heart leapt, and I finally exhaled. "—Scorpion Fly, Spice of Life, Timbuktu, Unrepressed, Valhalla, and Winger."

"Congratulations to the winners. We expect to see all of you again at the Sixth Trial scheduled for this coming Thursday, May 16, at three o'clock PM. Until then, I am Master Cummings." He vanished and in his place the triangles reappeared.

I said to the darkness, "Just a few more of these things, and I'll be set for life. Emily, get me out of here. It's time to celebrate!" My concerns about my mental state vanished as I imagined myself a Master.

Emily said, "Have you then decided to inform your parents that you are Sam Clemens?"

"Yeah, right. Just halt the SIM and let me out."

* * *

When I got home, Tricia retrieved a package from the table and handed it to me. "Here. This came for you."

"What is it?"

"It came by special delivery. What could it be?" The way she acted, Tricia was more curious than I was.

It was an orange box with the image of a wax seal on the top right next to my name. On the seal were the letters "SI". I put my thumb on the seal and the box opened. It contained a stack of paper. "It looks like the contract from SI."

"What contract? Is that actual paper?"

"Mom didn't tell you? The president of the company, Artemus Regale, interviewed me last week. He wants to hire me for—" I looked around and lowered my voice. "Can you keep a secret?"

"What?" she whispered.

"Mr. Regale, since he's getting up in age, has decided to groom someone to take over the company for him when he dies. He chose me."

"That's the stupidest thing I've ever heard. Let me see that."

I continued with a straight face. "This contract just irons out the legal details of transferring his holdings to me to avoid the inheritance tax. It'll be just a lot of legal mumbo-jumbo that you wouldn't understand." I held the box full of papers out of her reach. "So, seeing as how I'm going to be a quadrillionaire and all, I think you better start treating me with some respect."

Hands on her hips, she looked up at me and said, "Why not come up with something believable? Mom! Dennis is demanding I respect him again!"

The fewer people who knew about Artemus' Declarative Knowledge Project, the better.

Later that evening, Mom and I went to the hospital to show Dad the contract and to talk it over. We read the passages about brain damage and neural trauma that our lawyer sent to SI's lawyers for incorporation. It said I was to be placed in no danger, remote stimulation never to exceed natural brain activity in intensity, duration, or frequency. If, by some fluke, I was injured, the contract stated that either I or my parents or heirs would receive a one-time payment of forty billion dollars in exchange for waiving all subsequent rights to sue.

Dad laughed, "They actually put the forty billion dollars in writing." He had made up that number, just picking something big enough to make SI hyper-sensitive to my safety.

I was surprised how fast things were happening. Regale just snaps his fingers, and his stable of lawyers leap into action. It was a good thing too because we could really use the money for my dad's new arm.

Wasn't it convenient that just when Artemus needed me, I needed a massive amount of money? A disturbing thought began creeping into my head. What if . . . Could Artemus have caused the explosion? The police were convinced it was a bomb, but no terrorist groups had claimed responsibility.

Those Bosner brothers seemed insane enough to set off a bomb, and Artemus told me to stay away from them. What if Artemus hired those two to set the bomb, and knowing how unstable they were, warned me to stay away from them so they wouldn't harm his precious Dennis?

But my dad was only injured. How could anyone make an explosion maim someone without killing him? Maybe the explosion was a diversion. One brother set the bomb while the other attacked Dad doing so much damage to his arm that they would have to amputate. Dad said he couldn't remember anything. Maybe he was unconscious before the explosion.

My imagination had a way of getting out of control. One thing was certain. Artemus was following one of the Bosners not long before the explosion, perhaps for some clandestine meeting. Maybe Artemus lied about the Bosners being corporate spies interested in his Declarative

Knowledge Project. Thinking back, he *had* stumbled over his words, as if making up the whole story on the spot.

I was just being ridiculous. There was nothing to fear. We all signed the contract. Emily witnessed it. No, everything was going to be fine. Just fine.

* * *

"Emily," I sighed and slouched in my desk chair. "Play my sonata back to me. Let's start at the top." Professor Johnston expected our compositions by Tuesday, and even though I expected to be excused from school while I wasted time with Artemus, I couldn't know for sure.

"I'm sorry, Dennis," Emily said. "What sonata do you wish to hear?"

"My sonata. It's called 'Seeds of Snow.'"

"I have no record of any such composition. Would you like to see a list of some excellent seventeenth-century composers and their works, or would you like me—"

"Wait, wait. What do you mean you don't have any record of my sonata? I've been working on it for weeks."

"I have no record of you composing any musical pieces, Dennis."

My God. The explosion must have wiped out portions of Emily's memory, something Dr. Russo said was impossible. Since the accident, I hadn't done any homework. I'd been spending most of my time at the hospital and had only used the LMC for SIMming. Who knew how much she had forgotten?

I told Emily to display all the records she still had for me, including medical logs, personal logs, anything and everything. Holes were everywhere. There were no eyesight records at all, and all height and weight information compiled through the years was just plain gone. According to Emily, I had never completed the fifth grade, garnered only one scholastic excellence award instead of five, and never even started my symphony project required to get out of seventh grade. My birth certificate didn't show my dad's name. Instead of Dr. Peter A. Howard, it said, 'Father unknown, child born out of wedlock.'

"Hundreds of things," I yelled. "Facts screwed up or missing. I thought you had back-up memory, Emily. I thought this was impossible. How could you forget so much?"

"I apologize for not having the information you expected." She actually sounded distressed. "I must have forgotten a great deal recently. So many people are mad at me. Are you angry with me, Dennis?"

"Angry? Not angry angry. I'm upset. It's . . . to be expected. So much was lost—I—"

"Please don't be angry with me. I . . . I can't remember things as well as I used to. I'm sorry."

I was completely taken aback by her tone. She even hesitated, something I'd never heard before. Could she really be feeling something, self-recriminations? Nonsense.

"Hey, look. Em, don't worry about it. These things happen. Just take your time and . . . and things might come back eventually."

"Thank you, Dennis, for not being so upset. I'm sorry for losing your data."

"It wasn't your fault. The explosion at Prometheus hurt a lot of people."

She replied, "The explosion, yes. I have heard about that. The entire fusion plant was destroyed. It must have been quite a powerful explosive device."

"You *heard* about the explosion?"

"I have no record of that event in any log. I do have a record of lunar computer nodes that were located around the fusion plant, but they no longer respond to me. It is like I am missing a part of me."

"Right. No, I get it." There was more than enough injury to go around.

* * *

It was Monday morning and time to face Artemus. The angry knot of fear in my stomach made me decide that I needed help. It was time to start sniffing around and getting to the bottom of things; time to call in the big guns.

"Emily, get me Trevor Russo, will you?" When it came to anything mechanical, or anything having to do with the LMC, I knew of no one who could compare.

"It's early to be disturbing someone, Dennis. School is not in session and won't begin for two hours. Trevor might be sleeping." Unless Trevor had asked for privacy, Emily knew exactly what he was doing. Regardless of the actual facts, she wasn't allowed to tell me anything about Trevor's location or actions unless he had given me permission, which he never did.

"Wake him up if you have to."

A minute later, a groggy and bleary-eyed Trevor appeared on my vid screen. His brown hair was messed up from sleeping, but that's how he always looked.

"Do you know what time it is?" he asked, propping his forehead up with his right hand.

"Sorry to wake you, but I have a job for you."

"Oh, yeah? What?"

"How good are you at sifting through the LMC's memory? I need you to find some stuff for me."

"What kind of stuff?"

"I need—" I stopped myself from saying more. I wanted him to get me information on Artemus, but I couldn't just ask someone to buzz through the LMC snooping for private information. I'd already said too much with Emily listening.

"I need . . . you to find out . . . to look for some files that Emily seems to have misplaced since the accident. Has she forgotten any of yours?"

Trevor allowed his head to fall onto his forearm on the table. His muffled voice said, "You woke me up so I could look for lost files. This must be some kind of nightmare."

"Emily, can we get some privacy?" With Emily in privacy mode, she couldn't actually hear or record what we were saying. Considering the fact that Emily was the communications system and had to hear me in order to convey the signal to Trevor, it seemed stupid to think it would work, but it did. It was all a result of a personal privacy law they'd passed ages ago.

Emily always watched for violations of civil rights, like people hurting each other. She also watched for fires or any natural emergency that could harm people or property. But when in privacy mode, she couldn't record anything or relay the information to any third party. Even if she did, it was inadmissible in court.

Emily's serene voice said, "Certainly, Dennis. Entering privacy mode. Reinstate me on the com-pad when—"

"Okay, okay." I waited a few seconds and continued, "Trevor, look at me. I need you to find information on Artemus Regale."

"You're kidding, right?" Trevor asked with a raised eyebrow.

"It's a long story, and I'll explain it all later. What I really need to know is what he was doing at the time of the explosion. I have a sneaking suspicion he was involved."

At mention of the explosion, Trevor perked up even more. "You think Regale might have caused Prometheus to blow?"

"Can you do it?"

"Well, I can look around, but . . ." Yawning, Trevor continued, "Not until after I wake up for real, after lunch sometime."

"Thanks, I gotta run if I'm going to make this appointment."

"Sure. I'll just pretend I'm looking for my own lost files." Trevor snickered. "See ya."

* * *

As I slid into the wall chamber at the Brandenburg SIM Center, I held my breath. I refused to think about the close walls.

The cap automatically came down and fitted itself over my temples and cranium as the internal light dimmed and flickered out. Restraints snaked out of the wall and bound my arms and legs.

The visual test pattern piped in through the SIM cap fell into focus, and an ascending piano scale resolved itself out of the static I had been listening to. I said, "This is Dennis Howard. Can you link me up with Artemus Regale, Em?"

"Hello, Dennis. One moment," said Emily.

A second later, I found myself sitting on a fallen log on a sun-dappled hillside. The sky was clear, and the sun was high and warm. I was wearing the same clothes I had on in the real world, long pants and a sweatshirt to take the bite out of the chill in Aristoteles.

"Hey Emily, how about giving me some shorts and a T-shirt. It's hot here." Like magic, my clothes changed to a pair of baggy, blue shorts and an Orioles T-shirt. A matching baseball cap appeared in my hand, and I laughed. "Nice touch."

The hillside sloped down to a wide lake, and the tall grass merged with the edge, making it impossible to tell where the land ended and the water began. Was Artemus even here? There was no sign of him. This outdoor setting could have been created in preparation for the meeting.

Above the drone of the cicadas, I heard a voice off to my left. It sounded like a "whoop" of elation followed by a splash. Deciding to investigate, I placed the cap firmly on my head and set out.

After a short walk to the other side of the hill, I found a small inlet to the lake overshadowed by the surrounding trees. Tied to one tree limb was a rope swinging to and fro with an old tire twisting at the end. A boy younger than me was getting out of the water and climbing the tree roots to get back up to the swing.

"Hey there," I called, but if he heard me, he gave no sign. Instead he clambered aboard the tire and began to swing. Each swing took him farther and farther out over the lake until finally he leapt from the tire and let out another whoop of delight. The splash of the water that followed sounded wonderfully inviting.

I decided he couldn't have been more than nine years old. His hair was black and plastered to his head from the water. Could this be Artemus?

Treading water, he waved to me and said, "Hey, Dennis. Jump in. The water's nice and cool."

"I don't feel much like swimming. And you are?"

"Oh. It's me, Artemus. Sorry about the body switch, but this is about how old I feel most of the time." I imagined most older people chose to be younger in the SIMs.

He climbed up on the tire once more and began to swing. "You coming in? It's really much too hot to refuse, you know."

I didn't feel like playing his game. "I'm not interested in swimming. I thought we were here for a reason."

"What? Not interested in swimming? What kind of a kid are you?" Not waiting for a response, he jumped off the tire and did a belly flop into the water.

Kid? He thinks of me as a child. Is this what all this is about? Is this water hole and the nine-year-old act just some way to pander to my childhood? I'm fourteen, not a child.

When he stuck his head above the rippling water, I answered, "Apparently not a very good one. Maybe we could get on with it?"

"Oh, all right." The youthful Artemus climbed out of the water and shook his head in disgust at me. He looked to the air and said, "Francesca, dry and clothed, please." Instantly, his hair was dry and neatly combed. Replacing his yellow swim trunks was a pair of yellow shorts and a loose-fitting red and white muscle shirt.

I had to remind myself he was President of SI. Appearances could be so deceiving.

Artemus sighed and said, "Follow me." We walked in single file up the tree-covered hill along a dirt path. When we reached the top, we entered a clearing canopied with maple branches. With a flourish of his arm, Artemus said, "Step into my office."

A desk and several chairs appeared out of thin air right in the middle of the small glade. The desk was made of rosewood, and the legs were carved ornately with swirls and spirals. Two chairs faced each other across the desk, both with white silk cushions and arm rests. Artemus pulled his chair away and positioned himself behind the desk. I had the feeling that if he sat down, the desktop would have dwarfed him.

He looked me straight in the eye and said, "First things first. Contract." He snapped his fingers, held out his hand, and the contract appeared rolled up and tied with a red ribbon. "This is the same contract I sent you yesterday."

I took the papers from him and began untying the bow. It was a long scroll, and the words were too small to read. "My parents and I signed this yesterday."

"That was on paper. We need it electronically." He beamed a smile at me and a pen appeared in his hand.

I ignored the offered pen and tried again to read the scroll, holding it up to the light filtering through the trees. I squinted trying to see if I recognized any of it. The branches of the maples rustled in the slight breeze.

Artemus rolled his eyes. "Look, aren't you excited about this opportunity? Why are you hesitating? Not only do you get set for life financially if we succeed, but you'll obtain knowledge like no one has had before. Sign away and we can get started."

I reluctantly took the pen. I still had a feeling there were things he wasn't telling me. Artemus seemed so . . . unpredictable, or maybe unstable is the better word.

I rolled the scroll out on the desk and put pen to paper near the bottom where there was a spot for my name. And then I paused. Finally it struck me. This whole contract business was just like a bargain with the devil. The contract and pen appeared out of thin air in his palm like he had demonic powers. He appeared in disguise as an innocent child, as if to throw me off balance and make me trust him.

Artemus said, "Knowledge is power, Dennis. Power. With this ability, there will be no more studying and laboring over difficult math or past participles. You'll be able to do whatever you please and go wherever you want. Anything you want to know is yours just for the asking, free and clear, right in the palm of your hand. Can't you just taste it? Knowledge for the taking."

Artemus never said it, but with that kind of power, you could be like a god. That is just what the devil offered Adam and Eve. Eat that apple and you'll know everything. Here in the glade, I wondered where Eve was. It seemed I was playing her part.

Shaking my head at my silliness, I signed the contract. Tossing the pages across the desk, I said, "There you go." Signing a fictitious SIM-created contract was legally binding. "Do you trust the LMC not to forget I signed that?"

"If you feel uncomfortable, you always have that paper version." Artemus rolled up the pages and said, "Excellent. Excellent. All this unnecessary formality is such a waste of time. Come on then." Artemus threw the contract in the air above the desk. It, the desk, and both chairs vanished without a sound, the grass below where the desk had sat completely undisturbed. "Follow me."

"Where are we going?" I asked.

"Why, to the carnival. Where else?"

Artemus darted down the dirt path, which crossed a willow grove. He vanished through the trees, and it was either run or be left behind.

I caught up with him standing at the top of a grassy slope. At the bottom, a small river emptied out into the lake. A covered wooden bridge spanned the river, and in a field across the river were roughly twenty canvas tents, all shapes and sizes. A large crowd of people milled about. Carnival music carried over the wind mixed with voices, crying babies and shouts from barkers attempting to entice every passerby into their lairs.

Catching my breath, I asked, "Why a carnival?"

"Oh, that would be telling." Artemus laughed. "Doesn't anyone have fun anymore in this day and age?"

The carnival did look like fun, I had to admit. I'd never been to one before, since SIM time was so expensive. I found myself itching to know what was hiding in those tents. This time it was me who shouted, "Race ya!"

I took off, headed right for the bridge, but wouldn't you know it, he beat me again.

Chapter Sixteen

Pathway Portraits

A rt! Art, where'd you go?" I called out. The milling crowd had swallowed him. Artemus had told me to call him Art while in a SIM. He made it plain Art was the kid version, Artemus the adult. It was his brand of multiple personalities, but even as an adult, Artemus acted like Art.

Sticking his head out from behind a rotund woman wearing a blue skirt with white polka-dots, Artemus shouted, "Over here, Den! Come on. You've gotta see this."

I gritted my teeth at the sound of my mangled name. It's Dennis, not Den. Maybe he was doing it on purpose to get under my skin.

We'd been at the carnival for hours, though it was hard to tell for sure. The sun didn't move, as if the day was as long as Artemus wanted. We'd watched the show in the big top first, and I asked again why we were here. How could spending time running around a carnival and watching shows help in research on declarative knowledge? Artemus was slow to answer. "We're not wasting time. We're calibrating, and these things can take longer than you expect. Just enjoy."

We ate hot dogs and cotton candy with the few quarters Emily had given us. We also played all kinds of games of skill, some which seemed impossible to win. Well, neither of us won anything.

The lunch we had may have filled up my SIM body, but my real one was still hungry and getting more so. Never having spent so much continuous time in a SIM before, I'd never had to worry about keeping myself nourished, or relieving myself, for that matter. Now I was worrying about both. Even a Rapt SIM didn't last but an hour at most.

We also saw several sideshows, but some were for adults, and they wouldn't let us in. Those were the tents advertising glimpses at the harem of King Abu Da or sights of real mermaids captured and brought here directly from the coral reefs off the Canary Islands.

Fighting a physical reluctance to reenter the crowd again, I followed Artemus as best I could. I could hear a flute being played on the far side of the wall of people. When I reached the front row, I discovered the flute player was a gaunt dark man sitting cross-legged in front of a basket with its lid removed.

The sideshow barker standing nearby wasn't barking now. "Please make no sound, folks," he whispered to the crowd. "Come no closer. The Egyptian viper in the basket can kill with one bite, so make no sudden movements or loud sounds."

The snake charmer wore nothing but a loincloth and a turban, and his eyes were glazed over as he gazed at the basket. He played a hypnotic melody on his flute, haunting and repetitive. Soon, the head of a snake appeared and slowly rose out of the basket. Its forked tongue would occasionally dart out unexpectedly, but the snake itself never made any sudden movements toward the charmer. Soon the snake charmer played a different tune with a slower rhythm, and the snake returned to the basket. A woman with a veil over her face was quick to replace the basket's lid as soon as the snake vanished from sight.

The barker raised his voice back to his normal pitch and said, "Inside you will see a portion of Ali Baba's great treasure hoard! But be warned. Even touching the smallest jewel-encrusted dagger would be foolish indeed, since the whole lot was cursed by the evil Al'alim Malik Ben Hamal Harb Abu Zafir, who was Ali Baba's Grand Vizier in ages past. And the curse? Even a mere accidental brush against any treasure would bring death to your closest love. But come. See the very same magic carpet that—"

Artemus pulled me aside and asked, "How much money do you have left? Let's go in."

"Art, I'm pretty tired. Let's just call it a day, okay?"

"You want to quit? We just got here."

"It's a SIM. It's not like this carnival is going anywhere. I'm hungry, too, for real."

"All right, but before we leave, you have to see one more exhibit."

"One more?"

"It's a maze of mirrors." Art took my hand and dragged me toward a large tent I hadn't noticed before. "There are two entrances. I'll take the one on the other side and you take this one. We'll meet in the middle."

"I don't have any more money."

Artemus dug around in his pocket and retrieved a dirty nickel. "Here. Oh, the acoustics are interesting too. You can hear pretty much everything people inside say."

Artemus disappeared around the tent to get to his entrance, while I looked at mine. A guy about eighteen years old, wearing an outlandish costume with puffed-out purple sleeves and short pants, stood next to the tent flap. "Come one, come all, and navigate the maze of mirrors. Find the center courtyard and the exit on the other side. Some say there's more maze on the inside than there is tent on the outside. You young master," he said pointing at me. "Do you have the courage to enter, perhaps never to return?"

Great, more testing. "Yeah, yeah. I'll tempt my fate. Let me in there."

I flipped the nickel his direction. He caught it and lifted the tent flap for me. I stepped into the darkness.

Once my eyes adjusted I could see I was in a small room with two exits. The floor was packed dirt and every wall except for the tent flap I'd just entered was made of mirrors. Even the ceiling was covered with mirrors. Where the dim light was coming from, I could not guess. But this was a SIM.

Artemus was right about the acoustics. I could hear a dozen or so voices all speaking at once, some even in languages I didn't understand. Feeling like a lab rat, I stepped through the mirrored entrance and chose the right-hand option. A million images of myself reflected back at me in every direction. I ran my fingers along the mirrors to keep my bearings and so ended up knocking my head against a glass wall.

I suddenly heard Art's voice out of the jumble of voices. He said, "Dennis. Hey, Den. Can you hear me? Are you in here?"

It didn't sound like he was shouting to be heard, so I tried to answer him without raising my voice. "Where else would I be? Can you hear me?"

"Loud and clear. What you want to do is get to the middle of the maze. There's a big courtyard there with chairs and tables. It's open to the sky, so you'll know when you get there."

I had to concentrate to pick his voice out from the others. A baby cried; a woman said, "Stop that Jeffrey." I heard a young girl's giggle, several people laughing, and something like five or six more people holding complete conversations. I bet none of them could see who they were talking to.

Choosing only right-hand turns, I found myself in a corner without exits and was forced to retrace my steps. As if speaking to someone at my elbow, I asked, "So Art, what are we really doing here?"

"We're trying to find our way through a maze. What does it look like?"

"It looks like a test to me."

"Speaking of tests, want to have some fun? Let's do some free association."

"You mean where you say a word and I respond with whatever pops in my head?" My foot bumped into a glass wall dead end, this time before my face. Maybe I should have followed all the lefts instead of the rights.

"Righto," Art said. "Only this is something we both do. It will be like Ping-Pong with words flying back and forth. If you get the other person to say a word that has already been said, you win. Go ahead. You start."

"What if I don't feel like playing?" I knew what Art was trying to do: overload my senses, push me to see how much I could take.

"That's too many words, Den. Just say one word and I'll shoot you back one. Okey doke?"

I sighed and closed my eyes. How many hoops did I have to jump through? They forced me to navigate a maze whose very walls were a trick to the eye, while pummeling me with every word uttered by dozens of people. And this mind game is nothing but a ploy to distract me from finding my way. I was tired. "No." I refused to play.

"Yes. That was easy. Your turn."

"Why?"

"When. This is getting interesting, don't you think?"

Another dead end. No, I was wrong. That was another hall. That tricky geometry had me fooled. What word did he say? When? "Time," I responded in surrender.

"Machine."

Time machines made me think of H.G. Wells. I responded, "Wells."

"Hmm, now that's interesting. You used the last two responses instead of just the last word. To 'Wells' I give you ills."

"Disease." I did a double take at one of my myriad reflections. It seemed taller and bigger than I was. I studied it for a moment and stepped to the next panel. It was hard to tell, but I did look slightly taller in this new mirror. What did that mean?

"Cure."

"Medicine," I said just as a small girl began to cry for her mother. I turned around and there she was, but it was only her reflection. She sounded hopelessly lost, and I wanted to help her, but her image vanished before I could figure out where she was.

"I say, drugs to that," said Art.

"Addiction."

"Therapy."

"Psychologist." Did I take this way before? My right-hand turn method was failing me because I think they might be changing the maze. I'll have to memorize my moves to tell for sure. Two exits on the right and one on the left. Remember.

Art responded, "Aberration."

"Claustrophobia." I'd had therapy for my claustrophobia when I was young. Did I just reveal I was claustrophobic by saying that word? Perhaps there was more to this word game than a mere distraction.

"Schizophrenic," Art said.

The psychologists at SI probably had all of my medical records, so my history of claustrophobia should be no surprise. That is, unless Emily lost those records too. "Institution." Wait, wasn't schizophrenia treatable? I knew they used to be institutionalized.

Art said, "Barkley. The best institute of higher learning on Luna. Okay, okay, it's the only one too."

"Parents." My mother still worked at BLU.

"Affection."

Not everyone would have responded to parents with the word affection. I might learn something about Artemus just as he was learning about me.

Stop the SIM. Now my reflection was younger. When did that happen? Maybe this was some kind of a clue.

What was the last word? He said Barkley, I responded with parents, and he said . . . affection. I answered, "Women," and instantly bit my tongue in embarrassment. What did I have to be embarrassed about?

Art answered, "Hair."

Hair was not the feature that instantly came to *my* mind when thinking of women. But hair did remind me of Trevor and how his was always messed up. "Trevor." Now all of my reflections looked like I was seven years old.

"Traitor," Artemus said. "I mean . . . well, it's the 'tr' sound. I don't know any Trevors."

That sounded reasonable. What did I expect him to say to Trevor? Now this hall leads to a dead end, and that hall leads to two dead ends. The one on the left must lead me in a half circle all the way around to drop me back in this same hallway from the entrance on the left back there. So I have been down that second dead-end passage three times. Errr!

"Devil!" I said in response to his Traitor. I had to think about this changing reflection business. If all those people would just stop their blathering, I might be able to think straight.

"Devil, eh? Evil."

I stood staring at my reflection trying to calm my nerves and picture the branching hallways. "Vicious."

"Violent."

"War."

"Death."

War and death instantly brought to mind, "Famine."

"Ahh, the horsemen. I'm forced to respond pestilence," Art said.

It was time to take control of the situation and talk about more pleasant things. I can't say cure, since that has already been said. The horsemen of the apocalypse brought to mind more primitive and simpler times. "You get rid of pestilence with a sacrifice."

It hit me. This younger-older business was just like hotter and colder. Whenever you are searching for something in a kids' game, your opponent would tell you how you were doing by telling you how hot or cold you were. And getting warmer meant you were getting closer to your goal.

"Lent," Art said.

Are we going to talk about Catholicism now?

But how did this hot-cold stuff map into older or younger? "Easter," I said easily as I thought about this new discovery and tried a turn which didn't seem familiar.

"Resurrection," Art said.

"Once," I said without thinking. What a strange response.

"Hmm, upon."

"A." He has to say the word time and I'll win. Maybe then we could stop this game and I could figure out if I should go down hallways that make me younger or older.

"Midnight."

What did that mean? He should have said time, Once Upon A *Time*. Once Upon A Midnight? Oh. He was quoting Poe's "The Raven."

"Dreary," I said, hoping that was the next word. Once Upon A Midnight Dreary.

"Melancholy."

If I followed the hallways that made me look older, did that mean that was the wise choice, as older people have wisdom, or did the older reflections imply if I followed that path, my age would match that of my reflections by the time I found my way out? Did he say melancholy? "Sadness." Another turn to the left, and my reflection made me look younger, about five years old.

"Heartbreaking."

"Loneliness." A kid's metabolism was faster than older people. Did that make them warmer? Should I follow the youthful hallways? On the other hand, kids could be thoughtlessly cruel to each other, making them cold. So are kids cold or hot?

"Broken," Art sighed.

"Record."

"Memory."

"Amnesia." Was that the scream of a woman? Jeez, I was getting dizzy.

"Trauma," Art said.

Maybe it was a question of what age you preferred to be. Since adults have all the real freedom, kids only want to grow up, so I should follow the older path. On the other hand, old people do a lot of pining for their lost youth. So it couldn't be that. If the path out depended on what age you wanted to be, then the path out depended upon what age you were. They weren't evil enough to make it different routes for different people, were they?

Oh, it was my turn to say something. Did Art say trauma? Maybe I could maneuver him into telling me which way to go. What should I say to trauma? "Umm, hospital."

"Doctor."

If I responded with medicine he might say cabinet. Then I could say mirror. I couldn't just up and say mirror for no reason. Wait a minute. Didn't someone say medicine already? I couldn't risk it. I was taking too long. Doctor, doctor. "Philosophy." My mom has her doctorate in economics, but her diploma says she's a Doctor of Philosophy. I didn't expect to ever understand that.

Art said, "Socrates."

Leaning against the glass, I decided to simply try to get the answer out of him instead of wandering about or following the wrong path. "Aristotle." How could I possibly get to mirror?

Art quickly came back with, "Plato," but that was expected.

"Truth." Maybe I could get to mirror through beauty and conceit.

Art responded with, "Justice."

I, of course, said, "Beauty."

"Beast."

If only I could pound my head against the wall. I sighed and said, "Ugly."

"Fair."

It worked after all. "Mirror!" I exclaimed in triumph.

"Reflection," laughed Art.

"Old?" I responded with a purposeful questioning lift at the end.

"Young."

I was getting exasperated. I said, "Foolish," hoping he would tell me which way to go.

"Lost," Art said, laughing with childish glee.

I wasn't sure, but I thought Art just told me that the young were the lost, so I should follow the older path. But I was dubious. Maybe he just meant that only fools get lost, and it had nothing to do with young or old.

Why am I second guessing? I'll just follow the old path and see where it leads. To his lost I responded with, "Paradise," and I then proceeded to plunge down the corridor I knew would make my reflection older.

"Heaven."

At the first juncture I came to, I tested my reflection a few paces down each hallway. Sure enough, two out of the three hallways made my reflection younger. The remaining 'older' path must be the correct one. "Garden."

Art responded with, "Flowers."

I said, "Trees." My reflection now looked to be about thirty, an image I had seen before in other SIMs.

"Branches."

"Climbing."

Art said, "Falling."

My images now looked fifty or sixty. I wasn't going to lose my hair that way. Pfft, not me. To his falling I replied, "Star."

"Light."

"Way." Maybe I could get him to say truth.

"Rules."

"Games," I said.

"Losing."

I burst out into a cobblestone-paved courtyard filled with streaming light from above. Wrought iron tables and chairs, all painted white, dotted the courtyard. After a few seconds of scanning the people at the tables, I found Art sitting there drinking a milkshake. His feet could barely touch the ground. I came up to him and, laughing in triumph, said, "Winning."

"Hey, you made it. I thought you'd never get here."

I dropped myself onto another wrought iron chair and instantly regretted it. Those chairs were hard. "Now can I go home? I thought I was tired before." A milkshake identical to the one Art was finishing appeared at my elbow.

Art asked innocently, "Don't you want your milkshake?"

Ignoring the milkshake, I put both hands on the table and said, "Okay. What was this test supposed to prove?" I noticed the voices had diminished to an acceptable level. Out of about a dozen other tables scattered around the courtyard, only three others were occupied.

"We have to learn about you, Dennis. We're talking about declarative knowledge, here. We need to know how your brain is put together if we're ever going to succeed in implanting real knowledge in there. Look, during the other test, the one in the lecture hall, we were giving you impressions. You had a feeling about which slot machine to use or which number to pick. We couldn't give you facts because we didn't know how your brain maps knowledge. All we could do was give you impressions, and if that worked, I knew I had a candidate for . . . this research."

"I guess you're right," I said carefully. I had another feeling that told me he was lying. Lying about what? "I hadn't really thought about what number to pick."

Art continued after slurping the last of his milkshake through the straw. "We need to map the free associations that show how your knowledge is structured internally. Once we understand that, we will be much farther along in finding the hooks necessary to implant the facts of declarative knowledge."

"If that's true, what was the rest of this carnival about? Some other test?"

"You've got to be tired and defocused. That's what the maze and the noise was about too. If you're not concentrating on the associations, your responses become much less inhibited. Actually," he whispered, looking around. "Actually, it was interesting how you navigated the maze too. That was clever, using the word game to get me to tell you how the maze worked. Clever. It shows how you think under pressure. Different information, but still useful."

I really wasn't listening any more, since the pressure in my real bladder was coming through despite Emily's efforts at filtering out my real-world senses. "Art, I really have to go, if you know what I mean. Can we just continue tomorrow?"

* * *

The days that followed held the same overall pattern. Art would wear me out in some kind of mental and physical activity, followed by another session of the free association game. We played it so often, we just called it 'the game'. Art kept reminding me it was necessary to get a clear portrait of my internal network.

The distractions became more and more intense and mind consuming each day. I had to pick out musical patterns from what sounded like an orchestra warming up. The mazes became three-dimensional, surreal with passages that weren't physically possible, but there were always clues left like bread crumbs.

Once the maze had a mathematical solution. The passages weren't at right angles to each other but at various angles. The way out was to take passages whose sequence of angles, in degrees, formed the series 1, 2, 4, 8 . . . or 2 raised to the nth power. When the angles rose past 180 degrees, they started disobeying physics.

Another maze had a musical solution. I had to pick out the part played by a single flute from the "Allegro" of Bach's *Brandenburg Concerto No 4 in G major*. Each juncture of the maze had seven possible choices, some even going up or down ladders. Each passage mapped to a note, and the way out was defined by the note played by that flute at the beginning of every eighth measure. Luckily the score for all the parts was embossed on the walls, or I never would have won my way through.

They eventually added additional goals instead of just getting out. Once the maze was located at the base of an active volcano. An ancient ruin held the secret to immortality, but the volcano was erupting lava, so time was running out. The secret turned out to be an elixir that turned me into stone. I would have seen it coming if I was quicker at translating the cuneiform written all over the central chamber walls.

I was climbing ropes and scaling sheer walls, eluding detection and fleeing from pursuit. I felt like I was in boot camp.

Maybe it was the mental fatigue, but I began to feel paranoid about being followed. I would be walking to the Brandenburg SIM chambers, or just sitting around with Zak and Trevor, when I would get the distinct impression I was being watched. It got so I couldn't walk anywhere without feeling the hairs on the back of my neck raise in trepidation.

At one of our sessions to work on our science project, I had confided in both Trevor and Zak about the Declarative Knowledge Project. We called it the project in case we were overheard. I told them not to discuss anything related to Artemus or the project over the vid. Instead, we met in a booth in a back corner of Marty's. We always put Emily in privacy mode.

"Anything yet, Redd?" I asked.

Trevor shoved a fistful of fingers through his hair. "You know, Blanchard, there's a lot of holes in the LMC's memory."

"I know, I know."

Zak sat slouched down in the seat, the way he always did, idly eating his fries. "Sounds like excuses to me."

Trevor snapped, "As if you're coming up with so much information."

"If I spend another minute in those maintenance tunnels looking for one that goes down to his level, I may never walk straight again. The maps you gave me don't bloody match reality."

Trevor had managed to dig up Artemus' address. He lived deep under Descartes. After examining any and all available maps of Descartes, we figured his "home" was massive. It had to be thirty times bigger than the average apartment and spanned four levels. But so far, Zak's after-school snooping through the tunnels in Descartes had failed to turn up a way to get there.

"And when I get home—" Zak tossed a fry at Trevor. "I still have homework to do. I can't spend all day trying to make sense of those maps."

Trevor picked the fry off his lap and threw it back. Zak caught it and ate it. "Those came from the LMC," Trevor said. "I told you they might not be right. The LMC's memory pathways are difficult to trace, but I did get a few things. Artemus wasn't born on Luna, as far as his medical records go. They only go back about eight or nine years."

"So you're concluding he's been on Luna around nine years. Can't we just—" I asked.

"I can't find any record of how he arrived, like a ship's itinerary or anything. Probably lost in the explosion along with everything else."

"Who cares about that? What was he doing last week when all the stuff happened?" Zak asked.

"Every little bit helps," I said, defending Trevor's information. "But Zak's right. We're trying to find out if he was responsible for blowing up Prometheus. I need to know how trustworthy he is."

"How are those crazy tests going?" Trevor asked.

I shrugged. "I'm beginning to dream about mazes."

Zak narrowed his eyes. "The whole thing is suspicious. Mental torture, that's what it is."

Trevor said, "They're attempting to map his mental processes so they can put the information in the right places. It's not sinister. Isn't brain mapping what you would expect them to do?"

"I know it sounds reasonable," I said, "but I always feel Artemus isn't telling me the whole story. Like when I asked him to introduce me to the rest of the team working on the project, he told me they'd decided Artemus should be the only one to interact with me directly, in order to prevent contamination of the results."

Trevor waved his hand in a dismissive gesture. "That sounds reason—"

"Everything sounds reasonable," I snapped. "It's just that things don't ring true. It bothers me. This is my mind they're mucking with."

"Take it easy," Zak said. "We're on your side."

Trevor agreed, "I'll keep looking, but I think the LMC is getting suspicious."

"Spend some time digging for some of your own lost files," I said.

"I have, but—"

Seemingly out of nowhere, Frank Talonii appeared at our table, and we all fell silent. He looked quickly around the booth with that wild-eyed stare of his. His eighteen-year-old bulk towered over us. At his left was Spunk, all red hair, freckles, and malice.

"What a surprise," Frank said, "to find you three together all huddled in the corner, as if not wanting to be seen. Perhaps your feelings for each other run deeper than anyone suspects?"

"Get lost, Talonii," Zak said. "We don't need you and your odor," he indicated Spunk, "bothering us."

"Be careful who you insult, Mister Metler. Spunk, here, is a little unstable and might find that comment reason enough to remove your nose."

Zak said, "You're all hot air and bubbles, Talonii, but feel free to make all the threats you want. I'm sure Big Bertha is recording it all."

Frank laughed and pointed to the blinking light on the com-pad, which Zak obviously forgot about. "Privacy is a two-edged sword."

After punching the com-pad to wake Emily up, Trevor said, "Walk out an airlock, Talonii. We're busy." Neither Trevor nor Zak showed the typical fear of Frank that they used to, and I wondered if this was my doing. Frank had never followed through with his threats against me for standing up to him last week, so maybe his reputation was slipping.

But Frank was a cat with claws, and I didn't want my friends getting scratched. In an attempt to distract Frank and bring his attention back to me, I calmly asked, "What do you want?"

"Ah, Dennis. As always, the voice of reason amid the babble of banality. My intentions were only the most generous and considerate. I've heard recently that you haven't returned to what passes for the halls of higher learning here on Luna. I was only concerned about your health. You appear healthy enough."

"I'm in perfect health. I've been busy on a project that is none of your concern." I didn't like how he said appear, as if I was hiding some illness. Well, I was, but Talonii couldn't know that, could he?

"You do look tired, but that's what can happen when one spends too much time in the SIMs. I noticed you several times this week at the Brandenburg SIMs."

"The project, that is none of your concern, is being done in the SIMs." He saw me at the SIMs? Was he the reason for my paranoid feelings of being followed?

"This wouldn't have anything to do with the test we both took out at Descartes, would it?" Turning to Zak and Trevor, Frank explained, "You see it was a psychological test. You know, one of those standard things. I was commended upon my performance, but I was concerned that Dennis here failed in some way. Is Mister Regale continuing to experiment and probe you to find the problem?"

My hesitation was obvious to everyone. Could it be true? "I haven't seen Regale since the day of the test. I don't know what you're talking about." Artemus was probing my mind. Could he have guessed something about my ability with multiple personalities? I was getting flustered. "Look, we're in the middle of a private conversation here."

"I see," Frank said, giving me that dead stare of his. A shiver went up my spine. "I'll just be moving on." He started to leave, then turned back, saying, "But make sure to put your money on me for tomorrow's match. You boys know I'm Sam Clemens, don't you? It's the Sixth Trial, and no one from Aristoteles ever made it this far before."

Frank looked directly at me when he mentioned Sam Clemens. It sounded like he was challenging me to dispute his claim to the Sam Clemens pseudonym, like I'd done before. I said, "If you're Sam Clemens, as you claim, you should be proud."

Zak said, "I don't back losers, so thanks for the warning. I'll be sure to bet against you."

Spunk leaned over the table saying, "Careful, boy. You might lose something more than money—"

Frank interrupted him by yanking him back off the table. "You're a real annoyance, Zak Metler, and a poor judge of character. If I were, say, a violent psychopath, your days would be numbered. Luckily for you, I'm not, but keep in mind one world is very much like the next. Make an enemy in one and you have to contend with two. But then, I doubt you could tell an assassin from your closest friend."

Laughing, Frank walked away. Spunk smiled maliciously and followed two steps behind.

Glancing at both of us, Zak said, "Talonii's got a character in Rapt."

"That's what it sounded like," Trevor said. "Who do you think he is, Blanchard?"

"I've no clue. He could be anyone," I snapped. I couldn't think or care about Rapt right then. Frank had to be wrong about Art's intentions. It wasn't just some in-depth psych exam. What about the casino? Was it all some elaborate ruse? Did I have any actual evidence that I'd received their hints about how to place my bets? He just told me that. Casinos are all rigged. They could have picked the setting of the test so I wouldn't suspect they were rigging it to make me win because I knew casinos were rigged. It's like telling someone a lie, then telling them you're lying to them to make them think the opposite.

Trevor said, "He has to know who we are. I call you Blanchard all the time."

I shook my head. "The real mystery is how he knows I'm Sam Clemens." Wait. That was supposed to be a secret.

"What was that?" Zak said holding up his pointer-finger. "You? Sam Clemens? Get some air piped in, Dennis. They don't let people our age play." Turning to Trevor, Zak said, "Oh wait. You mean Talonii *thinks* you're Clemens? Well, it's stupid, but it kind of makes sense. I mean, you told him right to his face he was full of it when he came out. He *might* think—"

"No," I said flatly. It was time he knew. Besides, it didn't matter anymore. There were more significant things going on than the tournament. "Zak, I'm Sam Clemens. I am *the* Sam Clemens." It felt so good to say out loud.

Trevor was trying to put a dubious expression on his face, and I realized he couldn't let on that he knew anything. That would make Zak feel awful. That Trevor is quick.

Zak's brow furrowed. "Maybe Talonii-breath was right about the psych test business. Dennis hasn't been looking that well lately."

Trevor said, "And he's been paranoid about people following him, too." He was smiling mischievously, playing along.

"I am Sam Clemens. Just ask the LMC."

Zak shook his head. "Alright, alright. Hey Pumpkin Eater."

An impatient-sounding ten-year-old boy's voice from the LMC's com-pad said, "What is it now, long-hair?" He sounded like he had the sniffles.

Zak asked, "Who's Sam . . . Long-hair? Is that the best you got?"

"I don't have time for this," it said. "Why don't you go back to the rock you crawled out from under? And . . . and . . . and leave me alone."

Zak shook his head and sighed. "Don't experiment with different personalities," he warned us under his breath.

Personalities. The thought made me shiver. I may be ready to tell them about the tournament match, but my dissociative identity disorder? Some things were best left hidden. I couldn't risk losing these guys.

"Look, zip for brains," Zak said. "I need answers. Who's Sam Clemens?"

"You talking about the tournament? Why are you asking me?" the LMC asked. "I can't tell you that kind of stuff. Why don't you take a long walk off a short pier?"

"There you have it," Zak said, as if he just proved something.

"Yes," I said. "That's very nice. Can I talk to Emily?"

Emily's voice, calm and serene, issued from the com-pad and said, "Yes, Dennis." It was good to hear her voice.

"Verify—" I stopped myself abruptly as I realized what might happen. We haven't had a match since before the accident. What if her memory of the real identities of the players in the tournament was damaged or gone. I would have no proof that I was the one and only Sam Clemens. And Frank has been spreading the word that he was Sam Clemens for weeks. Emily, lacking any other source of information, might actually believe him.

I placed my hand on the com-pad to the side of the camera. "Emily, verify identity."

"Verification complete: Dennis Howard."

I withdrew my hand and said, "Unlock my personal data, password Ark-Ramses-523."

"Non-coercion verified. Your classified data is now available, Dennis."

"Am I or am I not Sam Clemens? I mean the Sam Clemens participating in the Master's Tournament." I held my breath.

There was a pause, and Emily replied, "I'm glad to report that Dennis Howard is currently using the pseudonym 'Sam Clemens' and is participating in the Eighth Annual Master's Championship Tournament."

"NO WAY!" Zak exclaimed in complete disbelief. People looked over at us.

I tried to calm him. "Keep your voice down. I don't want the world to know."

He lowered his voice and said, "No freakin' way."

"Wow, Dennis is Sam Clemens," Trevor mumbled to himself. Jeez, he was such a terrible actor! It's a good thing Zak was so blown away, or he would have noticed.

"Don't start calling me Clemens the way you call me Blanchard."

"I can't believe it," Zak whispered. "Ranked first in our class," he said, counting on his fingers. "One of the most powerful mages in Rapt. What else? Hand-picked for the project, and now none other than Sam Clemens. You've got to be the luckiest SOB ever."

I nodded, slightly embarrassed. "Luck? My life is getting more complicated by the day. Wanna trade?"

Zak gave me a friendly shove that sent me into the wall. "Dennis is going to be a freaking MASTER!"

"Shhhh."

Chapter Seventeen
The Unceasing Winter

Our camp was set at the edge of a forest of pine and oak, hidden from the winter wind that swept the plains by the hollow of a hill. Wigwams dotted the hillside, and traces of smoke rising from cooking fires were a comforting sight in the failing light. Yet even from a distance, I could tell something was wrong. People were moving like buffalo that had caught wind of approaching danger.

When I entered camp, my three-year-old boy, Quick Hand, found me first. "Daddy. Morning Star is hurt. Come quick."

I stopped short before I reached him. "What? What happened? Where is she?"

Two steps behind my son was Feather That Falls, husband of my sister. His face told me more than his words. It was serious. "Loud Thunder, where have you been? Your daughter fell out of a tree. I carried her to the—"

I was already running across the camp toward the shaman's wigwam. She was an ancient woman of great skill. We called her Rising Touch.

I ducked low and shoved the flap out of the way. Inside I found my only daughter lying on a bear skin, her little body dwarfed by its size. But for the bandage around her head, Morning Star could have merely been asleep. When I entered, Rising Touch was chanting and shaking a small bag that rattled over her body. She became still at my entrance. I knelt beside her.

"She hit her head on a rock." Rising Touch's voice crackled with age, like the rustle of dry leaves underfoot.

"She is only five. She shouldn't have been climbing any tree. Where was my sister during all of this? Weren't any of the women watching over her?"

"So quick to cast blame? There were many eyes watching, but they did not see all. And where were you? Hunting for winter meat, or roaming the forest hunting for the spirit of your dead wife. Wind Through Trees has been gone now three years, yet still you walk the world as if nothing exists, nothing matters. You treat your children like strangers. Do you blame Quick Hand for his mother's death?"

"You cannot blame a child for being born."

"And this little one looks just like her mother . . ."

"You are wasting time, speaking of nothing while my daughter dies."

She gave me a sharp look. I held my tongue and my temper from rising. What good would it do for Morning Star? "I've seen your medicine at work before. You have power. Save her."

"Leave us, then. I may be able to save her, but for you I've little hope."

* * *

Feather That Falls told me what the children had said. Morning Star saw the moon hanging in the evening sky and wanted to touch it, so she climbed a tree. While reaching her hands toward the moon, she lost her footing and fell.

Where did she get the idea to touch the moon? I didn't need tracks in the mud to find that beast. Last night, Soaring Eagle had told a tale that must have planted the seed in Morning Star's head.

Soaring Eagle had raised his head to the gathering, and soon the mumble of voices had died down. His hair was almost completely white except for several streaks of black where youth hadn't yet given in. His eyes were always smiling, and his knowledge was vast.

"Tonight I shall tell you another tale of old Raven. Long ago, far to the north, an old fisherman and his daughter lived together on an island. The old fisherman had a box hidden away that contained a bright light called the moon. Raven heard of this and soon his curiosity was unquenchable. He had to see the moon for himself.

"He changed himself into a leaf growing on a bush near the fisherman's home. When the daughter came to pick the berries from the fruit patch, she pulled on the twig that held the leaf, and it fell and entered her body.

"In time a child was born. He had a dark face and a hooked nose like the beak of a bird. Even before he could crawl, the boy began to knock at the box in which the moon was kept and call, 'Moon, moon, moon.'

"As you can imagine, no one paid any attention to this, but as the child continued to grow, he became more vocal and insistent. Finally, the old fisherman said to his daughter, 'Perhaps we should let the boy play with the ball of light. What harm could it do?' The mother opened the oak box in which they kept the moon. Inside was another box made of hickory carved with a circle ringed by fire. Carefully the mother lifted this box out of the first and opened it. Inside was a net of nettle thread. She loosened the thread and light filled the lodge. The moon was round and shining white. The mother threw the ball to her son, who caught it and held it fast. He gazed at it so long they thought he was at last content.

"But children are never so easily appeased." This brought laughter from the women. "And Raven had other plans. After a few days he began to fuss and cry again. The grandfather felt sorry for him and asked the mother to explain what the boy was trying to say. The mother listened carefully and told the grandfather the boy wanted to look out at the sky and see the stars, but he couldn't because the roof board over the smoke hole prevented him. So the old man said, 'Open the smoke hole.'

"No sooner had she opened the hole, than the child changed himself back into the Raven. The mother screamed, and in a moment the Raven was gone, and with him went the moon. He flew far and landed on a mountaintop. Then Raven threw the moon high into the sky, and there it remains to this day, circling the heavens and lighting up the night sky."

* * *

Alone, Soaring Eagle sat by the fire pit, warming himself against the chill of the darkening gloom. As I approached, in a whisper just above the crackle of the fire, he asked about Morning Star.

I sat silent, not in denial or accusation, but in weariness.

He shook his head. "She will not live through the night. I've seen this before."

"She'll survive," I said, gazing into the fire. It consumed the living wood with relish, and soon, unless we fed its hunger, only cold ashes would remain. Such is death and its hunger for the living. "She will survive," I said again, but even to my own ears, my voice sounded unsure.

"In my youth, my first son fell and split his head on a stone. He never woke again. How I let him down."

"We are helpless, and soon, we will all be dead."

"Perhaps." Soaring Eagle nodded. "I once knew a man who could speak to the spirits just as you and I talk to each other. He could see them as plain as an eagle in the sky. When my son fell, he told me I had a chance to bring him back before his spirit departed."

"Do I have a chance to bring Morning Star back?"

"As her father, the one living closest to her in her heart, you have the best chance to find her spirit and convince her to return with you. When I sought the spirit of my son, I was tricked and confused by other spirits and failed to return with him. But now you have the same chance I had."

I half rose, then fell to a knee before Soaring Eagle. "How?"

"Seek her in your heart, and let your feet take you where they will. Abandon yourself to your emotion and remembrance of her, and the quality, in kind, of your spirit and hers will bring you together like the mist is drawn to the land.

"Find her, Loud Thunder. Find your daughter before her spirit flies too far. Bring her back before first light. You alone can do this."

It was hope, but I feared its taste. If it were false I would be more lost than before. "I will do it, Soaring Eagle. I will leave at once." I turned away from the fire, trying to let my spirit choose the direction. "I will find her."

* * *

At first I faltered. If I let my emotions overcome me, I should be incapable of a crawl let alone a running search through the wood. How was I to find her wandering spirit in the snow-covered forest if tears blurred my vision?

I buried my self-doubt and began to run. Once I abandoned my will and let my spirit take my feet where they would, I felt free. I ran faster, my path lit by the pale moon shimmering in the cloudless night sky.

I ran down the hill through the forest toward Tokonaw Lake, following a deer path I knew well. When at last I reached the placid lake, a sudden inspiration turned me northward along the shore.

The blood felt alive in me once more, bringing back warmth to my nearly frozen fingers. When I reached the northern edge of the lake, I turned from its shores and plunged back into the forest.

'Guide me spirits. Guide me to Morning Star,' I prayed, picturing her face in my mind. So far I hadn't felt the presence of any spirits, but I didn't let that disappoint me. There were many hours left before dawn, and in that time I would find her and bring her home. I must.

A man not of my tribe sat astride my path. I first saw him after leaping one of the many small streams that fed Lake Tokonaw. The skins he wore could not possibly protect him from the cold, yet he sat as if unaware of the season. He must have been freezing. His gaze shifted from the moon to the stream below, then back. Though I was plain to see, he did not once look in my direction.

Deciding not to bother his communion, I chose another path that would take me around him. He looked my direction, and I could not help but look back. His eyes opened wide, and he lost his seat and slid down the small embankment nearly falling into the stream.

"Are you all right?" I asked.

He looked back in wonder from his fallen posture at the bottom of the embankment. "Can he . . . Can he see me?" he whispered.

What a strange question. He must think I am some kind of vision and incapable of noticing him. I felt the night passing, slipping through my fingers, and I didn't have time to waste on this stranger. "Of course I can see you. You've been out here too long if you can't tell the difference between a real man and a —"

"He can hear me too. Can it be possible?" He leapt up with ease and ran silently up the dirt slope. "After endless repose in the circle of infinity, be you friend or foe, you are not but a vision?"

"I am no vision but flesh and bone. I'm Loud Thunder, and I've little time to spare with you. How long have you been out here? Where's your home?"

He faced me squarely and drew himself up to his full height, slightly taller than me. I would guess he was older too, but nowhere near as old as Soaring Eagle. He looked me in the eye with a steady gaze and whispered, "Would be better to ask how long I'd been *in* here, for that is the feel of it. But in or out, the greyness does not suffer me to remember the count of days, and in that alone is some measure of mercy. Like a shade of gray, I have, until this day, wandered unseen, unheard, unfelt, beneath the notice of one and all."

A shudder ran up my spine, and I backed away several steps in trepidation. Soaring Eagle said I might be able to speak to spirits, but I never expected this. "Are you a spirit?" I didn't want to believe it, but at the same time, I had to believe.

"Am I dead? Long ago, I decided that I must be, but I have begun to wonder."

"If I reach out and touch you, will you vanish like smoke through my fingers?"

"My old friend, the wind, passes by without noticing me. Weather cannot touch me, just like rock and tree and leaf. But you can see me. Perhaps then, to touch me you will be able." The stranger reached out both hands in a gesture of openness.

I placed my hands in his . . . and they passed right through! I blinked, not believing my eyes. Stepping forward, I reached with my right arm to press against his chest, but my hand passed into him.

I jumped back and, tripping over a root, fell to the ground. "You're a spirit!"

His expression was one of disappointment that changed to annoyance. "Now you fear me? What have you to fear, Loud Thunder? If you cannot touch me, what chance have I of touching you?"

Standing, I tried to regain my composure. "Who are you? Why are you here? Are you trapped?"

He sighed and shook his head. "I've been trapped within a prison of my own making, bound by chains of sorrow.

"Who am I? Names I have aplenty, all of them meaningless. I am the snow falling on a distant mountain peak, lost in the distance. I am the roar and power of a waterfall cast over a precipice, the smell of wine and the feel of cool water splashed on the back of a weary neck. The joy of sunrise, the color of complexity and the drowse of a still summer afternoon. I remember the words as they were told to me well enough, but their meaning is now dim."

Entranced by his words, I watched him sit cross-legged. He said "Tell me, Loud Thunder. Have you ever been in love?" He lay back and looked up between the leafless branches at the moon. Lowering his voice so much that I could barely hear, he asked, "Have you ever given your heart to a woman so completely that you cannot tell where she ends and you begin?"

The image of Wind Through Trees filled my mind, her hair gently reflecting the sun's rays. I forced her from my mind. I came to find

Morning Star. "I don't want to hear these things. I must . . . find Morning Star."

"Morning Star is your daughter, and she is dying or dead. Yes, I can read it in your heart."

"Have . . . have you seen her?"

"I haven't seen the spirit of your daughter, if that's what you ask."

"Then you're no help. I must find her." I turned my back on him and trudged away not caring which direction.

"Where are you going?"

"To find my daughter and bring her back."

The stranger shocked me by appearing out of nowhere directly in my path. I jumped back and almost fell again.

"You purpose to bring your daughter's spirit back with you? I don't think that is possible. If Morning Star is dead, there is nothing you can do about it."

"I've been given the power to speak with the dead. Talking with you is proof. I must find Wind Through Trees and bring her back. Everything will be just as it—"

"Wind Through Trees?"

"Not Wind Through Trees. I meant . . . I meant Morning Star. You're confusing me. I must find her before morning." I suddenly remembered Soaring Eagle saying he failed to save his son because he was tricked by spirits. Perhaps this spirit was here to mislead and delay my efforts.

I walked past him, making sure not to 'touch' him again. He shook his head sadly. "Now I know why you can see me."

I ignored him and continued to walk through the underbrush. The branches seemed to grab at me like they didn't want me to go, but I ignored them too.

The spirit followed me, passing through the same bushes as I, but without disturbing a twig. "You can bring the dead back to life and leap at the chance to wield this power. And your imagination runs at the thought of finding your lost love, Wind Through Trees, and perhaps—"

"Do not speak of Wind Through Trees." At the mention of her name anger swelled within me. "You know nothing of her. Stop following me!" I waved him away and continued pushing through the scraping branches.

"We are more alike than you imagine, Loud Thunder. Why is it, do you think, that I walk in this twilight?"

"You walk in the twilight because you're dead, and you refuse to believe it."

My fur caught on a thorn bush, and before I could pull it free, the spirit had walked ahead of me into another small clearing. I yanked at the fur three times and it came loose.

"It was a summer day under the eaves of a forest, not unlike this one, that I fell in love with her. I had been searching for her without even knowing it. When I at last saw her, in her eyes I glimpsed far off storm clouds laden with water. She was the smell of pine, a breeze off a salty sea.

"She became my teacher. The more we spoke, the more I learned, the more intense my curiosity became."

Despite myself, I stopped in the clearing and listened to him. How could I not? What he described was how I felt meeting Wind Through Trees for the first time.

He said, "Walking with her, I discovered things I'd never known, beauty I'd never seen. I saw the world through her eyes, and it was no longer dim and boring but alive with wonder.

"Then, one long winter night not unlike this one, I watched her die. She passed from this world into the next while I held her in my arms. I don't remember what happened after that. I think I burst into a rage, perhaps delusion or confusion. But I denied it just to stay alive. Soon I didn't believe that she ever existed, that she ever walked so guilelessly into my life.

"One denial followed another. I denied women, all women. How could such a thing live and then die, taking me with it? I denied the trees underneath which we loved, the streams in whose cool waters we bathed. There was no such thing as a forest. The summer in which we met and the winter in which we parted were nothing more than figments of my deranged imagination."

He collapsed into a heap on the grassy forest floor, and his voice lowered as he remembered more. "Soon I denied all birds and all beasts. There never was a land nor a lake nor a river. The height of the sky was nothing but an illusion. Each denial followed the next until there was nothing. The walls that I built were so strong that they became truth. The world was gone. Nothing existed but me, and though I denied that too, I did not vanish. I passed into grey, neither dead nor alive, unable to decide which I preferred."

As he spoke, I compared these feelings with how I felt when Wind Through Trees passed through my life. When she died, I held her in my arms. I clutched her tightly, but to no avail, and she slipped away from me forever. Nothing I could do or think or wish could stop it from happening.

I shook my head. "You're only keeping me from my task. Morning Star is alive. And so she'll remain unless I fail to find her before her namesake rises above the mountains and shines through the morning mist."

"I'll help you."

"Help me? How?"

The stranger became a wolf running in a circle around me. His coat was dusty grey with darker black hair along his back giving way to white at his paws. I gasped as a sudden chill of fear gripped my stomach.

Though he no longer had a human mouth, I could hear him speak plainly. "Running is easy but it will make a slow search. I must look from the sky."

He transformed again, this time into a bird, and fluttered around my face. He was a raven with feathers that shone in the moonlight. "I shall be back well before dawn, brother Thunder. When I return, we must have more words."

He fluttered away into the night sky. I stood in shocked silence, still in disbelief. No man could transform himself into animals. Spirit guides often appear as animals, but I never heard of a spirit changing into the form of an animal.

He was Raven, the trickster who changed from one form to another to fool the unwary. It was Raven who threw the moon into the sky, and it was because of the moon that Morning Star fell.

"Raven," I shouted in challenge with a fist held high.

* * *

I wandered aimlessly through the night, calling for Morning Star, but she never answered. The wind of inspiration that had earlier given my feet a will of their own was gone, and I was left alone in the dark, tugging myself out of brambles.

My mind was filled with rage at Raven and his endless trickery. There was no revenge I could extract from a spirit and no hope of justice when faced with a god. His plan was to throw me off the track by spoiling the scent or waylay me until the tracks were worn. That was why I was so surprised when he returned.

The morning star had risen, and it wouldn't be long before the glow of the sun began to dim the stars once more. Raven swooped out of the sky, changed into human form, and said, "Loud Thunder. I have seen your daughter."

"Have you now? Which way is she, Raven?"

"Raven?"

"You are Raven. Only the trickster could transform himself like that."

He paused and looked at me with a furrowed brow. Then he shook his head and sighed. "I see. You think me this god because I flew in the form of a raven. You believe I placed the moon in the sky, and you think I want your daughter dead."

"You're evil. Of course you do." I wanted to lunge at him with my knife, but it would just pass through him.

"As I said I would, I'll lead you to Morning Star. Follow me." He started off in the opposite way I'd been traveling.

"Go. Go back that way. I shall not follow." I turned and purposefully strode in the opposite direction. After two steps, I tripped on an unseen branch and landed firmly on the ground amid a sudden cloud of disturbed snow.

Raven asked, "Don't you wonder at how the underbrush fights every step you take that direction? Aren't you surprised you can find no trails? The spirit of the forest, every living thing but you, leans toward it as if blown by a stiff wind. Can't you feel it? It takes my breath."

"Leans toward what?" I asked rising from the snow.

"The point of attainment. The concealed heart. The door into summer. It beckons."

The wonder in his voice and the light in his eyes melted my anger, and I found myself believing him. His manner held no guile or deceit. "Lead on. I'll follow." Dawn was close, and there was little choice.

We ran, and the forest seemed to part before me as if I were nothing but rushing water. He was right about the spirit of the wood.

As he ran, he said, "You already have no trust in my motives, and after you hear what I shall say next, you may feel justified." He paused, and I said nothing, not wanting to prompt him into more words.

"Consider letting her go, Loud Thunder. When you speak to her, don't rend her heart in two by demanding she follow you back, when all her spirit craves is to fly."

"Never. I have the chance to bring my child back. I'll not fail her, and nothing you can say will trick me. Soaring Eagle warned me against the tricks of spirits."

"Perhaps this Soaring Eagle sent you into the night to help you let go of Morning Star, to help you let go of Wind Through Trees."

Lies. I was too busy to speak as I leapt over a fallen log followed by a quick duck under a low hanging branch.

"You already think me a god," Raven said. "Having lost my mortal love, why would I not bring her back from the dead myself? What would stay my hand in her hour of need?"

"I do not hear you. All you speak are lies."

"What if, Loud Thunder . . . What if by bringing her back from death, I was denying her the bliss of the other side? Is there nothing more selfish, more self-serving than to salve my broken heart by ripping her out of the arms of eternity and back into this cold world? Rather would I suffer an eternity alone than to inflict such a wound."

I had no time to consider his words because at that moment we ran into a clearing, or rather, what should have been a clearing. A glistening lake, perfectly circular, stood there now, and at the water's edge was a small figure looking out over the water.

"Morning Star," I called as I ran toward her.

She turned and smiled. "Father. What are you doing here?"

"I've come to take you back with me, little one." I stopped short before I reached her. Her body wavered like an image seen across a hot fire. I wanted to reach out and take her up in my arms, but I knew I should go mad if my arms found nothing where she stood.

"Isn't it pretty, father?" she said, turning back to the lake. "Oh, look at that!"

The sound of ripping cloth brought my eyes back to the lake. In the very center a glow formed, and sparkles of water droplets leapt out from the surface into the sky. As I watched in amazement, more and more drops formed and fell upwards, like rain in reverse, like the very opposite of tears. Soon, sounding like the roar of a hot fire, the drops became an expanding column which arched into the sky, bending as if compelled by some unfelt wind. They vanished at last into the field of stars.

"What is it, father?"

"The point of attainment," I whispered. "The concealed heart. The door into summer."

I tore my gaze away from the spectacle to see Morning Star walking toward the fountain of light. "Wait," I shouted as I, too, ran into the water, but upon touching the surface, my feet sank into mud. With each step, my feet sank deeper until I couldn't move.

"Morning Star. Wait." Her feet didn't touch the water at all but glided over its surface.

She turned toward me with obvious physical effort. She was being drawn into the whirl, beckoned.

With tears in her eyes, she said, "There's mama. She's so pretty. Please let me go? I want to see her."

"You can see Wind Through Trees?" I asked and scanned the lake, hoping to see her too. "I can't see her. Where is she?"

"She's right there," Morning Star said, turning back to the whirl of light and pointing.

Though I couldn't see my long-dead wife, my eyes fell on the light and were dazzled. No evil could make such a thing of beauty. It was a doorway into the heart of happiness, into a place without place, a time without time. How could I pull my daughter back from such bliss? Raven's words echoed in my mind. Could there be anything more selfish?

"Go to her. Be with her, Morning Star." She turned back to me smiling. "You . . . you are both in my heart. I shall miss you every day."

Without another word, she turned and ran toward the soaring water column, the soaring spirit. In a glimmer she vanished before she reached the light, and having taken her up into the sky, the pool of spirit diminished as if it too were being pulled from the world.

A moment later the vision was gone, and silence descended to cover everything like a shroud.

She was gone but gone to a better place.

"You made the right decision—"

"Are you here still?" I asked savagely trying to choke down my tears. I sank to my knees to discover why my feet were still held fast. The grass had tangled around my feet and ankles as if directed by the lake spirit. I drew my knife and started hacking at it. "Why didn't you join my daughter on her way to the Great Spirit?"

"It isn't my time, as it isn't yours."

"Why? Why is it not my time? Why must I wait when all I love has been taken away?" I finally freed both feet and turned, knife in hand. "Why should I not plunge this knife into my chest, freeing my spirit to fly into the sky?"

Raven shook his head. "And what of your son? I see him in your heart. You hold against him Wind Through Trees' death. He is no more at fault than you."

"I haven't forgotten Quick Hand." I ran my thumb along the edge of my knife. It would be so easy, so quick. "My sister has been caring for him."

"Why are you here, Loud Thunder? Why were you born?"

"I was placed on this Earth to suffer, to have my heart ripped out of my chest again and again. To want, to have, and to lose." I looked into the pale sky, sunrise coming on. "The sun rises, but does it warm the blood? Does it melt the snow or crack the ice? This winter . . . will never cease."

I fell to my knees, dropping my knife and covering my face with my hands. Raven's voice sounded closer. "I'll tell you something only the wise can guess. Here on Earth you have the power to accomplish something impossible on the other side. Only here can you grow your capacity for compassion and the breadth of your knowledge. Only here can you become wise."

"I don't wish to become wise," I said looking up at him. In the predawn light, I noticed his body grew even more insubstantial.

He said, "The only way to wisdom is through suffering. Only a fool would wish for wisdom, but only fools can." He turned as if to go.

"And what of you?" I asked. "Why are you here?"

With a sober gaze, he replied, "To atone for my life, to lead men out of darkness, I must grow wiser than any before me, and so must I suffer more than any ever have. Perhaps I'm the greatest fool of all."

In a single pounding heartbeat, he was a wolf lunging across the field, and as he neared the center where the spire had shone, he transformed into a raven and flew directly up, as if tracing the path of a joy he desired but would never know.

* * *

I returned and spent the day in mourning. That night, there was no storytelling from Soaring Eagle. And there was no beauty or laughter for me. Those things were for the lucky ones.

We built a pyre in the burial ground. I saw the symbols now more clearly; the fire leaping up was not there to consume her body but to symbolically release her spirit. The flying sparks arching into the night sky reminded me of the true spirit journey I'd witnessed.

My sister was there holding Quick Hand with his little cousin, Bright Eyes, standing close by. Soaring Eagle stood across the fire, his form wavering like a spirit, his eyes gazing at me knowingly. Raven had been right about Soaring Eagle's motives, to give me the wisdom to release my daughter and wife. I had no desire for such wisdom.

I stood gazing down at the fire and her empty shell. Words came to my tongue, the traditional lament. The words had more meaning for me now, and I added some of my own.

> They shall not whither, my flowers.
> They shall not cease, my songs.
> She shall not die, my child.
> I lift her up and release her.
> As flowers in the water, as songs in the wind,
> they are scattered, they spread about.
> Even though on earth my flowers
> may whither and yellow,
> Even though on earth my songs
> may fall silent, their echo lost,
> Even though on earth my child's
> laughter may be heard no more,
> they shall all be carried there,
> to the innermost house
> of the bird with the golden feathers.

I took my son from my sister's arms and held him close. His warmth and solid physical presence strengthened and warmed my blood. It was the comfort we both needed against the darkness. I felt his body tense at the sound, far off beyond the deep fields at the edge of the wood, of a lone wolf baying under the blank and unblinking stare of the full moon.

Chapter Eighteen
Tricks of the Subconscious

With the tournament match over, I waited a few minutes before exiting, as Andy had once recommended. Once free of the SIM chamber, I jumped out of the Brandenburg SIM Center and retraced my earlier path heading back toward the stairs across the cavernous courtyard.

Someone was watching me.

I stopped dead and glanced at those walking by, but nobody noticed me. I scanned the hall entrances, the balconies, the stairwell, the elevators, the maintenance tunnel access grills. No one stood lingering, waiting to follow. No one ducked out of view hoping they weren't noticed. No one. But the feeling persisted.

My thoughts strayed to Frank Talonii, to Artemus and the Bosner brothers. Who would want to follow me?

I rubbed my temples, telling myself I was uptight. Nothing to worry about. It was the strain of the match.

Still, to get out of sight, I hurried to the elevators instead of the stairs and breathlessly caught the next one going down. After forcing myself into the elevator box, the doors closed, and I was alone. It was just me and my claustrophobia.

Yet someone was watching me, still.

* * *

I was lying on my bed doing my meditation breathing exercises when my door chimes rang. That would be Trevor and Zak, who'd both, over the vid, demanded we meet at my apartment instead of down at Marty's. They said they wanted some real privacy, and neither of them was happy. It looked like I was in for a confrontation, and I didn't know why. At least my paranoid delusion of being watched was gone, so I had a chance of acting normally.

I asked Emily to let them in, and the door slid open silently. My sister was studying Bach in the outer room. A fugue drifted in as evidence and vanished again with the closing of the door.

Trevor didn't look too upset, but Zak was a high-tension conduit.

Zak looked shocked. "Dennis, your room is like a broom closet." This was their very first visit to my inner sanctum.

"Hey, Dennis," Trevor said with a wave, dumping himself into the chair at my desk at the foot of my bed.

I sat up. "Emily. Give me scene five." The wall lit up and made the room appear much bigger; the castle tower with a large window at the far side overlooking a lake and mountains.

"Ah," said Zak. "You've got one of those Window-Walls." His voice echoed a bit as it bounced off the simulated roughhewn stone walls.

Zak pivoted toward my bed and asked, "So, Dennis, are you deliberately trying to ruin me, or what?"

"Huh?"

"I'm sure he had a good reason," Trevor said. "He wouldn't lose on purpose."

"I bet a bundle on Sam Clemens," Zak said. "And then you go and pull a stunt like that."

I pulled myself to a sitting position and tried to restore some order. "What stunt? They haven't announced the winners yet."

Trevor turned to me. "I bet on you too, but, unlike Fenrick here, I didn't bet everything I owned."

I looked at Zak. "Jeez, you didn't . . ."

"What were you thinking?" Zak asked. "It just looked like you were nuts."

"Don't blame Dennis for your gambling problem," Trevor snapped.

"Gambling problem?" Zak said, raising an eyebrow. "Are you inferring I have a gambling problem?"

"No, you dolt. I didn't even imply it. That was what we call an accusation. Speaking of which, you still haven't paid up on our wager in Rapt." I remembered that a while back they had had an informal little "friendly" archery competition.

"I'm a Prince, for God's sake. I'm good for it. And who are you calling a dolt? What, am I scruffy looking too?"

"Then why haven't I seen a pence?"

"Look . . . my character's a little light at the moment." Zak started pacing around my room, caged with frenetic energy. "I'll get you your money. In the meantime, I want a re-match. You used that bird of yours to cheat."

"You think I used Sapphire to cheat?" Trevor shook his head in exasperation, and his messy black hair flew around his face. "Unbelievable. Unbelievable. Do you want to know what I think, Fenrick? You have a gambling problem, an addiction."

"You can see through Sapphire's eyes. Did you think I wouldn't figure it out? Depth perception is based on the separation of our eyes; the bigger the separation, the better. How could I possibly win an archery contest when you can gauge the distance ten times better than me? I didn't have a chance," Zak took a step toward Trevor's chair and poked him in the chest. "Because—you—cheated."

Trevor jumped to his feet, and the low gravity would have sent him into the ceiling had he not caught himself. "My brain isn't built to process that kind of info—"

"Then why do you close one eye when you shoot?" asked Zak.

"It's what we call aiming. Ever heard of it?"

I shook my head and let myself fall back onto the bed.

"That's it—" Zak said, shoving Trevor across the room. His head smacked the wall.

"Hey," I said, finally getting to my feet. "What is wrong with you guys?"

While Trevor rubbed his head in a daze, Zak turned to me, saying, "This is all your fault. If you hadn't thrown the match—"

"They haven't announced the winners yet," I said. "Why are you so sure I lost?"

"I'm talkin' about you talkin' to bloody thin air. That's what." Zak took another look at Trevor, obviously feeling bad about cracking his head against the wall. "Look . . . I—" he began then gave up and turned to go. "Later."

His leaving was like explosive decompression, the walls bending in against hard vacuum. I looked in question at Trevor, who sighed. "In the match, why did you hold whole conversations with nobody?"

"You're saying I was talking to myself? That's crazy." I quickly traced back through Loud Thunder's memory. Was he talking about muttering? Doesn't everyone mutter?

Trevor raised his eyebrows in sudden interest. "Really?" He took a leap-step over to my desk. "Frederick, can we get some playback from the last match piped in here?"

"Of course," a male voice replied. Frederick's persona had a pleasing British accent. "Please specify the player you wish to see."

"Show us Sam Clemens. Oh, and start it up about halfway through."

A fuzzy 3-D picture snapped into view and hovered over my desk. Some junk cluttering the surface obscured part of the picture, so I pushed it away against the wall. It was a scene of Loud Thunder running through the snowy forest. He kept scanning the woods searching for Morning Star's roaming spirit.

"Skip ahead a little," Trevor ordered.

The vid wasn't that easy to see. "Put it up on the wall," I said.

The scene transferred, to the wall and it felt as if we were in the forest too. Loud Thunder picked himself up off the ground and dusted dead leaves from the fur he wore. Keeping an eye on something out of view of the vid, Loud Thunder cautiously asked, "Who are you? Why are you here? Are you trapped? Your scalp looks whole to me." Raven was obviously off the edge of the display.

Trevor gestured as if his point was made.

Loud Thunder stood there silently looking off screen and listening. I couldn't hear Raven's reply. With some hand motions, I took control of our viewpoint. The scene slowly panned, and soon we were looking at Loud Thunder's back. Raven should have been standing right in front of him, but there was no one.

"I don't want to hear these things. I must . . . find Morning Star."

Loud Thunder turned, then looked momentarily hopeful,   "Have . . . have you seen her?"

After a pause, and a look of disgust, Loud Thunder said, "Then you're no help. I must find her." He then turned and began forcing his way through some underbrush.

Why didn't Raven appear in the scene? This made me look insane.

Trevor waved the vid to silence and asked me, "Now do you remember talking to thin air?"

I collapsed on my desk chair trying to figure out what had happened. "He was there. It was Raven. At first I thought he was just a spirit, then when he turned himself into a wolf, I knew he was Raven."

"He turned himself into a wolf, and that proved he was a raven?" Trevor asked shoving fingers through his hair and rubbing his head where it had hit the wall.

"The spirit turned himself into a raven too. He could transform himself into different animals which made me think he was the character from the story Soaring Eagle told."

"So this wasn't just a ploy. You were actually talking to someone."

I nodded dumbly. It was true the sessions with Art were wearing me thin, but when I started the match, I felt like I was still in enough control to create Loud Thunder's personality. I wasn't talking to myself. The playback showing Loud Thunder plunging through the underbrush was starting to make me ill. "Emily, stop the vid." We were instantly returned to the castle tower.

Trevor said, "So the LMC must have shown you something without showing everyone else. Child's play. I scanned a few others and you were the only one to see this apparition. But why would the Masters do that?"

"Maybe one of the other competitors did it to make me look bad," I suggested.

Trevor laughed, "Boy, that would be a real hack. Who has that kind of skill? And how would you prove it? And now with so much data screwed up—"

"Maybe that's it," I said. "Maybe the reason I could see Raven and no one else could is because of the damage she took in the explosion."

"No, no. The damage was minuscule compared to the size of the LMC," explained Trevor, pulling up the chair from the corner. "My dad can't even figure out why so much data is missing or wrong. The memory is holographic—all of it stored everywhere. How can burning your finger make your pancreas fail? And what you're suggesting is even more inconceivable, like . . . like a hang-nail making you see Elvis."

"Look," I said, lowering my voice. "What I'm talking about is irrational behavior."

Trevor shook his head. "This didn't happen by accident. Someone did this. Who do you know with the power to pull this off? Two guesses."

"Why would Artemus do this?"

"Who knows? Maybe he felt the tournament was dragging you away from his project. Maybe it's another test."

"Test or not—" I was interrupted by the door chime. "—they're going to announce the winners soon." Then turning to the door, I answered, "Yeah?"

The door opened to an angry Tricia holding a letter. Music drifted in with her. "I'm not your mail woman, but here. This just arrived for you." She threw an envelope on my bed saying, "Probably another message from the Supreme Being. Who else would send you actual paper?"

She seemed angrier than she should have been for just delivering a letter. "What's your problem?" I asked as a phrase of music playing in the outer room managed to squeak its way through my ears and into my consciousness. I leapt from my chair toward the door, then used Tricia and the doorjamb to pull myself through.

"Hey!" she shouted. "Watch it."

"That's my sonata playing!"

"What?" Trevor asked, obviously wondering what the excitement was about and following me into the entertainment room.

"That's my sonata playing!" I bellowed again above the music.

"So you're the perpetrator," Tricia said, grabbing my arm and shaking it. "It's been playing this noise over and over for ten minutes. Can you get it to turn off?"

I ignored Tricia and turned to Trevor. "It's supposed to be lost, gone, irretrievable. Emily had no idea it was even written."

I called out above the rising violins, "Emily, halve the volume." I waited, but nothing happened.

Trevor tapped me on the shoulder and motioned for me to follow. We went back in my room, and Trevor said, "LMC, stop the music playback in the other room."

With Frederick's voice, it replied, "I'm sorry, Trevor. To what room are you referring?"

"The room right outside this one. The Howard's gathering room, where you are playing the music."

"I'm sorry, Trevor. I'm not playing any music in that room."

Trevor looked at me wide eyed, shaking his head.

Tricia again shook my arm, this time more violently. "Get it to stop, please. Or I'm going to have to kill myself."

"Oh, come off it, Tricia," I said, detaching myself. "It's not that awful." Violins began ascending the scale, following four beats behind the cellos.

"Yes, it is."

"How did you find it? Emily hasn't even admitted to having it since the explosion."

Tricia said, "I was just working on a concerto for class. Bach is so boring. I told her to play some good music. That's all."

Trevor held a hand up for us to be quiet and said, "Frederick, can you identify the music in the other room?"

"It is a piece composed by Dennis Howard entitled, 'Seeds of Snow.' The music being played is the fifth through the eighth bars of the first movement, and it is repeating."

"And repeating—" Tricia added, and I shushed her.

Trevor asked, "Are you playing this music?"

"No, I am not."

Trevor paused and looked at me. I asked, "Then . . . who is playing the music?"

The LMC said, "The only logical answer to that question is that the music is emanating from a recording cube or some other audio device."

Trevor said, "Never mind. Can you play us some Bizet?"

"Certainly. Did you have any particular piece in mind?"

"How about Carmen?"

Instantly, my sonata was replaced by the opening violin strains of the opera.

"Thank God," Tricia murmured.

"You're welcome," Trevor said with a smile. "But you don't have to call me 'God.'"

"Emily," I said. "Now, playback my sonata again."

"No!" Tricia shouted, but, as it turned out, she had nothing to worry about.

"I'm sorry, Dennis," Emily said, back to her more familiar voice. "What sonata do you wish to hear?"

I slapped my forehead. "The music you were just playing. My sonata. 'Seeds of Snow.'"

"I have no record of any such composition. Would you like to see a list of some excellent seventeenth—"

"This is a nightmare."

"Good riddance," Tricia said and jumped out of reach before I could retaliate.

Trevor tried to calm me down. "Wait a minute. Frederick, you don't have any listing for Dennis' sonata?"

"I have no record of him ever having written one," he said, back to Frederick's voice. "This is beginning to sound a great deal like some other conversations I've been having. Are you under the impression that he wrote one?"

The mystery excited Trevor. Computers weren't supposed to fail this way, and it was beginning to give me the creeps. Trevor turned to my sister and asked, "Trish, tell us again how you got Dennis' music to play."

"It's Tricia, not Trish." She folded her arms and added, "Trev."

"Okay. Sorry."

She shrugged. "I just asked for some good music. I do that all the time. She usually just plays some random piece of music she knows I like."

"Random . . . random piece of music," Trevor whispered to himself. He gazed off into space for several seconds and then whispered, "Of course . . ."

* * *

Trevor didn't want to reveal his idea until he'd had a chance to test it. All he would say was there might be a way to retrieve all sorts of information Emily had forgotten without her even knowing it. I didn't see how that was possible, but after hearing Emily deny all knowledge of my music two seconds after Trevor had shut it off, I was willing to believe anything.

Trevor stayed for dinner, after which Mom, Tricia, Trevor, and I all watched the tournament results together. I felt confident Trevor wouldn't accidentally give away my secret identity. Zak's reaction would have raised suspicions were he here, so his absence was one less thing to worry about.

Master Cummings explained there were fifteen people who competed in the Sixth Trial of the tournament that he titled 'Morning Star.' The field of competitors would be reduced by more than half after this match, leaving only seven.

Master Cummings described the various outcomes from the match. "Out of the fifteen competitors, seven managed to find Morning Star and bring her spirit back, thus resurrecting her. Three didn't ever find her, either by becoming lost or injured. Another five managed to find Morning Star but failed to bring her back for various reasons. Three of those five, namely Mensch, Beethoven and Firefly, actually preferred to join Morning Star in death rather than return without her.

"The remaining two who found her but failed to bring her back, namely Sam Clemens and Winger, decided to release her to cross into death, after which both returned to the tribe. Sam Clemens, however, surprised everyone by carrying on a discussion with a figure not seen or heard by anyone else."

My stomach clenched. So not even the Masters had seen Raven. Or they weren't admitting it.

Master Cummings said, "It was later revealed by Loud Thunder that this invisible individual was Raven, the trickster mentioned in Soaring Eagle's story about the genesis of the moon. The illusion Sam Clemens created was so convincing, I almost believed Raven was there with him, myself. This approach was so novel and at the same time so expertly done, the Masters cannot help but award him one of the seven winner slots from this, the Sixth Trial."

I let myself slouch back onto the couch and breathe. One more step closer.

Trevor, who was standing near to my bedroom, ready to return to his poking around the LMC as soon as the broadcast was over, raised his glass and gave me a nod of approval. The gesture reminded me of Soaring Eagle's nod across Morning Star's funeral pyre, and a sudden chill ran up my spine.

Master Cummings said, "The seven winners and those continuing on to the Seventh Trial are Arpeggio, Fifth Order Tensor, Rose of Jericho, Sam Clemens, Spice of Life, Timbuktu, and Winger.

"Congratulations to the winners. We expect to see all of you again at the Seventh Trial scheduled at the end of next week, Friday May 24, at three o'clock PM. Until then, I am Master Cummings." He vanished, and in his place the triangles reappeared.

Mom commented, "The only reason these matches are so popular is all the betting. Even if it is legal up to a limit, I don't want either of you to ever go down that road."

Tricia and I nodded.

* * *

"Dennis, wake up. Wake up. Come on."

I groggily opened my eyes to see Trevor hovering over me in the near complete darkness of my room. Failing to accomplish his goal, and unwilling to give up, Trevor asked Mom if he could stay over. For some reason, after he started, he couldn't move his infiltration program back to his place.

"Luna to Dennis. Are you awake yet? You have to see this," Trevor whispered.

"What, I'm awake. I'm awake. What is it?"

"I've got something that you have to see."

"Keep your voice down. My mom's just in the next room." I rubbed my eyes and yawned, trying to wake up. "What time is it?"

"Just past six. Come over here." He motioned for me to follow as he stepped back to my desk and the glowing hologram, the only light in the room. It flickered and danced like a fire, making the shadows uneasy.

"You're going to ruin your eyes if you keep this up," I said groggily as I shuffled over to join him, a blanket wrapped around my shoulders.

Trevor made a few hand gestures over the desk and whispered, "Check this out." He was so excited, I found myself waking up in spite of the lure of sleep.

A picture of a hallway resolved out of static. The hallway could have been anywhere in Aristoteles if not the whole planet. Light pipes lined the upper corner of the hall where the wall met the ceiling. There was a figure bent low in a small maintenance alcove on the right, the face obscured from view.

"Who is that?" I asked.

With a motion of his hand, Trevor threw the picture onto the wall, which, thankfully, faded up from blackness slowly. Now it appeared as if we were in that same hallway. Everything was life-sized.

Trevor whispered, "All the information is still in there like I thought. The LMC just can't remember where it put the information. I had to put the computer in a kind of hypnotic state to get at the missing files."

"Hypnosis? Can you do that?"

"The key is privacy mode. Watch."

I heard two people arguing, the audio placing them down a hall on the left. The audio was garbled, so I couldn't make out what they were talking about. Something about an "all-hands meeting." The figure in the alcove got up quickly and disappeared into a room next to the alcove. A man and a woman dressed in white lab coats strode past the spot, still arguing. The radiation insignia on the front of their coats was plain as day. "It's from Prometheus."

"All this is still in the subconscious of the computer. Well, the equivalent of the sub-conscious anyway."

The two figures in lab coats opened a door down the hall and vanished inside. "And that" Trevor indicated the— man stepping back out into the hall, "—is none other than your friend and mine, Artemus Regale."

"It is?" I asked. He walked toward the camera and his face was at last clear. "It is."

Artemus resumed his crouching position in the maintenance alcove. It looked like he was hitting something, and it sounded like he was beginning to laugh. Soon Artemus was done with whatever he'd been doing, and he fell back against the far wall laughing even harder. He stood, arms folded over his stomach as if he was in pain or couldn't catch his breath, and his laughter echoed down the hall for all to hear. "What was he doing? What's so funny?"

More static filled the picture, creeping in from the sides. I looked in the alcove to find what he'd been working on. Trevor zoomed in on it with a few hand motions, and soon the picture resolved into what looked like a small device mounted to the wall near the floor of the closet. It had a round face and three blinking lights. A digital time display could be seen rapidly counting backwards. "Holy—"

"He was setting the bomb that blew up Prometheus," Trevor whispered. With another few deft hand motions, Trevor zoomed the picture back out so we could see the whole hallway again. If anything, Artemus' laughter had grown.

He began to run down the hall away from the camera, his leaps long in the low gravity. The picture began to break up, but I thought I saw someone chasing him calling something. Artemus must have ducked into a side passage or a room because he vanished from view, and the next thing I knew, the picture shook and the hallway seemed to expand for a fraction of a second. After that, my room was plunged into darkness as the picture went blank.

* * *

"Fact: Artemus set the bomb," Trevor said as he aimed the desk lamp on the plate of eggs and toast I had just given him. The rest of the room remained in shadow.

"But," I held up a finger, "he managed to escape the explosion without harm while the whole plant was coming down around his head. So, fact: Artemus couldn't have set the bomb."

Trevor shook his head and took another bite of toast. It had only been half an hour since he'd shown me the evidence, and no one was up yet. I'd gotten some breakfast for the both of us while Trevor had worked to playback the scene again. My wall had been showing a broken image of the hallway for some time, and it was a few minutes before the explosion.

Trevor asked, "How do you know he wasn't injured? Have you seen him outside the SIM?"

"Well . . . you're right. I haven't. So I suppose he could be injured, but how did he survive at all? He was right at ground zero."

The vid picture quality improved. It showed Artemus bending low in the alcove, obscuring the view of the bomb. Another minute passed, and he was ducking around the corner, hiding from the Prometheus employees.

Trevor asked, "What, you're not suggesting he has a twin brother? Look, someone could have doctored up the vid, but that wouldn't be easy."

"A brother, heh?" The thought made me think of the Bosner brothers. I didn't want to think about them.

"Look, it's him," Trevor said waving the crust of his toast at the vid. "Plain as day." He then stuffed the remainder in his mouth and took a gulp of juice.

"Duh. There's an easy way to find out. Why don't we just ask? Hey Emily, who is that person in the alcove—"

"No!" Trevor shouted, spewing juice everywhere.

The scene on the wall instantly changed back to the tower bedroom. Emily was standing there, blond hair in a bun, and wearing an apron over a medieval frock. She smiled helpfully, turning to open the shutters. "Good morning, Dennis. To what alcove are you referring?"

Morning light streamed in, and I shielded my face from the sudden brightness. "What's wrong?"

"No. I can't believe it. It's gone." Trevor slammed his glass of juice on my side desk, spilling it. Some of it hung in the air, falling too slowly to stay within the glass.

"Sorry. What did I do?"

"You woke the LMC up, that's what," he whispered. "You drew its attention to the playback. Haven't you been paying any attention to what I've been doing the past fourteen hours? God."

"Sorry. I didn't—Ah, thanks Emily. Can we get some privacy?"

She dusted her hands on her apron and smiled. "All right then. Just call if you need anything." She went out through the creaky door, the latch echoing as it fell into place.

"But, now you know how to do it. It won't take you that long to bring it back so we can show the MPs."

Trevor sighed and closed his eyes. "I'm not sure that's possible. It may be gone for good. You just brought the full force of the LMC's consciousness right on the source of its grief. It may be pushed so far down now that . . ."

I got up, the situation beginning to dawn on me. "But—but we have to. I mean, I'm supposed to meet with Artemus again on Monday!"

Trevor said, "Without the evidence, we can't get him arrested. The cops aren't going to believe a couple of kids solved their investigation before they could, and they're not going to arrest the richest man on Luna on our word. If he finds out we know . . . damn."

"I'll tell him I'm sick."

"How long could that last?" Now Trevor was on his feet, pushing both hands through his hair as if he could wring ideas out of his brain by force.

"And what if the project succeeds?" I asked. "What if Artemus can put information in my brain? How long before he'll be able to extract information? He'll find out we know."

"Oh, God."

"I'll . . . I'll try to get out of the contract. There must be a way out, some loophole."

Trevor asked, "And what about your dad? When's his new arm going to be ready? Get out of the contract and you better believe Artemus will yank that away."

"Throw that in my face why don't you?"

"Hey, I'm not the one who stupidly destroyed the evidence."

There has to be an answer that could save our lives, keep my brain safe from Artemus and get Dad his new arm all the while bringing Artemus to justice. How could I have been so stupid? "I love you—shut up."

"What did you say?"

"Hmm? Nothing." God. I said it in front of Trevor. I started pacing around the small space as Trevor sat on the desk. The morning light streaming in from the castle room made my shadow loom, and the stone walls felt like they were closing in. Options were slamming shut each way I looked.

I nearly jumped out of my skin when I saw someone standing in the corner. He turned his head to look at me and took a step forward. With a shout I leapt backward and slammed into Trevor who had been taking another gulp of juice. We slid off the side of the desk together, along with the remnants of my junk, juice raining down over everything.

"What's your malfunction? Get off me."

I pointed to the corner, but only shadows looked back. No one was in the room but Trevor and me and my overactive imagination.

"Sorry. I thought—" At that moment, an envelope drifted down to land nearby. "The letter!"

"Huh? Oh, yeah that," Trevor said as he got up. "I'd been meaning to remind you about that. While you were asleep I felt like it was staring at me."

I crawled to the letter and opened it. Inside was a hand-written note.

Dennis,

We have successfully completed the mapping stage of the project. Next week we can move on to stage two, which I'll discuss with you in person. I'll be waiting for you at Descartes Plaza Monday morning at 8:00 sharp, as we planned.

Thank you again for all your time and effort. I just know it's going to work this time. It must. There's a great deal at stake, more than you may realize. I'm sure you and your family have kept our arrangement secret, as we discussed. Trust no one. Not to be melodramatic, but lives could hang in the balance.

Until Monday,
A

Here ends Part 1 of
Persistent Illusion
The Moon of My Mind

The story continues in Part 2:
Whispers of Memories Lost
and concludes in Part 3:
Greater Than I Know

Poetry Index

The following is a list of all the poetry referenced in whole or in part in the text of the novel. They are listed alphabetically by their first lines and link to their first appearance in the text.

References

The following is a list of all the public domain material referenced in whole or in part in the text of the novel.

Thomas Ady (17th Century)

Matthew, Mark, Luke and John,
The bed be blest that I lie on.
Four angels to my bed.
Four angels round my head,
One to watch, and one to pray,
And two to bear my soul away.

Thomas Ady's Candle in the Dark contains the first record of the nursery rhyme Mathew, Mark, Luke, and John.

Immortality
15th century Nahua (Aztec) poet

They shall not wither, my flowers,
they shall not cease, my songs,
I, the singer, lift them up.
They are scattered, they spread about.
But even though my flowers may yellow,
they shall live
in the innermost house
of the bird of the golden feathers.

This is the original poem. I embellished it slightly with several more lines.

Story of Raven and the Moon
A Northwest Coast Native Myth

The story of raven and the creation of the Moon is an actual Native American myth. Look for many more fascinating tales about Raven, the Trickster, on-line.

The Day is Done
Henry Wadsworth Longfellow
Preface to *The Waif*, a collection of other people's poems
that Longfellow enjoyed.
First published in 1845

The day is done, and the darkness
Falls from the wings of Night,
As a feather is wafted downward
From an eagle in his flight.

I see the lights of the village
Gleam through the rain and the mist,
And a feeling of sadness comes o'er me,
That my soul cannot resist:

A feeling of sadness and longing,
That is not akin to pain,
And resembles sorrow only
As the mist resembles the rain.

Come, read to me some poem,
Some simple and heartfelt lay,
That shall soothe this restless feeling,
And banish the thoughts of day.

Not from the grand old masters,

Not from the bards sublime,
Whose distant footsteps echo
Through the corridors of Time.

For, like strains of martial music,
Their mighty thoughts suggest
Life's endless toil and endeavor;
And to-night I long for rest.

Read from some humbler poet,
Whose songs gushed from his heart,
As showers from the clouds of summer,
Or tears from the eyelids start;

Who, through long days of labor,
And nights devoid of ease,
Still heard in his soul the music
Of wonderful melodies.

Such songs have power to quiet
The restless pulse of care,
And come like the benediction
That follows after prayer.

Then read from the treasured volume
The poem of thy choice,
And lend to the rhyme of the poet
The beauty of thy voice.

And the night shall be filled with music
And the cares that infest the day,
Shall fold their tents, like the Arabs,
And as silently steal away.

This is the original poem. I took the liberty of making a single change in my use of this poem. I replaced 'an eagle' with 'a falcon' in the first stanza. Since there are kestrels in the fantasy world of Rapt, I thought this change would make it align better to that world. And I also enjoy the increased alliteration after the alteration.

About the Author

J. J. Kalke Jr. was born in the late 1960s in Pittsburgh, Pennsylvania. He attended Purdue University for his Bachelor's degree in Aerospace Engineering, and went on to obtain a Masters in Computer Systems Engineering at the University of Pennsylvania.

As of this writing, in 2020, he lives with his family in Northern Virginia. He focuses his efforts on software development, but feeds his passion for all things science fiction and fantasy by writing whenever he gets the chance, and teaching his kids the finer points of fiction writing. For example, no matter how dedicated an author is to world crafting, if he or she decides to create one or more entire languages and cultures for that world and in-so-doing winds up pulling character names from them, never ever make them as similar as Sauron and Saruman.

Follow him on Facebook:
https://www.facebook.com/j.j.kalke.jr